THE
RESERVE

Also by Jordon Greene

Novels
They'll Call It Treason
To Watch You Bleed

Short Stories
Anywhere But Here
The Maze
Forbidden
Far From Home

THE
RESERVE

A NOVEL

JORDON GREENE

FRANKLIN/KERR
CONCORD, NORTH CAROLINA

The Reserve: A Novel by Jordon Greene

Published by Franklin/Kerr Press, LLC
349-L Copperfield Boulevard #502 | Concord, North Carolina 28025
1.704.659.3915 | info@franklinkerr.com
www.FranklinKerr.com

For information about special discounts available for bulk purchases, sales promotions, fund-raising and educational needs, contact Franklin/Kerr Press Sales at 704-659-3915 or sales@franklinkerr.com.

Edited by Christie Stratos, Chelly Hoyle Peeler & Nancy Tulloch
Cover Image © 2018 andreiuc88/Shutterstock.com
Cover Art & Interior design by Jordon Greene

Printed in the United States of America

SECOND EDITION

ISBN-10: 0-9983913-7-9
ISBN-13: 978-0-9983913-7-3

Library of Congress Control Number: 2018905733

Fiction: Horror
Fiction: Thrillers & Suspense
Fiction: Science-Fiction

To Curtis Fore,
without your help this story would not
have been the same, literally.

ACKNOWLEDGMENTS

This story took me into some new territory and I'm glad to have had the support and help of a great group of friends and associates to ensure that it's the best it can be.

I want to thank everyone at Edition Bookstore and Coffee Shop in Kannapolis, North Carolina. I swear you're all awesome. You always make me feel like family while I take up a table for hours once or twice a week (sometimes more) to write and even more so when you come and visit me at festivals. The "fangirling" is hilarious, even if I don't know how to respond and try to act like I don't know you when you do it.

Thanks to my friend Curtis Fore for helping make some core changes to the characters and story that really helped solidify and strengthen the plot early on. The story would definitely not be the same without your help. Thanks as usual to my mother, Kim Greene, for helping me form much of the story's ending when I was having a "little" self-doubt.

I had another great round of beta readers again who tested the waters before things got too far. Thanks to Pat Armstrong, Emily Scott, Gavin Evans, Beth Tallent and Justin Dutton. Of course thanks to my editors Christie Stratos and Chelly Peeler, for fixing all my mistakes and other unfortunate issues. Last, I'd like to thank Nancy Tulloch, my proofreader, for catching everything that the rest of us didn't.

Prologue

A branch buffets Omar's neck and cheek as his feet pound the moist soil. He stretches his stride, pushing the bounds of his endurance. Steamy puffs of breath streak past his face as another branch attempts to swat him down. Omar ducks, and a cluster of towering tree trunks, black behemoths under a leafy canopy, force him to make a quick course correction.

Behind him an eerie half moan, half scream screeches over the thumping of his feet with an almost feline whine. Leaves and branches ruffle as it rushes closer.

"Shit!" Omar curses between heavy breaths, his mind a blur.

What the fuck is that thing? Where's Joe?

Only minutes ago, Omar Laity and Joe Corban, his photography intern, were trouncing through overgrown vegetation and through decaying buildings, looking for the perfect nighttime shot among the deteriorating structures. Then the first scream broke the silence. Before Omar could look back, a horrified grunt reached his ears. Joe was gone. Then *it* appeared in the shadows in a full sprint, heading straight for him.

Omar didn't take the time to question its intentions. Its guttural moan and determined sprint told him all he needed to know. He ran.

Ahead, Omar catches a glimpse of moonlight breaking through what appears to be the edge of the forest. His heart lifts and he pushes forward, slipping around another bush and jumping over a fallen trunk.

It's getting closer. Its panting breaths and crackling footfalls grow louder. Omar squints as another scream cuts through the night. There is something primal, a rage in that scream that elicits a chill down Omar's spine. He presses onward, swinging his arms to the beat of his legs, trying not to panic.

The ground falls from under his feet without warning. His body tumbles forward, crashing hard against an outcropping of rocks. With a groan, Omar lifts himself back up, ignoring the throbbing pain in his side, and takes off again. Agony spikes through his arm. Reflexively, his body bends over the limb, his lack of attention sending his shoulder into an unyielding tree trunk. His body pirouettes around the thinly barked trunk and hits hard against the ground.

He grunts as his face slams into the coarse soil and he inhales a gulp of dirt. He coughs, choking on the grime, as he tries to get back to his feet.

You've got to get up, Omar! Get up!

Willing himself to ignore the pain, Omar plants a hand on the ground, bracing himself as pain gushes down his arm. As he gains his footing, an unwelcome cry echoes from behind as the harsh footsteps come to a halt. Omar's green eyes shoot open in the dark as a massive hand grasps his ankle, and claws sink into his skin.

"Ah!" he yelps as his tendon snaps.

Omar digs his fingers into the ground, desperate to escape its grasp. Dirt grinds under his nails, but he can't break free of its iron grip. Instead, his body wrenches back a foot. Another spike of pain blossoms up his body as the meat and skin around his foot is stressed beyond its limit.

No, no, no!

The creature howls again, clenching his ankle tighter. Omar refuses to loosen his futile grip on the forest floor, grasping at any faint hope of survival.

A sharp ache shoots through his back as something sharp slices between his shoulder blades. Omar contorts, shoving his shoulders back and throwing his hands out, trying to about-face and guard his back from further pain.

Unable to move, skewered to the ground, a cold, stiff hand clasps his forearm, sinking one lone claw between the bones. Omar shrieks in terror as a heavy weight grinds into the small of his back, wrenching his body into an unnatural angle with his arm bent backward in the creature's grasp.

"Get off me!" he yells.

In response, it moans and yanks at his arm. The muscles strain beneath the skin as they bow backward, a tendril of electricity shooting up his shoulder. Then it snaps. A pain unlike anything he's felt before cracks like lightning up his shoulder as the bone snaps and his frayed stump flops in the air in the creature's grasp.

"*Fuck!*" He forces the word between gasps.

The weight on his back grows as the object penetrating his skin twists. He tries to turn, to escape the pain, but the creature's foot is planted firmly.

"Please! Stop!"

Tears pour from his eyes, mixing into a puddle of mud beneath him as his spine takes the brunt of the pressure. The creature yanks again and again in a savage rage, moaning and screaming like it's some wicked game. Unable to stand the stress any longer, the skin around Omar's shoulder tears. Crimson races along the seam of torn flesh. His skin rips like paper under each pull.

Omar's eyes widen in shock as an unbearable agony rumbles through his hefty frame. Warm liquid pellets dribble over his face, dropping from above, and his other arm tumbles to the ground at the edge of his sight, its bloody stump laughing at him.

The weight lifts from his back, and the razor-sharp claws rip from his back only to come again. They pierce deep into his back, ripping, pulling, shredding into his body. The savage roar almost deafens Omar as the creature goes to work on him, thrashing deeper into him, slashing into his stomach and reeling out a yard of Omar's intestines.

Omar's eyelids grow heavy as thick shadows overtake his vision. He fights to keep breathing, to will past the pain and focus on living. His body convulses with another barrage of ravenous clawing. A warm liquid seeps up his throat and into his mouth, then begins to pour out. It tastes of iron, bitter and wretched. He gasps one last wet breath as a victorious teeth bears down on his lifeless form.

Three Weeks Later

1: Cooper Bay

A shudder jolts me from my dreams. I spring upright before anchoring my palms to the armrests and shooting my eyes about the cabin. I sigh, scanning the rows of passengers in the cramped space. I'm not the only one waking up. A series of yawns and grumbles whisper around the deck.

I let a yawn escape my lips before peeking out the petite ovular window to my right. At first all I see is a layer of faint clouds lit unusually bright for this time of night, but in a matter of seconds they lift to expose New York City's brilliant cityscape, its grand skyscrapers, and the perpetually packed streets filled with headlights and people.

I rotate the soreness from my shoulders, trying not to bother the lady sitting next to me. She grins broadly, wiggling to get into a more comfortable position.

"Morning, Cooper," she says.

I can't remember her name, but I'm not too worried about it. She's in her mid-forties, a little plump around the waist and short, and she seems like a nice lady, but she's definitely too talkative. I only met her five hours ago after boarding this red-eye flight and finding my seat next to her. After the usual pleasantries, it took me nearly an hour to ask her politely to let me go to sleep. I may only be twenty, but boarding just before midnight is still exhausting.

"Morning," I reply, feigning a small grin, sleep still calling to me.

Ahead, the SEATBELTS light comes to life followed by the captain's voice over the plane-wide intercom announcing our descent to JFK International. Minutes later, the plane touches down and I scan the baggage track for my single black suitcase with COOPER LEE BAY stamped on the luggage tag. Most people call me Cooper or Coop, but at times my mother calls me Cooper Lee. That usually isn't a good thing.

After I find my bag and step off to the restroom. Another yawn breaks my lips into a wide "o" before I can crack the door open and slide by a tall, slender man at least thirty years my elder. He avoids my eyes as he slips by. I stop at the sink and place my palms on the slick black countertop. I bend, leaning my weight on my elbows and let yet another yawn work its way through my throat.

In the mirror, my tired eyes peer back at me. The late hour compounded by the time change from Texas to New York has drained the luster from the cognac brown around my pupils. I try to blink away the fatigue, but it refuses to let go. Instead, I drag in a breath of heavily scented air, citrus I think, and run my hands under the automatic faucet. Bracing myself for the cold, I splash a handful of water against my face. It trickles over my taut, light mocha skin and dark pink lips and sends a chill spilling down my neck and back. I'm the only member of my family that can maintain a tan; the rest only transition from a pale white to an uncomfortable red, including the brother I'm about to meet.

I swipe a hand through my dark brown hair, throwing it to the right in a small wave before grabbing a paper towel and dabbing the remaining water from my face.

"Hell of a way to start summer break, huh?" I ask myself. "A red-eye flight to New York. Damn."

I'm a freshman acting major at UT Austin. Well, a sophomore now I guess. With finals behind me, I'm spending the next few months with family starting here in the Big Apple. It's been almost a year since I've seen my oldest brother, Nicholas, so I was excited when he offered to let me spend the first couple weeks up here. Other than myself, he's my only sibling so far to leave our hometown in Concord, North Carolina just outside of Charlotte. I'll get down to Concord again in another three weeks, but I'm looking forward to the next few with Nick first.

I turn and leave the restroom, heading toward the exit where Nick is sure to be waiting for me. This summer's going to be good for me. Just getting away from UT will work wonders, or rather away from her, Addison Richards, my ex-girlfriend. We dated since November of my junior year at Northwest Cabarrus High, and to be honest, she's hot. She's so hot. But I'm not that shallow, or at least I like to think I'm not. I thought she had a good head on her shoulders and even a great personality, but apparently I was wrong. I mean the bitch seriously dumped me with a text message the day before my calculus exam in December. Had it been history or something more technical, I know I would have failed. Lucky for me, I guess, I barely scraped out a low C. I could have easily aced it had she not fucked with my heart the night before.

Stop, Cooper. Just forget her. She's not worth the energy.

I have to keep reminding myself to let it go, to move on, all that quotable bullshit. I'm doing better, and I'm probably better off without her anyway, but it still angers me to think about it. I mean, who does that shit?

I squeeze past a family of four and barely avoid running into a young blonde chick. I was apparently in between her and her boyfriend, or husband, who she's now wrapped around and kissing like she hasn't seen in him years. Ahead I search the sparse crowd, looking for a head of shoulder-length, curly brown hair and a complementary mustache and beard. I spot him just before he sees me.

"Nick!" I yell across the large room and quicken my pace to meet him.

"Hey, Coop!" he yells back, a broad smile painting his pale face, his dark brown eyes significantly more cognizant than my own. "How you doing?"

"I'm good. Tired, but good." I bob my head lazily. "Four a.m. is way too early for me though."

"Hey, it was a cheap flight," Nick retorts. "How am I supposed to pay the rent here if I fly you everywhere first class during normal hours?"

"You always were the cheap one. First, you didn't fly me first class this time. Plus, I'm happy with coach as long as it's not the ass-end of the night."

"Oh." Nick crinkles his brow and then grins. "So, we're already hitting with the low blows, are we? You didn't even wait for breakfast."

I chuckle, pinning up the corners of my mouth in a smile, and pat Nick on the shoulder.

"I think you'll be okay, man."

"Let's get on out of here." He shakes his head and waves me forward. A few minutes later, my luggage is stowed in the trunk of Nick's late '90s model forest-green Jeep Cherokee, and we're roaring down Interstate 678 toward Lower Manhattan, where Nick's small one-bedroom apartment is nestled between a dozen other identical flats. The sun is beginning to break the horizon, a faint glow of its brilliance lacing the road. To my left is the iconic skyline of New York City. It's not my first time in the Big Apple, but the view never ceases to amaze me.

"So how's school going?" Nick asks.

I pull my eyes away from the cluster of steel buildings jutting into the sky and run my fingers through my hair.

"Good. It's going good," I tell him. "I'm officially a sophomore now, aced all the exams this time."

Nick knows exactly what I'm talking about. He was basically my pillar when Addison dumped me. I don't have to complete the thought and bring it all back up again, thankfully.

"Well that's great. I never aced any exam," he says. "I simply passed them. That was enough for me."

"Hey, that's better than the alternative." I smile. "Oh, and did I tell you about next semester's acting class?"

"Uh..." Nick thinks but comes up empty. "No. Don't think so."

"I can't believe I forgot!" I exclaim. "Matthew McConaughey is teaching part of the class! I mean, I knew he taught some classes at Austin and all, but I thought it would have been harder to get in."

"That's awesome! You get to learn from a real pro then."

"I know, it's exciting!" The thought alone makes me jittery. To our right, a tiny Honda flies by well above the speed limit, snatching my attention, its high-pitched exhaust blaring the whole way by.

"So you still liking Austin?" Nick asks.

"Definitely," I tell him, and it's no understatement. I really do like it. Concord is great and all, but it's no Austin. "There's so much more to do in Austin. Of course, it's nothing like it is here. The music scene is so much better than Charlotte though."

Nick smiles and nods his head, one hand on the wheel and his elbow propped on his door's armrest. The car is engulfed in a large steel bridge, with catwalks for pedestrian traffic above us. Unfortunately, with the sun rising, the traffic is thickening, and our pace is already slowing.

"Oh, speaking of music. How's it going over at *FU* Records?" I ask, purposefully emphasizing *FU*. It's technically Falling Up Records, but with an acronym like that, you've got to use it. And they do.

"Great," he tells me. "It's a job and all. It's not all awesome, but how many can say they get to work with music for a living, and rock bands at that?"

I cock my head to the side and shrug. "True. Any worthwhile new bands lately?"

"We've had a few come through, nothing big, but not too bad." He looks at me before putting his eyes back on the road. "I did hear a rumor that we might be signing one of the bigger indie bands soon though. No one's saying who, but I hear it's going to be big."

"That'd be awesome!" I agree. "Be sure to let me know who it is when you find out."

The Jeep emerges at the end of the tunnel-like bridge, crossing over the East River. Rows of multilevel apartment buildings hewn out of brown stone rise on both sides of the street, and the city continues to rise into the sky ahead.

"Is Autumn driving you crazy yet about the wedding?" I prod. Nick proposed to her back in December, and it didn't take long for his fiancée to decide on this upcoming September for the wedding. She wanted to avoid the summer heat and the winter chill. I can't say I blame her. Fall, or autumn funny enough, sounds so much better than a hot summer wedding or freezing your ass off in the middle of winter, especially up here.

Nick takes his eyes off the road — we're barely moving anyway, so it doesn't faze me — and lifts his brow, giving me a piercing expression. I grin.

"Do you really have to ask?" he said. "Of course she is. She's fretting over everything."

I chortle and look out the window at the never-ending sea of buildings, cars and people. The sun is higher now, its rays bathing the city in warm reds and oranges.

"Well, that's your fault for asking her to marry you," I retort.

"Oh, I'm still good on that," he tells me. "It's just a universal female thing, I think. I mean, no decision is easy. I swear that's why some guys prefer other guys."

"You considering it?" I ask, eyes wide and a smile spreading across my lips.

"*Fuck* no!" he comes back.

I shake my head with a quiet laugh. Minutes later, Nick parks the SUV in the deck and I tote my bag to the elevator and finally his apartment. Nick places a lone finger to his lips as we cross the threshold.

"Shh…" he warns me, leaving the lights off as we pass through the entry hall, which opens into an overfilled living room. There's a large body on the couch, chest rising and falling rhythmically. "Grady's here, too, for the next few days."

I nod, pursing my lips. I don't know the guy well, but we

have met. He's one of Nick's college friends from the UNC School of Arts. I think he's a cameraman or something now.

"You'll have the loveseat." Nick points to the smaller of the two sofas.

Of course. That's what you get for getting here last, even at your brother's place.

I deposit my bag on the sofa and glance at the lump on the other couch before following Nick into his tiny excuse for a kitchen. Grady's thick, rather chubby body, if I remember it correctly, lies under a thin sheet with his head propped on one of the sofa pillows. His curly brown hair looks almost black in the dark and his mustache and beard nearly take over his mouth and chin.

In the kitchen, a little six-by-six space, I lean against Nick's steel-faced fridge. On the opposite counter is a microwave and an overworked and spotted stovetop-oven combination. A set of knives and a drying rack sit next to the sink and the occasional doodad dots the counter, courtesy of Autumn I'm sure; it's definitely not Nick's doing.

"Tell me about this movie you're filming." I plant my hand on the counter and cock my head to the side. It's one of the reasons I'm here at the beginning of my summer rather than later. Mom wanted me to come home first, but Nick found an opportunity for me to watch the production of a real film and I couldn't resist.

"Ah, yes," Nick whispers. "I think you'll like it. I couldn't say much the last time we talked, a lot was still in development then. It's a horror flick."

That immediately piques my interest. Of all the genres, horror is my favorite, hands down. Give me the blood and the gore, scare me, scar me. I love it.

"Sweet," I say.

"So the basic gist is that the movie follows a group of friends in a post-apocalyptic world, trapped on an island, who come upon a killer who's willing to do anything to have them." Nick pauses for emphasis. "Let's just say cannibalism is a common theme. Your character, Carter Hawkins, is the lead, and the female lead — "

Did he just say, "your character?" No, he couldn't have.

"Woah wait a second now." I stop him, speaking a little louder, forgetting that Grady's just around the corner, even though he is snoring up a storm. "Did you say *my* character?"

"Well, technically I said, 'your character,' but yes," Nick comes back like it's nothing big. Then a sly grin breaks the serious look on his face.

"Are you serious? How?" I ask, my voice growing louder.

"Shh," he reminds me, then wobbles his head and looks up at the ceiling like he's thinking about it before meeting my excited brown eyes again. "The guy who was supposed to play him dropped out last week before he signed the contract."

"Okay, but how the hell is it my role?" I ask again, trying to keep my voice quiet. "I mean I didn't even audition or anything."

"Luca needed someone to fill in," Nick started, "so I suggested he give you a try. I gave him your audition tape for that screamer movie you tried out for and he loved it. Said you looked the part, plus you're cheaper on a short notice. We start filming tomorrow, well tonight I guess. They'll work out the details then."

"Are you serious?" I step back, gripping the counter so I don't start jumping.

This has to be a joke.

"This is as real as it gets, Coop," he confirms, and then repeats himself. "And we start filming in less than twenty-four hours."

"Woah! I..." My voice stalls out as I try to gather my thoughts. "Thanks, man! This is awesome! I mean, this is so great!"

"What did you think I needed your shirt, pant and shoe size for last week?" Nick asks, an amused smile staring back at me.

"I don't know." I shake my head. "Thought maybe you were planning early for Christmas, or for the wedding maybe."

"Nope," he smiles. "Autumn and Mom already got all the suits ordered. I had to give the costume people some idea of your size. Speaking of which, we have to be up in a few hours. We've got to get you fully sized for your clothes and let Brooklyn take a look at you. She's the team's makeup artist. Plus, I want to grab breakfast first."

"Yeah, sure," I agree, still in a daze. He could tell me he saw a UFO last night and I'd probably be agreeable right now.

"Get some sleep, Coop. I'll see you in a few." He grins and pats me on the shoulder. "It's good having you up."

I nod. "You too, Nick, I mean, uh, yeah. Thanks for letting me come."

He chuckles at me before disappearing down a small hallway. For a long moment I just stand between the fridge and stovetop staring at a blank wall. Finally, I shake the shock from my head and let a sigh escape my lungs.

I'm going to be in a movie. I'm going to be in a fucking movie.

2: Cooper Bay

I can barely keep my eyes open even with the sky covered in low, gray clouds. Arriving early this morning and then getting up bright and early the same morning has put my internal clock in chaos.

A light drizzle plays with the Jeep's wipers as Nick steers us out of the parking deck and into heavy traffic. I yawn, my mouth full of hash browns. I'm sure it's a beautiful sight.

"So basically, my character's a badass," I tell, more than ask, Nick after swallowing. I read over the movie script twice before letting myself go to sleep. So yeah, I can't exactly put all the blame for my exhaustion on the red-eye flight. But it was worth it. I mean it was surreal, noting the little details and habits of Carter Hawkins, *my* character. He's a regular guy, a year younger than me, good looking but totally unaware of it, and he has a habit of sticking his foot in his mouth at just the wrong moment. That aside, he's the hero of the story, but he doesn't begin that way, not at all.

"I don't know if I'd put it that way," Nick chuckles. "He saves the day in the end, but that's not without loss, a lot of loss."

I nod. Nick's right. Most of his friends and family are dead and gone by the end of the movie, but he makes it in the end with his girl. Typical B-horror material, but that works for me.

"Well, yeah." I shrug him off. "I'm still the hero though."

I glimpse out the window at the mass of people trekking down the sidewalk, a rainbow of umbrellas forming a make-shift ceiling over their heads. This place is amazing. Every ethnicity, every creed, every religion and orientation, all of it is represented on every street, under every towering sky-scraper and gigantic electric billboard. The massive structures seem to reach up to the darkening clouds to announce the city's unimaginable breadth and inclusiveness.

"This place is incredible," I change the subject, awed by the massiveness of it all.

"Yeah, it's pretty cool," Nick responds. "It just takes for-ever to get anywhere in this traffic. I swear I could walk across town on foot quicker sometimes."

"Well, why don't you walk then?" I ask, barely masking my sarcasm.

"You want to get out? Be my guest." Nick smiles and waves toward the sidewalk.

"I'll pass." I shake my head.

At the next traffic stop, Nick picks up his phone and swipes past a few screens.

"You heard the new Bad Omens song yet?" he asks.

"No. Are you serious? How'd I miss that?" I crinkle my brow. They're *only* one of my favorite bands.

"Yesterday. Don't worry, you're not that behind. Here we go," he tells me and taps the screen.

My eyes light up as a series of chest vibrating booms break the silence. Bathed in bass and the band's signature in-dustrial lilt, we creep down the street and Nick swings the Jeep onto a side road before jerking into another parking deck.

"Damn, that's sweet!" I almost yell when the last beat falls into silence.

"Yeah, they're definitely holding on to their momentum from the first album," he agrees, twisting the ignition off.

I step out and meet him around the back and follow him to an enclosed staircase that leads back down to street level. With our heads under the cover of a small black umbrella, we cross another side street and take a left down West 37th Street before Nick veers off under a blue fabric awning attached to an eight-story gray stone structure with a mismatched upper half constructed of brown brick. The top half of the building must have been constructed years after the lower levels, and no one apparently gave thought to acquiring the same stone or even following the same design pattern. The vision is stark, but all the buildings in the vicinity seem to have fallen victim to the same inconsistency, a quilt of dull, mismatched grays and browns.

Inside, Nick leads me down a busy hallway. The walls are painted a neutral green and covered in posters advertising everything from the local mobile hotdog stand to an upcoming musical. We pass door after door leading into local businesses and shops. Halfway down the corridor Nick takes the stairs and we exit onto the third floor, stopping before a nondescript door in the middle of a largely empty hallway.

"This is Brooklyn's place," he tells me. Brooklyn Davis, the makeup artist he had told me about, or more warned me about. Apparently, she's a bit of a flirt.

Nick knocks on the wooden door and seconds later I hear quiet footsteps on creaky floorboards approaching on the other side. A lock clicks and the door slips open about two inches before a chain lock grabs it.

A young girl peers around the corner, brown eyes and free strands of brunette hair greet us. She sees Nick.

"Oh, Nick, it's you." Her bright eyes light up and she pushes the door closed to lift the chain lock and then lets it swing open. "So, I assume this is your brother. Cooper, right?"

She's pretty. Well, cute might be a better word for it. Petite dimples dent her cheeks when she smiles and her thin frame sways gracefully.

"That'd be right," he tells her and then introduces me. "Coop, this is Brooklyn."

"Nice to meet you, Cooper," Brooklyn extends her hand. I take it and give it a shake. "Nice firm grip *and* handsome. This should be easy."

I'm not sure what to say, so I just grin sheepishly, which earns an amused chuckle from Brooklyn.

"Hey," I say.

She grins and lets us in.

"Now don't give him a big head," Nick tells her. "He's already hard enough to deal with. If nothing else, bring him down a notch for me."

I shake my head and follow Nick into the apartment. It's small but neatly kept. The walls are teal, scattered with simple wooden frames and beach memorabilia. One such piece depicts a cartoonish fishing pole hanging off a pier, and a simple pair of red and blue sandals, presumably cut from a bit of driftwood, hangs a few feet over.

We round the corner. It opens into a tiny living space decorated much like the hallway, except the walls transform into a deep shade of mocha, and two tall windows dot the opposite wall. I can see the other building across the street through the clear panes. On the largest of the two sofas cramping the space sits a small man. His face is square except where the slopes of his chin form a hard V, and his pale skin comes dangerously close to whitewashing his Hispanic blood. The set of mindful chestnut eyes appear small under his thick eyebrows.

"Luca!" Nick nearly yells. "I wasn't expecting to see you here."

"Hey, Nick," the man rises and grabs Nick up in a bear hug. He looks even smaller wrapped around my brother. "I had a little free time and I wanted to see who you swindled me into casting for my lead role."

Oh, it's Luca, the director.

I straighten and put on a stupid caught-off-guard grin. Brooklyn holds back a laugh and steps around the sofa.

"I just need to get my stuff. I'll be right back," she says before walking off, leaving us with Luca.

"Well, I don't know about swindling you," Nick raises his hands and then points at me, "but here he is. Cooper meet Luca Sanchez. He's the director of the movie you're starring in."

I take a step forward and offer my hand. He takes it and we shake. His hands are cold and clammy, but I'm too nervous to care.

"Good to meet you, Cooper. When Logan dropped out at the last minute I thought I was going to have to postpone shooting," Luca tells me, still holding my hand in a firm grip. Finally, he lets go. "But your brother told me about you. He says you're in acting school down in Colorado, right?"

"Uh, no, sir. I'm at UT-Austin," I correct him. I'm not sure if Nick told him wrong or if Luca's just got a bad memory. It doesn't matter.

"Oh, that's right." He points at Nick apologetically. "That's what he said. Texas. I knew it was one of the southern colleges. But as I was saying, your brother mentioned you. He says you're good, a natural. What do you say?"

I don't know what to say. I've never confronted a director in the real world, only in school projects, and for those, Jacoby or another one of my schoolmates were the director. I let the initial shock fade and work on presenting a confident front, not wanting to appear unsure.

"I'm still learning, sir, but I believe I can do the part," I tell him. "I've read the script twice since Nick gave it to me last night."

"Well that's good. Just remember that this isn't school. This is real-world acting. It might not be a big studio picture, but we're going for quality. So are you sure you can do it?" His tone and demeanor become serious.

"Yes, sir," I tell him. I know I can. Well, I hope I can.

"In that case, stop calling me sir," Luca says. "I'm not that damn old. It's Luca."

"Yes, si..." I stop myself. "Luca."

"That's better." He smiles and pats me on the back as he walks past me and into the hallway. "In that case, I'll see you both tonight at Amicci's."

I nod without thinking. *Amicci's? What's Amicci's, and am I going?* Nick and Luca exchange goodbyes and I hear the door open and slam shut again down the hallway.

I guess that means I'm going to Amicci's tonight.

"You'll like him," Nick looks at me. "He's a lot of fun. Big into the music scene."

"Seems like a nice guy," I tell him.

"A good director, too. If he keeps going like he is, he'll

make it into the big leagues eventually. He even got Jaylen Walker to play a part in this one."

"Jaylen Walker? You mean *Attack of the Zombie Sharks* Jaylen Walker?" I ask, grinning from ear to ear.

"Yeah," Nick grunts. "He's had some big roles, despite that one minor mishap."

"That's a pretty big *mishap*."

Footsteps signal Brooklyn's return. She is hauling a small tote box under her arm, filled with all manners of makeup, I'm sure. This is the one part of acting that doesn't excite me. Makeup.

"Sit," she tells us, and places the tote on a generous brown coffee table before taking a seat where Luca had been. She pats the cushion next to her and looks up at me. "Cooper, if you'll take a seat here so I can get a good look at you."

I do as she asks and sit down. I hate makeup. Oh, how I hate makeup.

3: Cooper Bay

Amicci's is dark. Shadows jump from table to table as half-drunk and shit-face-drunk patrons pass among the crowd. The music is loud, pushing patrons in and out of the bar with its thumping, rhythmic undercurrent.

"Luca said they got a table near the back," Nick shouts over the cacophony of voices and music. He says something else after looking away, but the words fade into the crowd before they can reach me.

"Okay," I yell back, trailing behind, winding in and out of the sea of bodies and tables.

A few drunks later, I catch sight of Luca in the back of the bar sitting at a large corner table, positioned away from the main crowd. There's a stately older gentleman sitting to his left. The start of wrinkles tug at his forehead just below a full head of salt and pepper. He sits up tall and proper, eyeing Nick and me down as we approach. I take a seat next to Nick on the opposite side of the table in between Grady and a blonde-haired guy I don't know.

"Hey, man," Grady says, like we're old friends, from behind his rimless glasses. "How ya been?"

"Good. You?" I ask, at least a little more comfortable around him than the others.

"I can't complain." He shrugs his shoulders and I return

my attention to Nick.

"Luca, Mr. Williams." Nick nods to Luca across the heavy wooden table and then the man with the salt and pepper hair.

"Hey, Nick," Luca yells over the noise. It's quieter back here, but the music and the buzz of the other patrons still makes it hard to hear.

"Nick," Mr. Williams says. He has an air about him, nothing too uptight, just old school. I can't substantiate it, but I bet he smells like old cigars. He points at me. "So who do we have here?"

"This is my little brother, Cooper," Nick tells him before looking at me. "Cooper, this is Marshall Williams, the executive producer for the movie. AKA, the money."

Nick says it with a casual flippancy, but that's Nick. I guess the man really isn't uptight after all. I grin and nod.

"Good to meet you, Mr. Williams." We shake hands across the table.

"Thank you for joining the cast on such late notice," the older man says, dropping back to his seat. "I trust that you have signed the contract by now. The last boy to agree to the role bailed on us just before signing. This late in the game we really need you."

"Oh yes, I did," I nod, settling my ass back in the poorly cushioned chair and placing my hands in my lap, admittedly a bit nervous. I signed the papers a few hours ago. "I really appreciate the opportunity."

"Oh, don't thank me," Williams tells me, waving his hand broadly to his left. "Thank Luca and your brother here, and…uh… What was that kid's name that bailed on us, Luca?"

"Logan," Luca answers, eyeing the table irritably.

"Yes, and Logan. They're the ones to thank."

I nod, not really sure what else to say. I know I wasn't exactly the first choice, but really?

"I guess I should introduce you to the rest of the crew." Nick takes over, saving me from an awkward moment of silence. He angles his head toward Grady, who's sitting in the seat next to him. "You already know Grady, and I think you know of Jaylen. He'll be playing Kaden Harris."

Nick swings his gaze back around the table and points to the imposing figure sitting to the right of Luca, Jaylen Walker. His black skin is taut and he has a broad chin and smile. He quickly puts his stein down and looks up at me, then extends his hand.

"It's great to meet you," I say, shaking his hand and trying not to look so awestruck. "I'm Cooper."

Jaylen grins. He has a firm grip. "And I'm Jaylen, but I guess you knew that. Good to have you. You looking forward to filming?"

"Oh, yes. Definitely." The words rush from my mouth, exposing my excitement. "It'll be my first film outside of school."

"Well that's comforting," Jaylen says, still all grins.

I want to retract the statement immediately.

Are you fucking *stupid, Cooper? No one's going to take you seriously if you lead with that.*

Out of the corner of my eye, Mr. Williams shifts uncomfortably in his chair and Luca avoids looking toward the producer.

Dammit. Wonder if they told him that little tidbit?

"And this is Gabriel Meadows," Nick cuts in before I can say anything else stupid, waving his hand toward a younger guy who appears close to my age, "but pretty much everyone calls him Gabe. He'll be playing Sean Brewer."

Gabe is thin with messy brown, almost black hair, amber eyes and a smooth baby face. He's pale like my brother. Not I've-never-seen-the-sun pale, more like I'd-prefer-to-sit-inside-and-play-video-games pale. The small black mole set below his pink lips is the only hint of imperfection I can find in his complexion, at least beyond the lack of sun. He immediately gets up, leans across the table and shakes my hand.

"Good to meet you, Cooper," Gabe says. His voice betrays his age. It's not high or anything, just youthful, boyish still. "Don't worry, this is my first film as well. I just graduated from acting school last week. I'm just glad I'm not the only newbie in the cast."

I force a grin. I guess I'm not getting out of that one anytime soon. "Great to meet you too, Gabe. I guess we've both..."

"And this is Helen Harrison," Nick cuts me off and waves past Gabe to the woman sitting next to him. She's the I've-never-seen-the-sun type of pale, like seriously stark white, and her platinum blonde hair exacerbates her ghostly color. Then again, everything about the woman feels gaunt and discolored, including her high cheekbones and bony frame. Bright green eyes provide her face with a glimmer that her complexion and thin facade otherwise deny her.

"It's a pleasure," she says, the remnants of a British accent lingering on her tongue. Despite her pale and skinny exterior, I can't help but find something attractive in her. I mean, she's at least in her forties, but she's still pretty in an odd sort of way I can't really put my finger on. Plus, I might break her if I did.

In the seat to my immediate right sits another guy. I think he's older than me, but it can't be by much. Nick motions toward him.

"This is Riley, our gaffer. He'll also be playing the part of Tanner O'Brien."

"I prefer light tech. Gaffer seems so unprofessional." Riley's steel blue eyes rise to meet mine, framed by short, dirty-blond hair, a small nose and unusually generous lips for a guy. Unlike Gabe across the table, his skin has a healthy tan to it, though his ears are a tad pointy. He smiles, spreading his thick lips across his face. "It's good to meet you, Cooper. I'll be sure to keep you lit."

"With light I hope," I try at a joke. I'm actually surprised when Riley erupts in laughter. It wasn't even a good one, but I guess he's probably laughing more at me than at my joke. Gabe snickers across the table, along with Luca and my brother. Helen is obviously trying to hold herself back, while Mr. Williams sits stoically with an eyebrow raised. At least the others are trying to humor me.

"I like him already." Riley pats me on the shoulder before looking back at me. "We can talk about *being* lit later."

I smile, the load finally off my shoulders.

"Yeah, later," Nick agrees, and then points to Brooklyn, who's sitting at the edge of the table between Riley and Helen. "And of course you've already met Brooklyn."

She nods, and I do the same. I look around the table, counting off the acting roles in my head. Four. We're missing someone.

Seeing the look on my face, Luca pipes in. "Ava couldn't make it in time for dinner. She's going to meet us at the docks in a few hours."

I nod just before Helen jumps in.

"She's playing Grace Bishop, your love interest in the film." Helen grins suggestively. "I think you'll like her."

"I'm sure I will," I say, trying to sound agreeable but not too eager.

"No, Cooper, you don't understand. You'll *definitely* like her, she's built like an hourglass." Nick stops talking and waves both hands in front of me, imitating the form of an hourglass.

"Oh yeah," Riley nudges my shoulder with a knowing grin.

"Oh," is all I can think to say.

"Oh, come on," Brooklyn argues after casting a hateful glare at Riley. "Is that all you guys think about?"

"Well. I mean." Nick feigns contemplation. "Yeah."

I chuckle, but it's okay. Everyone at the table, even Marshall, is laughing. Only Brooklyn remains nonplused.

"It's okay, Brooklyn. We're in a group of guys. They can't help themselves," Helen assures her between giggles. "They only think with their dicks, you just have to learn to overlook it and move on."

No one bothers to argue with Helen's prognosis. What would be the point of that when she's right? Brooklyn huffs, but her beaming glare doesn't lighten on Riley.

The two must be a thing.

Minutes later, a new round of drinks spot the table and our food arrives on black trays. I lift my Blue Motorcycle and take a generous sip of the cold, citrusy blue liquid. I still haven't gathered the courage to order it by its other name, *Adios Motherfucker*. One day, though, I'll do it.

They're an interesting bunch from what I learned

throughout the night. Gabe's definitely the gamer in the group, maybe a bit on the nerdy side, but with his looks it hasn't hurt him. Apparently, he's been with the same guy since his senior year in high school, which is more than I can say. Jaylen isn't at all as serious as most of his movie roles. He might even be a worthy rival of my brother's humor.

I've sort of known Grady for a few years, but I didn't realize he could be so oblivious until tonight. Riley, on the other hand, is neither humorous nor oblivious. Sure, he's made a few jokes, but he really seems more reserved than I originally thought. And the more I pay attention to him and Brooklyn, I'm getting the feeling that he's less interested in her than she is in him.

Helen seems nice, but there's some type of tension between her and Luca. It's low key, but I swear it's there, especially when she cut him off before he could finish talking about snagging the directorial role on the film. Then there's the money, Marshall Williams. He seems like a fun guy if you get past his traditionalism. I swear he's just old school, though, and rich.

"I'd like to make a toast," Luca announces and raises his stein. The table quiets down, but it seems like the rest of the restaurant only gets louder. "We're about to make a great movie. I can feel it. So this is to each of you."

Glasses and steins rise around the table and clink against each other. I join in on the chorus of cheers, and down the last bit of my drink.

"Another round," Luca calls out to the waiter walking by. "On me."

The stick of a man nods and walks off to get the drinks. I realize I still don't know where we're shooting. I can't believe

I never thought to ask.

"So," I start, "where exactly are we filming, and when?"

Devious grins make their way around the table. I scrunch my brow, confused. Mr. Williams speaks up first.

"North Brother Island, tonight."

North Brother Island? Where the hell is that?

I can feel my brow raising before I ask, "Tonight?"

My question is met by nods around the table. Trying not to sound like I'm complaining, I pick back up with, "Oh, that's great. The sooner the better, right? So where's this island? I've never heard of it."

"Right here in New York City," Helen pulls my attention away with her cool accent. "It's a small island in the East River, in between Port Morris in the Bronx and Rikers Island."

"It's an abandoned island—" Luca joins in before Brooklyn cuts him off.

"Off limits, too, technically," Brooklyn injects, her tone accusatory. "It's an avian sanctuary, a reserve. It's been abandoned for like fifty years or something."

"Can I finish a sentence?" Luca asks, palms up and a half grin perched under his nose.

"Sorry..." Brooklyn smiles and looks away.

"Seriously?" I can't help but blurt it out now that I'm finally starting to feel comfortable around them. "It's been abandoned for fifty years? In the middle of New York City?"

It seems too crazy to be true. An abandoned island right nestled up by one of the largest cities in the world. How the hell does that happen?

"They're not joking, Coop." Nick pats me on the back. "I swear it's real. The place is totally uninhabited. Just a bunch of birds, though I hear there aren't as many of those either nowadays."

"So…how?" I ask.

"Ava knows more about it than any of us," Helen answers, "but basically it was the home of a quarantine hospital, Riverside I think, in the late 1800s. It's where Typhoid Mary was quarantined, is what Ava says. I think it shut down and became a couple other things until it finally closed for good in the late sixties and the city declared it off limits to the public, and voila, it became a bird sanctuary."

"Yeah, for some bird that's since moved off the island, too," Luca says. "Some heron, I think. At least that's what I think Ava said."

"That's right, they're gone." Gabe nods.

If one thing is apparent, it's that no one at the table is one hundred percent sure about the island except Ava, who isn't here. I chuckle inside even though the island seems a bit ominous, with typhoid and all.

"Damn," I mutter.

"If you can't tell already, Ava's the resident historian, too." Nick nudges me. "That's why she's not here actually. She had to work tonight. She handles educational programs over at the Brooklyn Museum."

"Ah," I mutter, frowning contemplatively. That makes sense I guess. "But she acts, too?"

"Oh yes," Helen jumps in. "She has a degree in history and acting from Berkley. She's not just a pretty face."

"She's definitely got us all beat on both the looks and the smarts," Grady points out, exaggerating his southern drawl as he leans back in his chair. His statement is met with questionable glances from both Helen and Brooklyn. "Except for you two, of course."

I shake my head. I think I've officially become the least awkward guy at the table, but I don't think Grady is one to really give a shit.

"So if the island is abandoned and off limits, how exactly are we filming there?" I ask, scrunching my brow.

"By boat," Mr. Williams states succinctly and then looks at Luca.

"Well, our presence on the island isn't exactly sanctioned or legal," Luca fills me in on the details of their plan. "It's the perfect location though. We don't have to fight with locals wanting to get into the movie or with having to clear out an area to start filming or ask for permits and junk. It's just empty, and it's perfect, really, for the movie. I mean, it's deserted, how much more post-apocalyptic can you get?"

Nick obviously realizes how nervous the idea makes me, placing a reassuring hand on my shoulder. My eyes haven't left Luca.

Are you serious? What if the authorities catch us? I don't want to go to jail or have this on my record.

"It's okay, Coop," Nick tells me. His eyes are soft and comforting when I finally pull my mine from the director. "We've got it all planned out. We're taking three small paddleboats over tonight and we're only staying for two nights. We'll be out before anyone thinks twice about it."

What the hell did you get me into, Nick?

"But if we get caught, what happens? Jail? Fines? What?" My speech quickens with each word. "I mean, it is off limits, right?"

"You signed the contract, Mr. Bay," Williams's voice changes into a deeper, ruder gruffness. "You've already agreed to it."

"Yeah, I have, but this is illegal," I tell him, surprised at the words coming out of my own mouth. "If it's illegal, I don't have to fulfill the contract."

"Coop... Man." Nick shakes my shoulder gently to get my attention. I look at him and let him know I'm not happy with him at the moment, but he continues anyway. "It's going to be okay. We're just going to slip in, film a movie, and slip out. It's okay. We're going to have a great time."

I break my eyes away and look at the food sitting in front of me. A plate full of jumbo shrimp and a heap of french fries. It's fried to a golden perfection just like in the picture advertising it on the bar's menu. I take a deep breath and grab one of the large fantails and shove it into my mouth. I chew, letting the worry slip between each chomp of my teeth.

Once my heart settles, I sigh and look back up at Nick. "Okay."

4: Cooper Bay

The stuffy cab bounces over another pothole. Out my window in the back seat, a set of empty, fenced-off basketball courts pass by followed by a row of drab multi-colored buildings. We crossed the Harlem River into the Bronx maybe a minute ago, leaving the busy hustle under the skyscrapers and flashing billboards behind for a more level landscape. Nick sits to my left and Luca sits shotgun, directly ahead of me, next to the black cabbie who's without doubt a New York native.

The driver takes a right at the next traffic signal, swinging us under a freeway, its support beams painted in a deep forest green. I try to catch the street name, but all I manage is *149* as the cabbie accelerates and I'm pushed against my seat. Traffic is lighter here. In fact, our three cabs are the only vehicles crowding the road as far ahead as I can see with the moon looming overhead.

The driver slows next to a brown and white-walled factory building with the Coca-Cola logo stamped discreetly on the side over seven closed loading bay doors. I can hear him sigh before accelerating again.

"Are you sure this is where you want to go?" he asks Luca.

"Yes," Luca reiterates for at least the fourth time since leaving Amicci's.

Ahead, a dimly lit gate rises from a path of weeds and grass to the right and the road veers off in the other direction behind the factory. In the dark I can just make out the silhouette of a guardrail directly ahead as the cab's headlights glare against the fence's metal struts.

The cabbie swings to the left, leaving the gate behind us. I take a quick glance over my shoulder and out the back window. The others are still right behind us. Skyscrapers rise in the background against a gray sky, its stars obscured by the city's intense glow. The light doesn't seem to reach here, though, and the few working streetlights set between the guardrail and another chain-link fence only emit a dull, coppery luminescence that barely illuminates the pole they're mounted on.

"Are you sure you want me to leave you here?" the cabbie asks again, dragging his words.

"Yes." Luca glares at the driver, the dull light slipping over and past his irritated eyes. "Just drop us off right here actually."

"Ah... Okay," the cabbie says, throwing up a hand in mock defeat. "You want me to wait or come back?"

"Nah, we'll call another cab when we're ready," Luca tells him.

The car comes to a stop. I barely register the brakes before Luca opens his door and climbs out. Nick follows along, so I do the same, swinging my door wide and stepping out onto the pavement. Lights flare up around me as the other two cabs come to a rest and the remainder of our posse unloads. I lift my backpack from the back seat and situate it over my shoulders. It contains my life for at least the next two days, my clothes, supplies and food.

"I know it's none of my business," the cabbie starts, but it's apparent he's going to ask anyway. "But why did I bring you all out here? There's nothing out here."

"Like you said, it's not for you to worry about," Luca tells him calmly and lets the cab door clunk shut before the driver can say any more. I see his lips moving inside the car, and I can imagine all the nice things he's calling Luca right now. It brings a tiny smile to my face, not that Luca's likely getting blessed out in secret but the simple notion that he's blessing someone out in general.

The cabs pull away, bouncing over the uneven pavement, and finally the red glow of their taillights disappears behind a grouping of bushes and trees. What we're doing sinks into my mind again and I'm suddenly nervous. It's not like I've never done anything illegal before but with a bunch of people I just met, that's definitely new.

I take a breath and force myself to push back the unease. Packs in tow, mostly slung over their shoulders, the rest of the crew gathers around Luca expectantly. The sound of the river sloshing just beyond the road beckons to me. Gabe brushes up against me as he takes the spot to my right and Nick claims his spot to my left. I nod at Helen, who's eyeing me across the circle.

Does she think I'm going to be a problem? No, you're just nervous, Cooper. Stop it. You're being stupid.

At my ten o'clock, my eyes catch someone new. She's beautiful. Shoulder-length dirty-blonde hair with brown roots fighting for control. Her eyes appear so vibrant even though I can't identify their color in the dark, but I'd take a guess and say they're blue. Prominent bare lips form a confident smile across a sloping jawline, complimenting her soft skin and super cute nose.

A light blossoms next to me as Helen switches her flashlight on, followed by a flurry of other glows around the circle. I pull my eyes from the girl.

Ava?

It was only a second, but it felt like so much longer that my eyes were locked onto her. I let myself take another quick glance, swiftly diverting my eyes to Jaylen at her side the moment after I find her, trying to be inconspicuous. Yep, blue eyes, or crystal blue to be exact. But that's not all the light illuminated. Nick was right, the girl has nice form. Her sloping hips thin into a small waist before blossoming again in the form of plump breasts under the unforgiving fabric of an off-white t-shirt.

"All right, everybody," Luca interrupts the silence. "We're here. It's time to get over to the island and film a movie."

A round of shouts come in agreement to Luca's proclamation. I keep my eyes focused on the director, trying not to be awkward again, trying to focus my attention on anyone, anything but the new girl.

"Oh, how rude of us," Helen jumps in, leaning in to the middle of the circle and raising a brow toward the newcomer, then finding me. "We didn't introduce the newest member of the team to Ava."

It is *Ava.*

Nods make their way around the group, and I let my eyes find her again. It's no longer awkward now that everyone expects it. Her eyes meet mine with a warm smile.

"Ava," Helen goes on, pointing toward me with her palm up, "this is Cooper Bay, Nick's little brother. He'll be playing your love interest, Carter Hawkins."

"Good to meet you, Cooper." Her voice is like chocolate, smooth and silky, and I can't help but want to hear it again.

"Thanks, you too," I say, trying not to sound like some awkward middle schooler and failing.

"Well, at least you didn't recast Logan with some ugly fucker." Ava casts a raised brow at Helen after her eyes travel over my body, then level with my eyes again. "Not bad at all, actually."

I take an involuntary gulp and tighten up my shoulders and hands. I don't have a clue how to respond to that. In the corner of my vision I can see Nick biting his lip to hold back a burst of laughter before he pats me on the shoulder.

"Glad you approve," Luca said with a barely perceptible shake of his head. "Well, no point in wasting time. Let's get going."

Without waiting for us to reply, Luca turns and mounts the barricade set between the road and the river, then plops down to a slim, rocky coastline. The others start after him, but I remain behind a moment to peer over the water. I squint, and under the veil of night a faint coastline comes into view just beyond a scattering of grass and old pylons, but the dark hides the details from my eyes.

I trudge forward, still unsure about all of this, flashlight in hand, and climb over the barricade. Even in the middle of June the night air along the coast carries a slight nip as it caresses the back of my neck and whips around my back. I try to keep my gaze away from Ava a few feet ahead of me, but I keep failing.

Seriously, Cooper. Stop acting like a fucking teenager.

I pull my eyes away and distract myself with idle chatter with my brother.

"So we've got to row over to the island?"

"Yeah..." Nick says quizzically. "Unless you want to get caught, that is."

"No, I just...uh..." I stutter, trying to find something to say, something to keep my attention off Ava. Quickly I find the words. "I was just wondering. I don't think I've ever been in a rowboat, that's all."

"Yeah, I don't think so, at least not that I remember." Nick grins with a nod. We were more of the gaming type. Not just video games, but sports, too. Boating, and especially rowboating, had never been on our list of things to do, at least not mine. "Me neither, now that I think of it. Can't be too hard though."

I shrug. The foliage at the edge of the bank gives way to the East River, and at the tiny shore's edge sit our three rowboats. There's nothing spectacular about them, just regular metal boats, like you might find at an outdoors shop, with two sets of oars mounted near the front and back of each. Luca is the first to climb on-board.

"All aboard!" he calls. All eyes land on him, heads lowered, eyes saying, *really?* Luca purses his lips as he settles down in the boat, vigorously shaking his head and muttering something I can't quite make out.

I follow Nick and Grady and take up residence in the boat with Luca. I take a seat at the rear between the last set of oars before thinking about the spot. Examining the cheap metal oars, I chew on my lip, wondering how easy it is to screw this up.

"Hey." I tap Nick on the shoulder, leaning forward, and whisper, "You wanna switch places?"

I can't see his smile, but I can tell by the tone of his voice that he's laughing at me inside. Yeah, I don't want to row. I'd prefer to go the right direction rather than in erratic circles. Who could blame me, right?

"Sure, I'll try it."

"Thanks!" I say, rising from my spot and cautiously switching places with him, careful not to rock the boat. I really don't want to get wet, especially not with all the clothes I have packed in my sack still on my back.

I settle down on the plank between Nick and Luca before stealing a glance to my left, where the rest of the group is mostly settled in now, except for Brooklyn, who seems to have made the same move I just did, switching places with Riley. Gabe sits at the head of the boat, looking at the oars suspiciously. I grin. In the last boat sit Jaylen, Helen and Ava, but I divert my gaze back to the dark river in front of me just beyond Luca before she realizes I'm looking.

"All right, guys," Luca announces. "Let's cut the flashlights and get going. North Brother Island is just ahead."

As the lights go out and my eyes adjust to the darkness — as dark as New York City can be, at least — Nick pushes off the shore and the oars comes to life, sloshing back and forth. The water churns beneath them, forming tiny waves as the boat drifts forward, black under the clear night sky. Despite the lack of clouds, I note the stark absence of all but a handful of the brightest stars.

Damn light pollution.

Nick taps me on the shoulder and points across the river where a mass of land sits.

"There. That's North Brother."

I nod. It looks big. I was expecting something smaller, something insignificant. How could an island that big in such a populated place remain uninhabited? It just seems crazy.

No one says a word as the island grows closer, its shore expanding with every swish of the oars. Ahead, clusters of wood jut up from the undisturbed surface of the water, washed in shades of gray. Behind them, a grand archway, ravaged by decades of abandonment, comes into view followed by a long wooden dock stretching to the island's bank. Its towering arch is decayed and rusted, pieces of metal and wood dangling from its side in a gentle breeze, a whole section at the top gone, its battle with time lost.

Along the shoreline my eyes catch a two-story structure growing from the surface and a large, unused cylindrical smokestack towering above it. I think it's made of brick, but between the dark and how the forest has reclaimed the structure, I'm not sure.

"Over this way," Luca utters just loud enough for everyone to hear and motions to the right. I let my eyes follow his hand, landing on an outcropping of rocks just beyond a manmade wall that was meant to hold back the river.

I drag in a deep breath. Here we go.

5: Cooper Bay

"There should be a road just past the trees here," Ava points ahead.

Behind me, Riley pulls the last boat onto the shore and hides it beneath a grouping of bushes.

"You wanted to shoot at the church first, right?" she continues.

"Yes." Luca nods, stomping up the bank and settling by Ava. He pulls a piece of paper from his left pocket and unfolds it. Swiveling on his feet, he searches the woods before finding what he's looking for: the brick structure I saw from the river with the massive smokestack atop it. He moves back to his right, pointing. "So, the church should be that way?"

"Round about." Ava nods slowly, the type of nod that says *yes* and *I'm not totally sure* in the same instant.

Standing behind them in the shadow of the impending forest. I can only see their silhouettes against the glare of their flashlights jumping between the trees. I flick on my own light and move forward with the others, keeping my eyes high and my beam sweeping the rocky coast. A few feet ahead it transitions into an overgrown combination of dirt, grass and weeds.

It's incredible seeing this much green in any part of New York City. Even the building to our left is literally covered in vines and the trees hugging its walls. The thick tendrils scale up its walls, breach its broken windows and disappear over its roofline. In the dark, it's almost like the building is not even there, but instead it becomes a massive bulk of plant life.

"Well, let's move on out," Luca raises his voice. "We'll start at the church and move from there."

"Is that all that's on this side of the island?" Riley asks, taking up a slow trot behind me.

"No," Ava starts, turning just enough to look back at us. "It's one of the few buildings on this side, but there's a lighthouse and greenhouse farther down the southern tip as well."

"Ah," Riley grunts.

I keep my pace even with Nick, sweeping my light between the trees while I push stray limbs out of the way. It's dense, a scattering of tall, spindly trunks covered in leafy vines coating the forest floor and the occasional knee-high bush, or maybe a baby tree.

The noise of the city is a distant echo, the beeping and swoosh of cars flying by, the voices, all of it but a whisper. This sounds more like home. The insects chirping loudly, birds squawking and singing, the light breeze rustling the leaves and pushing at my shirt. A tree branch ruffles and sways overhead as a bird takes flight, disturbed by our presence. I flinch before I realize what it is, glancing up at the now-empty branch and then at the Nick. I'm relieved to see Gabe and Brooklyn were apparently spooked, too.

"Are there any animals on the island, besides the birds?" Gabe calls from a few feet behind me. His boyish voice possesses an inkling of worry.

"Ah..." Ava thinks aloud.

"Nothing dangerous at least?" Gabe interjects.

"No," she says. "As far as I know we're not going to run

into much except some birds, and insects of course. So if you don't like spiders you might be in for a treat."

Spiders. Dammit.

I cringe at the thought. Of all insects, spiders are my least favorite, the fucking spawn of Satan himself, if you ask me. Oh, and we're going to be camping tonight.

Wonderful. Again, Nick, what have you gotten me into?

"This island isn't that big, right?" Brooklyn speaks up, her tiny voice barely carrying past me. "It's pretty small, isn't it?"

"Yeah, it's small." The voice is Luca's. He doesn't bother to turn around but instead keeps stomping through the forest. "It's not even a tenth of the size of Rikers Island."

I dodge a loose limb that Grady pushes to the side and right into my path. The forest is thicker here. Then suddenly it ends, spilling us out onto a cracked and crumbling paved road just wide enough for a single car.

A crisp wind whips by, ruffling my hair and caressing my cheeks. I look up, expecting to see the night sky, but instead my eyes are met by an entanglement of tree limbs casting their own sort of night sky over the roadway.

"We'll head right," Ava directs, stepping onto the road and leading on. "There should be an intersection up ahead. We'll cross back over into the woods there and the church should be just a few minutes out."

No one answers. Either everyone simply trusts her or, like me, they don't have a clue where to go on their own. I keep my light low, casting its glow on the crumbling road and Luca's and Grady's backs. In the dark, I let me eyes settle on the best sight in this night-encased forest. Ava's rear. I don't claim to be a connoisseur of ass exactly, but hers has to be among the top. The way her thick thighs mold into the slope of her buttocks and back up into the small of her back is exquisite. Watching her walk causes the blood to surge down to my crotch. I have to look away.

Calm down, Cooper. You're not in her league.

Up ahead, the intersection appears in our flashlight beams. Ava takes off toward the tree line and waves for everyone to follow.

"All right, back into the woods," Luca says and steps past the tree line after Ava. Grady and Nick follow, and then me, with the others close on my heels. Within five minutes, weaving in and out of trees and vines, the forest opens up again, carving out a small clearing. In the center is part of an old structure, but mostly it's a pile of debris. One lone wall stands at the opposite end of the clearing. It's dirty, a stained white with countless vines overtaking it just like the rest of the forest. At the base of the wall is a heap of crumbled building material, presumably the structure's former roof and fallen walls. I follow the others closer to the structure.

"This is the church." Ava's voice is higher than before, a note of excitement breaching the surface as she douses what remains of the structure in light. "There's not much left, but this used to be the island's sole church."

"Must've been small to begin with," Helen notes, eyeing the building's petite footprint. It can't be more than ten yards wide and maybe twenty or twenty-five yards long, even during its prime when the walls stood tall and proud.

"You've got to remember, the island's permanent population was never that big, especially compared to the surrounding city," Ava explains. "And there used to be a bridge connecting the island to the mainland, too, so not everyone who came to the island stayed all the time. There were about 1,200 inhabitants during the peak of Typhoid fever, but even then, most of the island's residents were patients who *weren't* exactly attending church."

"That's a good point," Helen says, stepping over a decaying four-by-four and peering into the ramshackle ruins.

The sky is visible here, the occasional star shimmering down through the nearby light pollution. I look around the opening. Other than the decaying structure, it's more of the same. Vines, wild flowers, more vines and even a few saplings beginning to take root within the church's former walls.

"This is where you want to shoot first, Luca?" It's Riley. He walks back to the tree line and deposits his bags against a trunk.

"Yeah, we'll start at scene four," Luca says, stepping away from the church and eyeing what remains of the building and tree line across the opposite end of the clearing. His gaze breaks from the building and turns toward the rest of the group. "It's not exactly what I had in mind, but it'll still work great, I think. This is where Grace and Carter are running from Kaden after they realize he's planning to kill them."

That means I'm up I guess. I take a deep breath and try to psych myself up. I'm actually about to start my first acting role. How awesome is that?

6: Cooper Bay

"Run, Grace, run!" I yell between ragged breaths, my feet pounding the dirt and wild undergrowth.

She's ahead of me by less than a car length, weaving in and out of trees. Slivers of moonlight penetrate the forest canopy and glide past her shoulder as she swats another branch away. I duck to miss a branch of my own and swerve to dodge one of the hundreds of trees dotting the forest.

He's behind us, chasing us, running with a determination that I've never witnessed before in a man. I take a glance back and almost miss his ebony skin, his natural camouflage in the night. But there he is. Broad shoulders swinging, thick legs covered in tattered trousers, with an unwavering look in his eyes above the horrendous scar running from his chin up to his left ear. Kaden, the one they warned us about.

Something snags my shoe. My body starts to tumble forward, but I catch my balance with a hand slapped against one of the trees, and I fix my eyes back on escape. We've been cut off from what's left of the world's population, a small rag-tag group of survivors after everything went to shit. We were told never to go into the forest, this forest, but my curiosity got the best of me and I dragged Grace along with me.

Ahead, she breaks free of the woods. I hammer my legs harder against the ground, stretching them to their max. I glance back again. He's so close, maybe six feet away now. I swing my gaze back to my twelve o'clock. With hands clenched into tight pumping fists, I fly past the tree line and into a small outcropping in the center of the forest.

I find Grace to my right so I veer off to follow, but something solid and heavy smacks against my back. My body flies forward. I throw out my hands to brace myself, but it does little to break the fall. My face pounds the ground, and my cheek takes the brunt of the impact. I groan and shake my head as the pain blossoms up my face.

For a moment I forget where I am and what I'm doing here. Then it all rushes back as a massive black hand latches onto my shoulder and wrenches me around. Before I can struggle, he's on top of me and his blade is slicing through the air on a direct path for my chest. I throw my arms up too late to avoid the knife entirely, but maybe I can make it miss its mark.

I scream out as the sharp edge slices against my lower arm. It hurts like hell, but it's enough to keep me here, in the present. I grapple for his knife-wielding wrist and clamp on tight, pushing upward, heaving as hard as I can to keep the blade from touching me again. I'm staring directly into his eyes, that nasty crooked scar, those wide crazed eyes.

"It's your destiny, boy!" the man's deep voice bellows in my face. "Let it happen. Everything in this forest is mine, and that includes your soul."

There's a scream. It's Grace, she must have stopped.

"No!" I scream into his face. "I'm not your fucking bitch!"

"Cut, cut!" The words break through the moment and I swivel my face to the left, brushing my ear against the grass and dirt. The pressure on my hands eases as Luca steps up from crouching just behind the remains of the church building.

Jaylen rolls off my chest and clambers back to his feet, and I sit up and inhale a deep breath, then let it out again. I've not run like that in years. I look between the director and Jaylen, brow raised. Jaylen looks down at me with a wry grin. I think I know where this is going.

"'I'm not your fucking bitch?'" he repeats my line, which *might* have been a bit of a last-second improv. "*Really?*"

I don't know what to say, it was the first thing that came to mind once my original line slipped into the inaccessible crevices of my mind. But the nervous energy in my chest releases when Luca bursts out laughing.

I hope that means it's okay.

"I..." I start but then stop.

"Man, it was all I could do not to break down laughing the moment you said it," Jaylen whoops and then extends his hand.

I take it and let him pull me to my feet.

"I sorta forgot my line at the last minute," I tell him, squinting my right eye.

"Oh, I know." Jaylen grins.

"'I'm not your *fucking* bitch?'" I hear my words repeated again a few feet away. It's Nick, with the others in tow. I open my mouth to say something but notice the amused looks on their faces and choose to smile instead. Ava, or Grace, is standing a few feet behind the others. She gives me an approving nod and I catch the giggle that jumps from her lips just before it vanishes.

"Your line was 'Get off me, you fucking inbred,'" Helen reminds me. She's the only one not grinning.

It was only the third take, so all in all it's not that bad, right? However, I did get the line right the first two times.

"So I take it we need to shoot the scene again?" I ask. I'm in shape, I even enjoy a good run, but taking that sprint on top of getting slammed to the ground a fourth time doesn't sound too exciting right now. I cross my fingers mentally, hoping by some miracle that he doesn't want to.

"Why?" Jaylen interjects, throwing an arm around my shoulder. The moonlight glints off the knife still in his hand. I ignore it, it's fake anyway, one of those ones where the blade moves in and out of the handle. Jaylen shakes his head. "I like it actually."

Luca scrunches his lips and chin and looks up toward the sky. "I don't know. I think Jaylen might be on to some-"

"You can't be serious!" Helen interrupts him. "You really want him to call Kaden a *bitch*?"

"I don't know, Helen." Luca waves her off. "But I think it actually works. I mean the character doesn't exactly know what happens to people when Kaden catches them. He just knows that they disappear. And Carter can be a little sarcastic at times, right? Plus, maybe a little comic relief wouldn't be bad thing."

"But…" Helen starts, and Luca cuts her off with an upheld hand.

"I like it," he tells her. "And if we decide it doesn't work later, we can cut it out and splice in one of the other takes."

I can see the decision tugging at Helen. She's definitely not happy about it. Nick stands back, arms crossed over his chest, grinning at me. I lift my shoulders, telling him that I don't have a clue. Next to him, Grady's and Riley's eyes bounce between the director and producer with more amusement than concern. Brooklyn is holding back a giggle, and Ava now stands next to her, a satisfied grin across her lips. I can't help but smile, but I pull my eyes away from Helen first.

"I agree," Grady chimes in with an emphatic nod, the roll under his chin bouncing.

"Me too," Ava throws in her support.

The look on Helen's face is both dumbfounded and angry. I can't imagine why she's so uptight about it. She seemed so carefree at dinner.

"Yeah, that's the one. That's our shot," Luca says, nodding, talking more to himself than any of us. He turns and faces the group again. Jaylen and I walk over and join them. "All right, let's call it a night."

A round of hoorahs sound out into the empty space above the distant sounds of the city.

"Let's camp out around the church tonight," Luca continues. "We'll start shooting at the beginning of the script tomorrow morning. Get some rest."

I let out a stuttered breath, excited both for a little sleep and to have just finished my first scene in a real movie. The realization floods over me and the notion carries me away. My body shivers with excitement, and my heart beats harder than it did seconds ago when I was sprinting through the woods.

I actually did it!

"Good job, man," Jaylen says, throwing his hand out. I take it and smile, hoping there's not more to the handshake. "You might have a future after all."

I'm not sure how to take that, but I don't let my smile waver. Instead, I thank him and then head over to join Nick and

Grady. Before I can reach them, Ava weaves through the group and steps in my path.

"Good job, Cooper," she tells me. "I don't think I've ever seen anyone run that quickly before."

"I used to run track back in high school," I tell her. I was never that great at it, but I ran anyway. It was one of those things I did after not making the basketball team. "I wasn't that good, but I enjoyed it. It's been a while, though, since I've run like *that*. I feel like my legs are going to fall off."

She giggles, the left side of her lips rising slightly and her eyes narrowing. The crystal blue around her pupils catches a tiny glint of moonlight, and I have to swallow back the feeling that rushes through my chest.

Damn, she's pretty.

"You'll be running a lot for this movie, so I guess it's a good thing," she says. "You shouldn't have as much trouble at it, right?"

"I...I guess not," I tell her, not really sure what the question was. I divert my eyes and look at the ground but realize that looks suspicious so I look at her again, but I feel like I'm staring.

"Well, we'll see. Time to get some rest now," she says and turns around. I nod and watch her go. Before she makes it more than a yard she turns back around and smiles at me, her legs still carrying her away. "Night, Cooper."

I start to avert my eyes, but instead I force myself to nod, a little too vigorously, and grin back. I don't know what else to do so I wave. As she twirls around again I bite my lip, feeling stupid, and I take off.

I could have at least said "night" back. Fuck you, Cooper!

A few minutes later, still feeling like an idiot, I spread out my sleeping bag, the dull brown one I bought yesterday after leaving Brooklyn's apartment. I didn't have one before, didn't need one. It's not like I ever go camping, or I ever really *wanted* to. I'd prefer a nice air conditioned room and a soft mattress with four walls cutting me off from the outside world if it were up to me. I don't ever remember any bad camping experience as a child, as if camping in itself isn't bad enough, it's simply that we rarely did it because my family hates it.

I even out the corners of the sleeping bag and prop my sad excuse of a pillow at the open end, hoping for at least some semblance of comfort. But my mind is still on Ava. I can't stop thinking about how she twisted around and told me goodnight. I replay the sound of her voice for the tenth time and let a wave of excitement rush through me. I clench my fist and roll my eyes.

Stop it, Coop, you're being stupid.

I sigh, settling into a crouch next to my sleeping bag. In the restricted glow of the flashlights lying around the camp I can see the rest of the group settling in. I can almost make out each person. Ava's already bundled up on the far end of the ruins opposite me, I've unconsciously, and consciously, kept an eye on her.

Don't be a damn stalker, Coop.

Brooklyn and Riley are setup next to her. Luca and Grady are a few feet away from Nick, whose sleeping bag is set next to mine. Helen looks to have taken up her own spot at the base of the church's last remaining wall away from the group.

Damn, I guess she took that pretty seriously.

As I drop to my knees and start to slip into my bag, I hear another bag unrolling and flopping onto the wild grass beside me. I look over to find Gabe setting up his bed.

"Do you mind if I setup right here, man?" he asks.

"Uh, sure," I say, waving my hand at the spot next to me. "Have at it."

He finishes emptying a few items onto the grass. A pillow, about as useless as the one my head is lying on, a few candy bars—Snickers, Twix and even a Fifth Avenue bar, I think—and, of course, his phone.

He slips into the bag and wiggles around to face me. My first thought is how I'd prefer him not to face me like that, like he's about to talk all night. I'd really like some sleep.

"So how was it? Playing the role?" Gabe asks. I can't help but think he's younger than me instead of a year my senior, but his voice, despite its boyish sound, is deep enough to betray his youthful looks.

"Uh… I mean…" I stumble for the words. I know I enjoyed it, but trying to find a way to say it without sounding too grandiose or stupid is harder than I expected. I try to keep my voice down. "It was great. I mean it almost felt real, especially being out here, on this island. It being deserted and all. I can't lie, though, I guess it was a bit euphoric to have finished that first scene, after it hit me and all."

"I bet so," he agrees, an excitement building in his eyes. "I can't wait until tomorrow. I'm so ready to get started!"

"I know what you mean," I agree. He's not so bad, maybe a little nerdier than me, but I think I can deal with him.

"Hey, do you know anything about Helen?" I ask him. From the sound of it, Nick and Grady have already dozed off, as well as a few of the others. Oh, how I wish I could fall off the edge into sweet sleep so quickly, but apparently that's never been for me.

"Not much," he says. "I mean she's one of the producers."

"I know that. I mean, look at her." I point over to where she's lying, segregated from the rest of the group of her own accord. "She's separated herself off from everyone else. Did it really make her that mad that I changed the lines?"

"Oh, that." It's like a light flicks on in Gabe's head. "I don't know for sure, but I think it's more that Luca let you after she disagreed. See, she wanted the director's role for this film. From what I hear she almost begged for it, but Marshall gave it to Luca. I mean Luca *does* have more credits under his belt and all, but he passed up Helen and hired her on as a co-producer with Luca instead."

I nod slowly, some of the pieces beginning to fit into place finally. So basically, she doesn't get the artistic input she wants. She got passed up for the real creative control of the script and directing but placed right where she has to watch it happen.

"I see. I take it this could be an interesting production then."

Gabe tilts his head and lifts his shoulders. "We'll see, I guess."

"Yeah," I huff. "Well, I'm going to get some sleep. See ya in the morning, Gabe."

"Night."

I lie back, looking up into the vast sky of light pollution and the occasional star, bordered by a continuous line of towering trees. The sound of the occasional insect and a few birds chirp their way into my ears. I have to unzip my bag. It's like a sauna inside, but suddenly I'm thinking about how many spiders are out here. I cringe and close my eyes. I already miss my room, any room actually.

7: Cooper Bay

My eyes flutter open. The sky is still veiled in black and gray, and the subtle cadence of insects serenades my ears. I reach for my phone and check the time. *1:04 a.m.*

Nice, I made it a whole...what, hour or two without waking. I guess that's better than it could be, considering the pain evolving in my back, a byproduct of lying on the hard, uneven ground. I stretch my shoulders and twist my neck from side to side, earning a fleeting moment of relief.

I'm not sure I'm going to be able to stand sleeping here a whole night like this, let alone two. I swipe my phone open and tap the Facebook icon. What better way to waste away my night than to drift aimlessly around social media? It's not like I'm really going to sleep tonight anyway.

I swipe through my feed, but no one's really posting right now, at least no one I know. I close the app, already bored with it, and let my hand and phone fall to my chest as I lift my eyes to the sky. I squint and trace the stars I can actually make out beyond the gray haze.

How many more hours of this?

Sighing, I twist onto my side, eliciting a flurry of swishing sounds from my sleeping bag trying to find a comfortable spot on my pillow. After a dozen tries I give up, a scowl undoubtedly slipping across my face. Then an idea slips into my head.

I raise my phone again and unlock the screen before bringing up a web browser. The glow of the phone intensifies as an empty white window opens and asks for a URL. The hard light forces me to peek at the screen through narrowed lids. I type in *North Brothers Island*. It takes me two tries to get past AutoCorrect's "corrections" of my spelling, but finally Google comes to life. When the search page loads I realize AutoCorrect was right after all this time. Apparently, it *is* North Brother Island, not Brother*s*. Live and learn, right? I press the link to correct the spelling and let the page fill up with links.

At the top is a Wikipedia entry. I grin mischievously, thinking back on the paper I had to write about Friedrich Nietzsche and John Locke in my political philosophy class. The professor was very clear about the unreliability of the online information hub, it wasn't to be used as a source. So naturally, I click on the link and the Mecca of knowledge replaces the search results. I read the first few sentences set below a picture of the island showcasing the very building we passed at the dock. Apparently there's a South Brother Island, too. It's significantly smaller, and according to this article, was used as a dump for garbage, manure and dead carcasses to help clean up Manhattan back in the mid-nineteenth century.

Well, isn't that lovely.

I keep scanning the page, getting much of the same information that Ava and Helen explained earlier. It was home to a quarantine hospital called Riverside, then later a veteran's hospital before its last venture as a youth drug rehabilitation center. The largest part of the article is dedicated to the island's most famous patient, or infamous as it might seem,

Mary "Typhoid" Mallon, the first confirmed case of Typhoid Fever.

A minute later, I back out of the Wiki article and slide through more search results. I take a quick glance around me to make sure I'm not bothering anyone. The closest person to me, Gabe, seems to be sound asleep. Nick's and Grady's snores assure me they're good, too, so I go back to my impromptu research.

I stop at an article titled "A 30-Photo Tour of the Abandoned North Brother Island" and tap the link. The page opens, and I'm immediately faced with a familiar sight again, the same picture from the Wikipedia page. I scroll down. I want to see what I'm getting myself into. Better late than never.

An old abandoned building. It looks like a house almost, small with white, dingy wooden railing around what must have once served as a porch. The roof is caved in and most of the windows seem to be in shards, the frames bowed and broken. I move down the page. The entry to some old building scrolls into view. It looks more institutional, more like a business structure with cold, circular metal railings lining two leaf-covered concrete sidewalks leading up to a set of damaged double doors. They hang open under a hollow awning, the cloth since rotted away. The next image shows a dirty brown room, its floor covered in nothing but books, like someone tipped all the shelves and made a dash for it, and a long metal bench sitting against the wall situated perfectly in the center.

I scroll farther down, passing a picture of a two-story structure covered in vines, but stop on what looks like a locker room at first glance. I tilt my head, studying the picture.

No, it's not a locker room. I read the caption underneath it. *OPERATING ROOM.*

It's empty, void of the tools, tables and machinery I'd expect in such a place, but its cold tile walls and what I now realize are hanging lights agree with the caption. The sight sends a chill up my spine. It's creepy. At either side of the open entry door are sets of cabinets built into the walls, their glass doors, or what's left of them, hang open, exposing the empty shelves inside.

What was that?

A groan slithers out of the woods, past the slender tree trunks. I twitch my head up and look past Gabe toward the border. It doesn't sound like any of the noises I'm accustomed to out here, the crickets chirping and other insects buzzing about. No, it's different. Almost guttural.

I rise to my elbows and angle my head toward the woods. There it is again, a groan, but this time it's followed by another, lighter noise. It sounds faintly different now, almost rhythmic. I bite my lip, trying to stave off the worry growing under my skin. I sweep my gaze over the clearing and the other sleeping bags. Everyone else is asleep.

The noise pushes through the trees again. I huff and slide out of my sleeping bag, even while I try to tell myself to stay in bed. I switch off the web browser and pocket my phone in my shorts as I get to my feet. I glance back at the other sleeping bags again, hoping that someone else will wake up and hear the noise, too. I'm not going to wake them on purpose, but if someone does wake up you better believe I'm making them go with me. I look around. No such luck.

I return my eyes to the trees and gulp down an imaginary batch of saliva before forcing my feet forward. The groans reach me again, then I hear a twig snap.

Fuck!

I halt.

Fuck this. Just go back to bed. Are you seriously this stupid?

I start to turn around, but something in my head, an itch, whispers to me, telling me that I need to check it out. What if it's something dangerous?

Well, duh, in that case I sure as fuck don't need to check it out!

The conversation continues in my head, but this time it makes a little more sense to my less-than-rational, fearful brain.

But if there is something out there, I should check, in case I need to warn the others.

The groan whispers over the leaves again, but this time I take two steps, then three. I know I could stay in my sleeping bag, but if there really is something out there, I can't go to sleep, not without knowing. I continue forward, keeping my eyes on the edge of the forest. The noise slips by me again.

I retrieve my phone and activate the flashlight. I'm not worried if it, whatever it is, knows I'm coming. Maybe that's a good thing, maybe that'll scare it away, make it leave. With my path lit in a glow of white, I break through the tree line. Shadows crawl away from my light, morphing like water over the trunks and bushes.

My hand grabs hold of the nearest trunk, pulling me forward, fighting the need to go back. Another groan grates against my ears. It's louder now, closer. Suddenly, a higher-pitched groan interrupts the silence and another twig snaps. I freeze, clenching my fists into fierce balls.

Just move, Cooper!

I ebb forward, letting the current of my curiosity control

my feet, stumbling over the rarely tread path. The dark sky overhead feels like it's pressing down on my head, and the forest devours me from behind, surrounding me with trees, branches and every life-ending scenario. I grab hold of another branch while pushing a lesser one out of the way, allowing my light to drop to my feet for a moment as I move past them. The noises intensify and a sudden urge to turn off the light throbs in my head. I consider it for a second and decide to err on the side of my instincts. I flick off the flashlight beam.

Sweat beads down my forehead and I can hear my breaths rasping through my lungs. I close my eyes and try to focus on breathing when a piece of wood snaps under my foot. My whole body quakes, as my feet fix themselves in place, unwilling to move. I clench my closed eyelids tight, as if not seeing the world around me will somehow protect me from whatever called me into the woods in the first place. I hold the air in my chest, and for a moment silence engulfs me. That's when I realize that the insects aren't chirping anymore and the adrenaline pumping through my veins has blocked out the sounds of the city, filling my head instead with the unusual groans. I release my clenched fists and open my eyes again. The air releases from my lips in a stutter and I tug up my feet, unrooting them from their foundation.

More careful now, I dart my eyes from my feet as they touch the ground to the woods before me, and then back again. My hand trembles against the bark of a thin tree as I sidestep a small bramble. The groans are louder now, but the closer I get something about them grows familiar.

Ahead I catch movement, and I dash behind a tree that's barely big enough to conceal my form, my back to its bark, facing away from the movement. The noise is more distinct now. I crinkle my brow as a moan passes me by, followed by another along with the shuffling of leaves. It sounds sensual.

What the hell?

I take a deep breath and inch around the tree, barely peeking around the corner.

Are you fucking serious?

In an instant the tension in my muscles relaxes and I feel utterly stupid as the sounds of passionate lovemaking echoes by.

Ahead, where I saw the movement just seconds ago, Brooklyn lies against an old fallen tree trunk, not an ounce of clothing on her body. Riley's on top of her, thrusting into her again and again. Their mouths are open wide between kisses, releasing erotic moans as their bodies writhe together.

I reel back around the tree. Well, at least it wasn't some animal, well, non-human animal. I shake my head in disbelief. I just walked out into the woods in search of an animal but instead found two of my new friends fucking. Yeah, I definitely won't be telling anyone about this. I can just imagine how that exchange would go.

Oh yeah, I mistook Riley and Brook fucking for some animal stalking us in the woods.

I'd never live that down, ever. Shaking my head, I creep off through the trees, weaving between the thin trunks and over the underbrush back to the campsite. I don't want to think about her, but my mind forces Addison into my thoughts. The sweet curves of her waist and hips, the taste of her lips, the smell of her hair. The *bitch*, I remind myself before I get too invested. She did screw me over and leave me to dry.

With a puff of air, I break into the clearing to find the others still soundly asleep. My eyes scan over the crew, and I quickly erase Addison from my thoughts and replace her with Ava's soft face. I know it's stupid, but it helps. I'll probably never see her again after filming this movie, and she's just a sudden crush, but it keeps my mind off Addison.

I slip into my sleeping bag and turn on my side. The groans still filter through the woods. Knowing what they are now, the noise offends my ears. I hope they're about done. Otherwise this is going to be a long night.

8: Cooper Bay

"Can someone wake Grady?" Helen calls from across the fire where a metal pan sits atop a wire frame. A massive helping of eggs sizzles in the pan, sending a pleasant aroma to my nostrils. "He's going to miss breakfast if he sleeps much longer."

My first thought is, *why can't* you *wake him?* but I keep that to myself. Before I can exchange looks with the others, Nick rises and trots off toward Grady's sleeping bag.

"I got it."

It's early, but the sun is already shining through a faint assortment of white puffs against an otherwise clear blue sky. A handful of birds fly overhead, little spies, daring to tell on our little excursion on their island. Riley stirs the yellowy-white mess in the pan and scoops a helping onto a plate. He holds it out to me and I take it with a nod.

A minute later Nick returns, alone.

"He up yet?" I ask.

"Yeah, he'll be here in a little," Nick tells me, shaking his head with a wry grin.

I nod, assuming that waking Grady isn't the easiest task, and fork a bite of egg and chew off an inch of limp bacon. It's not crispy enough.

Next to Riley, Brooklyn munches on a meal bar. I found

out this morning that she's apparently a vegetarian. Riley, on the other hand, is most definitely not. At least the handful of bacon he just shoved into his mouth says he isn't.

I stretch my shoulders, trying to release the tension in my back from a night on the ground spent staring at an empty sky. I wince as a tiny sting pricks my shoulder.

"You okay there?" Ava asks. She's sitting next to Brooklyn across the campfire, dressed in a pair of ragged khaki shorts and a torn crimson t-shirt, her costume for the day. The shorts are short to say the least, and her dirty blonde hair hangs wildly over her right eye, which causes my chest to tighten.

"Yeah," I say, a little more confident now after chasing her through the woods in our scene last night. I try to forget the line snafu. "Just didn't get much sleep last night, that's all. The ground apparently hates my back."

"I take it you're not much of a camper then?" she asks with a sly grin on her face.

"Cooper? A camper?" Nick interjects. "He's barely an out-doorsy person."

"Hey now," I defend myself, putting up a hand. "I'm not the one that stayed inside all the time listening to my music and playing video games."

"Yeah, but I hardly think trying out for basketball and running track in high school really qualifies you as the rugged outdoorsman type." Nick slaps me on the shoulder and plasters a grin across his face.

"You played basketball?" Gabe jumps in, his voice excited. "For your high school team?"

I shake my head. "Nah. I tried out, but that's as far as I got. I was tall enough and fast enough, but my shooting game just wasn't there. I was always more of a runner, so I got on the track team instead."

"Ah, gotcha. I played varsity my senior year, point guard." Gabe's eyes light up, a topic that he apparently enjoys. "It was a small rural school down in Virginia. 'Course I wasn't out then, otherwise I doubt they'd even let me on the team. It was *that* type of town. Locker room was great though."

Gabe grins mischievously and bites his lips. I'm not sure what to think, but he picks up quickly. "Our team sucked, but damn did I enjoy it."

I can laugh at that, so I do. It's not what I expected to hear, especially after the locker room mention. Ava leans forward and takes back the conversation.

"Yeah, your brother's right," she says. "Sports definitely don't make you an outdoorsman. Athletic, maybe. Outdoorsman, no. I'm not either really, but I do love it out here, the history at least. I mean, it's cool, right?"

She looks around the group, expecting an answer, an affirmation. Instead she gets a round of questioning glances, including mine.

"You know, we're sitting in New York City. I mean, when you get down to it we are." She eyes us some more and finally earns a few nods and noises, which she takes as agreement. "And there's nothing here, nothing. It's abandoned, forgotten, a relic of time."

I can see the historian in her surface. The creases in her jaw tighten as her lips form a smile.

"Other than a few photographers, and maybe the occasional trespasser like us," she sweeps an open hand around the group with a raised eyebrow, "the island's not been occupied for at least six decades. It's just us and nature, us and history."

"And spiders," Brooklyn speaks up.

"Yeah, that's nature," Ava goes on, unperturbed.

She's looking straight at me. It's like she's talking to me directly, wanting me to respond. I don't know what to say, and I can't truthfully say I'm super excited to be outside in *nature* like this, except for the acting part.

"Yeah, it's cool, that's for sure," I lie, mostly at least. I stumble to find more to say, something not too polar opposite but not too obviously false either. "I checked out some stuff online about the island last night actually. It's pretty neat really...well, creepy is probably a better word for it. Supposedly they keep trying to open the island back up as some sort of history tour, but the city keeps shooting it down for some reason."

"Yeah," Ava starts, and a frustrated huff escapes her lips. "They don't seem to understand the historical significance of the island. I mean it's where the infamous Typhoid Mary was kept, and so much more. Did you realize that she was quarantined twice?"

A flurry of shaking heads indicate that none of us knew that, except mine. I nod enthusiastically, a little too excited to know what she's talking about. It's one of the tidbits I found on my second sweep of Wikipedia last night after tripping over Riley and Brooklyn's little getaway. She grins at me, and I can't help but hold my head a little higher.

"Yes," Ava continues. The excitement in her voice is almost hypnotic. "Typhoid Mary, actually Mary Mallon, was the first identified asymptomatic carrier of typhoid fever. When they first brought her to the hospital here, on the other side of the island, they kept her for three years. They tried to remove her gallbladder where they thought the typhoid resided, but she refused, and there was nothing they could do at the time to make her. Eventually the New York Commissioner of Health, Eugene Porter, decided that carriers like Mary could be let out of quarantine as long as they took on jobs that kept them from passing on the fever."

I listen. I'm not sure whether I'm interested in the topic, or if it's just the movement of the speaker's lips that has me mesmerized. At the edges of my sight, Gabe and Luca look bored to death.

"Mary was a cook, though, and she didn't listen. Instead she changed jobs every time a typhoid outbreak popped up. They finally caught her again in March of 1915 while she was delivering food to a friend on Long Island. She obviously didn't seem to understand how much of a danger she was or she just didn't care. They brought her back here to Riverside where she remained confined for the rest of her life, another six years before she died of pneumonia. They think she directly infected somewhere around a hundred people, maybe more. That doesn't even count those infected by those she infected."

"So that's basically how this island got started? Typhoid?" Jaylen asks.

"Largely, yes," she says. "It started off as the Renwick Small Pox Hospital on the mainland, and then moved here in the early 1880s and became Riverside. The island acted as a natural barrier to passing on the disease, so it was perfect. Later, it served a few other purposes too."

I finish off the bacon and remaining eggs on my plate and wipe the grease from my fingers.

"Well, that's interesting," Gabe says, feigning curiosity, his face telling another story. I shake my head as he smears his sleeve across his lips and plops his paper plate on the ground. "I can't wait to see the rest of the island, sounds creepy."

I nod.

"All right, let's get to work, guys," Luca jumps in, "and gals. Time to get shooting."

I get to my feet. I'm ready, excited to get back into the game. I follow Nick back to our bags next to the remains of the old church. I packed up my things earlier, so I tug the pack up and throw it over my shoulder. I chuckle inside as Grady rushes to pack his bag, having just risen from his sleep.

"You having fun, man?" Nick asks, an expectant look under his raised brow.

"Yeah!" I say, maybe a little too loud. "This is great, aside from sleeping on the ground."

"I can't argue with that," he agrees, shaking his head. "But you gotta do some crazy shit sometimes in the movie business. Just think what the big names do."

"Yeah, really," Gabe jumps in, literally wedging in between us to get to his pack. "Especially if you do your own stunts."

I grin and nod, wondering how many stunts the kid could have done, considering his first acting scene ever would be today. I shrug it off. I'm just glad this film, so far, has only required a little running and sleeping on the ground.

We head back toward the fire where Luca and Helen are waiting. Helen is smothering the flames and Luca is drenching the frying pan with water. Steam billows off the black metal over a popping hiss. Riley, Brooklyn and Ava arrive just before we do, and Gabe is on our six just a few yards behind with Jaylen ambling up a moment later.

"I guess this means we're just waiting on Grady, right?" Helen purses her lips.

"Yep." Nick shrugs with not an ounce of urgency or apology. Instead, a satisfied grin rises at the corners of his mouth.

Luca smiles at Nick, hiding his expression from Helen's aggravated gaze.

"We're on a schedule, people," Helen starts up again. "We don't have all day to lollygag around. We only have so mu—"

"Calm down, Helen," Luca interrupts her. "We're going to be fine. It's just a few minutes."

I hide a grin as Helen crosses her arms and investigates the forest, lips pursed again and annoyed. There is something regal under all that frustration, something left over from her British heritage. At the same time there's something ugly and high-minded there, too.

A few moments later, Grady walks up to the circle.

"So what're we waiting on, people?" he asks, looking around the group.

Luca grins as Helen's eyes go wide and laughs are stifled around our wide circle. I hold back my own, but my lips gape in a big smile anyway.

"All right, people," Luca calls out. "Let's go."

9: Cooper Bay

The morning sun cuts through the treetops in tiny slivers. It's warm for early morning, enough that I'm sure I'll be sweating soon.

I dodge another limb and continue through the woods behind Nick. There is no path, no roadway, just the trees around us and the ground beneath our feet. I can hear Grady huffing a few yards ahead of Nick, already out of breath, and I doubt we've covered half a football field yet.

We're headed for the nurses' dormitory now after finishing up a few of the opening scenes focusing on Ava and Riley's characters, before my character enters the picture. The two are close friends, according to the script, and my entrance later in the movie is supposed to bring its fair bit of strife between them. We haven't made it that far through the script though.

"Up ahead," Ava's soft voice sifts through the trees. "We're almost there."

"Is that it?" another voice echoes by. I think it's Luca, but this far back I'm not sure. It's either him or Riley.

"Yes," Ava replies, this time quieter.

I guess we've arrived at the nurse's dormitory, but all I can see is the forest. I quicken my step and crane my neck around Nick to see if I can find the building. I still don't see anything.

A few steps later the trees separate as the edge of the forest comes closer, revealing a two-story structure surrounded by more trees. It's built of brick, covered in rectangles of red, brown and something in between. The doors, and what's left of the windows dotting its walls, have no trim. Instead, each is recessed inside the thick brick wall like sunken eyes. I break past the tree line and slow my steps as I take in the rest of the structure.

It looks mostly intact. Besides the absent sheets of glass in most of the windows and the half-rotted doors, the building has withstood the test of time better than the old church. Vines rope up the side of the building, twisting in and out of the broken windows and open doorways, and tree branches hug the brick.

"All right, guys," Luca calls to us. "I want the next scene to be shot inside."

"Is that even safe?" Jaylen asks before Luca can continue.

"Well, that's what I hope to find out," Luca tells him. "Let's split up into two groups and scope out the building, see how it is. If it appears safe, we'll go forward with shooting here. Otherwise, we'll just have to improvise."

That earns Luca a round of nods, me included. I imagine what it looks like inside from the pictures I saw last night. My mind conjures up images of debris, half-rotted floors, creaking panels, peeling wallpaper and fading paint. Creepy.

"Everyone to my right goes with Helen," Luca announces. "And everyone else is with me."

I guess that means I'm with Luca. I check the others. Nick and Grady are already next to Luca, and Gabe quickly jumps up between us. I sigh quietly when I realize Ava is with

Helen's group as she joins the others around Helen, who's already making her way toward the building.

"We'll take the north half," Helen yells back as an afterthought, not waiting for Luca to give any further instructions.

Luca nods toward her with a huff as he silently mouths a single word through pursed lips. He turns and treks off toward the entry a few yards behind the other half of the group.

"Let's go, guys," he says.

He takes the door from Jaylen. It's an old slab of wood with a long-faded design carved into its surface, and its bottom edge is molded and full of rot. I take the door in turn, and cross into the building. Sunlight streams into the open space, a plaza or common area, through what used to serve as windows. Now the wind wafts through the holes unhindered. The room is empty, and a dank and sour aroma assaults my nose.

Something made of paper sits half immersed in a pool of stagnant water. I step closer to the tiny pool and crouch down. It's an old newspaper. I cock my head to the side and check the date. *May 5, 1963.*

Fingering the edge of the paper, I straighten the wet sheet and flip it over. I mouth a silent *wow* as I read the headline: "COMPLEXITIES CLOUD BATTLE IN VIETNAM". It suddenly hits me how long this place, this entire island, has been abandoned. I mean, I believed Ava, but the newspaper brings it to life.

"Look at this," I tell the others, still bending over the pool staring at the paper. I try to scan what's left of the story, what's not faded away.

"Whatcha got?" Nick asks.

I hear their steps close in, so I shift to the right to get out of the way.

"A newspaper," I start. "It's apparently from just before the island was abandoned. Look at the headline. It's about the Vietnam War."

"Cool," Gabe says. "Ava did say it was abandoned in the mid-sixties, right?"

"Yep," Nick replies. "That's odd though. I wouldn't think they'd have just abandoned stuff when they packed everything up and left."

I nod and rise back to my feet, dropping the paper back to rest in its watery grave.

"Let's go," Luca says and heads off to the right, obviously not interested in the little piece of history.

I take off after them, lagging a few feet behind to take one last look at the paper. It's like history stopped on the island back in the sixties. Something about it strikes me as fascinating.

It's cooler inside than outside, but not by much. Vines curl over the windowsills and down the walls, eventually crawling their way through the hall and under doors. They've literally invaded the entire island.

Out of the corner my eye, I catch a staircase. There's something familiar about it. I squint and crinkle my brow before it hits me. It's the spiral staircase I saw in the pictures online. It's small, single-file, ascending to the next floor in a tight vortex. Its metal rails are rusted with yellow and red patches overlaying intricate shapes that used to decorate the base. Like so much else, rot has overtaken the stair planks. Entire steps are missing, revealing a darker space below.

"Looks like we won't be going upstairs any time soon," Grady says. "At least I ain't."

"I *ain't* either," Nick agrees with him, mocking his Southern friend's choice of words.

"Don't worry, guys, I *ain't* going to make you." Luca laughs.

"Really, guys?" Grady grins. "Really?"

"Hey, it's just because we love you, man." Nick slaps him on the shoulder and chuckles.

"Yeah." Grady laughs too. "Sure."

10: Ava Thompson

Ava crouches, shifting her weight from side to side as she sifts through a collection of books left behind on a surprisingly still-upright bookshelf. She strokes the old wood, displacing a thick layer of dust and letting out a sigh. The room is musty, filled with the aroma of trees, mold and rust, but it's the smell of the books that excites Ava.

"If I didn't know any better I'd think that some of these people left in a hurry. I mean why the hell did they leave behind all this stuff?" Ava says more to herself than to anyone standing in the room.

"They're books, I'd leave them behind too." Riley smirks.

"Seriously?" Ava rises to her feet and faces Riley with a deep scowl.

"Yeah, seriously," he replies. "I mean, movies are so much better, not to mention they don't take fucking forever."

"You do realize that a good half or more of the movies you watch are the result of a book, right?" Helen chimes in as she peers out the second-floor window before turning back to her own bookshelf.

"Maybe so, but not all of them," Riley reasons, kicking aimlessly across the floor. Dust sparkles in the air as it inter-mingles with the light streaming in past Helen.

Ava rolls her eyes. "Yeah, sure."

"All right, let's move on, it seems safe enough in here," Helen orders.

Brooklyn is the first to exit the room, followed by Helen and the others. Out in the hallway it's darker. Rooms line both sides of the hall, and only the occasional open door allows light to flood into the corridor. Ava moves carefully behind Helen at the tail of the group, trying to avoid the pools of water that scatter the uneven boards, checking each step for weaknesses. Falling through the floor back to the first level is not the way she wants to end the film.

She watches Brooklyn and Riley walk ahead of her. She can see the look in Brooklyn's eyes when she glances at him, especially when she seems frightened. There's a longing there, a need. Ava unconsciously grimaces, thinking how Riley seems to not share the same feelings but is leading the girl on when he looks at her.

She doesn't even realize she's just a body *to him. I've seen his type before. All he's interested in is how quickly he can screw her and run.*

Coming up to another room, Ava pushes the thought out of her mind and peers around the corner. The others move along, having already had their fill of the room. It looks much like the others except for the notable absence of any books or other personal belongings. She moves on as well, carefully catching up with the group.

Ten minutes pass and the end of the hallway greets them. A staircase sits in the corner, its rusting rails curling down into the floor.

"Looks like that's it," Helen announces. "Let's head downstairs."

No one answers, instead following single file to the staircase. At the edge, Helen leans over the precipice of rusted railing, peering down to make sure the stairs are traversable. Satisfied, she takes a step onto the stairs and tests the first plank. It protests but holds true, so she puts her full weight on the plank and slowly moves down the steps.

Riley, followed closely by Brooklyn with her hand on his shoulder, takes the stairs behind Helen, stepping gingerly on each riser. The planks groan and creak under their weight. Ava pauses at the edge and takes in a deep breath. It's been at least sixty years since these steps have felt the weight of humans stomping up and down their wooden supports. She purses her lips and steps out onto the first step. It bows a little but holds like it had for the others. She takes the next step, then the next, working her way down the spiral.

"I've always loved spiral staircases," Brooklyn says, grinning from ear to ear and sliding a hand over the rough brown metal railing, the other hand still lying on Riley's shoulder. "They're so majestic, just like you see in the old—"

Crack!

The plank under her foot gives way, splitting in two. Brooklyn screams and drops through the opening quicker than Ava's eyes can follow, but her body stops short of tumbling all the way through the wooden planks. Riley spins around, eyes wide. Without thinking twice, he darts down and grasps Brooklyn under her shoulders.

"Brook!" he yells.

"Help! I'm stuck!" Brooklyn screams in his face, confusion and panic setting in.

"It's okay! We're going to get you up," Riley assures her. He breaks his concerned gaze from her brown eyes and scans where her body and the wood merge.

One leg disappears beneath the stair, engulfed by whatever lies below, while her free leg sprawls down the lower risers. A plethora of wooden splinters jab into her thigh, holding her in place. The skin moves, slipping over and around the thick shards of wood, holding her in place. Ava refuses to move, but she peers over Brooklyn, catching sight of the fresh blood seeping from her thigh. Riley moves to touch her leg but thinks better of it.

Gulping back the needle in her throat, Ava crouches on the stair above, one hand holding firmly to the rail. She shakes it once to test its resolve. It seems steady enough, so she leans forward to check on Brooklyn.

"Are you all right?" Ava asks, scared that putting a hand on her would send her falling farther.

"It hurts," Brooklyn almost yelps and begins to squirm.

"No, no, Brooklyn," Helen chides, a pained expression painted over her face. "Don't move, you don't want to risk the wood breaking further."

"Here, I'll pull her up," Ava tells Riley, trying to break his gaze from the wounds on Brooklyn's thigh. She grits her teeth, still horrified that any movement might send the entire staircase crashing down, but what choice does she have? "Riley! Get with me here."

"Uh, yeah. I got it." He blinks away the trance. "You pull her up and I'll push her from the waist. Once her leg is clear, I'll pull her forward."

"Okay," Ava agrees. "Helen, can you try to push away the wood, so it doesn't..."

"I got it," Helen confirms, obviously understanding that Ava doesn't want to worry Brooklyn.

Ava nods appreciatively. "On three."

Riley nods, placing his hands firmly around Brooklyn's tiny waist. Ava hooks her arms under Brooklyn's armpits and pulls up just enough to get rid of the slack between them. She nods at Riley.

"You ready, Brooklyn?" Ava asks, gritting her teeth.

"Uh... I think so," she says, but her voice is scared.

"All right. One...two...three..." Ava heaves upward. Brooklyn's small frame is light, but at this angle she seems heavier.

Riley assists from below and Brooklyn begins to rise from the floor. Ava keeps lifting and finally her foot clears the hole, and Riley reels her forward. He pulls her against his chest and wraps his arms around her.

"Are you o—" he starts.

The stair creaks beneath their combined weight and the wood begins to snap.

"Move!" Helen yells.

Riley looks down as the board begins to fracture under his feet. He wrenches around, holding Brooklyn close to his chest and pounds down the stairs. Ava skips over the hole left from Brooklyn's leg and her weight comes down hard on the next step. The plank screams under the pressure, a series of high-pitched cracks piercing her ears. She yanks her foot away as the board splinters open, and speeds down the stairs.

With only a few boards to go, Riley races down the stairs as fast as he can with Brooklyn in tow, limping along beside him. The foot of her injured leg scrapes against a plank, and she shrieks, yanking her leg up on instinct and missing the next riser. Before Riley realizes what's happening, Brooklyn's weight jerks him forward. They tumble down the old wooden stairs, flipping and crashing down the hard edges until the bottom greets them with an unwelcome thud.

"Oh fuck!" Riley grunts, eyes clenched shut in pain.

Horrified to put her weight on another step, Ava leaps from the last board, catapulting herself to the ground floor. She barely misses Riley and Brooklyn before her body smacks against the wall, her shoulder taking the brunt of the impact, and tumbles to the ground like a rag doll. She groans, clutching her shoulder.

"Are you all right?" Helen cranes over Brooklyn and Riley to check on Ava. "Ava!"

"I'm good, I think," Ava croaks, waving her off. "What about Brooklyn?"

"Brooklyn." Helen nods vigorously. "Are you okay?"

"It hurts!" Brooklyn whimpers. She moves an inch, but retracts in pain, curled up into Riley's chest.

"I'm good," Riley says right before Helen can open her mouth to ask. He squirms to the side to get a better look at Brooklyn. She's wincing, reaching for her leg. She groans with the action.

"Is she okay?" Riley asks, worry clear in his eyes. He twists to get to his knees, a cry escaping his lips. "Damn, that hurts!"

Helen eyes him. "You're probably bruised up pretty bad from that fall."

He nods and gently rubs his shin, wincing. He ignores it as best he can and moves closer to Brooklyn. Scratches etch her calf and thigh in a flurry of spots and lines, all serving as an outline for one long gash where the wood dug in deep and kept her from falling further. It's a vivid crimson wound, running three inches vertically and another half inch wide, ending in a slab of loose skin and meat at the top. Blood dribbles onto the floor, connecting a line of red blotches back to the stairs.

"Oh hell." Riley's face becomes pale as his eyes lock on the wound. "What do we do? Do you have the first aid kit? We did bring one, right?"

"Luca has it," Helen says. Her eyes grow scared.

"We need something to stop the bleeding," Riley screams.

"Calm down, Riley," Helen demands. "We'll…"

By the wall, Ava rubs her shoulder and stretches her limbs. It hurts, but she moves anyway. On her feet, she reaches for the wall to balance herself as the world spins before her eyes. Finally, it stops, but then the pain kicks in. She grits her teeth and tries to ignore the ebb and tightness in her muscles. She scoots over to Brooklyn and eyes the wounds along her thigh.

"Do you have any bandages?" she asks before realizing that's why he asked about the first aid kit.

"No," Riley almost yells. "I don't have a damn thing."

She knows he's hurting, so she ignores the anger in his voice. Instead, Ava scans the empty room but finds nothing but broken windows and empty space. She throws the bag off her shoulders to check its contents, hoping to find something of use, but before the bag hits the ground a tearing noise reaches her ears.

Her eyes shoot up to find Riley ripping at a piece of his shirt. He pulls and reels, stripping at least four inches of thin fabric from the bottom of the garment. He bends down and begins applying his makeshift bandage to a whimpering Brooklyn. Ava gets to her knees and lifts Brooklyn's leg up to help, which earns her a plethora of curses. She ignores them.

Riley wraps the cloth under and around Brooklyn's leg,

careful to cover the entire gash. He makes another pass and ties off the cloth.

"It's too thin," Helen says, now kneeling by them. "It's already bleeding through."

Mixed with a pained groan, Riley huffs and lifts the remainder of his shirt from his body and begins tearing at the fabric again. Another band of fabric snaps away from the cloth, now nothing more than half a tube top. He wraps the new strip around Brooklyn's leg, doubling up the new band, and tying it off just above the last strip.

"I think that'll do for now," Riley hopes, examining the bandage and wiping away the remaining blood with what's left of his shirt. "That should help a little, Brook. You think you can get up? I'll help. Just lean on me."

"Yeah," she nods with a hard grimace edging her lips. "I think so. It'll beat staying here at least."

Riley gets to his feet and crouches back down, looping his arms under her, and lifts. From behind, Ava guides Brooklyn to her feet under Riley's grasp and after a little struggle, Brooklyn's standing up. She nearly drops back to the ground as the foot of her injured leg touches the floor, but Riley holds on tight.

"I got you," he says with a smile, though Ava can see the pain behind his eyes.

Maybe I was wrong.

11: Cooper Bay

"What the hell was that?" Gabe blurts as a shriek echoes through the hollow space.

I spin around and face the open door. It was a scream, a girl, I swear it. My eyes meet Nick's and Luca's as we exchange glances.

"The others," Luca says under his breath, and, without warning us, dashes out of the small dorm room.

I wind around a discolored metal bed frame, the only item housed in the tiny room, and shoot into the hallway. Nick and Luca are a stride ahead. I hazard a glance behind me to ensure the others are following. Gabe is on my heels and Grady lags behind but moves as fast as he can.

What's going on?

Door after open door whizzes by, flashing oblong rays of sunlight across my skin. Following the leader, I skip over a capsized metal chair without losing speed. Seconds later a clattering of metal and wood assaults my ears. I take a glance back just in time to see Grady's leg knocking the same chair against the wall. The bull doesn't slow, unfazed by the collision.

More screams ring down the hall. This time it's more than one person. I look forward in time to catch Nick detouring down a side hallway.

I hang the left, skidding the soles of my tennis shoes across the aged floor, hoping nothing catches. All thought about the stability of the structure around us flees my mind as we barrel down the corridor toward the other group somewhere in the guts of this long- lost building.

"Do you know where you're going?" Nick yells.

"It came from this direction," Luca chokes out between labored breaths.

I slow my pace to stay behind Nick, forcing myself to calm down. Luca bursts through a door at the end of the hallway and comes to an abrupt halt. I'm on Nick's heels as he races through and slides to a stop by Luca. I stomp my feet against the wooden planks and halt my movement.

"Are you all okay?" Luca asks before he has time to take in the scene.

Brooklyn is leaning on Riley, who for whatever reason is now shirtless. Helen is standing by him with her hands out like she's ready to assist, and Ava stands next to Brooklyn with a hand on the girl's back.

Then I notice the bruise on Ava's temple, above her right ear, and the cuts along her ankle. I crinkle my brow.

"What happened?" I ask, before noticing the torn cloths wrapped around Brooklyn's thigh. Blood permeates through the fabric and a variety of smaller cuts cover her lower leg in reddened abrasions.

"The stairs fell out on our way down," Helen says, her face worried. "Brooklyn took the brunt of it. Her leg fell right through."

Luca steps between Helen and Brooklyn, eyeing the hurt leg, a scowl on his lips.

"Are you all right?" he asks carefully.

She nods vigorously, like it's too much to say. I can only imagine how much it hurts considering the blood staining the bandage. Grady comes running in, his eyes wide, scanning the scene before him. Nick holds his hand up and tells him it's okay.

"We do have a first aid kit, right?" Gabe asks, eyeing Luca.

"Yes." Luca nods, returning his eyes to Brooklyn. "I've got it in my pack. Let's get you off that foot and get you cleaned up."

As Luca and Riley lower Brooklyn to the floor and begin cleaning up her wound, I walk over to Ava. I can tell she's in pain by the way she's squinting, the action tightening her skin and deepening the contours of her cheeks, but she hasn't said anything yet.

"You okay?" I ask. "You look like you got beat up a little."

"I'm okay." Ava practically bites back. Her tone lightens, apologetic. "Sorry. Um... I'm good. Just a bump on the head and a few scratches, nothing too bad."

I glance down at Brooklyn's leg as Luca and Riley remove the last of what I assume used to be Riley's t-shirt. My face contorts when the torn skin and bloodied tissue come into view. I shudder and return my attention to Ava.

"You've got a pretty big bruise there," I insist, pointing to the black and blue blot on the side of her temple. "You must have hit something pretty hard."

"Well, yeah," she agrees, looking back at the stairs and then the wall opposite them where a piece of the sheetrock is busted in. A crumbled mess of chalky debris scatters the floor.

"Damn," I grin. "You must be more hardheaded that I thought."

"Excuse me?" She glares at me.

"Just kidding." I throw my hands in the air in surrender, trying a cheesy grin.

Yeah, that was probably bad timing. Damn, I hope it doesn't seem like I'm flirting.

"Ahuh, sure." She eyes my suspiciously, then lets a beautiful smile break through the charade and laughs. "Typical guy."

The others are still crowded around Brooklyn. Luca applies the bandage over a helping of antibiotic cream, then wraps a length of tape about Brooklyn's thigh to secure the fresh white bandage in place.

"So you just *had* to rip your shirt off now, didn't you?" Grady prods at Riley. "I mean, really?"

Riley shakes his head with a wide grin. "It was the first thing that came to mind when I realized we didn't have the first aid kit. Guess I've watched too many movies."

"It worked, that's all that matters," Helen says, her brilliant white teeth flashing in a broad smile.

"I, for one, am glad," Brooklyn thanks him, rubbing an open palm up Riley's chest. "I think I like it better like this anyway."

"Okay, that's enough," Luca jumps in, barely hiding a chuckle.

"Oh, come on, man, this was just about to get good," Grady argues.

"I think we'll be all right without more," Nick interjects.

"Yeah, that's plenty," Gabe joins in.

Riley doesn't comment. Instead he grins and helps Brooklyn back to her feet.

"Well, I think we've established that upstairs isn't the best bet," Ava says, nodding her head toward the battered staircase. There's a jagged football-size hole among a scattering of splintered wood about a quarter of the way up the staircase. Blood dots the shards of cracked wood, and there's no bottom to the hole in sight. That must be where she fell through. I turn back to the group and eye Brooklyn's leg.

Damn.

"Agreed," Luca says, taking in a deep breath and letting it back out. "Let's keep to the lower floors in any building we go in, okay?"

It was more of a statement than a question. No one seems to disagree either. I sure as hell don't. Not after this.

"Brooklyn, I don't want to sound insensitive, but you can still do makeup with a hurt leg, right?"

"Of course," she spits, nodding her head, eyes asking, *really?*

"Good, let's get set up for the next shot then. I want to use a few of the dorm rooms and the hallway at least."

12: Cooper Bay

Sprawled out on the filthy floor of the nurses' dormitory, I scan my lines for at least the twentieth time. I'm nervous. It feels like the first time again. But at the same time I'm amped, all in the same instant, like some battle between adrenaline and the mind.

The next scene is where my character and Ava's finally decide they like each other. Even with their rocky meeting early in the movie, the two are forced to work together, to complement each other even. It's the end that has me nervous though. It ends with a kiss.

I can already feel my heart pounding against my ribcage, and the camera's not even rolling yet. I look up and peer across the small room, past the broken staircase and Gabe, who's sucked into his phone. I find Ava looking at her own script. I let my eyes linger over her face, the gentle slope of her nose and how it pokes up just the tiniest bit at the end, the silky quality of her light mocha skin and gentle neck. She's on her feet, leaning back against the tattered wallpaper, one knee pulled up and a foot planted against the wall. She's mumbling something I can't hear. I'm guessing it's her lines.

A warm beam of light filters in through the window and highlights the natural beauty of her lips. I study them. I think girls call the color nude, but all I know is that they're a shade darker than her lightly tanned complexion. They form a generous bow, like the one Cupid aims in the movies and television commercials, around perfect white teeth as she silently mouths each syllable.

Reluctantly, I pull my eyes away and plant them back on my script. I shouldn't stare too long. I don't want anyone reading too much into it, and I especially don't want her to catch me.

Or do I?

I discreetly bring my hand to my chest and inhale a calming breath.

No, Coop. Stop being an idiot.

"Everyone ready?" Luca's voice saves me from myself. It trails in from the hallway and everyone in the room raises their heads.

He, Grady, Nick and Riley had all gone to scout out the final locations in the building, hoping to find a few more suitable settings for upcoming shots, the next scene in particular. The group saunters into the room and Luca looks to be in a better mood now. They must have found something of use. I think he was worried Brooklyn's injury would cause us some problems, but so far it hasn't. She's resilient. It's like opening up the makeup bag flushed away any pain she felt. It was only a matter of moments after before she was in our faces again, checking and re-checking us.

"In the next scene Grace and Carter barricade themselves in a room within the old motel. Are we all on the same page?" Luca asks, focusing on Ava and me.

Ava nods, looking up from her script long enough to acknowledge the director.

I nod too. "Good here."

The others do the same, and Luca turns and waves for us to follow.

"All right, let's go."

I push off the floor and get to my feet. I wipe the dust from my shirt, the same tattered gray tee I wore in my first scene along with the accompanying pair of cargo shorts. It's not much different from what I'd normally wear, minus the tears in the shirt exposing bits of my chest and stomach. I look at Ava and give her a half grin. I'm not sure why exactly. Maybe I want her to go first.

It is the gentlemanly thing to do, right? No, well yes, but no, she might see it as a bit too self-serving considering the vantage point. No, that's just you overthinking things, Coop.

Or maybe I just want to acknowledge she's ready to go.

Who the fuck are you kidding, Coop? Just go.

I break eye contact and fall in behind Gabe as they pass into the hallway. Her footsteps catching up from behind prompt the urge to turn around, but I don't.

"Hey," her smooth voice whispers behind me.

"Yeah?" I crane my neck around, silently thanking her for the excuse. I'm whispering, but I'm not really sure why. I squint as a sliver of light from one of the windows stings my eyes. It passes, and I find Ava again as the light causes her crystal blues to sparkle. I tighten and release my fists.

"You seem jittery," she tells me.

I hold back a sigh.

Is it really that noticeable? No, Coop, she's just talking about the next scene.

"It's still all so new," I say, slowing to let her come up beside me. It's not technically a lie. It *is* still all new to me, and at times I *do* find myself getting nervous about performing well.

Not to mention trying to remember my lines. She doesn't realize it, but that's not the real reason for my apparent nervousness. She's the real reason, but how the hell do I say that without coming off like an infatuated sixth grader with his first boner? "I'll be good. I promise."

"I hope so, this is one of the most important scenes in the movie." She's either trying to calm me down or scare the shit out of me. I'm not sure which it is, but it's rattling my nerves. Another shred of light glints off her bright blue eyes and it's everything I can do not to look away. "This is where our characters realize their bond. We need to create the right chemistry on set. It has to look like we *really* like each other."

"Oh, yeah! No problem," I assure her, trying to sound more confident than I am. "I'm sure that won't be too hard."

I wince inside, consciously restraining myself from physically grimacing. I want to throw my hands up and ask why the hell I'm so stupid, but I don't.

"Good." If she caught my internal outburst, she doesn't let on.

We walk in silence for what feels like forever, but it couldn't have been longer than a few minutes passing door after door. It all starts to look the same after the fifth or sixth one, and I don't see much else with my thoughts stuck on her. As much as I want to hear her talk, I don't know what to say.

A minute later, Luca stops in the middle of the hall and about-faces.

"Here we are." He rises on the tips of his shoes to look above the others and peers around them until he finds me. "Cooper." Then he finds Ava. "Ava. Can you two come on up? Time to get you set up."

Five minutes later, we're in position at the end of the hall by the opening to another common area. There's yet another set of spiral stairs in the corner, old papers and clippings rustle on the broken concrete floor. It looks like someone took a jackhammer to most of the floor; crumbled pieces of debris transition into large, cracked slabs of concrete the farther away from the stairs you move.

Grady positions himself approximately twenty yards down the corridor, a hulking camera on his shoulder, while Luca settles his smaller camera and tripod combo on the cement. Nick dangles the long, fuzzy microphone over his Southern friend. According to Nick, we'll probably have to re-record the dialog back in the studio, but this should at least grab the ambient noises and let us keep the spirit of the dialog. He smiles approvingly at me. I'm not sure how to take it; pride in the fact that I'm acting, just a little brotherly encouragement, or something to do with Ava. I brush the thought away. It doesn't matter.

"Rolling in three...two...one... Action!" Luca flips his finger forward, our queue, and his eyes disappear behind his camera.

I dig my shoes into the uneven concrete and jolt forward. For a split second my mind is free of the girl, focused entirely on hitting my mark. It doesn't last long. A moment later Ava's at my side, her legs matching me stride for stride. I keep my eyes set ahead, forcing myself to focus on Nick, the most familiar thing in this untouched part of the world, and head straight for the camera. I force my lungs to drag in deep breaths, pushing my chest in and out. The run has to look like a struggle, and the fear on my face has to appear genuine, so I tighten my brow and push forward, bobbing my head with each step for emphasis.

It only takes a few seconds to cross the small section of hallway. We skid to a stop across the broken concrete atop a predetermined line two feet from the camera.

A pleased expression washes over Luca's face as he screams, "Cut!"

What really surprises me, though, is the thread of a smile tracing even Helen's mouth.

"Very good!" Luca whoops. He twists around and looks at Helen. "I don't think we need a second take of that. How about you, Helen?"

"It looked good to me," she says. "We can review the film before we leave the building and make sure though. I'd say move on to the next scene. Keep things flowing."

"Let's get setup for the next shot." Luca smiles and waves his hands over his head.

"That's it?" I ask, not masking my surprise. I fully expected to make that short run at least three times before we got the take Luca wanted.

"Yeah," Luca assures me. "There wasn't much to mess up."

I shrug, lifting my left eyebrow. I guess not.

Before I can catch my breath, Grady is already hefting the camera around the corner, followed closely by Helen and Nick. Brooklyn hobbles along behind them, an arm slung over Riley's shoulder for support. I wave my hand forward in a gentle sloping uppercut with my fingers extended, signaling Ava to go ahead. A generous grin has taken over my face. The corners of her mouth rise as she steps forward. I fall in beside her and we meander down the hall just behind the others. It strikes me as odd that I'm intentionally walking beside her, but I work to ignore the thought. She probably doesn't think anything of it anyway.

"So far the only bad thing about this film is the dirt," Ava complains, glancing my way.

"The dirt?" I ask.

"Yeah, the dirt. You know, the stuff on the ground and smeared all over my face," she explains, her eyes set wide under a raised brow. She moves her hand in a circular motion around her face, emphasizing the sarcasm.

"Ah," I sigh, trying to catch myself. Luca wanted to make it look like we'd been wandering for days, so he had us go outside and rub dirt on our faces for realism. According to the storyline, the world has pretty much ended and our characters are running from a madman through some old abandoned forest. So yeah, dirt makes sense.

I try to measure my next words carefully, balancing what I want to say and what I probably should say.

"Well, you look all right even with all the dirt."

"Really?" she jests. "You're not hitting on me, are you? I mean, I'm pretty disgusting right now."

"No," I nearly yell. "I just... I mean, a little dirt doesn't hurt."

She chuckles but doesn't press it, thank God.

Minutes later, we're in the middle of the next scene. I careen around the corner, nearly kicking Ava's feet out from under her as I struggle to keep my balance. The first three attempts at that little maneuver didn't end so well. I lost my balance entirely on each count, once barging into Ava and nearly throwing her against the wall. Her skin was soft to the touch as my body tumbled against her and landed in a heap next to her. When my palm landed on her arm above the wrist, I wanted to find a reason to keep my fingers there, but I knew better and quickly retracted my hand like I was avoiding a mousetrap or some worse fate. The last take was the first that we both made the corner without slipping on pieces of stray rock. At first, Riley thought the strays added to the ambience, but after three failed attempts, he finally decided they just made it impossible to finish the scene. I was ecstatic when he and Gabe finally swept the rocks away. Even after that, it took two more takes before we got it right.

"All right, let's move along, no time to waste," Luca prompts, motioning to Grady and Nick.

"Do you want some water?" Helen slips around the camera as Grady repositions for the scene's final shot. She's holding out a cool bottle of spring water.

"Please." I take the bottle, unscrew the cap, and take a generous swig. The running had only been in quick bursts, but it hadn't taken long to wear me out. At least it hadn't been difficult to appear tired.

"Ava?" Helen holds out another bottle.

"Sure." Ava takes the bottle.

"You two seem to be working well together." Helen grins softly, her bright green eyes glowing. She winks at me.

Seriously? Give me a break!

"I think so," Ava agrees, eyeing me for a moment.

I shrug with a smile, not wanting to seem too enthusiastic.

"Good. That's helpful for the film," Helen points out, waving her hands around as she talks. "This next scene is a big one. People have to be able to feel the connection between you two."

"We won't disappoint," I tell her, speaking for both of us. If Ava minds, she doesn't show it.

"Well, I think Luca's ready." Helen motions toward the

director and walks off to line up against the wall.

"All right, take your places," Luca calls out.

I raise a brow at Ava, silently asking if she's ready. I get a smile in return and follow her around the corner, going out of sight from the others. We both turn back to face the corner about two yards away and await Luca's command.

"Three...two...one... Action!" The words echo off the wall and the scene begins.

Without waiting, I sprint forward. Ava keeps up just as she did before. In less than a full second, we bound around the corner. Before we finish the turn, though, Ava slips and slaps the ground. I hear the thud just as I lose sight of her in my peripheral vision. As planned, I skid to a halt and spin to find her on the floor, a look of stress masking her face. I sling my eyes to the left, back to the corner we'd just exited, acting like something horrible is following us, filling my eyes with fear. Then I lock my eyes with Ava's again.

"Help!" she screams, taking on Grace's persona. She's scraping her fingers against the floor. I close the gap, grasp her hand and pull her to her feet. We make off again, barreling down the hall and past the crew.

In unison, we careen off into a small room before sliding to a halt. I know I don't really know her and that I don't love her or anything, but I still want to hold her hand. I can already hear footsteps brushing closer, and I don't need any questions. I let go of Ava's hand.

"What do you think?" I ask her, just wanting to say something rather than standing here awkwardly waiting for the others to file inside.

"I think it was good." She shrugs. "It's not really for me to decide, but I think it could work. Felt real at least."

I wag my head from side to side, pursing my lips as if trying to determine whether I agree. I do. Luca's voice breaking around the corner saves me from further conversation.

"That was good. We'll do a reshoot in a moment, but let's go ahead and move on. I don't want to lose the momentum of the scene with the filming so close. We'll just jump back after this," he says. He doesn't waste time before explaining the scene. "This is where Grace and Carter finally admit to each other that they're in love. They're stuck in here, waiting Kaden out, hoping that he'll just leave them be."

He faces me and then Ava. He steps closer, putting all his attention on us.

"You're scared shitless. You don't know what's going to happen, if Kaden's going to bust through that door, and if he does you're done, dead, right?"

I nod quickly.

"Good." He grins and goes on. "You want to live, but in that same instant you stop hiding how you feel for each other. Between all the horror and fear, you both realize what's important."

Luca moves his eyes between us. I stifle a gulp.

"Ready?" Luca asks.

"Yeah," I reply, in unison with Ava. It's everything I can do not to grin.

"Well then, let's get to it!" Luca moves into the corner with the others and takes up his position behind Grady again. The lighting is not as good here, so Riley's holding up a small softbox light. It emits a gentle glow on the room to even out the light and allow the camera to pick us up better.

I follow Ava back to the hallway and take up my stance. We have to start outside the room so that Luca can catch us running in from the interior. I take her hand in mine, and she lags behind to simulate me pulling her along.

"Three...two...one... Action!" Luca announces, flicking his finger again.

I bolt forward, pulling Ava behind me. We make the corner and slide to a stop again in the middle of the room, but this time we don't stop acting. I search the wall for a way of escape, a window, another door, anything, but my eyes are met with four empty walls, no windows, and, as planned, no hope for escape. Only a singular six-foot-tall chest sits next to the entry, another relic from the island's past. Turning to face the door, I snap my eyes to Ava and try to recall my lines at the same time.

"We can't go back." I sound frantic, panting like I'd run a marathon. "He's too close, we don't have time."

Ava nods vigorously, trying to catch her breath as she shoots her eyes around the room. I sprint across the space and slam the old wooden door shut. It claps against the rotting doorframe and shudders on its hinges. For a second, I worry the hinges are going to break and the door's going to fall back on me. It doesn't, so I turn back to Ava, sweeping my eyes over the room, searching for a way out even though I know there isn't one. Apparently my character isn't too bright.

"The chest!" Ava, in character, shrieks, her hand pointing past me.

"Good idea!"

With an overemphasized nod, I rush to the old chest and heave my body against it. It doesn't budge, the damn thing's heavy. I keep pushing, but it's not going anywhere. This isn't good. It's supposed to move. I begin to worry, trying to figure out how I'm going to complete the scene if I can't move the damned chest.

Unscripted, Ava jumps from her spot and plants her shoulder against the firm wood next to me and adds her weight to the struggle. In a way I'm grateful, but at the same time it hurts me, or embarrasses me. I grunt, making it sound like the effort is straining me, which isn't exactly untrue. My eyes widen when, instead of inching forward, the chest begins to tip. I lean in to the heavy chest, trying not to focus on how close Ava's back is to me. Finally, the center of gravity changes and the chest topples over and crashes against the concrete. Wood cracks and splinters as we jump back.

Heaving, I dart my eyes to Ava and force myself to hide the smile that wants to surface, instead giving her a scared expression. We jerk around on Luca's queue, a quiet clap meant to simulate our adversary trying to break down the door. He claps again, and we press our bodies against the broken chest and push our backs against it. It's hilarious to imagine what I'm doing, but I keep an appearance of utter fear on my face.

Luca grunts, our signal that Kaden's gone. I slump against the chest and find Ava's hand, lacing my fingers between hers. I let out a deep breath and turn to meet her eyes.

"Are you okay?" I ask. Her crystal blues shine back brilliantly in the low artificial lighting. They're so beautiful.

"Uh, yeah," she stutters between breaths. The closeness of our faces, and the way her lips curl and move sends a tingle up my spine. Under all the dirt, grime and sweat, she stares into my eyes.

I'm supposed to say something, but my mind's racing with everything except my lines. The gentle slope of her cheek below her gorgeous eyes. The cute tip of her small nose. The almost imperceptible tremble of her lips. The way she's looking at me, like she feels it too. I know she's acting and I'm crazy to even think it, but I don't care. And we're supposed to kiss, so I let myself move in, closing the gap between us.

I find the warm surface of her lips just before my eyes close. I let go of all pretense and worry as her lips tremble against mine and my mouth parts. I swear she tastes of strawberries. Bending my torso, I scoot in and slide my hand onto her cheek. I let my palm feel her smooth skin, imprinting every sensation in my mind as my hand slides under the curve of her chin and finds her neck. She doesn't stop me. I scoot in closer, and kiss her more intimately, wanting her, needing her.

"Cut! Cut!" Luca yells. "Cut!"

I snap back into reality and jerk back. I scoot away, putting a good foot between us. I immediately miss the taste of her lips, but at the same time I sit back and cough, worried I did something unforgivable. I avert my eyes, not sure what or who to look at, so I pick Luca.

"What the hell was that?" he asks.

"Did you just decide to skip all of your lines?" Helen jumps in, her face half confused, half amused.

"Sort of," is all I can come up with, and my voice comes out like a child who got his hand caught in the proverbial cookie jar.

Dammit.

I dare to check on Ava, sweeping my eyes around and squinting with a half smile. It quickly expands, rising up my cheeks.

Ava's grinning from ear to ear.

13: Cooper Bay

Despite the shadows cast from the trees and the cool breeze rolling between their trunks, I'm sweating. I wipe my brow and cheek, ridding them of the thin film building on the surface.

Since my last scene in the nurses' dormitory, the team's shot two more sequences. I wasn't in either. They were mostly Jaylen's scenes where Luca delved into the inner struggle of the film's villain.

Ahead of me, Luca and Helen lead the pack, weaving through more trees and undergrowth, while the others trail behind. I can hear Brooklyn hobbling along a few feet back, still relying on Riley's shoulder to make it more than a step. He doesn't seem to mind though.

I reposition the pack on my shoulders and step over an emaciated log. Just how untouched this island really is has only now begun to set in for me. The excuses for roads are overgrown, the buildings are more and more falling victim to nature, and the hundreds of trees make the forest feel like it goes on forever in empty woods.

My gaze holds resolute to the path behind Luca and Helen, but I still can't wipe the grin from my lips. I don't think I've said more than a full sentence to Ava since our little *scene*, even with her walking next to me right now. And we haven't dared broach what happened behind the tipped over chest. But she's smiling too. I've kept a regular check, glancing to my right every few minutes, plus she's not avoiding me. After our lips had parted and the crew came down on us, it finally seeped into my brain what had happened. I was sure she'd stay as far away from me as possible and that things would get awkward, but so far, I've been wrong. I mean, it's not like I was the only one kissing.

Every few steps her shoulder or hand brushes against me and I can barely hold back a shiver, but I keep my eyes ahead. I feel like a stupid kid with a crush I can't quite put into words, and I definitely can't speak it to her. Still I relish the memory of her lips against mine, the slightest hint of strawberry under the musty scent of the forest, and the feeling of her skin under my hand.

She's holding a tablet now. I steal a glance. The island's likeness etches the screen, painted with a handful of semi-detailed block outlines. I'm guessing they're the buildings on the island here. Her attention is on the map, keeping us on the right path. I let my face angle toward her, trying not to be obvious. She's so beautiful. While she examines the map, I admire her strong legs below the tattered shorts and the smoothness of her stomach between the tear in her shirt. In the last scene Ava's character, Grace, barely escaped Kaden's wrath, the gap in her t-shirt being the primary evidence of her struggle. I'm not complaining though.

She lifts her eyes from the tablet and I start to open my mouth, but I catch Luca throwing up a hand. I shift my eyes up, lips pursed. He looks like a newbie platoon leader trying to warn us of impending danger. I come to a stop and he finally speaks up.

"Let's stop here. This should be good. There's plenty of room for running."

I look around, but all I see is more of the same, trees and wild growth. I don't presume to know what locations work best for the movie, but I guess I can see how it would work. There's plenty of cover, but the paths between the trees are wide enough to wind through easily. The next scene takes place earlier in the script and involves Riley's lone scene in the movie. Luca puts his hands up high and twitches his fingers to call everyone over. Ten minutes later, we're taking up our spots.

About twenty or thirty yards north of the group, I relax my weight against a tree. The sound of birds chirping bounces under the foliage, and I shift my stance and wiggle my back against the bark to scratch an itch. The others should be filming Riley's scene by now. In the next little bit, he'll come running around the corner — well, the trees — and Luca will have Grady reset his camera for the next scene. I'm supposed to be here when Riley bursts out, finding my character. I'm a stranger to him, but my character still ends up leading him to safety.

With time to spare, and finally a little privacy, I unzip my shorts and relieve myself on the roots of the closest tree. I stare into the forest, aimlessly examining the brown and gray tree trunks, sparsely leafed branches, the dark green vines scrambling up the canopy and the wild undergrowth. My eyes travel up the thin bark of a nearby trunk, following it to the top. I squint as the leaves up high sway and let a spark of sunlight through, and my gaze drops back to the forest floor.

It's so quiet out here.

As if to contradict my thoughts, a gentle breeze picks up

and whooshes through the trees, sending the forest into a reticent rustle as it breezes past my neck. At the edge of my vision, a low-lying branch sways and snaps back into position. I shoot my eyes toward the bough and my arms tense up.

What was that?

I peer around the trunk I'm pissing on and quickly finish up my business and zip up my pants. My survey is useless, I don't find anything, just more plants and trees. I tilt my head and step around the trunk anyway.

There it is! It moves too fast to get a good look at it, but I swear it's the size of a large dog, maybe bigger. It's only a shape in the woods, too far out for me to discern any details. I step forward as something scratches against a tree off to my right and the sound of leaves rustling ruffles my ears. I step back and swallow.

"Riley?" I ask, keeping my voice quiet. "Riley is that you?"

I wait. No one answers.

"Luca? Nick? Gabe?" I try. The birds return my calls with indecipherable warbles. I pivot on my feet, sweeping my gaze over every foot of forest floor. "Ava?"

No one answers. I can feel my pulse quicken. I'm alone, stuck in the middle of a forest that I can't hope to navigate my way out of, and I sure as hell don't know how to get back to the rest of the crew on my own. I close my eyes and tell myself to calm down. I'm about to open my eyes again when a quiet groan sounds through the trees.

"Guys?" I yell this time. "Are you out there?"

A stone's throw to my right a tree sways, and a low crunching betrays the culprit. I jerk my eyes toward the noise as something streaks beyond my vision, leaves and grass swaying in its wake. It's bigger than a dog, I'm sure of it now.

"All right, guys, this isn't funny," I tell them, forcing myself to step around the tree, starting in the direction of whoever's trying to scare me. There's no one. I scan the woods, finding nothing but more trees and dirt.

Suddenly, I'm horrified. I jump back, flattening my back against the nearest tree. I look up to the leafy canopy, my hands shaking, then force my eyes back down to keep watch.

What the hell are you scared of, Coop? Get a grip on yourself.

In the distance I hear foliage moving again, followed by a succession of heavy breaths. My teeth clamp together and I swallow back my nerves. I bend forward, daring to leave the safety of the tree, and search the ground for a weapon, anything. The best I find at my feet is a tiny twig I could easily snap with my pinky finger. The breaths go quiet. Then I notice that something is off. I look up and search the branches. The birds have gone mum and an eerie silence hangs over the boughs. I scoot up close against my tree.

A growl breaks the silence.

My flashlight.

I push off the tree just far enough to wrench the pack from my shoulders. I unzip it and pilfer through the contents, trying to imagine I didn't hear the growl. I push past a spare pair of shoes and underwear before my fingers grasp the cold metallic handle of the flashlight. It's one of those metal-housed, foot-long, heavy as fuck Maglites. I don't bother to zip the pack up or even throw it back over my shoulders. Instead, I drop it to the ground, causing a small dust plume, and twist around to face the woods.

The breathing gets louder and behind it the sound of racing footsteps and cracking branches startles me. It's coming right for me. I flatten my back against the thin but sturdy tree trunk again and hold the flashlight against my chest with both hands wrapped around the shaft, waiting. My breath comes in quick spurts.

I want to run, but it's too late. Whatever is clambering in my direction has already found me. Gathering my wits, I push off the tree and drag in a deep breath. Branches sway and crack while I tighten my grip on my flashlight.

I steel myself, raising the heavy light. The thing bursts past the trees and a small bramble. I'm about to swing when I realize who it is. I still my hands.

Riley.

"What the *fuck*, man?" I scream angrily.

He stumbles to a stop a foot from my face, his steel blues full of surprise. I'm not sure if he didn't expect to see me or if it's the sight of the flashlight held at the ready that confuses him, so I lower the flashlight and let out a pent-up breath. He does the same.

"What?" he peers back at me, a *what the hell* look growing across his face.

"Scaring me like that!" I accuse him, working the fear out of my voice and lowering my pitch.

"Scaring you? I didn't even know...where you were," he says, still catching his breath between words. "I've been...trying to...find you so I could...stop running."

"Sure, so who's been sneaking around out here then?" I ask.

"Sneaking around?" Riley replies with his own question, his brow raised above his left eye. "I just got here, and everyone else is still back there." He cocks his head and gives me a concerned look. "You look really spooked, man."

"Well, someone was out here watching me."

"Man, I don't know what you're talking about," Riley starts, "but there's no one out here but you and me, and I wasn't anywhere around until, like, a few seconds ago."

I eye him suspiciously for a moment and then drop my gaze to my feet.

Did I just imagine it? No. I heard something, and I saw something.

Maybe it wasn't as big as I thought it was, though, probably just some local rodent.

"Never mind," I tell him. Suddenly I feel stupid. "Don't worry about it. I must have just got spooked being out here by myself."

"Okay," Riley elongates the single word, separating the two syllables.

"Y'all over there?" A Southern drawl slithers through the tree trunks. I sigh. It's Grady.

"Yeah, we're over here," Riley yells back. He looks at me, brow still raised. "You sure you're okay, man?"

I nod. "Yeah, I'm good. Don't worry about it. Just forget it."

He seems to agree, swaying his head as Luca and Grady trek past the same grouping of trees he sprinted between less than a minute ago.

"You ready, Cooper?" Luca asks.

"Yeah, I'm good to go."

I think I am, at least.

"Gabe?" He raises his voice to be heard through the trees.

"Good here," Gabe comes back.

"I'm ready," Riley says before Luca can ask the question he knows is coming.

Luca nods and signals Grady to get set up. Nick follows along, working to find the best angle to capture the ambient noises of the forest and our voices. Brooklyn is propped against Helen's side a yard behind Luca, and Jaylen's preparing for his next scene somewhere nearby, I think.

"Remember, Cooper, your character doesn't know who Riley and Gabe are. You've never met them before." Luca's attention switches to Riley and Gabe, his hand out flat. "Same for you two. You run into Cooper, well, Carter, in the woods while you're running from Kaden. Let's put a good fifteen yards between you, give you some more woods to run through."

The two boys nod and move into position out of my view. I go to take up my spot when Helen comes up from behind and puts a hand on my shoulder. I startle.

"A little jumpy, are we?" She grins at me disarmingly, something I wasn't entirely sure she could do as the tension between her and Luca became almost palpable. "Let's have you a little out of view at first, like you've heard them coming, but you're scared of who it might be," she tells me, nudging me back another step behind a graying tree trunk.

"Okay," I say, taking control of my body again. I take a quick glance at Luca as Helen walks back behind the camera. He raises an eyebrow and purses his lips before nodding in agreement.

The forest goes quiet again as Luca conducts the countdown in silence, the digits on his fingers lowering one after the other before the snap of the clapperboard rings out. I peer through the leaves, watching for Riley and Gabe to come running in my direction. I hear the shuffling and smack of feet on the ground, then a rustle of leaves in the distance accompanied by panting. The first thing that comes to mind is the shape I saw before Riley appeared earlier, but I push it aside and focus.

I see Gabe first, his slim frame weaving between the trunks. He's a good two yards ahead of Riley who finally bursts from the forest a second later. Gabe yells back to Riley, in character, "Come on, Tanner! Don't look back!"

Riley doesn't respond as they continue to weave through trunks and undergrowth. They're a few yards away when I lose sight of them behind a thick grouping of trees. I set my eyes along the path I expect them to be on, predicting where they might come out. Finally, Gabe emerges into view. I snap back into my role, stepping forward as he reaches my position.

"Hey! Over here." Crouched by my tree, I wave him over.

He stays in character, pausing for an instant to weigh his odds. Either he keeps running, hoping to outrun Kaden, or joins up with some stranger in a place he's not supposed to be. Following the script, he chooses me and makes a sharp right, sprinting the remaining yard.

"Follow me," I recite my lines.

Gabe starts after me, but he looks back for Riley. I stop, too, and peer past him, squinting into the foliage. He turns and meets my eyes again, a spark of confusion lighting their dark centers. Riley's taking longer than he should, so Gabe adlibs his next lines.

"Wait, I can't leave my friend. He was right behind me."

I squint, not sure what to say next. It's hard enough getting my lines right, let alone making them up on the fly intentionally. I look over Gabe's shoulder, where Riley should have already passed, but there's no Riley.

"Cut!" Luca screams through the trees. I look to my right as the director comes into view, stepping over a small mesh of wildflowers. "Riley? What the hell are you waiting for?"

I furl my brow, snapping my eyes back to the trees, fully expecting Riley to race through at any second.

"Riley?" Luca complains, stepping in front of me.

His call is met with silence. By now everyone is moving, stepping closer to where Riley should have passed. Gabe and I join them, meandering around a set of trees.

"What the hell?" Luca's voice carries through the woods.

I quicken my step and find Luca. He's staring at the ground. He raises his head and his eyes pass over mine. The look on his face scares me. They're worried, unsure, but still holding on to something. Before I can ask, he turns around and slashes the silence. "Riley?!"

Gasps echo past me as the others gather around, their eyes following the same path. I see it too. A coating of blood drips down the thin gray bark of a tree, slithering down from about waist level. My eyes follow the fading stream down the trunk and I find another patch of red on the ground about a yard out. It's perpendicular to the path Riley was meant to travel.

"Riley?!" Luca yells again.

Nick and Gabe echo the call. I find Brooklyn hobbling around the corner. Her mouth gapes open when she finds the blood.

"What happened? Where's Riley?" She's already panicking. "Where is he?"

"Calm down, Brook." Ava pats a gentle palm on Brooklyn's shoulder and smiles for her. "It's going to be okay. He's got to be around here somewhere. I'm sure he's okay."

Ava looks away from the girl, sweeping her eyes around the forest until she finds me. Her blue eyes seem to search for validation. I want to be strong for her, to say something helpful, but I don't know what to say. I don't have a clue what happened to Riley, I don't know where he is. Is he okay? I don't know.

"Yeah, he's going to be fine." I shoot out the words, masking my doubt with mock confidence. "He probably just got turned around or something."

"What about the blood?" Brooklyn nearly screams.

"Yeah, she's got a point," Gabe blurts, motioning at the drying fluid on the tree.

"Maybe he lost his balance, ran into the tree and got scratched up a bit," Jaylen jumps in, while I glare at Gabe.

"Riley?!" Helen yells. I shrink back.

I cup my ear, listening for a reply. Luca yells again. Still nothing.

"Let's search the area, guys," Nick suggests, waving his hand in a wide semicircle. "He can't have gone far, and *if* he's hurt, he shouldn't be moving too fast."

14: Cooper Bay

"Riley?" I yell for at least the twentieth time. The words carry less force and immediacy than they did fifteen minutes ago.

I keep telling myself that it doesn't make any sense. Unless the guy kept at a full sprint, which isn't likely, he couldn't have gone far. I swear we've searched everywhere he could have feasibly made it already. Brooklyn tried his phone earlier, but it just rang until Riley's voicemail came on, and we couldn't hear his ringtone anywhere nearby.

Luca says that Riley probably just hit his head, citing the blood on the tree, and lost his direction. That he wandered off the wrong way. He's confident we'll find him soon if we keep looking. I don't know. I'm not so sure it's that simple.

"Riley?" Nick shouts.

I still think I saw something, heard something, before Gabe came running up.

"Ri—" Nick starts.

"Nick," I interrupt him.

"Yeah, man?" He lowers his shoulders, letting a slow breath lighten his chest.

"Do *you* think Riley just got confused and ran off in the wrong direction?" I ask.

Nick tilts his head and turns to face me. His eyes question me before his mouth opens.

"I mean, yeah," he says. "What else could have happened?"

"No, I get that, but," I start but then hesitate. It seems stupid now that I try to speak the words. It comes across like something you'd tell at night around a campfire, like a ghost story, but I continue anyway. "What about the blood? There was a good bit of it. You really think that was just from bumping his head? Not to mention, it was awful low for him to have hit head first."

"Well..." Nick starts, but lets his voice trail off. His eyes cascade to the ground, like he's intently examining the thick patch of clover and creeping vines. He scrunches his brow. "How else do you explain it?"

I nod, not so much in agreement as glad he's willing to hear me out. Nick's always been that brother, the one that tries to understand despite his tough exterior or how stupid something might sound. I still remember when my first girlfriend dumped me back in middle school, eighth grade, I think. When my oldest brother, Brendan, had just told me to suck it up because it wasn't even a real relationship, Nick had quietly sat down with me in my room and just let me cry for a while. He never said anything profound, he just told me I'd be okay. It seems silly now, but it meant something to me back then. The point is that he listens.

"I know Ava said there are no animals on the island, but is she sure? I mean, *is* there any wildlife on the island, besides the birds?" I ask rather than answering his question, stepping onto a felled log.

"I think she probably knows what she's talking about, but I don't know, maybe." He shrugs. "I mean people did live here for a while. Who knows?"

"Anything big though?" I persist, trying not to sound desperate, but leading him, wanting him to help make what I'm about to tell him not sound so odd.

"Maybe. I really don't know, Coop." Nick turns and sweeps his eyes over another patch of forest while I stand in place, watching him. I huff.

"I think there's some animal, something bigger. Like human-sized," I blurt. It comes out worse than I'd planned, but I didn't let myself think on it too much either. At least I didn't say Bigfoot.

"Huh?" Nick's head twists to the side, his brow crunched, his left eye opened a little more than the other. "What are you saying, Coop?"

I freeze. Now that the opportunity is here, I don't want to tell my brother the shoestring hypothesis I put together. My eyes dart to the ground, bouncing between the bases of the two trunks closest to me.

"Well?" Nick urges.

"I think…" I stop, but quickly force myself to continue. "I think something took Riley. I don't believe he hit his head and wandered off into the woods so quickly that we can't find him. I mean, I don't know him that much, but he seems smarter than that to me."

"You think something, on the island, took Riley?" Nick repeats my claim in abbreviated form, angling his head down as he speaks the words. I can tell he's not buying it by the look in his dark brown eyes.

"Yeah."

"What?" he asks. "It'd have to be a pretty big animal to literally snatch Riley up and get away so quick."

I nod furiously. His words hold a measure of doubt, but

he's at least following along for now.

"I know. That's what I'm trying to say," I explain. Now comes the hard part. "I heard something in the woods a minute or two before Gabe came running up, and I got a small glimpse. Whatever it was, it's big, like, our size big."

Nick shuffles his feet and cups his palm over his mouth in contemplation. I think he's at least considering it.

"Maybe there's someone else on the island," he suggests.

I don't think so, but I understand what he's saying. I tried to think along that line just minutes ago, but that breathing...it wasn't human. I debate for a moment whether to mention the breathing, maybe insist that it was some animal, but I keep it to myself. It truly does sound silly the more I think on it.

"I guess. I mean, what else could it be?" I agree.

The wind flutters my shirt as it whips through the trees. For a moment I think I hear it breathing again, but it's just the wind.

"I don't know, man," Nick admits, shaking his head. "But if there's someone else on the island, and they took Riley, then we need to get back to the others."

I nod in agreement. I can't argue with that.

"Let's go," Nick says, reaching for his phone and dialing a number.

I jump down from my perch and join him, walking back in the direction we came. Even though I can't see past the leafy canopy, I can tell the sun is on its western descent. The shadows are growing longer. I check my phone. 6:57 p.m. It won't be long until sunset.

A little over five minutes later, we're standing in the same place where I first saw whatever it was I saw — a man, animal,

I don't know. With everyone present, Nick and I relay our conversation to the others. Nods and confused looks paint their faces. Poor Brooklyn's crying again. I'm surprised to find her leaning on Gabe's shoulder.

"So you think there's someone else on the island, and that they took Riley?" Helen asks, the disbelief evident in her voice.

"It's not so farfetched," Grady insists, still getting his breath back from the trek around the woods. "I mean, *we're* here, right? There isn't much to stop people from coming."

"Maybe it's some homeless dude," Gabe picks up, throwing out what most of them were probably thinking. He's about to say more, but a whimper at his side stills his lips.

"Yeah, I mean, it make sense," I say. "I know I heard something, I saw something just before Riley disappeared. I swear it ran past me, but it kept to the trees, so I didn't get a good look at it."

"You keep saying 'it,' rather than 'he' or 'they.'" This is the first thing Luca's said since we met up between these trees.

"Uh... Well..." I look at Nick, hoping to see some hint of support, but I find his expression lacking. He doesn't want me to say it. Maybe I shouldn't. "Sorry, you know what I mean. It's just that I didn't get a good look at them."

Luca's head bounces up and down slowly. He pulls a half smile. I think he believes me. I sure as hell don't.

"Well, if there is someone else on the island and they've taken Riley, we need to find him," Ava interjects. "We should call the cops, too, right?"

"No!" Luca nearly yells, throwing his hands up. "I mean, no. We're not supposed to be here. If we call the police, then our asses get shipped back to the city, and depending on whether they charge us or not, this movie might be done with."

Lovely, I think. We're out here by ourselves on what we thought was an abandoned island, and now we need to play detective because we can't call the authorities. I'm not too fond of getting in trouble for being here, but I'm not sure I like the idea of traipsing around in search of some kidnapper either.

"Oh," is Ava's reply.

For a few minutes, Luca, Jaylen and Gabe debate whether we should just go ahead and call the police. Jaylen wants to bring the police to the island, let them do their jobs, but he wants to keep looking too. Gabe agrees with Luca that the last thing we need is the police. In the end, Luca wins.

"All right," Luca says, placing a hand on Gabe's and Grady's shoulders as he stands between them. "We need to split up. Three groups of three. We'll each head a different direction to search. Keep your phones on and call in to the other groups every half hour."

"What if we don't find him tonight?" Ava asks. Her eyes are worried. It hurts me to see her like this, but I notice she's standing closer than she was moments ago.

Luca sighs, taking a moment to think about the possibility while examining the forest floor. He raises his eyes back to Ava. "Then we'll continue searching in the morning. If he doesn't turn up by eleven, meet at the hospital on the north end of the island. You should all have maps. We'll call the police then if we have to."

I absently pat my pack where my copy of the map resides.

"But..." Helen starts, but Luca stops her with an upraised

hand.

"But nothing. If we can't find him by tonight, then we call the cops. Jaylen, Grady," Luca says. "You two go with Helen. Ava—"

"I'll go with Cooper and Nick," Ava interrupts. My face jerks toward her, barely holding back my surprise. She looks away, realizing too late how obvious the statement was.

"Uh... That works," Luca agrees, raising his brow. "Gabe, Brooklyn. You two are with me then. In case there is someone else on the island, be careful. Now let's go."

15: Cooper Bay

The shadows creep ever longer, draping the forest in a concealing shroud of gray as the sun inches past the horizon. Bugs chirp above the hum of the city, and a fallen twig snaps under my foot.

"I can't believe this is happening," Ava says.

She's an arm's length to my right, scanning the forest floor and the lower tree limbs.

"I mean, no one's supposed to be here," she continues.

"We're here," Nick answers, shrugging. "Who knows how many people have actually crossed over, maybe there's even a homeless population and we only now happened across them."

"I don't know about that." I shake my head and scrunch my brow. "I doubt many of the homeless have ready access to a boat or kayak. Plus, it wouldn't benefit them unless…"

I stop, wishing I hadn't even started.

"Unless what?" Ava asks.

"Unless they came here to die…" I let the words trail off.

"Oh." Ava looks away.

I continue along the northwestern trajectory we chose before leaving the others. If we're where we think we are, and I trust Ava knows what she's doing with the map, then we should be coming up on the old male dormitory soon. At present the scenery is dull, more of the same, a hundred copies of the same tree I swear I've seen a million times already. Their thin limbs are filled with countless shades of green. Vines choke their way up almost every trunk and braid between the sparse stalks of grass and patches of dirt-covered forest floor.

Where are you, Riley? I wonder. It's been nearly an hour since he disappeared, and deep down I feel responsible. It tugs at my chest and I can't stop chewing on my lip as my nerves work me over. I should have said something. I should have sprinted back to the group as soon as I saw *it*, before Riley had a chance to disappear. I should have warned them. It's my fault.

"Is that it?" Nick asks, pointing a bony finger past me to where the trees peel back and a stack of worn red bricks protrude from the ground.

"Maybe," Ava answers. She unfolds the map and traces a finger over the creased paper. "That's where it's supposed to be."

"Do you think he's in there?" I ask, knowing full well they don't have any better idea. I stop at the tree line and scan the structure. It's two stories, like the nurses' dormitory, but it looks like time has been much less forgiving here.

Trees brush against every edge of the building and vines crawl up the bricks, tracing a maze of green and faded rust red before wrapping over the roof's ledge. I squint, my eyes searching the thick edge of the flat roof. The whole top right quarter of the building is missing, crumbled in years ago from the lack of upkeep. The vines have taken hold, breaching the ancient bulwark, and a singular tree sprouts from within the building, its branches spewing over the breach.

"I don't know, let's find out," Nick says and steps past

me.

I pull my eyes away from the structure and follow. Ava's close on my heels.

The brush behind us shuffles, and I swivel on my feet. My eyelids narrow to tiny slits and I open my hands, holding them out to my sides.

"Did you see that?" I question, unwilling to turn around.

"See what?" Nick asks.

"I didn't see anything, but I did hear something." Ava moves beside me, her steps slow and careful.

"There was movement, something slipped behind us, in the woods." I jut my chin up, signaling toward the forest and step closer to the bush. Its leaves have settled, but all I can think of is the shape I saw earlier. Actually it wasn't even a shape, it was just something behind the trees. I blink, trying to remember, but it hits me that I didn't see anything but movement. Undeterred, my heart still racing, I take a drag of air, hoping to catch some unusual scent, but I find nothing more than the fresh aroma of an untouched habitat.

"Are you sure?" Nick asks. He doesn't seem worried.

"Yeah," I assure him. "I think it was…"

Nick gives me a disapproving scowl, so I cut my words short.

I keep my eyes set ahead, scanning the foliage where the leaves stirred, hoping to catch something in my sight. As hard as I try, all I find are trees and dirt. I step closer, placing a finger against my lips. I jerk back when the bush ruffles again, throwing my hand out to keep Ava back. I take another step closer, angling my neck to get a better look around the bush. I'm careful not to move too quickly. It ruffles again, but I hold my ground this time. My heart is racing, and my lungs pump with a burning ferocity. Another step. I'm only a foot away.

Suddenly it shifts, and leaves burst into the air. A squawk and flurry of feathers flap in my face. I stumble back, smacking into Ava, as the bird takes flight and finds a roost a few yards above my reach.

"Dammit!" I yelp.

"Did he get you?" Nick chuckles behind me. I glare into the woods, but I can't hold on to it, so I let me eyes soften and let out a small laugh of my own. Ava joins in when she realizes it's okay.

"A little bit." I shake my head before I finally realize there's a hand on my side. Ava. I shuffle forward, trying not to look embarrassed and then force myself to face her. "You okay? I didn't mean to run into you like that."

"I'm good. I have to admit, it startled me too," she chuckles. "Good thing I was behind you though. You might have ended up on your ass otherwise."

"All right now," Nick shakes his head, a wry grin painted across his face. "Let's check out the dorm's perimeter, okay? Then inside. Maybe he decided to find shelter."

I force a cough and nod, but Ava's still grinning at me, so I finally let go of my pride and enjoy the moment. Five minutes later, we slip around the building's last exterior corner, coming full circle, and I start for the entrance. The shadows fully engulf the building and the sun barely penetrates the thick layer of trees and greenery covering the rooftop and most of the windows.

I step onto the concrete platform and reach for the old metal door handle. With daylight fading, I'm not thrilled about navigating a creepy abandoned building by flashlight. Nevertheless, I swing the door open. The hinges emit a hushed squeal and the solid wooden panel scrapes the floor before coming to a halt a foot inside. I force it the rest of the way and step in. Before entertaining another step, I retrieve my flashlight and flip the power switch. The dilapidated interior blooms into existence within a fading cone of bright white light.

The walls are falling apart. Torn and rotting sheetrock hangs from the wood paneling, exposing the now out-of-code wiring. Its simple painted surface is dull and broken. A scattering of paint chips, slabs of sheetrock and dust line the base of the walls. I swear it looks like the male inhabitants took to rioting in their last days on the island and decided to use a sledgehammer on portions of the wall. It's in shambles.

Please be here, Riley.

16: Grady Maddox

"According to the map, that's the boiler house." Grady motions ahead at an imposing brick structure. In the dark it's menacing, its empty windows peering back like the eyes of a spider. He sweeps his hand across the path and points at another building about ten yards from the edge of the forest. "And that's the coal house. At least, I think."

Helen's beam lights the path between the two structures and settles on the coal house. It's smaller than the boiler house, but in the last rays of the falling sun its presence is still intimidating.

"You think he might be in there?" Jaylen nods toward the larger building and takes a step onto the cracked pathway.

"Maybe." Helen sighs. She takes a step forward, quick to be in the lead, and walks toward the coal house. Crossing the divide between the two buildings, she inches up to its dirty brick side and stops at the first window. She leans around the cracking windowsill and shouts. "Riley?! You in there?"

Her voice bounces off the interior before going silent. She angles her head, putting an ear between herself and the open window.

"Riley?!"

Only the cadence of insects coming out for their night songs reply.

"Dammit," she complains. Turning to face Grady and Jaylen, she sighs. "Guess we need to go inside and check it out."

"If he did hit his head, maybe he's unconscious," Grady reasons, trying to mask his own worry.

"But if there's someone in there with him…" Jaylen starts, stopping short of completing the thought. His lips part as he puffs out a heavy breath. "Fuck it, if he's in there we need to find him. Let's just be careful."

Grady and Helen nod, but no one moves. They all exchange glances, each waiting for the other to move first. Finally, Grady steps forward and stops by the entrance to the coal house. He turns to face them and moves, nearly stepping on Jaylen's heels in the dark.

"Well, Jaylen, would you like to take the lead?" He smiles, hands drifting toward the door.

Jaylen's brow rises. He hesitates for a mere second before stepping around Grady and shaking his head as he stomps past the threshold.

"Stay close."

17: Cooper Bay

It's dark. My flashlight beam reflects off the heaps of crumbling stone scattered about the floor. At my back is total darkness.

Nick passes through my beam and shines his light past an open doorway. Before I can reach him, he retracts back into the hall and shakes his head.

We've been at it for almost half an hour. The slivers of light that did get through the dusty windows are gone now. I swear it feels like I'm in a movie. I mean, aside from the fact that we're moving slowly and probably look like lost teenagers, I feel like I'm part of an FBI team sweeping an office building, clearing rooms, trying to root out some terrorist cell. At least that's how I'm trying to distract myself from the knot in my stomach.

I eye Ava at the edge of my beam. Having her here is the only reason I don't press my back against the wall like a scared little girl, fingers clenched around my flashlight, and swing around the doorway all dramatic-like with my flashlight held out like a gun; one part urge, one part terror. Instead, I inhale a gulp of stale air and force my legs to move calmly and deliberately around the bend.

"Riley?" I turn to find Ava peering around a doorframe. Her voice is quiet, a whisper, but it feels loud in the darkness.

I take a quick glance back into the room. It's empty, so I slip back into the hallway. Doors line the corridor, but my flashlight reveals little more than decay and rot. Half the doors are missing from the wooden molding that once outlined them, but none of the doors have escaped rot. Cracked and splintered boards litter the floor, and dust bursts in tiny plumes with each footstep like we're giants pounding the earth to a pulp.

"I don't think he's here." It's Ava again. She's facing me now. I hold my light low, just enough not to blind her but to still see her. She seems uncomfortable, maybe even scared. Deep inside it both hurts me to see the discomfort on her face and comforts me to have her so close.

"We're not even finished with the first floor." Nick sweeps his flashlight over the hallway, already spotting his next target. He doesn't bother to face us. "We still need to search upstairs."

"Upstairs?" Ava sounds indignant.

"He might have run up there," he comes back, his voice a little more stern.

"*Or* was taken up there," I insert myself, speaking before I let my mind catch up. "*Maybe.*"

"Is that really a good idea?" She ignores me, her eyes rooted on Nick.

I purse my lips when I realize what she's saying. The last time she went upstairs in one of these decrepit buildings, it didn't exactly end well. For a moment I think she could just stay down here while we search upstairs, but that seems like an even worse idea once I really think about it, especially if there is someone or *something* else on the island.

Nick tries to tread carefully, but he doesn't turn to face

Ava when he replies.

"We just have to be careful. What if he is up there? Maybe he's unconscious." He sweeps the light over a patch of broken wall. "I can go up by myself if it'll make you feel better."

"No," I say, maybe a bit too quickly. It's a bad idea. I know it somewhere deep in my bones. "We need to stick together."

Before I can speak up, Ava does.

"Cooper's right, I'll go. Let's just be careful."

"We've still got a few more rooms to check down here first." Nick keeps walking. "Let's finish that up first, then we'll check upstairs."

I don't bother to respond. Instead, I sweep my beam around and find the next door on my right. I step over a small hump of debris and peer around the doorframe, swinging my flashlight into the space. It's small, like my dorm back at UT, just older, much older. And we have air conditioning.

Hell, did they even have AC back in the sixties? My mind wanders before I rein it back in.

The room's empty so I twist back around and catch up with Ava and Nick a few steps down the hall. I'm almost used to the musty scent put off by the rot and mold encasing the building...almost. It's still offensive to my nose. I breathe through my mouth to filter out at least some of the smell.

A few feet ahead I catch sight of a staircase in the jittery path of Ava's flashlight beam. I concentrate my light on the stairs, helping to illuminate the risers as we step closer. It looks a lot like the one in the other building, where Ava and Brooklyn earned their scars. It's a spiral, nothing too ornate, except for the etching of burnt orange rust along the outer railing. The architect really must have had a thing for spiral staircases.

We stop before the staircase, our lights drowning out the dark and casting a patchwork of shadows behind the incrementing platforms.

"All right. Up we go." Nick mounts the first step but stops short of taking the next. His beam settles on one of the lower planks and he tilts his head.

"What is it?" I ask.

"Is that Riley's shoe?"

I step forward and peer around Nick's waist, letting my beam guide my eyes. Propped upside down on the third step is a tennis shoe. I blink, thinking I'm seeing things, but it doesn't change. Trailing up the stairs in small bursts are splatters of red. I swallow back a burst of alarm as the dots connect in my head. Blood. I lean in, trying to get a better look. A trace of uncertainty dampens the alarm. The splashes are dried and faded.

"You think..." I start, my eyes glued to the fading droplets. "It doesn't look fresh, it should be wet still..."

"I don't know, maybe." Nick shrugs. "Either way, that's the closest to proof we've had yet. Let's go."

Behind me, Ava shifts uneasily. I turn and grin at her, stupidly hoping my uneasy smile might give her some comfort.

Nick starts up the stairs. He tests each plank carefully before taking the next. I give him a three-step lead before urging Ava to go ahead of me. I want to be behind her in case she falls. She rolls her eyes but passes me. I pat her on the shoulder as she reaches the first stair and cautiously tests her footing. It takes her a few seconds to gain the confidence to move, but with fingers wrapped around the railing, she finds it and mounts the stairs. They groan under her weight. I close my eyes for a second, horrified that this isn't going to end well. I let my eyes open again and follow, keeping my beam on the stair in front of me, checking for any obvious imperfections or weaknesses before I let my foot land.

The droplets of blood seem to multiply. They morph from the occasional droplet into a gradual smear. It's like someone's throat was slashed and their killer towed the blood-soaked body up the stairs. The thought makes my stomach churn.

"Oh my God!" Ava's voice is shaking like the beam of her flashlight. "There's so much blood."

I yank my foot from the last step and place my palm on Ava's forearm, trying to steady her. She tries to reassure me she's okay with a smile, but she can't manage the simple expression. Her eyes are spooked and her arm trembles under my palm.

Ahead of us, Nick's beam still follows the wide crimson smear. The swatch of color smears from left to right, as if painted by some drunken artist. I train my light on the trail and follow, keeping a light grasp on Ava's arm. There's something fetid in the air, something worse than the mold, and it's getting fiercer with each footstep.

My light flicks into the first room. There's nothing. I keep walking. Nick flashes his beam around next room, gives it a quick scan and goes back to walking the hall. Passing by, I take a second look in the room and find nothing too. The smell is growing more rank by the second. I cover my mouth with my flashlight-wielding arm, refusing to let go of Ava.

Ahead, Nick comes up on the next room. I shoot my beam along the trail. It cuts off to the right, into the room ahead of

Nick. He turns, putting a hand up against the glare of my beam, and I can see his Adam's apple move, lips thin. I step forward as he turns and steps around the doorframe. Before he can cross the threshold, Nick jumps back and clamps a hand over his mouth.

"Oh fuck!" He throws up his free hand, urging us to stop.

I tilt my head, imagining the most horrible possible scenario. I step forward despite Nick's warning and make the bend. The smell smacks my nostrils like a freight car. Rot, but not that of wood or plants. No. It's the rot of flesh and meat. My eyes spring open, taking in all the blood.

My light bathes the floor, illuminating bright crimson pools and exposing a body, or pieces of a body. Nearest the door, about three feet past the entry, is an arm. Meat and torn flesh hang from its stump where a body should be. My gaze sticks on the hand, the fingers. Human. I feel my own hands begin to shake, and the beam from my flashlight starts to wobble. I clench my fist and rush back into the hallway.

"What is it?" Ava asks, stepping closer, ready to peer around the corner.

I throw my hand out and grab her arm to hold her back.

"No, Ava," I tell her. "You don't want to see, just stay there."

"Is it Riley? Is he okay?" Her voice is scared and worried. She pulls her arms away and wedges herself between me and the door, peering inside. If I could see the color of her face in the dark, I'm sure it would be white like snow on a winter day. "No, no!"

Her screams pierce my ears. She jerks back, flattening herself against the wall.

"It's not Riley," Nick says with no less disgust in his voice than if it had been him.

I pull my eyes from Ava just long enough to verify Nick's assessment. Beyond the severed arm, a body lays strewn against the corner of the room. The head is bent forward, its mouth hanging open in a perpetual tormented cry. Its eyes and cheeks are sunken, covered in dried blood. The torso is the definition of mayhem. Whatever did this ripped and tore with a rabid passion, clearing flesh from bone and expelling blood in equal fervor.

I twist around, putting my back to the corpse. I close my eyes and take a deep breath as Nick stills himself and enters the room. I hear his footsteps but refuse to take another glance. Swallowing, I let my eyes open to find Ava shaking, her body pressed against the wall. It doesn't take much to move, anything to get farther away from the rotting corpse. Stepping forward, I place my hands on Ava's shoulders and lean down, trying both to meet her eyes and return a semblance of calm to my own. She refuses to look at me. Instead, her blue eyes dart to every corner and crevice in the dark space.

"Ava." I call to her even though she's standing only inches before me. She's there, but she's not at the same time. I take another gulp to clear the quiver from my voice. "Ava. Ava!"

Something snaps, and her eyes finally find me. The crystal blue of her eyes seems hollow as they try to focus on me. I give her a gentle squeeze.

"Ava," I repeat now that I have her back. "It's not Riley."

She reaches up and wraps a hand around mine, pulling it from her shoulder. She rubs her cheek against the back of my hand and whimpers. I feel her trembling, the wetness of her tears trailing down my hand. I'm horrified. There's a mutilated body behind me and then there's this girl. I didn't know her from Eve until a day ago, but that doesn't disband the primal need to protect her that's burning in my chest—but I don't know how. I don't know what to say, what to do. So instead, I just lock my eyes with hers.

She's strong, but this is crazy. We're not meant to see stuff like this.

"It's okay, Ava, it's going to be okay," I tell her, hating that I don't have any way to ensure my words are not lies.

Slowly, she pulls away from the wall and I let my other hand slide off her shoulder. She lets go of my hand, but instead of coiling back she slides her arms around my back and leans her entire body into me, burying her face against my neck. Her tears trail under my shirt as her arms wrap around me. I feel her shivering as I turn to be certain she doesn't see through the doorway again.

"It's okay, Ava." I wrap my arms around her. She shudders in my grasp, but as we stand there, the shakes begin to subside. "It's okay. I've got you."

I feel stupid for saying it, but she doesn't recoil. Instead, she rubs her cheek against my neck again. For a moment I can't believe she's in my arms, and I can't think of anything I want more, but I quickly push away the selfish thought.

"Whatever did that is a monster." Nick trudges out into the hallway, dropping his hand from his mouth and taking a drag of fresher air. "What the hell lives on this island?"

The question is directed at Ava.

"Are you sure there aren't larger animals on this island?"

"Slow down, Nick," I bite back. He squints and starts to open his mouth again. I don't know what's come over me, but I don't stop. "No, Nick. Give her time."

"No, it's okay," Ava lifts her head. She keeps her eyes low as she slips back a step. She wipes the last tear from her cheek and takes a deep breath, clasping her hands. I can hear a stutter as she expels the air from her lungs again. A few seconds pass, and her eyes find Nick as she fidgets. "No. As far as I'm aware, there's nothing but birds living on the island. I mean, maybe there's something small, like rabbits or something, but it's mostly insects and birds as far as I know. Nothing that could do that. Nothing."

"Maybe something was introduced to the island later, after it was abandoned." Nick steps forward, his hands waving. He always moves his hands a lot when he's nervous. "It's possible, right?"

"But what's big enough and mean enough to do that, Nick?" I ask.

"Uh..." He thinks, eyes darting along the path of his light. "A bear? Maybe a cougar?"

"But how'd it get here? How did it go unnoticed this long?" I shuffle my feet. It doesn't make sense. How would something that big get here?

"I don't know, but there sure as hell is something else here, and it's not a giant fucking squirrel," Nick tries.

"Calm down, Nick." I hold out my hand palm down. "We'll figure it out. Whatever it is, it's big and it's obviously dangerous. I—"

"We need to warn the others!" Ava interrupts. She reaches into her pocket and retrieves her cellphone. When she taps the phone, her head angles to the side and she stares oddly at it. The look on her face makes me nervous. "I don't have any signal."

I cock my head and immediately reach for my phone. I

swipe open the screen before I check the bars at the top left corner. Nothing, just a tiny emblem of a tower with a slash through it.

"I've got nothing. Nick?" I motion for him to check his, too.

Before he can utter a word, I know the answer.

"Nada." He shakes his head.

"How the hell do we not have signal?" I posit, taking a step back. It feels like the world is closing in. We're stuck in the dark with only our flashlights to guide our way, Riley's missing, there's a fucking dismembered body in the room behind us, we're alone on this island and no one knows we're here, and our phones aren't working now. I force myself to breathe. "We're in New York City and not one of us has signal. I know I did an hour ago, and yesterday."

"There's something really wrong about all this. We need to go to the hospital," Ava urges, "meet up with the others. They need to know it's worse than we thought."

"I agree, they need to know."

"I know, but we need to check the rest of the building for Riley," Nick says. I can tell he doesn't want to stay, but he doesn't want to stop searching, especially with what we just saw. "If Riley's here, he's probably hiding. I mean..."

He doesn't finish the sentence, but his eyes trail off to the door, following the rotting stench. I look at Ava, trying to see if she agrees. She nods. I curse my luck and nod my own reluctant agreement.

"Let's make it quick."

Nick takes it to heart. He bobs his head for us to follow and is off down the hall without another word. I turn to follow, but before I can move I feel Ava's fingers clasp my hand.

I stop long enough to look back and offer a weak smile, and then take off down the hall.

18: Luca Sanchez

A breeze rustles the leaves, sparkling fractured rays of moonlight about the forest floor. Her leg propped atop a fallen trunk, Brooklyn leans back against a tree. She lets out a sore huff, wincing as her hand goes to her leg.

"We'll take a quick rest and pick up the search again in a few minutes." Luca steps over the same fallen log and takes a seat opposite Brooklyn. He eyes the bloodied bandage on her leg and grimaces. "How's the leg holding up?"

"It's…" she says between breaths. Even with Gabe to lean on, she's winded from the one-legged walking. "It'll be okay."

"You sure?" Luca prods.

She nods vigorously, but it's easy to see she's still in a lot of pain.

"It looks pretty bad." Gabe swoops around Brooklyn and leans against another tree. The wind stirs through the small hollow and whips through his hair, but it does little to dishevel it further.

"I'm good." She holds her head high, putting on a strained grin.

"Real smooth there, Gabe," Luca chides the boy.

"Sorry. I'm just tired." Gabe lays his head back against the thin tree bark and closes his eyes dramatically. He fidgets with his fingers and hands, releasing and clamping, releasing and clamping.

A minute passes with only the rustling of the leaves, the occasional bird chirping and the low howl of the wind interrupting the silence.

"I can't believe this is happening." Brooklyn lowers her head. "I mean, how? How the hell did Riley go missing? He's not a kid. He's a grown, capable man. And this." She motions to the makeshift bandage on her leg.

"I don't know, Brook, but we're going to find Riley and we're going to get you fixed up." Luca smiles. His voice is calm and empathetic. "Riley probably just got turned around and is trying to find us too. Right this moment, maybe."

Luca throws his gaze at Gabe, searching for backup, but finds none. With shoulders shrugged, Gabe opens his eyes wide and shakes his head.

"I don't have a clue what's going on here. I mean how *does* someone get turned around like that? He was *right* there. I'm telling you, he was *right* behind me and then he was just gone. Gone!" Gabe moves away from the tree, stepping into the middle of the small clearing. His amber eyes are dark under the dim moonlight, concealing the guilt in his eyes. "How the hell, man? I mean, really?"

"You're not helping, Gabe." Luca's voice gains a stern undercurrent, one he usually reserves for the eighth and ninth take of a scene when no one seems to want to cooperate.

"And not talking about it is really helping a lot, too, isn't it?" Gabe throws his hands in the air and rolls his eyes. He grumbles something indecipherable and turns, putting his back to Luca.

"We can talk about it, but let's try to keep our heads about us." Rising from the log, Luca sighs before continuing. "We don't need to spook each other."

Gabe spins around.

"Spook each other? You're worried about spoo…" He lets the unfinished word trail along the cool night breeze. Pursing his lips in a half grin, Gabe looks to Brooklyn and then back to Luca. "Brooklyn. You think I'm going to bother Brooklyn, don't you? 'Cause he's her boyfriend? That right?"

Luca doesn't answer, but the hardness of his face and the temperature building behind his brown eyes say enough.

"You've got to be kidding me!" Gabe almost yells at his boss, all respect tossed aside. "You're worried that I might bother Brooklyn? She's a grown ass woman, if she can't handle it she shouldn't have left the city."

"What?" Brooklyn yelps. "I don't need to be babied."

"I'm not babying you." Luca raises his hands in self-defense. "I'm just trying to be sensi—"

"And Riley isn't my boyfriend. We were just good friends," she interrupts Luca, throwing her eyes onto Gabe.

"Oh!" Gabe puts a hand over his mouth in mock dramatization. "So you're just a slut then?"

"Okay! That's far enough, Gabe." Luca steps between the two, but before he can say more Brooklyn begins to yell back.

"I'm no slut, you fucking asshole!" A tear streaks down her cheek but does little to dissuade Gabe.

"Really? So fucking Riley in the woods last night when he's not your boyfriend, that's not a slutty thing to do? Does Luca get a go next while I do Riley?" Gabe shakes his head, his deep brown eyes angry. "'Cause let me tell you, he must have really been going to town on you. Hell, I could hear you two fucking back at camp. You woke up Cooper, too, with all that moaning and gro—"

Gabe falls back as Luca shoves him against a tree and holds him there. "Shut up, Gabe! What's your fucking problem? It doesn't matter. None of that matters. It's her business, and that's that. We need to focus on Riley, on figuring out where he is and getting back to the others. All of this other random bullshit that you've got going on right now can wait."

Still propped against the fallen trunk, Brooklyn keeps her eyes down, trying to hide the tears. She sobs quietly. "We were going out, but only the past two weeks. We hadn't decided to make it public yet."

"Oh shut—" Gabe starts but Luca throws up a single finger an inch from Gabe's lips.

"Zip it, Gabe. We need to stick toge—" Luca jerks his head to the right, facing north, and peers through the tree trunks, past the almost imperceptible movement of the lower branches and leaves.

"Did you hear that?" he asks, releasing the pressure against Gabe's chest.

"Seriously, man?" Gabe steps forward. "You—"

"Shhh." He holds a finger against his own lips. Gabe squints, realization shining in his eyes, and turns to see for himself.

"What is it?" Brooklyn whispers.

"I'm not sure," he tells her. Luca examines the empty forest for a few more seconds before shaking his head. "Maye it was nothing. I thought I heard someth— There it is again!"

Leaves rustle and a branch cracks to the west. Their eyes dart toward the noise in unison.

"Did you hear it that time?" Luca asks.

"Yeah." Gabe nods, the anger in his eyes lost behind a film of building fear and suspicion. "What is it?"

"I don't know, but it came from over — "

The noise crackles in their ears above the rustling of the wind, and this time Luca catches movement again.

"You see that? Over there, that bush." His words are quick but quiet.

"It sounded closer too," Gabe comments, nodding his head.

Fixing his eyes on the bush, Gabe's eyes widen as the brush and leaves move again. Out of sight, a deep and gravely growl crawls past the branches.

"What is it?" Brooklyn cries out, louder than the two men appreciate; Luca throws up a hand behind him, palm outstretched, urging her to be quiet. She bites her lip and leans forward.

The bush stirs and the leaves separate, revealing little more than a growing shadow. The bush stirs and the leaves separate, revealing little more than a growing shadow. Deep in his chest, Luca feels it staring him down, examining him. His heart begins to race. Gabe takes a step back, probably feeling the same sudden desire to put space between him and whatever lurks in the shadow overpowering his thoughts. His heel catches a surfaced tree root and his body tumbles back. His heel catches a surfaced tree root and his body tumbles back. He lands on his ass, painting the butt of his pants in dirt and field grass. Startled, Luca takes a step back, his eyes darting back to Gabe quick enough to see what the problem is. When he jerks his eyes back, it's gone.

His gaze scurries about the bush, sweeping over the trees and nearby bramble where the shadow lurked, where something had surveyed them, sized him up.

"Where'd it go?" Luca asks, taking another step back.

Gabe climbs to his feet in time to put a hand out to prevent Luca from stubbing his toes. He joins Luca's search of the woods, looking for the shadow.

"Where'd it go?" Luca repeats.

"I don't know, it was there a second ago. Right?" Gabe replies, suddenly doubting his own eyes. All the malice is gone from his voice, and in its place is an almost childlike fear.

Without taking his eyes off the forest, Luca backsteps toward Brooklyn. The woods are quiet, and even the gentle swishing of the wind ceases as his heart accelerates. A twig cracks under his feet and Luca clenches his fist and grits his teeth, every muscle in his body contracting.

"Dammit," he grumbles under his breath.

He allows his body to relax and begins to move again. He throws a hand out to steady himself when his calf bumps against the fallen log, then twists around to face Brooklyn. Shaken from his trance, Luca fixes his eyes on her as he leans down and loops an arm under her shoulder. "We need to get you up. We're going to the hospital *now*. I'm not so sure it's safe out here."

"What is it?" Brooklyn asks, trying to see past Gabe.

"I don't know, but I don't plan on sticking around to find out." The deep howl plays in his head again. *Definitely an animal. But what? It sounded big.* "Come on, Gabe, let's go."

Gabe stumbles backward a step, then turns around without question. With the cool air nipping at his neck, his feet fall into rhythm with Luca.

"Let's keep it slow and calm. The last thing we need to do is spook *it*."

Luca pulls Brooklyn's arm around his shoulder and holds

her hand to his chest, bearing her weight around his neck. His eyes sweep each tree and branch.

Snap.

They freeze. It came from behind, and it's close. Luca bites down hard, grinding his teeth, the urge to turn around overwhelming. Then it roars. It's an animalistic, rabid howl that breaks the night calm and causes Luca's heart to plummet. Before its roar can evaporate into oblivion, the rhythmic pounding of heavy feet join in the chorus.

"*Fuck* slow! *Run!*" Gabe screams and races across the forest floor.

The others mimic him, but Brooklyn's swollen leg refuses to give way to the imminent danger. She grunts each time her injured leg struggles under her weight, her pace growing sluggish as Luca drags her forward.

"Come on, Brooklyn," Luca urges her. "You can do this. Let's go."

She grits her teeth and tries to pick up her pace. Her breaths come in quick gasps between audibly painful footfallls, but she keeps moving.

Twigs and branches snap behind them, the noise growing closer every second. Its howl ignites the night, sending a chill down Luca's back. He pumps his legs, trying to move quicker, but Brooklyn's injury won't let her move any faster. He peers forward, daring to take his eyes off the ground. Ten yards ahead he finds Gabe. He wants to scream for the young actor to come back and help carry Brooklyn, but his lungs are working overtime. He curses in his head as Gabe's form becomes nothing more than a silhouette, then disappears behind a black veil.

Luca leans forward, trying to balance his pace with the

weight on his shoulder. The woods explode with cracks and creaks below the thunderous boom of something's feet beating against the ground behind them, abandoning any attempt at stealth. It's so much closer. The sound of its footsteps crescendo as it rushes forward, closing the gap between them. Luca pulls Brooklyn to the left, dodging a low-lying branch and then the knotted root system of a nearby tree. He pants as he stomps forward, determined to get away, determined to keep his promise to a scared Brooklyn.

A growl breaks the air inches from Luca's neck, a tigerlike rasp lacing the roar. With the force of a linebacker, something solid slams into Luca's back. He defies gravity as his body soars forward. His arm slips from under Brooklyn's shoulder. He grapples for her arm, but his fingers slip over her skin uselessly.

Pain explodes in his face as his cheek and ear collide with an unforgiving slab of bark and his body is launched into a half spin before thudding against the forest floor. Momentum sends him skidding across the dirt and grass until his back slaps against the base of a tree trunk.

"Ugh..." Luca groans, body prostrate in the dirt. Every inch of muscle lining his flesh aches, and his face is on fire. He reaches to comfort the burning building in his cheek but wrenches back as the pain shoots through his face. His eyes drop to his hand, finding his fingers coated in blood, *his* blood.

A howl breaks out behind him. Needing little more motivation, Luca digs his fingers into the dirt and twists his body about, feeling a flurry of protests from every tendon. He screams, as if the mere vocalization of the pain could somehow dampen the sensation. His eyes narrowed, Luca sweeps a grouping of thick bushes. It's gone. The woods are empty, like it was all in his imagination.

Brooklyn! Where is she?

"Brooklyn!" he yells, raising his head a few inches from the ground. "Brooklyn! Gabe!"

"I'm over here!" she manages between heavy breaths.

Squinting, he follows her voice under the shadowed woods. He finds her less than a car length away, sprawled on the ground like him. Her body shakes, and salty tears drop from her eyes, wetting the ground beneath. She's staring into the woods, her eyes terrified. Luca follows her gaze, but he doesn't see anything.

Oh no! It must still be here.

Pulling himself around and grasping the closest tree, he gets to his feet, letting his body slump against its bark. He twists around, moving his face close to the trunk, careful not to let his injured cheek touch the coarse bark. He peeks around the tree inch by inch, bringing his vision closer to what lies behind, to what has Brooklyn struck with fear.

It's deathly silent again except for the beating of Luca's heart, the gentle breeze slipping through the trees and the gravelly breaths of some hidden thing in the night. He leans farther, but he's neither ready to see what lurks behind nor willing to hold himself back. He stops for a moment, clamping his eyes shut and fights the urge to turn and run. He shifts his jaw and swallows back the fear building in his throat. Shaking, he inches forward.

Snap!

Luca reels back as something bounds out of the dark. Under the cover of night, it's nothing more than a thick shadow sweeping through the dark. It's at least six feet standing upright, but he gleans little more as it clears the ten feet separating him from Brooklyn in the time it takes Luca to drag in another breath. Luca swings his eyes to Brooklyn as a massive hand wraps its thick fingers around her shoulder. His mouth falls open as thick claws burst through Brooklyn's back with a sickening squishing sound.

She screams in agony as the hand lifts her off the ground like a child's plaything and sprints into the woods.

"Brook!" Luca screams. Ignoring the lightning shooting through his nerves, he takes off after her and the creature. His mind races.

What the hell was that? Where'd it come from?

He stretches his legs, running as fast as the pain will allow. He pushes through the woods, ducking under a bough of low hanging branches and weaving through the trees. The wind slaps at his bruised and bloodied cheek. Brooklyn's screams echo back to him, their intense shrill growing quieter by the second. He hammers forward, unwilling to lose her.

Minutes pass, but Luca doesn't stop. Adrenaline douses the searing pain in his cheek and battered body. Suddenly, he realizes that he can't hear Brooklyn anymore.

They couldn't have gone that far.

Luca skids to a stop and closes his eyes, letting his hand grasp the tree next to him. He drags in harsh gulps of air. The wind whirls loudly through the trees. He listens, but only the whistle of the wind answers.

"What the hell am I doing?" he asks the trees. "I should just go to the hospital. Yeah, go back to the hospital and meet up with the others."

Stop it, Luca, he chides himself, trying to muster the courage to push back against the instinct to turn around and run, to forget about Brooklyn and save his own hide. Then, in the distance, he catches a flicker of light bouncing in the forest. He drags in another long breath, a pang in his gut cutting it short, and pushes away from the tree.

19: Cooper Bay

The wind is picking up. It howls through the trees, taking me back to the woods where Riley went missing. The movement of limb and leaf flashes in my mind and just as quickly vanishes, drenching the forest before me in the black of night. Then the vision comes again, this time veiled in crimson, and the branches part as if something is pulling at them with invisible strings. I try to blink it all away, but instead of disappearing, the image transforms from the grotesque and distorted form of the man we found in the dorm to Riley's body in the same state. Even with my eyes open I can't rid the images from my mind. Riley's gutted chest, entrails heaping over his waist and trailing over dead leaves and withering grass, the blood streaking between a severed thigh and leg.

I close my eyes, creasing my brow. I just want the images to go away. For a moment they subside, but I still can't help but wonder if I could have done something. Should I have warned him? Should I have run back to the group, flagged them down and told them all to go back?

No. I didn't know. How could I have known? I mean, what the hell *is* going on? I don't even know if the same culprit is responsible for both Riley's disappearance and the body we found, but it's hard not to connect the two. My mind is determined to put them together. If nothing else I'm now certain that Riley didn't just wander off, and Nick doesn't think I'm crazy anymore.

Our flashlights swing in wide semicircles, sweeping every inch of the woods around us. The thin, towering trunks, the mess of vines, the untouched wild grass and the darkness make me feel small. I swallow back a gulp of saliva.

No one says it, but we're afraid — no, we're terrified. The severed limb and filleted flesh digs its way into my mind just as much as I'm certain it does Nick's and Ava's. I can't be the only one it's getting to. The confirmation that someone or something is on the island pushes us to question every movement and every crack of a twig or curious whistle in the wind. I crane my neck to the side and scan the never-ending tree line. I find nothing out of the ordinary, but the veil of night casts a heavy melancholy over my chest, and the island's pervasive vines suffocate the life out of everything I lay my eyes on. Brashly, my mind conjures an insane image of the vines reaching from the next tree. They loop around my neck and constrict, cutting off my air until I'm nothing more than a heap of skin and bones.

Ava tightens her grip around my hand. A sliver of courage pumps up my arm and wipes the images from my brain, at least for the moment. I thank her silently with a dim smile. She hasn't let go of my hand since she entrusted me with her tears back at the dormitory.

"You okay?" I ask. I feel two-faced for asking, even a little selfish. I'm in no position to cheer anyone up, not with the heaviness in my chest, a guilt that I can't seem to reason away.

"Yeah, I just keep seeing that body." Her voice is small, almost a whisper. "Who was he?"

It's a relief to know that I'm not the only one whose mind

is ravaged by the brief encounter. I know her question is more of a statement, but I feel like I need to answer.

"I don't know, but once we get off this island we'll send the police," I assure her. I'm no coroner, but from the brief look I got it didn't seem like the man had been dead long. The blood wasn't fresh, but I don't remember any telltale signs of decay aside from that fucking stench.

The thought sends a chill down my spine, a reminder that we're dealing with something dangerous and violent. The realization that I have no clue who or what it is hits me hard, but I disguise the fear in my voice.

"They'll be able to figure out who he is and what happened."

She bobs her head but doesn't say anything. Her eyes are strong, but I can see the anxiety and unease behind their crystal blue sheen before she looks away. I squeeze her hand this time, hoping it does the same for her as hers did for me.

Ahead, Nick fumbles with the map and makes a slight correction to our heading. I duck around a low-hanging branch and lift it out of the way for Ava.

My body seizes up when a scream shatters the darkness. It was human. I snap my head around, my eyes searching for its source, but it's far off, obscured by hundreds of skinny trees and the night.

"Did you hear that?" Nick asks, aimlessly holding a hand out in my direction, his gaze searching the trees.

"Yeah," I gulp. "Who was that?"

"I don't know —"

"It was Luca's group." Ava points her free hand frantically at the empty woods. "It came from the east, that's where Luca and his group were headed."

"It sounded like a girl... Brooklyn," I say, my words slowing as her name trails off my lips.

Then it comes again. It's definitely female. It must be her. I step forward but stop short of a full gait.

"We... We...need to help them," Ava stutters. "She sounds like she's in trouble. We have to help!"

I nod and exchange a worried glance with my brother. He nods, accompanied with a quick exhale. I look back to Ava. "Let's go."

She lets go of my hand and we bound forward. In seconds I'm in a full sprint, head leaned forward, arms pumping, winding through the woods, whipping past trees, branches, bushes and rocks. A howl rises above the wind. At first it sounds like a heavy breeze catching in the trees, but it doesn't take long for it to build into a guttural roar, tinged with a high-pitched cackle. The hairs on my neck stand erect and my breathing becomes erratic. I force the air from my lungs and make myself focus on breathing as I propel myself forward, my flashlight beam bouncing up and down, jerking from the ground to the lower branches. In the corner, off to my right, I keep Ava in view. When she falls back, so do I, and when she gains speed, I push harder. Nick never was the runner in the family, but I know he can keep up, so I don't worry about him.

Twigs snap and break as I race past them, trying but failing to miss them as they scratch against my arms and face. I focus on the unsteady beam lighting my path, but it's mostly a blur. I can't keep it steady at this speed as my body jerks with each step. I can make out the trunks and most of the under-brush, but it's thick. Jerking to the right to avoid a small bush my eyes missed, my foot catches on something solid and I tumble forward. I throw my hand out, gripping a pencil of a tree and let the weight of my body tug at its roots. It holds, and I get my bearings. I take off again. It only takes a few extended strides to catch back up with the others, but it helps that they saw me fall and slowed their pace.

Brooklyn screeches again, followed by the wail of something far worse. The screams continue, merging into one disgusting cacophony of fear and dread. It's moving southward, so I angle to my right and dig in my heels, at the same time wondering why the hell I'm running toward this. Another scream punctuates the darkness, but this time it keeps coming, slicing through the night like the howls of some ghost eternally tormented by the flames of Hell. I steel myself as we barge through the forest, trying to focus on the screams and at the same time, dehumanize them as just another noise so I can deal with the fact that I'm running toward them.

Abruptly, the wails cut out. For a few yards we keep running, but now unable to track Brooklyn, I slow to a jog and then stop, resting my hand on a nearby tree. A yard or two ahead Ava stops, and then Nick a second later to my left.

"Do you hear anything?" I ask, drawing in a deep breath and squinting, trying to see past the thick veil that covers everything more than twenty to thirty yards out.

The grumbling howl rises again, then it's gone.

"This way!" Ava's running again before she finishes the sentence.

I stumble forward and match her stride as I come up beside her. Careful to stay with her, I work on keeping my flashlight steady and preventing my feet from getting snagged by another root or thicket. We run for at least a minute, maybe two, without a noise to guide us before we slow to a trot again, and then stop altogether. I listen for another growl or scream, even though I don't want to hear it. Without the noises it's impossible to know where she is.

Sweeping my light from side to side, I scan the immediate forest floor. My beam catches a crop of thick-leaved bushes and some low hanging tree branches off to my left. I step forward, lifting one of the branches over my head and holding it for Ava to step under.

"I think it was here. I mean this was the direction it came from at first, at least. I think..." Ava's eyes search the forest, looking for something, anything to guide her. "Maybe we can find something like a path that'll lead us to them."

I nod, then look to Nick. He cocks his head to the side and nods, unconvinced but willing to at least give it a try. I feel the same, so I shuffle past the bushes and scan the immediate underbrush and the ground, but I make certain to keep an eye on Ava. I find that my every thought is now consumed with worry for her, and Nick, but I know he can handle himself. I'm sure she can, too, she's a strong girl, but I can't help it.

My foot catches on something soft and I career forward. My face barely misses its fateful collision with a surface root when I throw my hands out at the last second, but the wind gushes from my lungs as my chest slaps the ground anyway. The dirt puffs away in a tiny dustbowl, and I suck in a helping as I try to drag the air back into my lungs. My body is racked by a series of coughs and dull throbs.

"Dammit!" I grunt, pushing myself up and back to my feet. I search for my flashlight, finding it only a few feet from where I landed, and go to pick it up. As I bend over to retrieve the Maglite, my eyes catch something red on my ankle. My foot doesn't hurt, but I clasp my hand around the flashlight and angle the beam onto my leg. There's a generous swath of red painted up my ankle and lower leg. I crinkle my brow and lean down to examine it better. I squint, not seeing a cut that could produce such blood flow; hell, I don't even see *one* cut. I stand back upright and turn around, shining the light where I fell.

My mouth falls limp and I jerk back, barely holding in a yelp.

"Oh my God!" I clamp my hand to my nose and mouth. There isn't a stench yet. It's too fresh, just having stepped through the doors of death, to produce the same acrid odor the body in the dorm had.

"What is it?" Nick swoops around.

"Uh... It's..." I stumble on my words. I know what it is, but who I'm not positive yet, or at least I refuse to admit what I already know as my eyes move to each severed piece of human flesh. First a leg that looks as though something ripped the limb away by sheer force, separating it from the knee down, the foot crushed awkwardly into the ground under an immense weight. Blood pools around the shredded knee where the bone protrudes an inch from the stump. Then a hand, wrenched from its home and dropped haphazardly on the ground under a thicket. Then her. Brooklyn. What's left of her body lays crumpled on the forest floor, neck craned gracelessly against the base of a tree trunk.

Before I can think to stop Ava from turning, I hear her scream. The piercing wail knocks me from my petrified state. Without thinking twice, I twist around and wrap my arms around Ava's shoulders, spinning her around to wrench her eyes from Brooklyn's corpse, my eyes still glued to it.

"Don't look, Ava, just don't look," I tell her. I have to

loosen my grip when I realize I'm holding her too tight.

"Why?" she bawls, burrowing her face into my shoulder.

I don't register Ava's words at first. My eyes are stuck on Brooklyn; though I want nothing more than to look away, I can't. Her mouth is slack, hanging open like the other body, except it's broken, unhinged. The flesh of her jaw under the left ear is torn apart, the sinew exposed and ripped, allowing the skin of her cheek to dangle eerily low, and the blood to trickle down her neck into the massive gorge where her stomach and chest used to be.

"Oh fuck!" Nick steps back, leaning over, hands resting on his knees. "Fuck!"

I refuse to look lower, instead focusing on her eyes. I remember them being such a soft brown when I met her back in the city, but now their softness is gone. In their place is an empty brown. I force my eyes away, finding the dull gray of a random tree, and placing my hand on the back of Ava's head. I lean into her, letting her closeness comfort me, only hoping I'm doing the same for her.

"I... I don't know..." I stumble over my own words. I can tell Nick is taking this hard. He knew Brooklyn more than I did, he worked with her in the past. They were friends.

"Oh my God." Nick drops to his knees, his voice becoming little more than a whisper as he leans closer to the girl's body. He slides his hands down her flaccid face, his fingers trailing through the blood. He closes her eyes as tears find their way out of his. "I'm so sorry, Brooklyn."

"I'm sorry, Nick," I tell him, not really sure what to say. My body is still shivering, or maybe it's Ava. I don't know.

In no hurry, Ava raises her head and looks me in the eyes. I feel like she's looking for an answer, a meaning from what lies a few feet behind her. I don't smile, I can't, and it seems as though it would be wrong to even try. She takes in a deep breath and releases her grip, but she doesn't turn around.

"What the hell could do this?" I ask. It's evident that whatever tore the other body to shreds had also done this, though I refuse to examine further. "I don't think people are strong enough to just...to do this."

It had to be an animal, something big and agile, something ravenous. But even that doesn't make sense. Animals kill to feed, not for sport or game, and certainly not like this. Neither the body in the dorm nor Brooklyn show signs of feeding. Every piece is accounted for, every organ, even if they aren't where they belong. In that respect, I can't help but feel it's the work of a man or woman. My thoughts go in circles, trying to make sense of it, but failing at every turn.

"I agree." Nick's voice shakes as he waddles back and stands erect. He turns, putting his back to Brooklyn, and faces me. "I don't know what type of animal could do *this*, but... Yeah. I don't think it's human. I'm sorry for doubting you, Coop."

I let my head bob lightly, no longer caring if anyone doubts me. At the edge of my vision, I catch the splatters of blood on the forest floor, up the trunk of a nearby tree and covering the bushes. I make myself turn away. Nick steps to my side and stares into the empty forest. Except it's not empty. At the edge of my vision I see a flicker, a bright twitch of light. My first instinct is to douse my beam, but Nick speaks up.

"Is that..." He starts to walk forward, but he doesn't have to go far before a human silhouette comes into view behind the blinding beam.

"Nick!" It's Luca. He screams, his voice as terrified as I feel. "Brooklyn. They took Brooklyn."

Immediately, my gut turns. He doesn't know. My minds races, trying to figure out the best course of action. Tell him, show him, redirect him. I don't know what to do.

"Luca…" Nick starts before I can make up my mind. It's best if it comes from my brother anyway. "She's… She's gone."

"What?" Coming to a stop before Nick, Luca's face goes stoic, his mind preparing for what he knows but refuses to understand. "What do you mean, Nick? It has her. It took off with her."

At first Nick doesn't respond, instead he looks down at the ground, his lips parting then closing, but the words don't come out. He raises his eyes to meet Luca's expectant but scared gaze. "She's dead."

"What? Where? Where is she?" Luca pushes past Nick, shoving him to the side. He only gets a few feet before coming to an abrupt halt. I refuse to turn, I don't need to see it again, it's already ingrained in my mind. His voice croaks next to me, "No…no. No!"

My heart sinks another level under the man's grief as he drops to his knees. Nick goes to him and puts a hand on his shoulder but looks off into the forest. We stand in silence for what feels like an eternity while Luca sobs, working through his emotions.

"I saw them." His voice is reticent but confident. Luca doesn't move from the reverence of his kneed position, but his eyes are no longer on Brooklyn. They search the ground, the blood, for some answer to the inanity of what lies just out of his vision.

"What?" Nick asks. "Did you say you saw them?"

"Yeah," Luca whispers again, and then slowly rises to his feet and puts his back to the corpse. He refuses to look at us directly, instead looking past us, his eyes angled toward the ground. "I saw it...them. There are at least two, I think. They move so quick. They're not too big, but they're damned strong."

"Two of them?" I gasp, stopping myself from falling back a step. The thought of two beasts, if that's what they are, roaming freely in this forest, stalking our every move, is almost unbearable.

"Yeah, they hunted us down. One scared us real good, and then the other came in and...and...it took her." I can feel in my chest how hard it is for Luca to utter the words with her body lying feet behind him. He looks up at the sky. "I watched. It never slowed down. It just ran at her. It...It grabbed her up by the shoulder... I saw its claws *dig* into her... Then they were gone. I ran after them. I *tried* to follow, but the one that had her, but it was too fast."

Nick looks up at me, his eyes apologetic. He doesn't have to say what's going through his mind. I know what he's thinking again. I was right. There *is* something inhuman in these woods, some animal that shouldn't be here, or at least that we didn't expect.

"What was it? Did you get a good look at it?" I'm surprised to hear Ava's voice. She sounds calmer than I expected. Maybe it's confirmation of what's happening or the realization that our hunter isn't human. I'm not sure, but whatever it is seems to have restored something inside her.

"Not a *good* look..." Luca stops to think, his voice finally rising above a whisper and his words coming more fluidly. "It wasn't anything I've ever seen before. It stood upright, at least mostly. It was maybe six feet tall."

He shakes his head, trying to visualize it.

"Yeah, about six feet. Uh… It had huge claws, I mean massive. I couldn't make out much else. It was too dark, and it moved too quickly."

"Was it hairy?" Ava questioned. "Maybe it was a bear standing on its hind legs."

Taking a moment to consider the possibility and probably recreate the scene in his head, Luca finds Ava. "No. It wasn't a bear. I don't know for sure, but I don't think it was hairy like that. I'm not sure really, but I don't think so."

The more Luca talks about the beast, the more my mind races with images of deranged creatures. Claws, incisors and gleaming red eyes flash through my mind, fantasies gone wild. I no longer feel comfortable standing here in the open forest, unable to see farther than a stone's throw.

"Maybe we should get to cover. The hospital," I suggest, gulping but trying not to show my fear.

"Yeah," Nick agrees. "I think Coop's right. We need to get out of the woods."

20: Helen Harrison

"Not in here." Jaylen's voice carries through the wooden doorframe.

Exiting the tiny side room, he props his shoulders against a network of cool pipes, long ago abandoned by the hiss of scalding steam. The metal is riddled with rust and eaten through in places.

"Anything back there?" he asks as Helen and Grady come down the hall. Grady ducks under a broken pipe and quickens his step to catch up with his slender colleague.

"No, it's all empty." Helen waves, a sigh breaking the thin line between her lips.

"There is a lot of junk though," Grady says. "Magazines, like really old ones, a bunch of empty cups…"

He lets his voice fade as the looks from Helen and Jaylen provide anything but approval. Helen shakes her head and rolls her eyes.

"What about you?" She juts her chin forward, aiming past Jaylen.

"Nah, it's just more of the same," Jaylen tells them, grunting in dissatisfaction. "There's still a number of rooms over there though."

He points around the corner to a hall that breaks off the main corridor.

"Well, let's get to it. The sooner we find Riley, the sooner we'll get back to filming…" she complains, then mutters under her breath, "*if* we get back to filming."

Helen takes the lead, more ready to be done with the search than determined to find Riley. Jaylen and Grady follow a step behind, flashlight beams bouncing gently across gruffly laid cement and poorly aged wood-framed walls. They step into the hallway, leaving the lofty open space of the boiler house's main floor. The ceiling here lacks the roadwork of interconnected conduits, instead plastered with falling ceiling tiles, riddled in black and weighed down by years of rain and mold. Windowpanes used to provide easy viewing into each office from the hallway. Now, where the glass still hangs intact, it's dingy, fogged over with grime, dust and more mold.

The producer, with a smug look on her face, approaches the first door and pushes it open with the tips of her fingers. It looks like an office, probably a plant manager or something. An old metal-framed desk sits in the corner. Its wood surface is warped and dirty. A swivel chair sits behind it looking feeble, like it would probably fall apart under a single finger. A set of open filing cabinets sit along the wall to the desk's right. But there's no Riley.

Turning back into the hallway, Helen finds Jaylen and Grady moving past, reaching for other doors. A shiver passes through her chest as Grady disappears inside one of the rooms. Helen purses her lips and stills herself before sweeping her flashlight down the hall. She moves past the offices claimed by Grady and Jaylen, evading a pile of fallen ceiling tiles scattered along the floor.

"Find anything?" She stops at the next door and calls back to the others.

"I don't got shit in here." It's Jaylen, his voice claiming an end to his patience.

"Nothing here either," Grady's voice echoes into the hallway.

Helen raises an eyebrow. *No surprise.*

Easing the frail door open, Helen bathes the next office in light. It's much of the same: an old desk in utter disrepair, a swivel chair, more file cabinets, and layers of mildew and fungi coating every surface. Helen tries to slow her breathing, hoping to inhale fewer mold particles. Unlike the main floor, the previous residents of these offices look to at least have cleared out their trash, even if they did leave the furniture.

Helen slides her hand into her back pocket and retrieves her phone.

Dammit. How the hell do I not have a signal?

The time to call in to the other groups is well overdue, but without a signal it's impossible. Jaylen's and Grady's phones hadn't provided any better hope earlier. She pockets the phone, sighing, and turns back to the hallway.

As her eyes land on the black opening of another room, a gray aura streaks by the door. Helen squints, wanting to rush forward, but something in the back of her brain tells her to be careful.

Jaylen?

She tilts her head and shuffles forward, taking care to step lightly. She spills her white beam across the floor, pushing back the dark. It seeps past the rotting doorframe, bending around the corners and lighting up the first few feet of the room. As the light cascades into the room, Helen steps next to the door and slowly cranes her neck around the corner. "Jaylen?"

"Yeah?" Jaylen calls, his voice spewing from an office down the hall before he exits the room.

Helen retreats into the hallway and peers through the dark. She finds Jaylen and her stomach tightens. He's too far away, but she asks anyway, pointing into the office in front of her. "Did you just go running by?"

"No, I just came from over there." He waves his hand back, indicating the same room Helen had watched him exit.

"Why'd you not think it was me?" Grady asks.

"Man, she said *run*." Jaylen doesn't crack a smile as he shakes his head and faces Helen. "Did you see something? Maybe it was Riley."

Grady grins knowingly.

"Yeah… I think, at least." She crinkles her brow, facing the last few offices set along the opposite side of the hall. "Or if Cooper's to be believed…someone else."

Helen takes a step toward the door again, placing each foot carefully.

"You don't really think there's someone else on the island, do you?" Jaylen questions, stepping between Helen and the office. "Taking people and shit like that?"

"No." Her response is quick, her opinion on the matter solid. Riley simply hit his head and ran off. He's as confused about all of this as they are, sitting somewhere in the dark, or moving from place to place, making it harder for them to find him.

"I've got it." Feeling ridiculous, Helen quickens her pace and strides up to the door confidently. Jaylen departs, taking an office behind the opposite wall. She stops outside the old door and leans around the corner again before coaxing the door the remaining few inches. An eerie heaviness pervades her chest, but she fights the sensation back. She draws in a deep breath and slips her foot across the threshold. An ear-piercing clash bangs against the floor down the hall. She jerks back, almost colliding with Jaylen. Their gazes fix down the dark hall, flashlight beams illuminating the remaining eight yards of stuffy corridor.

"Did y'all hear that?" Grady joins them, dragging his feet along the concrete floor as he stumbles out into the hallway.

Not bothering to answer, Helen forces her legs to move, creeping barely a full stride. Beyond the reach of their lights, a silhouette materializes against the far end of the hall. Helen takes another step forward but can't bring herself to raise her flashlight.

Riley?

She starts to form the name on her lips when the shape shuffles away from the glow and disappears into the last office. Helen stops and grips her flashlight tightly. The beam bounces across the floor and up the wall, bathing it in dull yellow. She flicks her eyes to the side to find Jaylen, silently asking what she should do. He raises his shoulders, and lets his mouth partially hang open. Helen releases a breath and takes another step forward.

It's probably just Riley. Stop bloody fretting.

Easing toward the door, Helen projects her voice down the hall. "Riley? That *you* in there? It's Helen."

Quickening her pace, she reaches for the door as a metallic crack jolts her back a step. Helen clutches her hands into tight fists and plants her feet on the concrete. Silence reclaims the room and hallway.

They stand, frozen in place, within arm's reach of the door. No one moves. Helen draws in a gulp of air, trying to summon the courage to reach for the doorknob. Sensing her fear, Jaylen steps forward and extends his arms, fingers outstretched, shaking. His fingertips brush the knob.

Without thinking, Grady steps back. Jaylen closes his eyes for a brief second and drags in another breath. Before Helen can command him to, Jaylen grasps the knob and thrusts the door in.

The beam of his flashlight floods into the diminutive office, but the knowledge of something lurking inside expands it into a bottomless abyss, every nook and cranny a potential hiding place. Jaylen sweeps his beam across the right half of the room. The beam trembles in his grasp, dancing along a set of empty bookshelves, a scattering of dust-laden printer paper sitting on the floor and a metal swivel chair just like the others.

Helen angles around the door and steps by Jaylen. She swings her light against the opposite corner, illuminating a wall of glass and its failing wooden framing. Her beam reflects off the sheer panes, exposing an empty wall stained in wet brown motes of dust. On the other side of the space, Jaylen's beam rolls over the chair and finds the beginnings of a wooden desk. He keeps moving the light, trailing over the dirty surface of the old bureau. Dust clings to its surface.

The beam flows against a solid surface towering beyond the desk. It glints off a long black curve. Jaylen frowns. The dingy bone-white form sways as if wafting in a gentle breeze. Jaylen's shoes scrape across the concrete. He leans his head closer to his right shoulder and narrows his eyes.

It moves. Jaylen freezes, barring his legs from dragging him back into the hallway and taking off. In a slow, deliberate motion the curve lifts, revealing another, and another. A spark of recognition ignites in Jaylen's breast as a handful of six-inch claws pass under his quivering beam. They clack against each other, rotating under the shadows. Jaylen grits his teeth and the light begins to quake in his hand.

He wants to raise the beam, to expose whatever is attached to the hand floating in his circle of light, but Jaylen can't bring himself to do it. Instead, he forces his free arm to move. He reaches for Helen, feeling aimlessly to his left for the woman, unwilling to utter a syllable as the claws sway. Out of the silence, a slow, steady grumble sounds in his ears.

How did I not hear that before? he thinks, forgetting about the tension that had gripped him in the hall.

His finger finds Helen. He paws at her back, pushing her, telling her to retreat, but she doesn't seem to understand. He grips her shirt and pulls her.

"Wha…" Her words are sliced through by a feral roar.

Jaylen's eyes race forward as the claws disappear into the night. He steps back without hesitation, the trance broken. He tightens his grip on Helen's shirt, reeling her around the corner. As she crosses back into the hall, her beam flickers across a tall figure looming behind the desk. Her eyes lock with its empty black orbs for a brief second.

"What the *fuck*?" she blurts as it pounces over the desk, target in sight.

Another hand grips her shoulder and yanks her again.

"Let's go!" Jaylen commands, pulling her away. Grady is already on the move, two strides ahead, his beam jumping from floor to ceiling. Helen blinks, trying to get her bearings.

Helen matches Jaylen's stride and bolts down the hallway. They fly past the next office as *it* skids into the hallway behind them, claws screeching and digging into the concrete.

Helen pushes her legs harder, lengthening her stride. She scrapes against the wall, but rebounds quickly, refusing to loosen her death grip on the flashlight.

Behind them, it claws at the ground. The scratching morphs into deep thuds on the concrete, but Helen refuses to look back. A thunderous growl howls past her as she breaks past the threshold to the main work floor.

Jaylen breaks off to the left after Grady and speeds off. On his heels, Helen is breathing hard, her arms swinging in time with her legs.

What the fuck was that? she screams inside.

She cuts off between a set of large pipes and an old concrete wall, daring a glance back as she skids around the corner. It's only a shadow about ten yards back, but it's still there, long legs hammering into the concrete, breaths coming in grueling drags. The sound of its feet slows but fails to relent.

Staying on Jaylen's ass, Helen makes the next left. Ahead, a staircase rises to the right. A glint of familiarity shines behind her eyes. She remembers passing them earlier with Grady. They lead to an observation loft overlooking the boiler house floor. For a moment she considers skidding to a stop and scaling the stairs two by two, but she gives up on the thought as the others sprint past. She nods to herself, giving Grady credit for remembering the poor state of the crumbling stairs and not repeating their ascent at a full sprint.

She hangs another left, winding through a maze of halls and offices. The sound of something heavy thudding against the concrete continues to echo past them. Helen swings her eyes around the hall, trying to remember where she is, cursing her inattention to detail when she had canvassed this side of the building. Other than a few unique pieces of debris, everything feels new and foreboding in the jumpy light of her beam.

She turns to check their tail, realizing the sound of its labored breath and footfalls no longer reaches her ears. Nothing. She slows, and Jaylen calls to Grady, urging him to slow down.

"It's gone." Helen allows her pace to drop to a jog, then a walk before coming to a stop by a large circular drum. Smaller pipes protrude from the drum's shell, twisting at hard right angles through rusty metallic joints. Some disappear above the ceiling, others extend the length of the hallway, evaporating into the shadows at the edge of Helen's vision. She stares into the black, waiting for it to show itself.

"Are you sure?" Jaylen questions. He raises his flashlight and paints the hall in dim white and yellow. At the end of the hall, the corridor breaks off to the left.

Helen stands frozen, eyes locked on the turn, flashlight hanging limp in her hands, coating the ground at her feet in a firm circular glow. She doesn't speak, she just waits.

"Helen?" Jaylen whispers, raising his voice when she doesn't answer. "Helen?!"

Her shoulder's shudder, and she blinks away the shock. "Yeah, what?"

"You okay there?" he asks as Grady comes up, bobbing his head to the left to see around them.

"Uh... Yeah, I'm good," she tells him. Its dark eyes are etched in the forefront of her mind. She looks around the dark space. The pipes trailing the wall and ceiling feel like they're closing in on her. Helen throws her eyes to the ground and drags in a deep breath.

Calm the hell down, Helen.

"Let's get out of here. The others will be at the hospital soon anyway," she sighs.

She pulls her gaze from the floor and looks down the hallway, where shadows engulf the pipes and floor, and then twists to look the other direction. She peers past Jaylen and Grady, her light flashing over their bodies and spilling down the other end of the corridor. Everything looks the same.

Where are we?

Helen takes a tentative step toward Jaylen but comes to a stop. She cranes her neck back around, second-guessing herself. In her mind, the feline-like grumble haunts her brain. She clenches her fists, trying to decide what to do. She eyes Grady at the edge of her vision, his chubby silhouette standing a few yards down the hall.

"Grady, do you remember how to get out from here?" she asks.

Grady nods. "Yeah, I think so."

"Lead the way," she instructs, throwing her free hand up, palms out, welcoming him to lead.

He lowers his face for a moment, his eyes racing back and forth, going over a mental map. Helen can't help but admire the quality. She mouths a silent apology for doubting the kid as he turns and starts down the hallway. Helen lingers a second before catching up, one question front and center in her mind.

Where did it go?

Four minutes later, they stop under the precipice of the building's main work floor. An assortment of pipes spiderwebbed across the walls and ceiling. Thick metal containers, empty rust-eaten drums, and fractured wood beams lie scattered over the floor. But the room's most expansive occupant isn't anything physical—it's the open space standing between them and the exit.

Helen reaches for Grady, gripping his shoulder firmly before he can step out into the open.

"Wait," she whispers.

Grady stumbles back and he cranes his neck around. "What is it?"

"What if it's still out there?" Her eyes shift and the Maglite shivers in her hand. "We don't know if it left."

"Would you rather stay in here?" Jaylen asks. There isn't a hint of sarcasm in his voice. He doesn't know either, and she can see in his dark brown eyes that he's scared too.

She thinks about the question for a moment. *Are we better here or out there?* She wrestles with it. Helen leans her head back and forth, scanning the dark opening, unwilling to swing her flashlight over the open floor and merit any unwanted attention. She squints, finding more debris and pipes winding over the floor and ceiling.

"No." Helen shakes her head and takes in a deep breath. "No, let's get out of here."

With only a nod, Jaylen takes the lead, leaning his body around the corner. He scans the floor with his naked eye, relying on the faint light filtering in through a handful of broken glass windows. He squints, guiding his eyes over a massive steel drum. It's draped in shades of gray. He moves past a set of containers at the far end of the room and then he finds it. The door, its perimeter marked by a thin band of faint gray light in the form of a rectangle against a wall of black.

"Okay, you two ready?" He doesn't give them time to answer before he speaks again. "I say we sprint for it, then run for the hospital. It's not too far, right?"

"I don't think so." Helen slides the pack from her shoulders and slowly unzips it. She digs past some clothes and finds the wrinkled paper map. She unfolds it slowly, careful not to make too much noise. She shines the light on the crinkled surface. The beam splashes against the paper and reflects, bathing their faces in a cool white light. They lean over the map.

Helen traces her pointer finger along the top edge of the island, her finger landing on the hospital. It's the easiest landmark to find on the map on account of its large size. She eyes the paper, trying to find their location, but nothing else stands out. She drags her finger to the left and finds the map's key. Helen scans the list, stopping at the line reading "6 BOILER HOUSE".

"All right, so we're in the boiler house, which is…" Helen draws her eyes along the map, past a simple long rectangle with a "22" printed within its walls, then number eight, and finally six, the boiler house, "…here."

She cocks her head, examining the building and her immediate surroundings, trying to orient herself. She glances at the key again, looking for number eight and five, the two buildings nearest the boiler house. Her eyes land on "8 COAL HOUSE" and quickly move up the list to find the listing for the small building along the western face of the boiler house. She frowns at the listing. *5 MORGUE.*

"Grady, do you know what side of the building we're on?" she asks, nodding toward the map. "I don't have any sense of direction in here."

Actually, I don't have any sense of direction on this island period.

Grady leans over the map, sliding his middle finger under

the coal house. The edges of Helen's lips rise at the use of his middle digit despite the pace of the blood shooting through her veins.

"Uh, from what I reckon, we're here, facing west." Grady taps the outline of the boiler house along the left edge and swipes his middle digit to the west, toward the morgue.

"Oh, just by the morgue," Jaylen laments. "Isn't that nice?"

"That's what it already feels like in here with…" Helen struggles for the right word. "With whatever it is."

Helen eyes the map again. The hospital is too far. The morgue just seems like a bad idea. Running out into the open woods feels better, but they would be left vulnerable. Her eyes shift past the rectangle box denoting the morgue, over a crease in the paper.

"What about the dock?" She lifts her eyes to meet Jaylen's, then Grady's, her finger resting on the paper. "We're here. Here's the morgue, and the dock is right behind it. That's not far from where we left the boats."

"Are you suggesting we leave without the others?" Grady pulls his head back indignantly. "You know that there is something here, something that might have taken Riley, and you want to just up and run without them?"

"We can send help." Her eyes plead with him.

"It'd be safer to get to the boats, but I don't think I can just leave them here, Helen," Jaylen explains, grimacing.

"I'm not talking about abandoning them," Helen tries again. She cranes her neck back in frustration. "I'm talking about getting off this damned island and alerting the authorities. They'll come and find them. We're not equipped for this. We don't know what we're dealing with and we're sure as hell not prepared to *deal* with it."

"I'm not going anywhere until we find the others." Grady lets his hand drop. The map crinkles and crackles as he flings it around. "Those are our friends, *your employees*. I'm not leaving them."

"Employees?" Helen steps back, the wrinkles forming across her brow barely visible in the dim light. "They're my friends, too, don't you dare try to insinuate otherwise."

"Really?" His Southern drawl becomes more pronounced as his voice fills with anger. "Then why are you so quick to ditch them?"

"I'm not trying to ditch them, you fucking hillbilly!" Helen bites back.

Grady's eyes widen, and he begins to speak, but Jaylen steps between them.

"All right, that's enough," he holds up his hands. "This isn't the time to be at each other's throats. I'm going for the others, either follow along or make a run for it. But I don't think you should go it on your own."

For a moment, Helen stares at the dark concrete floor, her lips pursed with frustration. Finally, she looks up and nods. She finds Grady, but she doesn't speak.

"Let's make for the woods and get to the hospital." Without waiting for the others to agree, Jaylen turns and faces the exit, focusing on the thin border of faint light etching out the door among the black wall. "Now!"

He takes off at a jog, then tilts forward into a full sprint, his flashlight beam sloshing over the floor. Helen and Grady take chase, careening around a plethora of fallen ceiling beams and scattered bits of concrete. Only ten more yards.

Something clangs behind Helen. She cranes her neck

around without slowing and sweeps her light about. Her eyes shoot open as the beam glints against black eyes and reflects over a pale humanoid face, minus the rows of fangs lining the creature's gray maw.

"Oh fuck! Run!" she screams as Jaylen's hands and then body slam against the exit door, sending it crashing around the corner. The faint glow of the moon sifts through the leafy canopy, spilling down the exterior wall and the ground. Helen turns and regains a few lost steps, thrusting past the exit.

"The other building! Not the woods!" she yells in quick bursts between breaths. "It's behind us!"

Jaylen veers off to the right without complaint, twisting on his heels. He slides to a halt at the entry to the morgue, looking back for the others. Helen and Grady speed across the small clearing and without hesitating, Jaylen swings the door in and they pile inside. The door slams behind him and he fumbles with the handle, trying to find the lock. He begins to panic as his fingers slip over the coarse, stained wooden door without finding his objective. He almost drops his flashlight but finally steadies it before lifting the beam to see the surface. He exhales, his eyes landing on the old deadbolt latch. He twists it, but it refuses to slide home.

"Come the *fuck* on!" Jaylen's voice pierces the room. He presses his shoulder against the door, compressing the old warped wood into its frame and tries again. Finally, it slides home. He jolts back when the door shudders, falling into Helen. He jerks around.

"It's just me!" Helen yells, gripping his shoulder to calm him. She steps back, her eyes locking on the door as the thing pounds against the thick wooden slab.

"What the fuck, man?!" Jaylen mutters, his attention back

on the door.

"Get down!" Helen orders in her quietest voice, motioning for the two men to keep a low profile.

Helen douses her light and lets the heavy darkness envelop the room. Only two thin windows line the east wall. They do little to illuminate the space. Gravelly breaths puff under the door, and the hinges strain under the creature's weight.

Helen clenches her fist and closes her eyes against the darkness, then opens them again, willing them to adjust. Abruptly the noise stops, and the door is still. Helen opens her eyes to the dark, finding the faint silhouette of the two windows and the slit of light creeping under the door. Beyond the wall, a careful, deliberate thud creeps under the door, followed by the *tink tink* of claws tapping against the concrete.

Maybe it'll go away.

A minute passes and the footsteps continue to sound off. They oscillate from one side of the door to the next like it's waiting for them to open up. Helen takes a step toward the door. She wants to turn her light back on, but she stifles the desire.

The door quakes without warning, expelling a high crack from its aging boards, but it holds against the weight. Its ragged, unnatural breaths, aggressive snarls fall like an anvil on Helen's ears. She throws her hands over her ears, wishing it would just go away.

Then everything goes silent for what feels like an eternity. Helen's heart thuds against her chest, but she refuses to move. Her eyes dart about the darkness. Finally, feet shuffle outside. They're close at first, but the sound begins to fade as it moves away. A howl rings out, but it's distant.

As the tension in her chest subsides, Helen allows herself

to move. She steps back blindly and jumps when her back thuds against something solid and tall. She squeezes her eyes closed for a second before she realizes that it's just the wall. Something feels off about it though. It's uneven.

She turns, daring to take her eyes off the entry, away from the last sliver of light in the room. Struggling to make out anything in the blackness, she takes a step back, narrowing her eyes. She angles her head as four thick metal squares, evenly spaced, form along the wall. Each is about two and half feet square, peppered in orange rust, painted black and gray in the dark. Her eyes widen when she puts two and two together. They're the old cold chambers to hold dead bodies.

"Dammit," she mutters.

"Well, we're in the morgue. Isn't that great," Grady comments, shrugging at their luck, but keeps his voice low. He raises a brow, trying to find the others in the dark. "Is it gone?"

"I don't know," Jaylen says, his voice even quieter than Grady's. "Did either of you get a good look at it?"

"Nah." Grady shuffles in the dark, examining the cold storage boxes. He traces a hand over the metal box and latch. "As soon as I saw the look on your face and you started to run, that's all I needed to know."

"You?" Helen can't see him, but she knows it's Jaylen speaking to her.

"Uh... No, not really." She considers lying. She doesn't want to think about it but decides against it. Its eyes and pale gray face rise in her mind. "I only saw its eyes, and a little of its face. But it was only a glance."

A long silence blankets the room before Helen speaks again.

"Let's stay here with the lights off for a little bit, just to make sure it's gone. Then we'll make for the hospital."

21: Gabe Meadows

Gabe's feet beat against the uneven soil, sending bits of dirt and scattered twigs into the air. Quick, shallow breaths wheeze between his lips. He ducks below a low branch and dodges another tree.

The animalistic howl races past him, sending another shiver up his back as he weaves between a patchwork of thick undergrowth and spindly trees. It sounds farther away now, more distant than only minutes ago, but he keeps running.

He throws up his arm, guarding his face from a low branch and almost fails to see the next tree, one of countless colorless gray trunks that seem to haunt his escape. Gabe angles to the left, and vaults over a small boulder, missing the trunk by inches. He doesn't lose a second as he pushes forward.

Unexpectedly, the forest shrinks away and a brisk wind blows the scent of saltwater under his nose. The coastline. He skids to a halt, scrabbling for purchase on the rocky shore. Past the loose mix of rock, sand and decomposing heaps of Styrofoam and plastic, the East River laps gently along the shore and around what must have once been a series of small white dikes, their purpose long forgotten. What's left is half crumbled, and large gaps let the river meander between them and the island.

Across the water, another island rises out of the river. A row of stoic buildings fenced in barbed wire line its coast illuminated by rows of high wattage spotlights.

"Help!" Gabe screams across the water. "Help!"

He stops and catches his breath. The moonlight glimmers atop the water and the city hums to the south. The stars are trying to peek from behind low-set clouds. Gabe squints, peering over the gently rolling water to get his bearings. To the north, a long man-made structure juts from the land across the river, a dock maybe.

The Bronx. That's the Bronx, so that's... He thinks, shifting his eyes rapidly to the east, across the river. *Rikers Island. The correctional facility.*

"Guys..." His lips fail to form the words as he twists at the waist, looking for Luca and Brooklyn. A timid scowl crawls over his face when his eyes only find the border of trees and an empty shore. "Guys?"

Gabe scans the beach and steps toward the forest, toward that ungodly howl. He stops.

Is it gone?

He waits for it, for the deep growl of whatever lurks in these woods, whatever it is that burst from the forest and made them its prey. All is silent, save the constant lapping of the water against the shore and the muted blur of cars, horns and sirens across the river at his back. He waits, standing like an ancient stone column, staring into the forest.

"Come on, guys," he whispers. "Come on. Don't leave me here like this."

He stands, waiting, begging them to rush from the trees. The forest seems to fade to black the farther Gabe's eyes try to reach. He waits for movement, for Luca or Brooklyn to come racing through the trees, to hurry onto the beach, but only the leaves ruffle in the gentle breeze. He stands for minutes, waiting. His body is shivering, eyes fixed to the woods.

"Dammit, guys," he curses. "Come on! Where the hell are you?"

Another minute passes and Gabe's eyes drop to his feet. Rocks line his gray tennis shoes where they sink into the loose sand, a sliver of water flowing around them. He snaps his feet up and trots to dry ground.

Something's wrong. They should have been right behind me.

Alone, Gabe turns and faces the water. He curls his lip under his chattering teeth. His mind wanders as he starts north along the coast with no real direction in mind.

It's all her fucking fault.

Unwilling to process his fear, Gabe focuses on the anger that had driven him into the clearing. It builds in his core, warming him and taking his mind off the now undeniable fact that something else, something big lurks in the woods. He kicks a small smooth stone and watches it hit the water. Tiny waves ripple against the mellow current, slivers of white shimmer along the precipice of each tiny crest as it settles back into a rolling black.

He closes his eyes and breathes, taking in each gulp long and slow. The wind surfs across the river and wraps its invisible tendrils around his calves and whips through his hair. Gabe stands still for a full minute before letting his eyelids slide open again.

"I have to find the others." Gabe turns to face the forest. He stares it down, meeting it blow for blow. He reaches around his side and pulls the pack from his back, retrieving his map. He unfolds it and moves his index finger across the home-printed paper.

His finger stops under "12 STAFF HOUSE" printed in petite, smooth-edged font under the map's small legend, and then he traces his fingertip from building to building until he finds number twelve. It's the last structure he remembers seeing before Riley went missing and they split off into groups, before everything went to hell. Gabe lifts his gaze to the forest and spins his body around in a slow three-sixty, taking in the sights. The forest. The beach. Rikers Island. The shore of the Bronx. Looking at the map again, he aligns its features with his surroundings, having only what he remembers Ava saying back in the cab for reference. He places a finger on the top right corner of the island, and nods to his audience of zero, hoping he isn't wrong.

"Now where's the hospital?" he asks, scanning the legend again. "4 TUBERCULOSIS HOSPITAL".

"Oh, that sounds just great."

He huffs and again traces his finger along the map, skipping over a deep crease in the paper before his finger lands on the largest building on the map. The shape of the structure from the vague aerial shot immediately conjures up images of the US Capitol Building, its two wings jutting east and west from a central core.

"How the hell am I going to do this without the others?" he asks. Gabe lets his eyes wander over the treetops, their leaves shuffling lightly in the wind, and down their thin gray trunks before looking past them where the dark engulfs everything. He bites his lip and sighs. Finally, a thought springs into his head and he rolls his eyes and smiles. "You stupid fuck, Gabe. *Google*."

Slipping his phone from his back pocket, he opens the device with a quick swipe of his thumb and launches the mapping application. He has no signal, but as Gabe discovered a year ago on a trip up the Appalachian Mountains on a backwoods road in North Carolina, GPS doesn't require a cellular data signal. The map zooms in on his location when the application loads, showing the same rugged shape of the island depicted on the map in his hands. He smiles victoriously and pockets the paper map.

He walks a few steps up the coast and then back, watching the map's movement to get his bearings.

"All right, now where am I in relation to the hospital?" he asks, staring down at the map. He slides a finger along the screen and then uses two fingers to zoom in. The shape of the hospital materializes atop the light gray of the island's outline.

West. He investigates the forest and all desire to breach its wooded border flees his chest. He gulps back the fear permeating his bones, his eyes locked on the numberless trees melting into the ebony woods.

Come on, it's just a forest. There's nothing unusual about that. Just overlook the scary monster. Yeah, Gabe, man the fuck up. Oh fuck, this sucks!

Gabe advances a foot and locks his shoes among the stones, facing down the abyss. "Okay. Just follow the map."

Biting his lip again, Gabe loosens his legs and takes a step toward the tree line.

"Fuck this shit," and he sprints forward.

22: Cooper Bay

"So Bigfoot basically?" Nick asks, sighing as he pushes another branch out of the way and holds it for Luca. His beam bounces over a copse and illuminates a dense coating of moss and vines.

"No, I mean... I don't know what it *was*, Nick." Taking the branch, Luca purses his lips, searching for the right words.

I take the branch next, holding it for Ava and then following behind. Under the thick natural canopy, Luca is trying to describe the thing that took Brooklyn, but he's struggling. Even after seeing something lurking in the woods earlier in the day, trying to see the human-like, bipedal creature that Luca describes pushes against my better judgment—and Nick's. Ava hasn't spoken so much as two sentences since we left what remained of Brooklyn to the island's flies and beetles. I think she's still fighting back the shock.

"It wasn't Bigfoot, man." Luca waves his hand in the air defensively. "I'm not a fucking idiot. I know what I saw, and it wasn't human, and it wasn't any animal I've ever seen before either. I'm not making this up, man. I'm terrified, not crazy."

I can sense Luca's sincerity, his fragility. The quiver in his voice. If I could see his eyes, I'm sure I would find a deep-seated fear.

"I know, man, I'm just trying to wrap my head around it."
It's Nick. I can barely hear his voice trickling between the trees, and I can only see his silhouette behind the light of his flashlight.

"I hate to ask, but—" I begin, but Nick cuts me off.

"Here we are." He holds back another branch and we each file by, spilling past the tree line.

I stop, a hint of awe seeping between the cracks of my apprehension. A massive brick structure rises four stories out of the forest, the very subject of my failed inquiry. The hospital. Compared to the city surrounding the island, it's small, but within the confines of the wildwood, its footprint feels massive. The trees appear to reel away from it, revealing the cool gray of the night sky around its flat rooftop, the stars blotted out by the far-reaching glow of the city. A scattering of bushes and vines spot the stone on the gray staircase leading to the entrance, and vines continue their conquest up the face of the building, finally disappearing over the roof's ledge.

The others are also standing still, necks craned back and flashlights canvassing the diamond-shaped pattern of the building's exterior and the consistent placement of half cracked, half missing windows. Luca moves first. I'm suddenly unsure I want to go, but it sure as hell beats the alternative—the looming overgrown forest at my back and whatever it is that haunts its depths.

Focusing his light on the entrance, Nick reveals a set of glass double doors at the summit of the concrete staircase. I'm surprised to find they hold an intact set of windowpanes, though a thick glaze of dirt and grime coats their surface.

"Maybe this place is haunted?" I stop in my tracks and twist to face Ava, surprised both to hear her talk and by the words she spoke.

No, that's pushing it.

"Haunted?" I ask. I'm surprised how well I mask the incredulity my mind wants to proclaim, but I can still see the subtle change in her demeanor — not hurt, but unsure. I immediately want to take it back.

"Yeah, I mean, think about it." She looks around me at the door and takes in a drag of mold-scented air before meeting my eyes again, and then the others'. "Whatever killed that guy back there... Brooklyn..." Her voice trails off for a second. She swallows and starts again. "Whatever it is, it's strong, inhumanly strong, and Luca said it's not any animal he knows. It's not Bigfoot, not a bear, not a mountain lion."

"But it's a ghost?" Nick butts in with a smirk.

I don't like his tone with Ava, but I can't help but agree with him at the same time. It can't be ghosts, there's no such thing except in myths and fairy tales. Sure, weird things happen, but there are rational explanations that don't include the spirits of the roaming dead. I mean, it's about as likely as the living dead bursting from their graves and going on the attack.

"I know how it sounds, I do!" She nearly yells it but keeps her voice down. "How else do you explain it? I mean just look behind you."

I turn, half-expecting to see some translucent apparition staring back at me, challenging my certainty. Instead, I find the hospital. My brow wrinkles in confusion.

"The hospital, the *Riverside Hospital for Quarantinable Diseases*." Ava rattles off the full name of the hospital in an expectant tone, emphasizing each word as her finger points accusingly at the structure. "Do you realize how many people died here? How many people were confined within these walls? Even after that, do you know how many kids were forced to stay here when it was a drug rehab facility? How many of them were abused, probably raped, or maybe worse?"

"But that doesn't mean it's haunted," Nick says with noticeably less conviction in his voice.

"You know, she might be right," Luca says, looking at Nick. "I know it sounds crazy, but so does a big monster in the woods. At least ghosts make some sense."

"Sense? Sense? You don't mean that bullshit, do you?" Nick comes back.

"Calm down, Nick." I put a hand on his shoulder. He jerks away and glares at me. He's scared. He's always hidden his fear well, but I can tell when something has gotten the best of my brother. I don't break eye contact, and gradually the intensity in his eyes fades and his shoulders slump.

"I don't know, man, I'm..." But he refuses to say it. "I just want it all to make sense. It has to make sense, and ghosts just don't cut it. They're not real."

I can feel the conviction in his words drain as he utters, *They're not real.* He wants to believe what he's saying and so do I, but what options are left?

"I know it's not popular, and I'm not even religious. I don't get into the ghosts and demons stuff except for the movies. Yeah, I believe in something else after this life, but... I mean, none of this shit makes sense," Ava explains, her eyes shifting to the doors leading into the hospital. "If it is something paranormal, this has to be the epicenter. Yeah, that's a big if, but all I'm saying is that I'm not so sure we need to go in there."

No one speaks for a minute. I think we're all having the same thought. *Fuck!* Or maybe it's just me, I don't know. I wrestle with the possibilities. If it is an actual physical creature out in the woods, something able to run us down and rip our bodies to shreds, is it safer to go inside the hospital for shelter, or safer to chance our way through the woods in the dark? But, if it is paranormal, if it's a ghost or spirit and this is truly the center of abuse and death on the island that Ava says it is, would we be walking into an even more dangerous trap?

It only takes a second for the scale in my mind to droop to the ground in favor of ghosts only being in the movies. Making a run through the forest quickly gets turned down. I'm not sure if logic or fear just came out on top, but I've made up my mind. I look at the hospital.

"I say we go in, take our chances inside," I announce, avoiding Ava's eyes until I've communicated my desire to Nick and Luca. Then I lock eyes with her and smile gently, trying to tell her without speaking that it's nothing against her. She awards me with the slightest of nods and a weak, almost saddened grin.

"I agree," Nick says, but I doubt anyone's really surprised by his decision.

"Me too," Luca says. He gives Ava another apologetic nod.

"Let's go then," Ava says. She puffs up her chest and swallows a deep breath. "I'm probably just overreacting. It's not exactly been the best day."

With agreement all around, Nick leads the way. I hang behind until Ava mounts the steps. She hesitates, and I place a palm on her lower back, plastering a supportive half-smile across my lips. With a sigh, she starts up the stairs and I follow close behind. My shoes crunch on a gathering of brittle twigs and the thick stalk of one of a hundred tendrils from the vines entangling the building. I sweep my light over the stairs and glance behind me. The beam illuminates the tree line and the crumbling road passing parallel to the hospital. Moonlight fades into the woods, its glow dulled by the gathering clouds.

At the top of the stairs, Nick stops and lets his flashlight penetrate the glass entry doors, past the dirty sheets of glass. I tilt my head to peer over Ava's shoulder. I was wrong earlier; the glass is cracked. One long fissure travels the height of the pane, with a handful of smaller fractures spiderwebbing out from it near the top. Nick's beam coats the floor and part of the walls in a dull brown glow, refracting through years of dust and dirt. It looks empty for the most part, save a few objects I can't make out, but I can barely make out anything from my vantage.

Nick looks to Luca, hesitating. Luca shrugs. My brother puffs a warm breath in preparation. He reaches for the door and gently nudges it forward. It creaks in a few inches before coming to a crunching stop. I step around Ava as Nick tries the other door. It inches open, scraping against dirt and something solid, but it keeps moving with a little pressure. He slips through the opening and we follow.

"Damn, this is creepy as fuck, man." Nick waves his light over the walls and floor.

"Yeah, fucking creepy," I imitate the sentiment, my mouth hanging open in a small "O". There is junk strewn across the floor and walls here. The other buildings, for the most part, were left hollowed out. Not so here.

The room is almost a perfect oval, except for the long, flat sides to the right and left like some great pressure fought back against the architect's plan, refusing to comply. In the dim light I find a single metal chair sitting off to the right, its thin, rusting frame sits a casket's length from the wall. It's one of those folding kinds with the padded back and butt, except most of the padding is gone. An ancient chandelier hangs at a dangerous angle from the ceiling, its arms painted in rust and specks of silver. Light shimmers off the pieces of glass under each of its arms, the ghosts of long dead bulbs still in place. I sweep my beam past the chandelier. A roll of carpet, caked in an eighth-inch layer of dust, lies under what appears to be on old serving tray covered in ripped gray fabric, or maybe white. Then again, it might be one of those portable laundry hampers. I don't know really and it's not important.

As my beam finds the entrance again, a set of brown benches comes into view. They look brittle, like it would only take one more particle of dust to bring them crunching to their doom, the years and rainwater pouring in the broken windows quickening their demise. Their boards are warped and splintered. The walls are the color of white-washed stone. The occasional patch of green paint under the white depicts a dull portrait of the hospital's former vibrancy. Whole pieces of the ceiling lie on the floor in varying sizes, but mostly in tiny crumbles.

It's not cold out, but I swear it feels warmer inside, and a musty scent hangs under my nose. I close my mouth and swallow absently.

"So this is the infamous hospital?" Luca sighs, unimpressed. "It's a pile of shit, that's what it is."

Nick chuckles and nudges his shoulder.

"Yeah," Ava speaks up. The imaginary weight of ghosts and goblins seems to lift from her shoulders. "I never thought

I'd actually be here, actually stand here. I mean, I knew we were planning on coming, but it was always off limits, one of those parts of history that's almost forgotten."

I watch her eyes run over the dirt and debris, the swollen wooden benches, the broken windowpanes, and the cracked stone walls. An excitement builds behind her crystal blues. The fear is still there, but somewhere an eagerness strangles the root of tension and anxiety that was there just a few moments ago. I almost smile at the change, but I hold it back. It feels wrong while Brooklyn's body lays among the thicket in pieces and Riley is still unaccounted for.

"Well, we're definitely here," Luca interrupts the moment. "And I'm none too excited about it now. Let's check out some of the rooms, really quick and then get back here and wait for the others."

"Let's not wander too far though. We don't want the others showing up and thinking we're gone," Nick comments.

I nod and start off toward the hall on my right under a large archway, but Nick and Luca are already heading toward the rear wing of the hospital. From what I remember of the map, the building is three-pronged with a shorter wing jutting out from the rear to the north and two larger wings jutting east and west. I redirect myself, unwilling to go it alone.

"Look at that," Ava urges before I have a chance to cross the threshold leading into the north wing. I let the quiet fascination in her voice work the rigidity from my muscles.

I look back to see what it is she's talking about and find her enamored eyes peering past me in the direction we were heading. I turn and focus my light. The doorway opens into a large open space. The walls are a similar stone white to the vestibule except for the large patches of rust orange. Surprisingly, this time it isn't rust though. It's peeling curls of paint.

"It must have been a waiting room or something," Luca says. His eyes scan the room, arching wide over the ceiling and back to the main floor where rows and rows of chairs are in various states of decay.

They're connected, barely, in rows nine wide, spanning the width of the room, leaving only a six or eight-foot pathway on each side for walking. It's obvious that they're built of wood from their swelling and rotting brown frames. Over half the chairs lie flat on the floor in a heap of decayed grayish matter that used to be wood.

"Yes," Ava says. She examines the room with a fascination I can't mimic and don't want to. This place is hell as far as I'm concerned.

I bend down to check out the chairs, I don't know why at first, but then it hits me. I pick up a piece of wood and grip it on both ends. I press the middle against my thigh, but it doesn't bow. I nod approvingly. Weapons. We need something in case that thing comes here.

"Something to fight with," I say, hoisting my wooden stake in the air above my head. I wince as Nick and Luca's beams flash in my face at the same time. "What if those...things come back? We need to think ahead a little, right?"

An expression of approval forms on Nick's face. He bends down and sifts through the debris, coming back up with his own stick. It's a bit larger than mine, probably sturdier too. He smiles knowingly.

Dick. I grin.

"He's right, the last thing we want is to be stuck in here with nothing but our hands to defend us," Nick tells the others before going back to looking through what presumably used to be the waiting room.

Ava leans down at the end of a row of the decaying chairs and tugs at the corner. I'm about to go see if she needs any help when the wood cracks and Ava falls back. I jump forward and throw my arms around her, catching her back against my chest, arms wrapped around her stomach. For a moment, my nose is lost in her hair, inhaling the distant scent of jasmine, and my mouth rests just under her ear, almost touching her neck. I gulp, waiting for her to jump away and tell me she doesn't need my help, but she doesn't. Instead, she takes a second to catch her breath and lets me lift her back to her feet. Reluctantly, I let her go.

Turning, she holds up a foot-long metal bar, the fruit of her near fall, and smiles. I nod approvingly, then glance down at my own stick. It's smaller. I shake my head and grin.

"Yeah, you got me too," I tell her, letting a quiet chuckle slip.

"Uh. Yeah." She raises her brow high and paints a beautiful grin across her lips. "We need to get you one, too. You can't be trying to fight off a beasty with a twig."

She goes to retrieve another bar, but I stop her. I crouch by the next row of chairs and begin working away at the soft wood. The wood here has withstood the test of time better than my first stick, but I keep at it, wrenching and pulling. Finally, it breaks away and the wood comes loose.

"I swear I could have done that easier than you just did." Ava gives me a sideways grin.

"Oh shut up." I smile back.

23: Helen Harrison

"Are you sure it's gone?" Helen asks, struggling to peek through the filthy glass on the east wall. It's too dark outside to discern anything of merit beyond the morgue's four walls. Her eyes find a patchwork of shapes, laden in obsidian shadows, each indistinguishable from its neighbor.

"I think so." Jaylen leans closer, placing his ear against the door's peeling paint. "I don't hear it anymore. It's quiet out there."

Helen steps away from the window and rests her hip against a metal table next to the cold storage units. At first, she hadn't wanted to be anywhere near the table, her mind conjuring up cold dead bodies called by death, lying rigid on their metal surfaces before a mortician callously shoved them into their frigid temporary internment.

"Do you think that creature is what took Riley?" Grady says somewhere on the other side of the room behind a thick shadow, his legs drawn pretzel-style before him on the floor. Helen looks toward his voice, finding the faintest silhouette in the dark. She still refuses to ignite her flashlight.

"We don't even know if anything took—" Helen starts.

"Don't give me that bullshit. We all know that something took him." Across the small space, Grady brushes a finger through the thick dust coating the ground. "Riley wasn't stupid, and if he just bumped his head and didn't know where he was, we would have found him by now."

No one speaks. Helen keeps her eyes locked on Grady's faint silhouette. You have to be strong, even stubborn in the film industry—any industry really—as a woman if you want to be taken seriously. She had learned through years of experience that if she wanted something she had to go for it, full steam, without remorse, and she had to be on the offensive and never give up. But sometimes she knew that mentality kept her from seeing what was right in front of her.

"Yeah, you're right," Helen mutters, hating the very sound of her words, of acquiescence. "Something took him, and yeah, it probably was that...thing. It sure as hell was big enough. The way it shook the door earlier... It's strong. Really strong."

"We can't stay here, guys." Jaylen shuffles in the dark. He checks the tiny glow-in-the-dark hands on his wristwatch. "We're going to have to leave eventually, and the sooner the better. The others are probably already waiting for us anyway. They're probably wondering what the hell is taking us so long."

"Are you proposing we leave now?" Helen asks, an indisputable layer of fear coating her voice.

"Yes," Jaylen affirms, his tone steady.

Helen's eyes gape wide. "You've got to be kidding."

"What do you plan to do? Sit here on your skinny ass for the rest of your life?" Jaylen steps forward, keeping a finger on the nearest wall, until he finds Helen. He sweeps his hand before him, as if to show her the contents of the room. "Do you really think you're going to make it in here? I mean, you do have your choice of four beds in the wall, five if you count the fucking autopsy table you're leaning on."

She doesn't answer, but her body twitches away from the table in acknowledgment.

"I know you're scared, Helen. We all are. I am. But let's think a little instead of running to rash judgments." He stops, looking for Grady in the dark. The cameraman comes around the opposite edge of the room and gulps. Jaylen returns his attention to Helen. "We have to get out of here. We *have* to. If that thing wants in here bad enough, eventually it *will* break down the door. It almost did earlier."

A single tear eclipses Helen's left eye and then slips down her cheek. She averts her gaze and wipes it away.

"I know." It's quiet, but the words still come. "Let's do it then…"

"That's more like it," Jaylen smiles and bobs his head.

"So are we just going to make a run for it?" Grady asks.

They each exchange glances, inwardly hoping that some-one has a better plan, but the silence speaks volumes.

"I mean, head for the hospital. So yeah, I guess so," Jaylen finally says, placing his hand on Helen's shoulder. "We'll make sure the coast is clear first, then we'll make a run for it. We'll stick close together, single file so we can guide each other through the woods. Do either of you know which way we need to go?"

He doesn't say it, but Jaylen doesn't want to check the map. That would require switching on a flashlight or cell-phone screen, and to do so would send a sudden glow past the windows. That cold, stark beacon in the night, like a lighthouse, would be an invitation rather than a warning. The very idea felt like asking the creature to return and might ruin their only advantage: surprise.

"Uh... Yeah, I think I do. It's on the north end of the island." Grady squeezes his eyes closed, visualizing the ink on the creased map in his pack. His cheeks push upward, obscuring his eyes in gentle puffs. "We need to go left when we leave. If we head straight into the woods, we'll be going in the right direction."

"Going *straight* through the woods is not an easy task," Helen says.

"Like I said, *if* we stay straight."

Helen licks her lips. "We'll have to stop and check our path eventually. The treetops hide the stars, so they wouldn't help even if we knew how to use them. This is not going to be easy."

"If I'm remembering right," Grady grumbles, lifting his left eyebrow a little higher than the other, "if we follow the road out front here, it turns east and goes by the other dormitory. The hospital is directly through the forest across from the dormitory. We should be able to stay out of the woods until then at least. Maybe that'll make it a little easier. I mean, it shouldn't be *too* difficult from there."

"How the hell do you remember all of this?" Jaylen grins.

"Just do."

"That sounds a whole hell of lot better than just running through the woods," Helen tells Jaylen. "I'm good with it."

Jaylen grunts. "Let's do it. I'll lead the way."

Without another word, Jaylen turns and fumbles along the wall for the exit. Helen holds onto Jaylen's forearm before he can recede into the shadows and lets him guide her toward the exit. Her foot kicks against something solid, emitting a metallic clink as the object rolls over the long untraveled floor.

A dim, warm orange radiates behind Grady's hand, glowing through his flesh. He slips his hand up an inch, allowing a sliver of bright light to illuminate the doorway. His worried eyes shine at Helen, then Jaylen. Clasping the door latch in his right hand and the deadbolt lock between his thumb and index finger, Jaylen leans forward and widens his stance. He looks back to his keep, his expression asking whether the others are ready.

Helen and Grady nod in turn, and Helen mouths a single word.

Go.

He slides the deadbolt back and shoves the door forward. Helen flips on her flashlight and jumps past Jaylen, out into the shadowy forest. The beam chases away the darkness, revealing the vine-covered forest floor and the decaying brick structure of the boiler house. She quickly redirects the beam to her left, the shiver in her arm evidenced in the erratic path of her light. She sweeps it over the red brick a full twenty feet before finding the building's end and the start of the forest where a wall of bark impedes her beam's reach.

Her eyes dart from left to right. It's clear. Another beam lights up behind her as Jaylen and Grady exit the morgue and sweep the rest of the clearing in a quick circle.

"I think it's clear, guys," Helen says, already inching toward the woods.

"Hold on, Helen," Jaylen reminds her, placing a hand on her shoulder as he passes her by, taking up the lead. "Let's stick to the plan."

Clenching tight to the small flashlight, Helen lets Jaylen

bypass her. She takes the time to slow her breathing.

Calm the fuck down, Helen.

"Come on," Jaylen waves and sets off at a quick jog.

Twigs crunch underfoot. The air is lighter, and the wind has picked up, whipping between the branches and cooling the fear on their brows. The feeble gleam of the stars disappears under the leafy canopy as they pass the edge of the morgue.

Just keep going. All you have to do is get to the hospital.

Something rustles the branches overhead. Helen ducks and glances up, eyes wide. A bird squawks and flies from a branch. Helen grunts as the fowl swoops low and then disappears back into the treetops. She fixes her eyes forward and locates Jaylen. He's only a yard or two ahead at most and she can hear Grady's hard breaths as he struggles to keep up behind her.

Helen's heart sinks when a feline-laced roar pierces the night and a shadow jerks around the nearest tree in a blur of movement. A warm, wet liquid splashes against Helen's face and neck, and before her brain can send the command for her legs to stop, she collides with Jaylen's shoulder. Her body flails to the right, spinning in a half circle before coming to a crashing halt on the forest floor with her back bent awkwardly across a thick root. A pained wail escapes Helen's lips as the wind in her lungs is forced out and agony spikes through her back.

Grady sees the commotion just in time and veers off to the right, barely missing Helen's prostrate form. He clutches the nearest trunk to stay on his feet.

Helen shakes her head, trying to expel the stabbing throb in her back, and raises her flashlight. She squints, partly dealing with the pain, partly pushing her vision to focus on Jaylen. He's standing still, exactly where she rammed into him. Her eyes climb his side, stalking the glow of her beam. The bright light spilling over his bulky form begins to quake and Helen's face goes white.

Two inch-thick, blade-like stakes protrude from Jaylen's skull, the skin rippling around the base in a mess of red, gray and black. Crimson beads dribble down the stakes, pooling over broken skull fragments and draining down his neck. A human-like hand grasps his face, one finger firmly planted inside Jaylen's right eye socket, and another impaling his cheek. His mouth hangs wide, slack and bobbing.

Behind the clawed fingers, a set of solid black orbs reflects the light from Helen's beam. Its mouth tears back in a bellowing roar. Helen's body flattens to the ground, pulling her face away from the beast, but unwilling to break eye contact. Frozen under its trance, she stares back. It cracks its head to the side, its black slits engulfed in a sea of silver-blue, studying her like it's trying to understand her. For a moment, a sliver of intelligence surfaces, a spark beyond the feral nature it exhibited in the boiler house.

Suddenly, its eyelids restrict, forming hard, thin horizontal gashes in the dark. It lifts Jaylen's body. His legs dangle lifelessly. Helen pushes back against the chill coursing through her veins as another thick, sinuous arm slices through the dark, interrupting the beam of her flashlight, and cleaves Jaylen's side.

Helen's mouth drops open as Jaylen's waist ruptures. Vivid crimson spills from the torn flesh as a whole slab of Jaylen's waist is axed away in a ragged medley of raw meat, blood and thick ribbons of torn flesh.

"What the fuck?" The words shake Helen from her stupor as an arm wraps around her waist and begins to pull her back. She strikes out, losing the grip on her flashlight, trying to connect with anything solid. The bright glow falls to the ground, shrouding Jaylen's tattered body in darkness.

"No!" she screams.

"It's me!" Grady whispers in her ear with authority.

She stops struggling, her chest rising and falling in quick gasps. Grady drags her through the dirt until two layers of trees stand between them and death. The woods engulf them in its ebony phantoms, casting a foul gray over the creature as her eyes adjust. She peers through the trees, hating the scene before her but unable to break the dark curiosity inside her. Its silhouette rises, the outline of its dense arms reaching for the sky before they race gravity back toward the earth, each clawed finger begging for flesh. Helen's mouth trembles at the sickening sound of those thick claws crashing into Jaylen's chest and ripping rabidly at his body.

"Come on," Grady whispers, reeling her back into the here and now. "There's nothing we can do for him. We have to go!"

Helen snaps from her shock and jumps to her feet. Grady pulls at her arm and she nods, dragging her eyes from the howling shadow and facing the dark.

"Let's go!" Grady urges.

24: Cooper Bay

I think I can hear the steady hum of the Big Apple wafting through the cracked and missing windowpanes. It's just a whisper, but I think that's what it is. Either way it feels out of place in the suffocating darkness. I know that I was only in the city for a day before we trekked off to this fucked up island, but the absence of the city's constant barrage of flashing lights and billboards is palpable.

I peek out the nearest window. The stars are gone, blanketed in dark clouds, prophets of an impending storm. So far, it's still dry outside. A meek breeze twists between the trees and breaches the hospital's aging walls, caressing my dirt-covered arms and face. I wipe a hand over my face, fruitlessly attempting to rid the grime from my cheeks.

I pivot my neck around, my shoulders against the vestibule's south wall. I'm keeping watch while Nick, Luca and Ava rest, in the hopes that the others will finally find us. Ava lies against my side, thighs close to mine and her cheek lying on my shoulder. It's a great feeling, one I've missed more than I cared to admit since Addison left me. I give Ava's hand a tender squeeze to let her know I'm still here.

Her fingers twitch, sending a warmth through my chest that I can't explain.

So you are *awake.*

I've barely known the girl a day, but I feel like I've known her for years. It doesn't matter that I don't know her mom's or dad's names, or that I don't have a clue where she was born, or what her favorite books or bands are, or if she'd get my *Star Trek* references. There is something I can't explain when I'm next to her and when I look into her striking blue eyes. The way her arm is laced around mine this very moment and how her hand rests on my thigh, and the warmth of her breath on my neck. It gives me something I've been missing. My lips twitch. It's stupid to feel this way, but I can't dispel it.

Think, Cooper. Don't be stupid.

For a moment I want to dip out from under her touch and put some distance between us, a barrier, a wall against potential pain, but I don't. Instead, I lean my ear atop her dirty hair and let my mind drift. I imagine leaning over without letting my body part from Ava and peering longingly into her pale blue eyes with equal parts need and passion, and then closing the gap between us. I imagine the lightning surging through me as our mouths touch and my eyes close, and all I feel is the caress of her lips and the taste of her mouth.

"Cooper. Cooper!"

I snap out of it, still sitting with my ass on the hard, cracked concrete and my cheek on Ava's head. I quickly raise my head and Ava wrenches her face up to meet my dazed eyes. I refuse to meet her crystal blues at first.

"Cooper, you okay?" she asks. I refuse to strike the serene grin from my cheeks as I finally look at her, her worried eyes finding me in the residual glow of a flashlight beam.

"Yeah, I'm good. Just tired," I tell her. It's not a lie, but not exactly the whole truth either.

"You didn't answer at first," Ava says. "I thought you

dozed off."

"Nah." I'm not about to tell her I was dreaming of kissing her.

How would she react to that? It's not worth finding out. You're being stupid again, Cooper, plus you've got real shit to worry about.

I notice the tiny patter of raindrops echoing over my head with a rush of cool air. Ava doesn't say anything else. I take in a breath.

"You okay?" I ask, not sure what else to say.

"Yeah..." There's an ephemeral pause in her words. "I think."

"It's going to be okay," I tell her. Immediately, I chide myself. I don't have a clue how things are going to turn out. I mean, Brooklyn's dead, fucking dead, and I tell Ava *it's going to be okay.* In what world is that okay?

But she doesn't seem to care as she pulls her eyes away and nuzzles her nose against my neck, just above my collarbone. I shiver at the touch of her lips against my chest, and an involuntary swallow betrays my trepidation. I want her so bad. For a second, my mind flickers.

Do I want her for her, or is it because of all the shit going on? Stop it, Cooper, you're not that fucking shallow.

"But is it?" she asks. Suddenly I feel like she can read my thoughts. Thank God, she can't.

"I don't know." I muffle the words, feeling the sting of the apology exiting my mouth. "I'm sorry, I shouldn't have said that. Nothing about this is okay. It's fucked up, really fucked up. I don't... I'm..."

She puts a lone finger against my lips and shushes me. A weak grin finds its way over her face.

"I am, too, you don't have to say it. And that's okay," she

tells me. I don't match her grin. Instead, I avert my gaze toward the dusty floor.

Across the room, Luca shifts in his sleeping bag, muttering something indecipherable in his sleep.

"Let's go in the next room so we don't bother them." Ava glances at Luca and Nick, then grins at me.

I nod and rise to my feet, no point in waking the others with our whispers. If the others do come, we should be able to hear them from the hallway. I lead the way. She grips my hand tighter, as if I might let go.

I'd never.

We pass under a rotting archway and I stop in the hallway. The floor is covered in dust. It looks like the scattered debris is the only thing holding up the walls in places. I turn around to face Ava.

"If you need to talk it ou — " I start, but Ava interrupts me with a finger pointing toward the adjacent room.

"Let's go in there." There is something different in her eyes, almost like her words are a question.

"Okay." I nod and lead the way, pushing the partially ajar door back with my free hand and letting Ava enter first.

Inside, Ava releases my hand long enough to push the door shut again, producing a gruff scrape of wood against wood, but it doesn't latch. Instead, the pressure of the old door against its warped frame holds it closed. When she turns around, I eye her questioningly.

"Are you okay, A — " I start, but before the second syllable can squeeze through my vocal chords, she lurches forward and pushes me back, pinning my body between her chest and the wall. Quicker than I can react, her lips clash against mine, and her hands grope at my chest.

For the briefest of moments my mind says to push her away, to stop, but I ignore its reason and let myself melt into her. I grip her small waist, sliding a palm around her side to the small of her back while my other hand cups her neck and pulls her closer. Under the odor of dirt and sweat, I find the subtle hint of strawberry on her lips again as my mouth parts and we merge into one.

My chest throbs at the pressure of my heart and the sensation of Ava's palm slipping under my shirt and across my stomach. As her hands drift higher, mine travel down her shoulder, discovering the gentle dip of her back before I grip her buttocks. I pull her in, and groan at the sensation of her body pressed against me.

The deep thrum of rain rises in the background, but I barely register it over Ava's increasingly labored breaths. It erupts into a downpour, slapping against the hospital's brick walls and wailing through the broken windows. She gropes at my waist just inches above my growing erection and lifts my shirt. I raise my arms and let the fabric pass over my head as a rush of cool air sweeps through the room and sends a chill up my back with the light touch of her fingers.

As her hands caress my chest, my eyes find the sloping curves of her breasts above her shirt's low neckline. I grin mischievously at her and pull the garment over her head. I lift her feet off the ground and twist around and taste her lips before letting her feet touch the dusty floor again. Her eyes shine back at me in the dark as I kneel before her and kiss her taut stomach, my gaze never leaving her perfect blue circles.

Ava bites her lips and a small giggle reaches my ears. She slides down the wall and I pull her into the dirt, sprawling out along the floor, our bodies pressed together. I lose track of time when suddenly my body shakes in ecstasy. I clamp my eyes shut as the sensation surges up my chest and a deep groan escapes my open mouth. As the feeling passes, I slump limply against Ava.

I open my eyes to find her staring back at me with a gentle grin. She's breathing heavy like me, but there is twinkle in her eye. I lean in and kiss her again.

Slowly, the sound of the pouring rain breaks through my euphoria, but I keep my eyes locked on Ava. I move my hand over her cheek, an intoxicated grin splashed over my face. She's so beautiful.

"Wow," I exhale.

"Wow?" Ava asks. "That's all you got?"

I chuckle and let my palm slither over her hip.

"I—"

"Where's Cooper and Ava?" The words come as a whisper outside the swollen door cutting us off from the hallway. It's Nick. He must have woken.

"Shit," I grimace. "They're awake."

Ava smirks and leans in for another kiss. I let my chest fall and release a quiet sigh as our lips part, giving her a reluctant smile before getting to my feet. Squinting in the dark, I find my underclothes in the far corner. I quickly retrieve them and get dressed while Ava does the same.

"Cooper?" Nick yells from the other room. A distinct concern rises in his voice. "Ava?"

I'd prefer to be dressed when he barges in, so I don't respond, but pull my shorts up more vigorously. As I'm threading my arms into my t-shirt, he yells again, but this time I hear his footsteps approaching. I shoot my eyes over to Ava. She's pushing her hair out of her face, but she's dressed.

I make for the door, swinging it open just as Nick's hand is about to press against the other side.

"Hey, Nick," I say, a huge grin slapped across my lips. Mentally kicking myself, I try to flatten my lips, but it only makes it more obvious when they pooch out like a duck's bill. *Fuck.* His expression changes from worry to intrigued suspicion in less time than it takes the second hand to click forward.

"Everything okay?"

Before I can respond, Ava peeks her head over my shoulder and says hey. The bewilderment in his face changes to a sly grin. I can see the approval in his eyes, and I give him the "seriously, man, not in front of the girl" look.

"All good, man," I blurt out, nervously twitching my neck and licking my lips.

"Uh, yeah." Nick continues to grin. He shifts on his feet to let us past the door and into the hallway. "I just didn't know where you two were. Woke up and you were both gone."

Ava slips by. I nod to her as she steps off down the hall.

"Could you tell Luca I found you two?" Nick casts his voice after Ava. "He went down the other hall looking for you."

She nods and disappears around the corner. I hate to see her go, and the thought of her wandering around these corridors by herself hits me hard in the chest. I go to follow, and Nick matches my pace, patting me on the shoulder.

"Good job, little brother."

"Oh, fuck off." I can't keep the smile from my face, so I stop trying.

Nick shrugs under an amused chortle, and the approval in his eyes doesn't fade. I quicken my stride, still shaking my head but laughing with him.

"Hey, you're making the movies come to life, Coop," he tells me, putting his hands up in defense.

"I hope not. This isn't exactly a happily ever after ending type of movie," I remind him with one brow lowered.

We exit the hall and find Ava only halfway across the main room. She calls out for Luca and a minute later we're all together again. I lean against the north wall along with Ava, facing the building's main entrance and watching the maturing rainstorm through the empty windowpanes. Droplets splatter on the floor, coating the dirty concrete in a growing slimy mess. My arm is wrapped around Ava's waist, and her head is propped on my shoulder. Luca and Nick stand directly ahead of us.

"It's 11:15 and the others haven't showed up yet," Luca complains, his hands gripped into small fists at his sides. "They should be here by now."

"Maybe they just got turned around, or they're sheltered up somewhere. It is raining," Ava offers, "and it's starting to come down hard."

"Yeah, and it could get worse. I know *I* wouldn't want to be out there if a lightning storm starts up," I tell them, glimpsing the sheets of pounding rain both outside and inside.

"I'm sure they're okay, Luca. Helen might be stubborn, but she's not stupid," Nick says. He kicks absently at a small piece of ceiling tile. It scratches to a halt a few inches away.

"I know, but I'd just feel a lot better about it if they were here." Luca stops and his eyes twitch like something clicked in the recesses of his mind. "And Gabe. He's out there too, all by himself. I shouldn't have left him out there. I shouldn't have let us come here until we found him. *Dammit!*"

"Stop, Luca," Nick raises his voice and places a consoling hand on the director's shoulder. "You did what you knew you needed to do. You can't change it and there's no point thinking about it. They'll all come when they can. It might be after the storm, or maybe they'll be here any minute, but they'll make it."

"You don't know that, man." Luca looks Nick in the eyes. I shift nervously, sensing the fear emanating from the director. I squeeze Ava a little tighter. "Don't try to sell me that shit, Nick, I'm not some eight year old who doesn't know any better. They might never be coming. That *thing* might have gotten them already. Remember, it's out there too."

Luca's eyes glaze over as they find me, but somehow he's not looking at me. The dark black centers of his chestnut eyes peer past me, through me, as if I'm not here.

"What if it ripped them apart like it did Brook—"

"Stop it, Luca. Snap the hell out of it, man," Nick shakes him, his voice bellowing with a barely audible quiver. "Don't talk like that. Yeah, I don't have a fucking clue what's going to happen or where the hell they are, but I'm not losing hope. We're still here, aren't we?"

I find myself nodding.

"They probably just got held up. Maybe they had trouble reading the map," I interject. I feel like some stupid jock the moment the thought breaches my lips, too late to reach out and retract it. It is possible, and it sure as hell beats the alternative.

"It's easy to get lost in the woods." Ava comes to my rescue. "Even if you know them, it's still easy. They probably just got turned around. We just have to wait."

A minute passes with only the beating of a million water

pellets filling the silence. He's scared. Fuck it, I'm scared. I'm not shaking, but my muscles are stiff and contracted, locked into a state of preparedness, waiting to spring into action at the smallest trigger. The tension in my right arm melts a little as Ava leans her weight on me. I catch her scent and remember the taste of her lips and the feeling of her body in my hands. For a moment I'm not here, I'm in that old, dark and dirty room on the floor with her again. It hits me how quickly my emotions can change, how easily fear takes root and shapes us. I close my eyes for a brief second and focus on the warmth of Ava's shoulder.

The moment passes, and I find myself standing shoulder to shoulder with Ava in the musty circular room. The others are still silent. Luca is leaning his weight against the dilapidated laundry cart sitting oddly in the center of the room. It shakes under his hand, but he doesn't seem to notice.

"Let's just wait out the rain, they'll probably sh—"

Crack!

The word freezes on my lips as every inch of my body stiffens and I pull Ava closer. My eyes streak past my brother.

"Was that lightning?" Ava asks.

It's possible, but I don't think the explanation is that simple. There was no flash of light, no vibration under our feet. Only a noise, like a piece of wood breaking or cracking.

"No," Nick mutters.

"I agree," I say, my mouth half open as I peer at the ceiling and then into the hallway shadowed in darkness underneath it. Suddenly, I get the feeling in the pit of my stomach that we're not alone. My body shivers, and inside I want to sink into the wall, to become one with it and escape the unknown. I squint, willing my vision to pierce through the dark veil, past the cracked stone and molded wooden doorframes, wanting and not wanting to see something in the same instant.

My head conjures up the most horrid of beasts. It's seven feet tall, its spine bent unnaturally forward, giving it a pained air. Its body is slick with mucus and slime, arms lolling at its sides with the long razor-sharp claws Luca talked of clicking and clacking against each other. I see it staring at me, crimson eyes lusting for my blood.

I shake my head, trying to wipe the fabricated image from my mind. It's still there, but I manage to press it into a recess.

"Riley?" Luca whispers. I barely hear him over the pounding rain, then he speaks again, a little louder this time. "Riley? Maybe it's Riley."

"Uh..." Nick stutters. I watch his Adam's apple bob as he swallows hard. "I don't know, man... Maybe."

"But what if it's..." The words trail off my tongue, leaving the rest to be filled in. I'm not sure if I really believe it, but somehow out of the pool of anxiety stirring in my chest, curiosity and wonder peek their ugly heads.

"Maybe they can't get inside." The words hit me as Luca utters them. He could be talking about anyone, maybe Helen or Grady, Jaylen or Gabe, but I know better. I think we all know better.

Maybe they *can't get inside*, I replay his words in my head. Somehow the thought that they *could* get inside had yet to break through the narrative my mind had settled on. I just assumed they couldn't. Now that assurance is broken. What if they can? I mean, why couldn't they?

Fuck!

I take a deep breath, steeling myself in the surrounding

darkness, but I don't say anything. I don't know the answer, so there's no point in freaking out the others if they haven't already come to the same conclusion.

"We have to check." My eyes snap to the right where Ava is looking up at me. She purses her lips in response to my scowl. "We need to know."

I don't want to agree. I don't want Ava anywhere near the possibility of danger that I'm somehow certain lurks in the recesses of that hallway. And I'm afraid for my own sake, too. I bow my head, ashamed of how I allow fear to push me around like a coward. My shoulders slump and I avert my eyes.

"She's right," Luca agrees.

I don't even bother to look at him. I can't help but think it's a horrible idea. But at the same time, I know Riley's out there somewhere.

I loosen my grip on Ava's hand and refuse to look at her. I want to be with her, to be hers, to be there for her, but I can't seem to break past the tightness in my chest and the shiver of my hands. Her fingers constrict around my hand, and she lifts my chin with her other hand, turning my face to meet her eyes. She gives me an uneasy grin, filled with an amalgam of sympathy, understanding, need and fright. I want to break away, but something won't let me. I swallow back the trepidation running through my veins.

You do what you have to do, Coop. Whatever it is, you can do it.

"I don't know, guys. I'm not so sure it's a good idea for us to go trekking around in here, especially at night." I can see Nick's hands make a small arc, moving with his words.

I want to say we shouldn't go, that Nick's right, that it's too dangerous, that we don't know the layout, that we don't know if *it's* inside, but with my eyes locked on Ava's blue eyes shadowed in deep grays, I can't. Instead, a grimace fouls my face.

"We should at least check," I say, earning my hand an approving squeeze. I wish I felt like it was the right answer, but I don't. Is there a right answer, or did I just let a feeling get in the way of logic? I don't know. Hell, I'm not even supposed to fucking be here.

"Okay." Nick nods, but I can hear the faint disapproval in his voice.

Oh please, just be Riley. Please.

25: Gabe Meadows

Dragging in a gulp of damp air, Gabe ducks beneath another branch. Mini eruptions of water burst around his jeans with each step.

It's pouring. Heavy droplets pelt his face and gush over his cheeks and neck. His clothes weigh him down, but he keeps running. The glow of his flashlight bounces between the trees and past a bramble, morphing along every surface. His thighs burn as he lifts his soused feet from the muddy ground and forces them to take another step.

A streak of scintillating white sears his vision an instant before a thunderclap deafens him. Gabe jerks to the left and his shoulder smacks against a slab of rough bark. His body spins around the trunk as he throws a hand out to break his fall, but his angle is wrong and his hip slams into the ground. A chill runs up his spine first as his back soaks in the gathering water, followed by the brutal impact of solid ground. His body rolls, flailing under the rain, crashing against roots, grass, thickets and dirt. A piercing ache explodes in his back as he comes to a halt, resting atop a half buried, notched rock. Rain shoots into his open mouth as he begs for breath, but instead chokes on the pouring rain. He gags and throws his head to the side, unable to move his body in so much pain.

Gabe groans, opening his eyes wide as the world spins

around him, then squints away the piercing raindrops. He twists, trying to get back up, but a sharp jolt of electricity bores up his side and into his shoulder. It drives him to the ground. He rolls onto his back, the small pack hanging from his shoulder arching his spine awkwardly to the sky. Prostrate on the forest floor, the rain beats against his soaked body.

"Agh! Shit," Gabe grumbles, rain pummeling his face. He shifts his butt on the moist yet still stiff bed of dirt and rock. Bringing a hand to his head, he rubs at the back of his skull, prompting a harsh prick of agony to flare in his brain. "Fuck."

He turns his face away from the sky to keep from drowning in the rain. A moment passes, and Gabe entertains the thought of just staying here, on the ground, wet and vulnerable. It can't be much worse than running. At least it doesn't involve voluntarily prodding his now pained body. But *it's* out here too. In the back of his mind he knows if he stays, it'll find him. It knows the woods, it must live here. He's just a visitor, a lonely trespasser in the wrong place. The vague form he briefly glimpsed over half an hour ago floats behind his eyes. Its large form, that shadow in the darkness, lurking through the forest, unbothered by the rain, seeking his scent. But is it any safer inside? A spark ignites in his mind.

Should I really be going to the hospital? The boats. What about the boats? I could leave.

His eyes shoot to the right, as if by some miracle he's looking to the shore where the boats are hopefully still beached.

I can make for the boats, go back to the city... I can get help.

Lightning flashes behind the treetops, its light somehow piercing through the dense canopy, followed a second later by a booming thunderclap. Gabe shudders, barely holding back a scared shriek. He chides himself. The thunder had never bothered him before and he damn well didn't need to let it get under his skin now.

No. You'll go to the hospital. Meet up with the others and then get our asses off this damned island. You already left Luca and Brook, you're not leaving all of them. You're not a fucking coward.

Twisting at the waist, Gabe attempts to turn over, but a sharp pain travels up his side.

"Fuck!" he screams, not caring if anyone can hear him. "Fuck it! Just get up, Gabe. Get the fuck up and go. It's not that bad."

Placing the pain spilling through his veins in the back seat, he throws his body onto its side and falls to his chest. He grits his teeth, holding back the agony stretching over his shoulders and down his waist. Scowling, he presses his hands against the mud and rises to his hands and knees, the mud slithering between his fingers and saturating the hems of his tan shorts. Gabe lowers his head and clamps his eyes closed, willing the burn to become nothing more than a deep throb. He takes a breath and rises to his feet.

"Just get to the fucking hos—"

Crack.

Gabe pitches his eyes toward the noise. He swallows absently, his eyes darting from bush, to tree, to branch, and back again, but he doesn't move. Half a minute passes and Gabe refuses to move. The rain falls harder, smacking against his skin and cascading down his back and chest, his clothes clinging to every curve of his slim form. It beats like an incessant drum, interrupted by pulsating flashes and the deep boom of thunder.

He snaps out of it just as it comes again. *Crack.*

"Hell no," he mutters. He swivels on his feet and almost loses his footing before sprinting in the opposite direction. A pang grips his thigh, unwilling to let go of its victim. It nearly sends him crashing into a nearby tree, but he catches himself. He weaves between the timber and past a thicket, then mounts a fallen log and leaps back to the forest floor. He grips his fist to bite back the flurry of pain coursing through his muscles.

He can barely see more than a few feet ahead. The blitzkrieg of thick raindrops bombards his vision and the sudden flashes of white make it almost impossible to stay focused in the dark. No matter how quickly he blinks, the trees, bushes, the ground, everything blends together, but he keeps moving.

A branch lashes his arm, sending a new sting up his shoulder and a ragged red scratch in its wake. He winces but doesn't slow. He tries to blink away the raindrops. He takes a quick glance to each side, letting his eyes take in the forest for any sign he's headed in the right direction. There's nothing, only more rain, trees and dirt, so he resolves to just keep moving.

Whatever spooked him back there doesn't seem to be following, at least it doesn't sound like it. He takes some comfort in the notion and slows to a quick jog.

At once the trees recede behind him and he stumbles into a clearing. Gabe stamps his feet to the ground and grinds to a halt. The dirt, muddy and slimy, moves under his feet, but he comes to a stop after a few inches. He pants, his chest rising and falling rapidly. His eyes squint behind the rain as they travel up the tall building rising from the dirt straight ahead.

It's large, at least four floors from the stack of black holes dotting the brick wall. It stretches in both directions past layers of leaves and vines, blurred by the rain, and disappears into the dark. He pauses at the edge of the forest and bites at his lip thoughtfully, debating whether to go inside, and then he sprints forward.

Gabe's shoes slap against the craggy concrete steps, taking them two at a time, skipping over the patches of vine and mold. Mounting the upper landing, he comes to a stop under the small overhang. He wipes a palm over his face and bats away the remaining water from his eyes before looking back. He searches for any sign of the noise that spooked him.

The dense rainfall makes it hard to see into the forest, but nothing breaks through the tree line. The leaves and branches toss in the wind and shake under the falling drops. He scans them for a full minute before letting his vision take in the man-made path set against the tree line and the overgrown lawn stretching between the building and the woods.

Hell, I don't remember crossing that.

He cocks his head and sighs, letting the adrenaline settle in his veins. Gabe pushes his shoulders back and grunts away the pain. He turns, finding the double glass entry door.

Please let this be the fucking hospital.

He peers through the dirty, cracked glass.

It looks abandoned.

He kicks himself mentally for the absurd assessment.

Of course it looks abandoned, dumbass, it's an abandoned *island.*

He turns and scans the clearing again, unable to shake the feeling that he's still being followed. He squints when a flash of lightning bursts across his vision, the thin bolt of electricity sprinting erratically in the night sky over the treetops. He blinks away the afterglow and keeps looking, not wanting to lead whatever that dammed creature is in with him. But there's nothing.

Satisfied, Gabe turns and pushes past the door. It creaks quietly, and he steps inside. It's darker here, but his eyes still make out a generous circular room, or at least it appears circular.

My flashlight! Dammit, I dropped it in the woods.

Gabe purses his lips in frustration and debates whether it's better to go it nearly blind inside or stay outside on the tiny porch under at least the light of the moon. He errs on the side of staying dry. Resolved to move on, Gabe steps away from the entry. Debris scatters the floor. He moves forward and nearly trips over something small and heavy. He regains his footing and aims his eyes toward the floor before taking the next step.

"Where the hell am I?"

Trying to be careful of the path ahead, Gabe advances, letting his eyes adjust to the near total darkness. He holds his hand out, fingers spread, and reaches for anything to guide him through the space. Finally, his eyes begin to adjust and shapes grow out of the dark. Blocks, stacks of odd-shaped items in deep shades of gray, and the shadow of rainwater flowing down the windows. There's an open doorway ahead, leading to a yet larger room, but he cannot make out any real detail.

The drone of the rain echoes past him as a sharp white flash sears the room into his mind. He squints as the thunder-clap sends a quake beneath his feet and Gabe instinctively ducks and covers his head.

"Fuck it!" Gabe screams back, a shrill noise compared to the thunder's mighty roar.

Coming erect again, Gabe exhales a long breath and shakes his head. In the brief instant of total illumination, his eyes found a room left long in disrepair. Rows of dingy brown chairs, mostly decayed or decaying along the floor. A stage-like area at the far end, bordered in crumbling tile and rotted wood, and a set of broken stairs leading up the right corner. Walls covered in scattered brown and white from chipping paint, and four sets of massive windows bordered by half-hanging, dust-ridden curtains that lost their color decades ago.

Not knowing what to do, Gabe twists around and lets his eyes adjust to the darkness again. He peers down the hallway off to the right. Beyond the empty archway it appears as little more than an empty black cave. Not interested, he pulls his eyes away and scans the first room again. There's some large blocky object near the center of the room. He continues past the broken windows along the circular front wall and the rain pouring in through them, to the hallway along the left side of the room to find more of the same.

This has to be the hospital, so where the fuck is everyone?

Gabe shuffles his feet along the floor toward the hallway entrance to his right. He stops at the arched doorway and peers into the emptiness. The faint shapes of five doorways materialize, two down the left wall and the other three along the right wall. Beyond them more undistinguishable shapes clutter the space.

"You should just stay here, Gabe," he tells himself. "No point in gallivanting around like some idiot in a horror mov-ie."

He steps back, retreating into the large circular room he had first come upon as another pairing of lightning and thunder shake him. As his heart settles again, his ears prick at a small, distinct sound emanating from the corridor. He leans forward, taking a step toward the dark again, and turns his face to put his ear between him and the hallway.

He waits. Was it just another sound in the rain, some animal, or worse? He refuses to back down, though, and keeps his ear aimed at the dark. Then, just above the drowning effect of the rain, it comes again. It's quiet but distinct. It's one of the others.

They are here!

Pushing aside caution, Gabe steps over the threshold and starts down hallway.

26: Cooper Bay

"You listened to that band I was telling you about, right?" Nick asks without turning around, his flashlight sweeping the next corner.

Trying to keep my mind off our fucked-up situation, I let my thoughts wander. I lean around the corner and peer into the dust-filled room, conjuring up images of drugged out teenagers and disease-ridden men and women lying under plain bed sheets.

"Which one?" I ask, raising an eyebrow. He gave me a list the last time we talked on the phone, a few days before I flew in to New York City. I doubt he really cares which one though.

"Villain of the Story," he says.

I'm glad for the distraction, so I play along. It's better than imagining the wretched residents of this abandoned facility.

"Uh…" I start, trying to place the name with a tune. It doesn't take long. A gentle medley interrupted by a crushing bass line, accompanied by a mix of clean and dirty vocals about not giving a damn what others say about you, more or less, comes to mind. "Yeah, they were awesome."

I feel my voice tremble, forcing out a phrase that would have come so easily just a day ago. They were awesome, but my mind immediately falls back into our present hell, making it hard to say it with much meaning.

"Yeah, they are," Nick agrees and takes a quick look over my shoulder. I glimpse back and find Luca. "Ain't that right, Luca?"

"Uh, yeah." The fear in his voice betrays his reply, but he keeps talking. "They're sweet. 'Grow,' I love that song."

"Villain of the Story?" I can feel the judgmental expression on Ava's face before I turn to meet her amused eyes. "Really? That's the name of a band?"

"Yeah, a fucking awesome band," I reiterate, a grin spread across my face and my brow raised. Something about her tone lets me break past the feeling that holds me back. "It's original at least. Right?"

"Well, yeah, I guess," she says. "So what do they sing? Pop? Rap?"

"What? Hell no! They're rock, metalcore." I squeeze her fingers before dipping around the next doorframe, shaking my head the whole way.

"What the hell is metalcore?" she asks, and my eyes go wide. I quickly remind myself that, for whatever reason, good rock isn't mainstream.

"I think we'll have this talk when we get off this island." I grin and take a quick look over my shoulder again with a raised brow. "You're not a rap girl, are you?"

Ava shakes her head in amusement. "No, I'm more of a pop and love song type of girl."

"Okay, I can deal with that." I catch Nick's attention and he shakes his head.

"Well, that's good I guess." Ava rolls her beautiful crystal blues at me.

"Guys, shhh!" Luca places his pointer finger over his lips

and pats at the air with his other hand. He looks at the ground, listening intently.

I listen too, searching the edges of my flashlight beam where the white blends to gray and then an oppressive black. Above the sound of nervous breath and Ava's feet shuffling over concrete, the only noise that reaches my ear is the continued drone of the rain beating on the roof before it sloshes over the edge. A thunderclap breaks the monotony, and my back goes rigid. I loosen my body as the building falls silent again.

"Did you hear that?" Luca asks. "I thought I heard — "

My brow rises as a voice echoes down the hallway, and my eyes shoot to my ten o'clock.

"Yeah," I say in time with Nick.

"Guys!" The voice comes louder this time. "Is that you down there? Luca? Nick?"

"It's Gabe!" Luca takes a step, his volume rising until he's yelling. "Gabe! It's us! We're down here!"

I start after Luca as he sprints down the hall. My light flashes past open doors, my makeshift wooden weapon swinging at my side. At Luca's pace, you might think we were running *from* something rather than *to* something.

"Guys!" Gabe yells as Luca's beam splashes over his pale skin and reflects against the amber flakes in his eyes. He squints against the bright glow and slings an arm over his eyes. "I guess this *is* the hospital then."

I skid to a stop next to Luca.

"Yeah." Luca's face glows with excitement, a weight lifted from his shoulders. "How'd you get here?"

"I just ran. One of those things was behind — " Gabe starts before Nick interrupts.

"Behind you? Did it follow you here?" Nick steps forward, breaking past the line previously held by Luca and me.

It takes Gabe a second to rebound from the interruption. His mouth hangs open for a moment before he shakes his head. "Uh... no, I don't think so. I heard it in the woods, way back, and I just ran. I didn't stop until I got here. I wasn't even sure where *here* was."

Gabe peers around Luca and me. I turn to see what he's looking at, but my eyes land on empty space. I turn back to face him with a crinkle in my brow.

"What is it, Gabe?"

"Where's Brook?" His eyes narrow.

He doesn't know.

It hits me harder than I expect. The image of her broken and bloodied body scattered on the forest floor weighs me down like an anvil in my chest. I swallow and avert my eyes. Ava presses her chest against my arm and lets her gaze fall to the floor.

No one speaks.

"Where is she, guys?" Gabe prods, lifting his shoulders questioningly. His eyes pierce through Luca. "Luca?"

"She's dead, Gabe." The words spill from Luca's lips and hit Gabe like a tsunami.

The boy stumbles back a step, his pallid complexion a mix of confusion and fear under a messy brown mop. His eyes shift under narrowed lids, and for a moment he looks like he might collapse under the news, but he steadies himself.

"What?" Gabe mumbles, an absent look in his eyes. "But how?"

"That thing... It..." Luca searches for the words but comes up short.

"It killed her, Gabe. Whatever's in the woods killed her," Nick blurts.

"No..." Gabe shakes his head and finds Luca again. "But she was behind me. You were behind me."

"What?" Luca furrows his brow and slides his foot an inch forward.

"You two were behind me," Gabe repeats.

"Yeah, right before you fucking ran off without us like a fucking coward!" Luca's eyes light up, his calm destroyed.

He leaps forward and clamps his hands about Gabe's neck. The boy stumbles, his back landing hard against the aged concrete floor, but Luca doesn't lose his grip. Instead, his fingers tighten around Gabe's thin neck, a snarl on his face and fury billowing in his eyes.

"It's your fault, you fucking little cunt!" he screams, spit smacking Gabe's scared face.

"I... I..." Gabe struggles through a constricted windpipe.

"Get off him, Luca!" Nick yells and jumps into action.

"Stop it!" Ava screams.

I release her hand and throw myself into the fray. As Nick wedges his fingers between Luca's hands and Gabe's neck, my palms find purchase on Luca's small shoulders. I reel back, thinking my weight and gravity will do the rest, but instead I find myself moving forward.

"Come on, Luca, it's not worth it!" I try to reason with him.

I can see Gabe's hands snaking under Luca's grip, pushing and pleading with the man. A flurry of tiny red veins storm through the white fields in his eyes and his lips gasp for breath.

"Luca, stop!" Nick demands, but his words are met with

deaf ears.

I wrench back again. Between Nick's prying hands and my momentum, Luca loses his maddened clutch. Gabe twists from under the director's weight. He sidles away on his ass, stopping only when his back flattens against the wall. I keep pulling back before I finally release my grip, and Luca crashes to the floor.

"What the hell, man?" Gabe barks, his hands rubbing his neck. "I didn't know! I promise. I just... I..."

He breaks into tears as Luca props a hand against the nearest wall and rises to his feet. Nick and I form a dividing line between the two just in case the fury in Luca's eyes fails to dwindle. He shifts from foot to foot. Through gritted teeth Luca huffs, but I can tell that the fire is out, only a smoldering ember left.

"I didn't know. I..." Gabe repeats between sobs. "I was scared."

I can't help but find it odd to see Gabe crying. Sure, he's not a weight lifter, or one of those big I'm-so-manly-I-have-to-prove-it types, but when I first met him at the bar he was so confident—young like me, but still confident. I take a step back mentally.

Didn't we all think we were strong before all this shit?

I look away to give him some privacy and give Luca another once-over. Satisfied that his temper has settled, I take up a spot next to Ava beneath the hall archway and realize we're at the start of the hallway again.

A flash of pure white permeates the room, splashing exaggerated shadows over the walls. The phantom of the overturned clothes hamper, the caricature-like ghost of the diminutive metal chair at the center of the room, and our monstrous silhouettes are plastered over the walls for the blink of an eye. The walls shake under the boom of the thunderclap that follows.

"It's okay, Gabe," Nick pats the boy on the shoulder but stands back, seemingly not really sure how to handle the situation.

"I'm...I'm sorry, Gabe." It's Luca, his voice barely audible over the pelting rain. "I just... I... Uh..."

"No, you're right. I shouldn't have run off," Gabe admits. He wipes the tears from under his eyes and sniffles. "I should have been there. Maybe I could have done something."

"No. There's nothing you could have done." Luca's words come hard, each one punctuated by a deep, tangible agony. "There's nothing any of us could have done."

With that, Luca turns away and stares down the empty hallway.

"But I shouldn't have have—" Gabe tries.

"Just stop, Gabe," Nick cuts him off. "There's nothing you or anyone else could have done. Nothing. Let's just leave it at that."

I put an arm around Ava's shoulder. For some reason I have the sudden need to hold her, to know that she's next to me, that she's still here. Gabe places a hand against the crumbling wall and lets his weight droop against it. His eyes dart along the floor, trying to reconcile the information and the guilt. I don't know what happened out there, but right now I'm not sure any of us really know what we'd do in response to the creature Luca described, except maybe Luca and Gabe, so I try not to judge them.

"What the hell is going on here?" Gabe starts again.

"Going on?" Nick asks. He turns, wiping a hand across his

face. "I don't have a clue. All I know is that there is something else on this island, and it isn't human. Whatever it is, it's dangerous."

"What do we do?" Gabe shifts on his feet and steps closer to the group. "I mean, what's the plan?"

"We find Riley just like before and then wait for the others," Nick tells him. "Then we leave."

A minute passes with only the incessant pounding of the rain outside reminding me that the world still moves on. It amazes me that beyond these walls, past the rain, past the trees and the vines, and past the small stretch of water lies the largest city in America, nestled up against the water, a bustle of activity even at this late hour. My stupor turns to fear when I realize not one of the tens of thousands of police officers on the mainland is going to come to our rescue on this forbidden island, not until it's too late, at least.

We're not even supposed to be here. The thought repeats in my mind like one of the massive LED bulletin boards in the middle of Times Square, but totally unseen.

"We need to keep searching the building," I blurt into the silence. I'm not even sure where it came from, but the words jump from my lips.

"What?" Nick looks at me.

"We need to keep searching. For Riley," I repeat.

"Yeah, let's keep searching." Luca backs me up.

He doesn't say it, but I can hear an unspoken conviction in his words. It's like he's saying *I need to find him*, like he feels it's his fault. Nick nods and gives Gabe a reassuring shake.

"You good to come?" he asks.

"Yeah, I'm good."

I look to Ava and before I can utter a word, she gives me a

half-grin and bobs her head, gripping my hand a little tighter.

"Come on," Luca almost whispers as he takes up the lead and trails off into the hallway without further debate.

I let Gabe pass me and fall in line ahead of Ava at my side. Nick takes up the rear. We settle on a brisk pace, quickly bypassing the rooms we checked minutes ago. Our beams bathe the hall in a gentle white glow that fades into absolute black yards ahead. I count off eight doors before Luca slows again. He creeps up to the next doorframe and peeks inside. With no light of his own, Gabe opts to fall back rather than sticking with Luca, locking step with Nick. They stop at the next door before Ava and I find our own along the opposite wall. I steal around the corner and shine my light over the room's contents. A rusting bedframe with the mattress missing sits in the corner, and a scattering of newspapers and magazines coat the floor. Otherwise, it's empty.

It goes on like this for another ten minutes before we reach the end of the hall, taking it slowly and carefully. Leave one room, approach the next, peer around the corner like scared little eight year olds staring into a dark bedroom before crossing the threshold to get a better look, then repeat the cycle again and again.

At the end of the hall, another set of spiral stairs rise into a murky black hole in the ceiling, presumably to the second and maybe third and fourth floors. I steal a glance at Nick. He crooks one eyebrow up high and shrugs. I let out a huff. So far stairs haven't been our greatest ally inside these crumbling buildings.

"Let's just do it." I'm surprised to hear the words spill from Ava. Her tone is low and aggravated, like she knows what we're all thinking, probably wants to say no, but decides against it.

"You sure?" I ask, trying not to patronize her. I'm genuinely concerned, but in the same instant I feel like we need to go. I mean, we don't know where the noise came from earlier, and if Riley is here, we need to find him.

But what if it wasn't him?

I sweep the thought into a dark corner of my mind.

"If you want, I can stay down here with you, and they can go up. Right, Nick?"

"Yeah, that would work," he says without hesitation. Victory one.

She shakes her head. "No, I'm good. We should *all* stick together." I can still see the reservation in her eyes under the low glow.

"Okay." I don't push it. If she wants to go, whatever her reasons, I'm not going to stop her. I drag in a generous gulp of moist air and give Nick a nod.

Luca takes that as a yes and mounts the stairs. He's careful, placing one foot on the first slat and testing his weight on the board. It groans and whines under more weight than it's borne in nearly half a century. He pauses before giving it a little more. It holds, so he plants his other foot on the stair and does a little jump, his feet never leaving the stair. He twists around and turns the corners of his mouth down in an expression that says *seems safe*.

I mouth an *okay* before stepping forward. Luca turns and starts up the steps, weighing each riser for any weaknesses before putting his full weight down. Gabe follows. I place a gentle hand on the small of Ava's back and urge her to go up first. I want to be behind her just in case. I don't know what I hope to do, but just being there, in a position to help makes me feel better about her going up in the first place. She walks up to the first stair confidently and mounts it, which is more than I can say about how slowly my foot hits the first plank. It's embarrassing how frightened I am to make the simple move, but after a few seconds I push forward and start up the stairs. Nick follows after me with considerably less delay.

Other than the cracks and groans of protest from the wood, we make it up without event. The second level is exactly like the first from my vantage by Ava and to the rear of Gabe and Luca. A deep hallway veiled by the absolute absence of windows. A handful of doors hang open along each wall, each emitting a weak shade of gray into the corridor, but it's barely enough to be useful.

"It's damn creepy up here," Gabe whispers.

"And it wasn't downstairs?" Ava quips.

He doesn't answer. I don't blame him either.

"Let's just get this over with." Luca waves his flashlight toward the first set of doors set opposite each other along the hall.

Without any indication of agreement, we all go to work. Ava and I take the right door. We peer around the corner. It's almost a copy of the rooms downstairs. This one doesn't have a bed though.

Strange.

It really shouldn't be strange. What's strange is the lot of bedframes still sitting in so many of the rooms we've already canvassed. Why would they have left so much behind?

I lead Ava back into the hallway and start down the corridor again. We pass Nick and Gabe at the next door. He nods, and we move on to the following room. More of the same. It continues like this for minutes before the hall spills out into an open space where a little moonlight flows onto the floor.

If my sense of direction is right, we should be somewhere above the entrance downstairs, but this room is square, almost perfectly square. The walls are bare here, too, the paint peeling back to reveal cinderblock walls. It looks like a river of rust poured down the blocks, staining them in waves of iron oxide. A set of bleak metal chairs and a scattering of magazines are planted along the far wall. Breaking the same wall, another hallway opens to the east wing. To the left a door hangs open, leading off into the north wing.

We meander into the open space and spread out. Ava follows me toward the sagging door. Gabe stops at the windows set along the hospital's face and looks out over the entrance, then angles his face up at the stormy sky. The rain pelts the windows with little mercy. It pours over and between the cracked panes, making puddles on the floor before it snakes out a path down the center of the room and veers toward the east wing and then back again. It disappears through the open door along the north wing. I take a step beside the little river, my eyes following its growing current.

Ava settles next to me. The space beyond is bare. I raise my shoulders at Ava and move forward, unconsciously avoiding the tiny stream.

In the moonlight I catch an unusual pattern on the floor and crinkle my brow. A quarter circle is wiped clean of dust and debris. An obvious ridge rises along the circle's edge where grime has piled up, the result of opening and closing the door. I squint.

How the hell?

I crouch inside the semicircle and hover my fingers over the raised dust, following the curved line. My hand stops over a break in the dust and I cock my head to the side. I look a little closer and find several distinct divisions. My eyes light up.

Riley!

"Guys!" I yell. I throw my hands up and wave the others over, almost slapping Ava. "Guys! Look at this. I think someone's been here, like recently."

They jog over, losing any interest they had just moments ago in their own quests. I point at the wide semicircle of clean ground, then the dirt-ridden space around it, then to the breaks in the pattern near the end where it appears feet or possibly shoes pushed the dirt aside.

"See, I think someone came through here. I mean if no one has in what forty, fifty years or whatever, then this door shouldn't have moved, right? Even if it did, how did the dirt get moved like that?" I continue pointing. I don't realize it at first, but an exhilaration floods into my body. All the time we've been trekking about this island without the simplest sign of Riley, and then this.

"I mean, yeah." Luca shoves his shoulder past me and bends over the veil of dirt. At any other time, I would have felt like a complete fucking lunatic to be so excited by dirt, but this is different. "Someone...or something."

"Couldn't the wind have just pushed the door open? The windows aren't exactly all there, guys." Gabe turns on the balls of his feet and waves a hand toward the windows.

He's got a point. Even now I can feel the slightest breeze blowing through the broken panes. The water dribbles down what remains of the rotten wood frames and trickles onto the floor. I'm nearly certain the shoe-size interruptions in the dust were made by something else though.

"I can see what you're saying, Gabe, but the breaks are awfully abrupt, and look at the size," I tell him, my palm up as if explaining a natural geological formation to a college geology class. "They're just the right size for feet, for shoes."

"You think it was Riley?" Ava's eyes gain a bit of their brightness back, and it brings a smile to my face. I let my shoulders rise in an unsure but hopeful gesture. She's completely forgotten Gabe's suggestion already.

"Maybe. Hopefully," I say.

I look back at Gabe. He's contemplating my words too. I can tell he believes me but doesn't want to get his hopes up much either. I can sympathize.

"If there's any chance it's Riley, we need to check it out," Nick speaks up, standing erect again.

"Well, what are we waiting for then?" Gabe steps around Ava and stomps through the open door, unsettling the neat border. A plume of dust puffs under his feet and quickly settles before his other foot splashes in a gathering puddle of water.

I start after Gabe into the north wing. It's darker here. Only a sliver of moonlight sneaks past the doorway, and the lack of windows shrouds the hall in shadows. I raise my flashlight and let it paint the space in a white glow.

It's small, maybe eight feet wide and another twenty feet deep. The air is less musty, but the exposed concrete holds the same familiar rusty tint. It looks like someone came through after the occupants left and pulled all the wallpaper down, leaving it scattered along the perimeter of the room to be eaten away by time.

"Well, there aren't many choices, so this should be quick," I mutter.

Nick and Luca filter in behind and waste no time making their rounds. Nick has the first door open before I reach for one. I grasp the worn doorknob and give it twist. It creaks but gives. Ava leans against me, peering around me as my hand guides it forward. I move my light into the room as the deep groan of time-worn wood sounds behind me, accompanied by a loud crack.

I spin around, nearly throwing Ava against the door. The light of Luca's beam splashes over Gabe as the planks beneath his feet snap further and splinters of wood jut up around his ankles. My eyes widen as the floor beneath him gives way to decades of rot. Realization floods into Gabe's eyes. He tries to move, but his body plunges between the rupturing planks.

"Gabe!" I yell, instinctively taking a step forward before a hand wraps around my upper arm and pulls me back.

Gabe's scream fills the north wing as he plummets through the wood. In less time than it took the wood to break under his feet Gabe is gone, swallowed whole, and a thick thud echoes up the rabbit's hole.

"Gabe! Are you okay?" Luca calls over the hole, keeping his distance, but the look in his eyes says he's considering stepping forward.

"No, Luca." I wave him back.

Nick steps up and places a hand on Luca's forearm. "Let's take it easy, man."

I tilt my ear toward the hole, waiting. At first all is quiet, then the sound of something barely struggling rises over the patter of the rainwater. A grateful half-smile streaks across my face when a series of grunts and curses start to fly from downstairs.

"Agh... Fuck." The words are quiet and gravelly, but after

watching Gabe literally fall through the floor and land some ten to twelve feet below, they're welcome.

"You okay, Gabe?" Luca tries again.

I can hear him shuffling, the pop and clack of debris he's disturbing ringing back to us. We wait for his reply.

"Uh... I don't know. I can't *fucking* move, man." The words are more pained now. "I fell on something. *Motherfuck-er!*"

I meet my brother's eyes, asking without words what to do. He thins his lips and faces the broken mess of the floor.

"Just stay right there, Gabe, we're coming to you," he yells.

"Really?" Gabe groans. "Did you not...hear a damn thing I said? I *can't* fucking move."

I cock my head to the side and raise an eyebrow at Nick. He winces, probably wishing he could take it back, then shakes his head.

"Let's go, guys." He motions us back.

"We're coming, Gabe!" Luca yells before catching up to us.

With a sudden fear of the floor, we take off at a slow jog. Passing into the open space we take a right, our beams coating the hall walls in a bouncing white. We haven't made it five paces down the hall before a panicked scream shatters the air. I skid to a halt, my body tensing. Ava collides with my shoulder and I throw my arms around her. I hug her, gripping tight, unwilling to loosen my grip for a second.

"What the hell?" Nick cries.

It comes again, but this time Gabe's voice cuts out prematurely, replaced by a distant gurgling. *What the hell* is right.

"Go!" Luca urges with his free hand.

I get the message and burst forward, but not before gripping Ava's hand and pulling her along. We sprint forward, Gabe's scream expunging the caution in our feet.

Just before my foot hits the top step, another weaker scream reaches down the darkened hallway. I want to unhear the wretched noise, to block out the wail, but I can't. I keep moving, barreling down the stairs. They creak below my weight but hold. I pause long enough to let Ava's feet find the floor and start off again.

"Oh God!" Luca yells behind us as one of the lower planks collapses under his foot. He rebounds quickly and jets off the spiral staircase. "All good, keep going!"

We swivel around and bolt down the hall again. I nearly trip over what's left of some wooden chair set against the wall, but I manage to whip around it. My heart is beating like I've run a mile, and my breath comes in heavy gasps under the weight of the wet air.

We cross the length of the hall in under half a minute with Luca barely keeping up the rear. Nick takes a hard left and bursts into the promenade. He doesn't see the old moth-eaten hamper or cart as he makes for the north wing. His knee makes first contact. I reach out, but I'm not close enough, and he topples forward. His entire body lifts into the air and his thigh glances off the stout metal edge. A hard clang sounds under Nick's surprised yelp and the basket careens into my path, slapping against the bare floor. I slow quickly enough to avoid it, my eyes immediately finding Nick.

I grimace when his chin meets the floor with a smack, followed by his shoulder and the rest of him. I slide to a stop, almost losing my footing on a scattering of stones. Once my balance steadies, I reach down and place a careful hand on

Nick's back.

"You okay, man?" I ask, not bothering to hide the quiver in my voice.

"I'm good," Nick groans. He grits his teeth and winces as he gets his hands under his chest and pushes up to his knees.

I shine my beam on his face, and frown at the gash running under his lip and down his chin. A steady stream of crimson trickles from the cut. Nick shakes his head and squints. He touches his chin, wincing as his finger realizes the wound.

"You got a nasty gash there, man," I tell him.

He nods, raising a sarcastic brow. Well, at least he still has his sense of humor intact.

"You okay?" Luca hovers over him, but Nick waves him off.

"Gabe." He grunts and gets back to his feet, but he lets Luca lead the way this time.

I shake my head at him but follow anyway. Careful to mind my surroundings, I reach the threshold separating the promenade from the north wing's lower level. We sprint around the rows of chairs. I barely have time to stop when Nick abruptly puts on the brakes. Ava spills in behind me, screeching to an unexpected stop too.

I eye Nick for a moment before noticing the confused expression on his face. I crinkle my forehead and follow his gaze. The shattered wooden planks, the tattered ceiling tiles, and a piece of cloth jut from the ceiling. I guide my eyes down from the gaping hole and my mouth drops open.

"Where is he?" Ava asks.

He's not here.

It's a stupid thought, it's obvious, but it runs through my

head anyway. In the middle of the room, wood scraps and ceiling tiles pile atop broken benches. I could have taken it if he was just missing, but the splattering of blood across the dilapidated rows and thick smear of red leading over the wooden heap are just too much.

27: Helen Harrison

A streak of electricity cracks the night sky, coating Helen's face in pale white and smoky shadows. The ground shakes beneath her panicked stride as the thunder washes through the trees. Helen wipes the pelting rain from her face only for a hundred more drops to bathe her skin.

She's shaking. The terrified expression on Jaylen's face, the way his mouth gaped open in search of air, and his chest impaled on a set of monstrous claws strobe behind her eyes. Her legs pump instinctively, mud and rainwater splashing against her small calves and thighs with each footfall, her fists clenched tight, her lips forming a hard, flat line across her face.

"Slow down, Helen!" Grady yells a few yards behind. He's breathing hard, panting, his diet of bacon cheeseburgers and onion rings no match for Helen's lithe movements. "Come on! Slow down, dammit!"

Finally, his words get through to her, breaking past the shock and the panic. Helen shakes away the water draining over her face, but the sky doesn't waste any time retaking its ground. She glances over her shoulder and slows her pace enough for Grady to catch up.

"Are you okay?" Grady questions, while he struggles to regulate his breathing.

She doesn't respond. Instead, she returns her focus forward.

Another electrifying bolt streaks the sky, and the dark vanishes for a fleeting second, the thunder rumbling through them a second later. Grady ducks at the suddenness of the heavy clap, but he keeps moving. Helen doesn't seem to notice, her feet never losing their rhythm as they pound out a path they hope leads to the hospital.

Pushing back a branch, Helen dodges another tree, quickly regaining speed and pushing through the limbs. Grady follows her lead, stumbling clumsily with each step, but somehow managing to keep up. His face and arms are covered in tiny scratches and a handful of small bruises where limbs and thorns hit his body.

He pushes back the same branch but fails to see the next one. Its rough bark strikes his forehead and the skin splits under the pressure. Grady's feet continue forward, carrying his momentum, while his head slings backward. He yells as his body flops to the ground. His voice cuts out abruptly as his head and body strike the ground and the air in his lungs rushes to meet the rain.

Misery leaps up his spine behind a blinding white in his eyes. His lips form a gaping "o", a tiny scrap of a groan pushing past his strained windpipe. He blinks away the white and straightens his glasses. He arches his back, about to rub a sore patch of skin when he remembers why he was running. His eyes dart around the forest.

Where's my flashlight?

He throws his eyes to the muddy forest floor and searches for any sign of his only source of light. Claustrophobia builds in his chest the longer the dark holds him in its grasp.

"Fuck! Fuck!" He curses his luck, wiping a hand over his throbbing brow. "Dammit, that fucking hurts!"

Glancing right to left between the trees, he finally catches the lone streak of yellow-white glowing under a dense thicket several feet ahead. His eyes cling to the small beacon of light and he inhales a relieved breath.

"Come on, Grady, get your fat ass up." He slaps a palm against the cold, muddy soil and takes hold of the offending tree to his right. He pulls his body from the ground and closes his eyes just long enough to let the aching in his back settle and the dizziness to subside, then opens them again to a friendless forest. Trees. Branches. Bushes. Rain. Mud. But no Helen.

"Oh, come on," Grady moans. He swings his head back for a quick glimpse. There's nothing. "Helen!"

He listens hard, trying to catch the sound of Helen's feet splashing over the hammering rain. He stumbles forward, his shoes sinking in puddles along the sodden trail and digging into the mud. He glances at the flashlight a second time and huffs before calling out again, his voice cracking.

"Helen! Come on, Helen, don't do this."

He shakes his head, water spraying from his drenched beard, and makes for the flashlight. He swipes it from under the thicket and casts the beam in a wide arc.

"Come on, Helen," he whispers, his eyes searching the rain. Not sure which direction he had been heading, Grady grunts and starts forward, careful at first, but quickly loses caution to the cold sensation burrowing between his shoulders.

I can't leave her. Fuck that, Grady, she'd leave your ass in a heartbeat. I think she did. No, Grady, she doesn't realize you fell behind. That's all.

He stumbles over something small and hard but keeps his footing with a lucky hand on a nearby tree trunk. Rain streaks down the lenses of his thin frames, which light up a brilliant white before thunder shakes the ground under his feet.

"Dammit!" he yells, his grip tightening on the rough bark.

He exhales, willing his body to relax. He takes a step away from the tree and he's about to take off when something in the air causes his hair to stand on end. He freezes, air rushing between his lips in tiny spasms. For what feels like minutes he doesn't move, he just stands in the pouring rain. Something tells him that he's not alone. Finally, he cautiously turns his head to the left. Grady squints, trying to see past the deep veil of night and the thick wall of rainwater. Low, ragged breathing brushes past his ears. He steps back, never letting his eyes leave the darkness, but refuses to raise his flashlight.

"Maybe I'm imagining it," Grady whispers, throwing a hand behind his back, palm out, ready to intercept any incoming obstacle as he retreats. "Maybe it's all in my head. Yeah, it's all in my head."

He takes another step back. Under the rain's drumroll, the breathing carries between the branches and through the deluge. A bough crunches and Grady goes rigid.

It's in your head, man, it's in your fucking head.

A flash of white erases the blackness and thunder cracks through the rain. Grady's heart skips a beat as every detail around him comes into pristine, monochromatic detail. Puddles of water gather like tiny lakes where the wild grass doesn't grow. A briar patch connects a thicket of dense bushes and weeds to his right. Each raindrop seems to slow its suicidal descent like a slow-motion video. Hundreds of branches jut from trees in crooked knots and forks. Every detail is a frame for the creature lurking in the center of it all.

Before Grady can retreat, its thick, wet, fleshy arms flex under the lightning. Light fractures off the deep contours of firm sinew under its pale skin. Water streams down its arms and drips from fierce, dingy claws. Its entire body cranes forward, pec muscles flaring, shadowing solid naked thighs. As the light vanishes Grady catches the gleam of its oversized cat-like eyes between a pronounced nose and thin, almost non-existant, flaring lips.

The forest goes black, dropping a palpable veil between Grady and the beast. The flashlight beam rocks haphazardly along the wet puddles at Grady's feet, his eyes fixated on the dark. His mind screams to run, to turn around and race for anywhere but here, but his legs don't respond. He can feel them shaking, ready to buckle beneath his weight, but he can't make them move.

Another deep grumble breaks through the trees, carried along a gust of wind as it whips by Grady's neck. An icy chill slithers down his spine and pricks his fear into high gear. He yanks the flashlight up and bathes the forest in light. It shimmers off drenched leaves and the glossy trunks of a hundred trees, but there is no beast. A branch cracks behind him and Grady spins to face death. His heart sinks when something grabs his shoulder, but his mind kicks into action. He lashes out with the dark end of the flashlight.

"What the hell, Grady!" Helen screams, dodging under the impromptu weapon. "It's me!"

"Helen?" he mutters, his mind finally registering who it is, and the excitement spreads across his face. "Helen!"

"Yeah, it's me. Why'd you stop?" She grips his shoulders for a moment and then lets go of him.

"I fell," Grady tells her after a quick pause. "I saw it. I saw what killed Jaylen."

Helen's eyes widen, and she grips his shoulders in both hands.

"It's here?" Her voice trembles.

Before Grady can respond, a roar rises from the tree line. Its massive eyes flash through Grady's mind.

"Run!" Grady yells, not wasting any time. "Run!"

28: Cooper Bay

"Come on." Nick's words fall back to me as he takes off.

"Wait a minute, Nick!" Luca shouts, his back to the rust-saturated wall. He doesn't budge, and Nick comes to a stop. "Gabe's gone, man. Look at the blood."

I hate it, but I'm glad *he* said it. The wails of pain that cut through the dark and then the abrupt silence spoke volumes. Then this, the blood coating the splintered boards where Gabe had fallen, the sight of something small and meaty dangling from one of the sharp edges, and the smear of the blood trailing out of sight behind another doorway.

Gabe's dead. He has to be.

Brooklyn's broken body flashes before my eyes. Unbidden, I imagine the upper half of Gabe's body being dragged behind some crazed beast, ribbons of tattered flesh mingled with a mess of greasy pink entrails trailing the dirty floor. I blink away the vision and swallow back the bile building in my throat.

"You don't know that, Luca," Nick snaps back.

"Nick." I try, keeping my voice quiet. "Maybe Luca's —"

"We can't just let him die! Let's go!" Nick interrupts. He

takes off, but not before shooting me an angry glare.

I purse my lips, letting a quiet moan slip through. "Shit." Then I take off after him.

"Stop, Nick!" Luca yells, throwing a hand out as if he could stop my brother by the mere gesture. "Cooper! Don't."

"I'm not letting him go alone," I throw back without turning. I'm relieved to find Ava on my heels, but guilt rushes through my heart at the same time. "We have to stick together."

A few seconds later, I hear Luca's sneakers pounding the floor. I stay a couple feet behind Nick, shining my light over the blood trail past an empty doorway. I find what's left of the door leaning against the wall on the opposite side and move on down a small hallway. There's no natural light here, only the unsteady beams of our flashlights bouncing over sullen walls and long-dulled nameplates next to some of the doors.

Inside, Nick slows. I try to lock my eyes to the back of his head, focusing on the thick ruffles of unruly dark brown hair rather than the floor and the gore, but my eyes are drawn to death like a magnet. I'm astounded by the sheer volume of spilled blood painted along the floor, interrupted by Nick's shoe prints in the still-wet fluid. Luca's words scroll through my mind. *Gabe's gone, man.* And if I hadn't really believed it a few seconds ago, I do now. There's no way his heart could still be beating if he lost this much blood.

Twenty yards down, Nick slows at a set of stairs. He considers them for a second, but quickly mounts them. There must be a subterranean level. It strikes me as odd at first, but I push the scrutiny aside. After all, I once thought creatures with half-foot-long razor-sharp claws that like to rip apart human beings with their bare hands on deserted islands was crazy, too.

My eyes catch a patch of fresh blood dripping from the stair railing just before I grasp the decorative metal. I reel my hand back and curse under my breath. The stairs groan under my weight, but they hold. My feet hit the concrete again and I wait for Ava before taking off after Nick again.

When I turn I find Nick standing still, his gaze fixed on the floor. I slow, placing myself in front of Ava. I can only think of one reason Nick would have stopped. For a moment, I contemplate turning around and rushing back up the stairs. I don't want to see, I don't need to. I just need to believe this isn't happening, to be back in the city, or better yet home in Concord or Austin, I don't give a flying fuck which, just not here.

But I keep moving anyway.

"Nick." The name escapes my lips as a whisper, but he doesn't answer, not at first. I take another tentative step forward.

"Shit," Nick mutters, releasing the word over one long breath.

He turns to say something, but I already see it. It's not Gabe, or at least not all of him. Lying carelessly against the right wall is a leg. No body, just a leg. The foot, sheathed in the same Nike that Gabe was wearing, is propped against the slab of wooden molding along the base of the wall. The bare calf is slack with droplets of red speckling the pale white skin under my beam. My eyes travel past the shoe and ankle. I freeze on what remains of his thigh. I can see the muscles spewing from the stump, chunks of red and gray intermingled with torn flesh. The muscle and fat stretch inches beyond the stump, as if reaching out for the rest of Gabe's body.

"Shit," I repeat, taking an involuntary step back. My body knocks against Ava, and I turn to face her. I can tell that she's already seen it, so I place my hands on her waist and look into her eyes. She gives me a small nod.

"We need to get out of here," Luca speaks up. "This was a bad idea."

"Agreed." I have to push myself to say it. "Let's go, Nick."

He nods without complaint, the severed leg wiping clear any vain hope that had clouded his mind. I put a hand on his shoulder and give it a caring squeeze before turning and heading back in the other direction. I pass Luca and lead the way to the stairs. I use my free hand to steady my flashlight when I notice the beam shivering along the wall.

Calm down, Cooper. Get a hold of yourself.

My feet move quicker, retracing our steps back, using the red trail as guidance again. Unbidden, the image my mind conjured up earlier of Gabe's upper torso surfaces again, then it's suddenly replaced by Brooklyn's burrowed out chest cavity, the blood and the meat intermingled in a pool of black and red. I clamp my eyes shut, willing the images to flee, but they stay, like an unwelcome billboard along some city street. I push forward anyway, coming up on the steps.

I stop at the base and help Ava up to the first plank with a guiding hand on her back. I step up after her, trusting Nick and Luca to follow. The old wood moans under my weight, and I feel it bow, weakened by a combination of moisture, disuse and time. I take the next step, and then the next, following close behind Ava.

I'm a few steps from the top landing when I stumble into Ava, and almost lose my footing. I reach out and grab the railing, forcing a shriek from the metal bolts and rods. Ava reaches back and wraps her hand around my arm, squeezing tight.

I shift around her shoulder and immediately understand the problem.

Not a hair dots the back of its head and the skin draping its skull is sickly pale. Taut, pallid hide stretches over dense muscle in broad tracks down the creature's shoulders, rising and falling in valleys and hills before smoothing out just above its naked buttocks and thick crouched legs.

It looks so human, is my first thought, followed quickly by, *Oh fuck!*

My legs stiffen. My hand grips the railing with the ferocity of a great white clamping its jaw around a diver's cage. I think the others have stopped behind me or ran off, but I can't seem to pull my eyes from the beast standing in our path to verify which. Its claws clack against each other above the dull drum of the rain, each click sending a shiver up my back.

I'm shaken from my stupor by a gentle prod at my shoulder. I hadn't even noticed Ava angling her body, slowly coming about to retreat back down into the subterranean depths of the hospital. I take a gulp and pull my eyes away from the creature and focus on Ava. With my light aimed south I can barely see her, but I make out the movement of her lips to form one single word. *Move.*

It's stupid, but in that moment instead of turning and creeping down the stairs, my eyes stop on Ava. She shouldn't be here. She should be back on the mainland, safe in her museum or apartment.

I turn to move, but the board below my left foot moans in protest. I freeze and hold my breath. With my teeth clenched, I carefully lower my weight onto the old wood. It protests again, but quieter this time, so I take the next step. Nick and Luca are already at the bottom. They stand at the base with their beams illuminating the last few planks, worry etched over their faces. Nick's eyes twitch from corner to corner, keeping an eye out on the opening above and us at the same time.

I take another step, squinting and clenching my jaw when the plank creaks again. I stop, drag in a generous breath and bite my lip. My eyes dart from right to left as if in search of something to quiet the noise, but my only hope is to move. Nick waves me forward, urging me to continue, so I bob my head and descend to the next riser. I keep moving. Only three more to go.

Crack!

My body flinches as the brazen disturbance fills the hollow space like a tiny lightning strike. I twist to find Ava. There's guilt in her eyes above trembling lips. I lean an inch to my right, peeking behind her and my heart drops to depths I've never known. My eyes lock with its wide cat-like orbs, a cacophony of olive and umber around long, slit pupils.

A lifetime passes while I stare into its eyes, frozen in place, wanting to move but stilted by fear. Then it blinks, and I break from my stupor long enough to see its chest lean forward, the muscles under its massive thighs contract, and its claws ball into awkward blood-coated fists.

Without turning, I scream.

"Go! Go! Go!"

29: Helen Harrison

"Don't slow down, Grady!" Helen screams over the rain. Her feet stomp against the sodden soil, the soles of her shoes scrambling for purchase in the water, dirt and felled twigs.

Grady answers by leaning into the deluge and clumsily stumbling around another tree, still lagging behind. His heartbeat quickens, a combination of exercise and fear-driven panic. His mind is a far more chaotic place. Thoughts bounce around, pushing him forward and holding him back in the same instant.

What the hell is that thing? I can't keep running like this. My legs feel like they're about to give out. It looked almost human, but with something more, something bigger, something more menacing. Damn your extra fucking hundred pounds, Grady. I'll be damned before I have another fucking donut. I'll be fucking damned.

A thick stalk from one of the native shrubs grabs at his leg, but Grady tugs free. His shoulder skids over rough bark, and for a moment his sense of balance escapes him. He stumbles at a full sprint, his feet doing a dangerous dance to keep up with the rapidity in his uneven gait. He staggers, nearly erring too far to the left and straight against another towering trunk, before his brain and feet manage a coherent conversation and he regains his center of gravity.

A twig snaps someplace behind him. Then a larger crack breaks past the rain. It sounds like an entire tree trunk snapped this time. A new shiver climbs Grady's spine and the hair on his neck stands on end.

He keeps his eyes ahead, squinting away the droplets with increasing frequency, struggling through water-coated glasses past the darkness. He doesn't dare raise his beam from the ground inches from his toes. The dirt, low-lying shrubs, and weeds speed by under his feet. Puddles of water erupt under each step, soaking into the thin fabric of his old sneakers. He searches for Helen, catching only a glimpse of her bright yellow blouse, now a dingy soiled yellow, matted against her back.

A flash of light illuminates the woods, bathing everything in blinding white for a tenth of a second before a deafening boom shakes the ground under his feet. His body tenses, but he manages to keep moving, pushing between the trees and the thickets.

Keep moving, Grady. Keep going, he pushes himself, heaving for breath.

A moment later, the forest breaks. His eyes shoot up to a broad structure that stretches east and west until it disappears under the canopy of encroaching trees. They lord over the rooftop and snake their leafy, vined hands past windows and broken brick like the forest is reaching out to reclaim what belongs to it. It engulfs the entire left face of the building in a blanket of greenery.

Across a small road, Grady finds Helen mounting a long staircase up to a set of broken glass doors and he follows.

"Come on!" she yells back, stopping long enough to turn and wave him on.

Three long strides later, Helen throws out a hand and pushes through the door. Grady bursts in behind her a few seconds later, coming to a halt in the middle of a circular promenade and breaking the building's long-held silence with his labored breath.

"Is this the hospital?" Helen asks, starting to move again.

A roar tears through the air outside, slipping between the broken doors and missing windowpanes. It rips up Grady's spine and he locks his eyes with Helen. She cocks her head, tension fleeing through her exhale. Grady throws his eyes to the forest as the creature breaks past the tree line. Branches and twigs explode into the clearing, scattering over the service road lying parallel to the building. Helen clenches her jaw at the sight of its silhouette plunging over the road, its limbs flexing with each swing with the ease of a seasoned hunter.

"Don't know, don't care!" Grady mutters, backing away from the entry. He twists on the balls of his feet and takes off. "Move!"

Helen doesn't argue, instead she turns and takes off after Grady, her shoes clapping against the floor. The dirty peeling walls give way to more peeling wallpaper in the hall to the right. Her beam flashes by piles of stone and rock, a discarded newspaper, a handful of rotten wood planks, empty rooms, and fallen ceiling panels.

A cacophonous explosion reaches through the corridor, bearing the bad news. *It*, that creature, is inside.

Helen quickens her pace. Ahead, another hall forks off from the main corridor to the left. She considers taking it, but Grady doesn't seem to notice as he rushes by. With a scowl, Helen sticks with the camera operator, pressing against the urge to leave him and save her own hide.

As if the growing stomp of the creature's feet wasn't enough to remind her of the monstrosity that hunted them, a blood-curdling wail fills the space, echoing against the aging walls and deafening her temporarily. Helen keeps running, coming up on Grady's heels in a few quick strides.

She steals a glance into each room as they rush by. A small square of a space that couldn't be more than ten by ten, followed by another two, each identical to the last. A slightly larger room, she thinks, but in her hurry, she can't be sure. They won't do though. She knows battening down behind their decrepit walls and doors hanging off their hinges would give them maybe a few extra seconds of life at best, not even minutes or hours, before the beast breaks through the door and stabs its bloody claws clean through her forehead.

A car length ahead is a set of winding stairs, a dark replica of those in the nurses' dormitory. They appear to float at the end of the hall, each spiraling riser one step closer to disappearing into the floor and the ceiling above it. If it wasn't for the rust and mildew plaguing their surface they might even appear majestic, something out of another age, but instead the dingy, scarred metal and sagging planks cause Helen's stomach to droop in anticipation.

"Up?" Grady asks doubtfully over a hard breath.

"Up!" Helen screams and charges forward, mounting the first stair.

Her feet stamp on the squishy planks. They cry in protest, drooping under her step. Helen pops her feet into the air after each step like some hyped-up ballet dancer prancing up into the upper loft, letting the boards relax just before Grady takes them on. They moan and crack against his trespass, the boards beginning to loosen and rift.

"Don't stop," Helen warns as she scales the last step, nearly jumping to the upper platform.

She turns and glances around the downward spiral to find Grady struggling up the stairs, his mouth hanging open, chest heaving with coarse breaths. She reaches her hand out as a roar vibrates under her feet and the sound of crunching wood and creaking metal jolts her back a step. She recoils, crossing her arms until the sight of a nasty clawed hand swipes around the corner. It goes for Grady but misses his ankles by inches. Helen jumps forward and puts her hand out again.

"Come on, Grady!" She urges him forward, taking his hand and dragging him up the remaining three steps as the creature barges around the bend, its body clambering against the old railing with the grace of a drunken football player.

Grady's feet leave the stairs as the railing gives way. The creature swipes again, its body suspended in air for a brief second before it crashes against the wall. It fights for the next step, but the risers rupture with a splitting crack. It falls like a boulder dropped from the sky. Its thick arms and hands wrestle for leverage, its razor-like talons digging into the risers with an earsplitting shriek, burrowing deep, splintered trenches and splitting the boards outright. It falls and crashes into the stairs below.

"Let's go!" Helen pulls at Grady and releases his hand. "We need to hide, now!"

Grady bobs his head spastically.

They turn and jog down the hall. Grady bathes the corridor with white light, illuminating a hallway identical to the one below. Paint peels from the walls, and the floor is covered in debris from the ceiling and crumbling walls. How the building is still standing strikes Helen as a mystery.

The beast's distant wail mixes with a flurry of cracks and screeches. Helen slows her gait enough to avoid a fallen beam and a heap of ceiling panels, keeping an ear out for any sign of the beast just in case it finds a way up.

Pepping her step, Helen maneuvers down the hall. She checks her six for Grady. He's hanging behind, but he's there. They pass another small empty room, another death trap, and Helen crosses it off the list.

This has to be the hospital, Helen thinks. The building's so much larger than the others, and all the compact rooms would serve as perfect patient quarters.

Five doors down on the left and four on the right, Helen skids to a stop, her head craned back. She places a hand on the room's doorframe and pokes her face around the corner. It's another room, but it's at least four times the size of the others, maybe larger. It looks like an old office space. She swallows, quickly deciding it's their best option, and breaches the doorway without giving herself time to renege on the decision.

The room is bordered by a series of glass-doored offices surrounding a mess of short-walled partitions in the center. She stops to take it all in as Grady stomps in behind her. He slows to a trot and falls in line before the maze of cubicles. Each one reaches just below Grady's five-foot-seven forehead. They're built of thin, layered plywood and rusty screws. They must have been painted at one point, but now their faces give way to the flavescent goldenrod of damp wood.

The first cubicle is empty, a hollow representation of the work that used to go on within these walls. The second is empty, too. The outer offices are shielded by generous sheets of glass that punctuate their walls from the waist up, giving an open view of their office workers.

Helen moves on, prompted by a victorious scream down the hallway.

Oh God! It's made it up. The words explode in her head.

With new determination, she rushes forward and urges Grady to follow. They pass a third cubicle. A simple old corroded desk sits in the corner, small enough that even within the tiny square there is still room for a trash can or maybe a filing cabinet. They pass it by.

"We can hide in one of the offices," she whispers, nodding toward the glass-edged rooms. She keeps her feet light on the floor, stepping over a ceiling tile and heads for the first office on her right.

"What about there?" Grady nods in the opposite direction.

Helen follows his gaze and finds the cubicle with the desk. She looks at him, brow raised and questioning, as if to ask if he was crazy.

"Well, not there, but maybe on the other side. Maybe it won't search the whole room," he continues to whisper. "The offices just seem like an obvious choice. They're covered in glass."

Crooking her head to the side, Helen finds herself agreeing with her plump companion and nods before her lips catch up with her mind. "Okay."

He takes off around the corner, disappearing behind the moldy dividers. Helen runs after him, the sinking feeling in her stomach threatening to drag her to the floor. She comes around the bend and peers into the first cubicle. No Grady.

The thud of heavy footsteps resonates down the hall and into the office space along with the creature's raspy breaths.

Something crashes in the hallway, causing Helen to miss a step. She rebounds quickly, flashing her beam along the pale dividers. She wants to cover her ears as the creature scrapes the tip of its sharp talons over the wall.

"Grady," she whispers.

He pokes his head from behind the next cubicle and puts one long, reproving finger to his lips. Helen grins like a kid with her hand caught in the cookie jar and ducks into the little space. Grady gets on his hands and knees and crawls under the desk, dragging his hanging stomach across the bare wooden planks. Once underneath, he quietly lifts the edge of the small desk and tries to move it forward. A low growl slips in from the hallway. Helen grimaces and ducks even though the top of her head doesn't reach the full height of the cubicle walls.

On the floor, Grady eyes Helen expectantly, his lips moving, forming the words *help me*. Helen steps forward, still crouching, and grips the desk. She gives it a careful pull and the desk scrapes its solid base against the floor. Helen grits her teeth. It sounds so loud. Unwilling to let the noise continue, Helen lets the desk down and slips under the opening. She wedges in beside Grady, not caring that she's compressed against him in the tight space with only their feet showing under the gap where a chair once sat.

They douse their flashlights and Grady puts his finger to his lips again as if Helen would blurt out any second about the most recent movie rumors or move of the crown in the United Kingdom. She purses her lips, but otherwise ignores him. The footsteps cease, but the heavy breaths continue to torment the air. It's at the door, Helen's sure of it. It moves again. The old floor planks creak under its weight. Helen squirms, trying to cram her body closer to Grady, needing him in this moment.

The moans of the floor grow louder, closer, and for the first time Helen can smell it. It's rancid, the scent of something dead, of a corpse decayed by time and nature. She covers her nose and fastens her eyes shut as her mind conjures up the sight of a dead deer crumpled into a pile of flesh and bone on the side of the highway with a flock of vultures forming a faulty perimeter as they viciously gore their beaks into the poor animal.

Helen pins her legs tightly to her chest and hugs them like she held her daughters when they were toddlers. A thought curls into her brain as the shadow of a massive clawed hand wraps around the rotting cubicle. Suddenly, the urge to see her kids again is unbearable. It's been months since she saw Alannah, her oldest, separated by a whole continent while she works on her Masters at UCLA. Helen was supposed to see her this week, but this producer role opened up, an opportunity she couldn't miss, so she had told Alannah she would see her a week later. Ariana, the baby by three years at twenty-four, hadn't shown her face in New York City for at least a year, something about her dad. She wouldn't talk about it and Helen hadn't prodded. Even fourteen years after their divorce, the bad blood ran deep. Maybe Ariana couldn't see it, but Richard Randall was a special type of low-life, a cheat.

The sight of its sharp claws brings Helen back to reality. She constricts every muscle in her body, trying to still herself from the shakes. Gradually, the rest of the creature slips across the opening, only a dark silhouette against a charcoal background. She can't tell if it's looking at her, at the desk, the wall, the floor. It's just a shape. But it stands there like it knows she's crouched behind the desk, like it can smell the fear running through her veins. Helen bites her trembling lips, grimacing at the horrid smell radiating off the creature's body.

Puffs of moist, acrid air bathe her face and arms, but she refuses to move. It's looking right at her, its maw inches from her face, probably dripping gelatinous saliva and blood. She clenches her fists against her mouth and snaps her eyes shut as if doing such might guard against the horrible smell and prevent it from clamping its teeth around her head. Her body trembles as she waits for death to come as a vice grip around her head or a stake through her heart. But death doesn't come. Its shape pulls back and its claws scrape against the cubicle wall.

Helen holds her position, refusing to move even an inch, both sure it would do no good to move and the will to do so gone. She waits for the piercing of claws, the sinking of teeth into her neck, for death. Instead, the creature's feet thud farther away.

When she opens her eyes, it's gone. She can hear it stop at the neighboring cubicle to glance inside, then the next, the sound of its dank exhales rolling over the short walls. It keeps moving, its footfalls growing quieter as it moves and finally exits the room, giving up on its prey.

Helen releases a pent-up breath, mouth wide, letting it rush from her lungs and then inhaling in quick spasms. Beside her, Grady does the same. She watches the barely visible Adam's apple in his throat move up and then back into place.

"I don't want to die here." The words squeeze past Helen's lips, her eyes set straight forward into the black.

"What?" Grady whispers, turning to look at the gray silhouette that defines Helen's form. He shuffles to make a little room, still not quite ready to leave.

"I don't want to die here," she repeats, blinking finally, a little louder and more of herself present in the words. "I don't—"

"You're not going to die, Helen," he starts, trying to think of something to say, some consoling half truth or one of those glossed-over fairy tales people tell each other when they know they're fucked. "All we have to do is get to the docks, send for help."

The fact that Helen had wanted to do just that only hours ago, that she had begged to leave, to let the authorities figure it out, doesn't cross her mind. Instead, she sees Alannah and Ariana playing together just off the back patio at one of the rental cabins overlooking the Adirondack Mountains that she and Richard frequented during summers in upstate New York. Alannah is ten, with her shoulder-length golden brown hair and bright pink dress, and Ariana is seven, complete with pigtails and flowers. She remembers thinking how perfect it all was, how much she wanted to keep it like this, to bottle it up and take it with her. Little did her girls know that the next two years would be a bitter war of custody.

"Ariana hates me," she tells Grady.

"Who? What?"

"Ariana, my daughter. She hates me." Helen stares into oblivion.

"No... She... Now isn't the time to go all sentimental on me, Helen," Grady tries. He doesn't know what to say, and he desperately needs her to be mentally present. "I don't know your family issues, and frankly right now I don't care. But if you want to see your daughter again, we have to get out of here."

He grabs her by the shoulder and gives her a shake. Helen stifles a frightened yelp and blinks away the glossy look in her eyes, mouth still parted and scared.

"I'm sorry, I'm just..." she tries. "I don't know. This shit is just really fucked up. I mean what is that thing? A monster? A yeti, Bigfoot? I don't even know what the hell to call it."

"I know, it's really shitty, but we've got this far. We can get out of here. Maybe Nick and the others are here," Grady offers. He hopes they are, letting his mind skip over the less enticing possibility. "We still need to find them before we go back to the dock."

Helen doesn't speak right away. The blackness burrows its way into the conversation, staring back at her from every direction, as if to say *accept it, this is your new home. Welcome to death.*

"Helen?"

"Yeah, yeah, I know." She nods spasmodically, wanting to flip on her flashlight and wash away the overwhelming darkness. "Do we even know where we are? Is this the hospital?"

"I think..." Grady's words trail off into the rain. "We started off in the right direction, but I couldn't keep my bearings. I just wanted to get away from *it*, you know. I mean, I think we are though."

We should just leave. Run for the docks and send back help. The thought runs through Helen's mind. *That thing is in here. We don't need to be traipsing around in here on some half-assed rescue mission. But what if something happens to them while we're gone? Can I live with that?*

"I think it left, Helen," Grady says a long minute later. "We should go."

"Okay." She doesn't argue, shifting her weight and lifting

her legs into a crouch. Using the desk, she stands up. Her mind is in a battle of choices. To stay or to leave, that is the question. Nothing so eloquent or profound as the opening lines of Hamlet's act three, but just as poignant to Helen.

Before she can nail down a choice, Grady grasps for her hand and tugs her from her stupor. They crawl over the desk, causing a tiny screech from its aged feet, and past the cubicle walls. Grady stops for a moment, face down, listening. With the footsteps continuing to grow quieter, he starts moving again, pulling Helen along. She doesn't resist, though on any other occasion she would have quickly recoiled her hand and lectured him for thinking she needed a man to help her. Instead, she follows, keeping her head below the top of the cubicle and allowing her free hand to glide over the divider's rough wooden walls to try to make sense of her location.

Quicker than expected, her fingers lose the wall and fall into the unoccupied air. For a moment she reaches aimlessly, hoping for some object to guide her. A second later she catches something solid. The next divider, another rough wooden half wall like the three before it.

If I've got this right, this is the last one.

Confirming her thought, Grady comes to a halt, stiffening his hand to stop her from colliding into his back. He leans around the corner and finds the door leading to the hallway, and the only sign of light in the room. It seems to fall past the doorway, painting a skewed gray trapezoid along the floor. He bobs his head, trying to psych himself up to leave their perch behind the abandoned workspace.

"All right," Grady whispers to himself, and marches around the corner. In nine strides they reach the door and pause. "You ready?"

"Uh... Yeah, I mean, we're not making a run for it, are we?" Helen asks, confused. She pulls her arms back. *Why the hell would he ask it like that?*

"No," Grady stutters. "I just wanted to be sure you were ready."

"Oh okay. Yeah."

"Let's go." He steps around the bend and angles away from the stairs, moving deeper into the building's interior.

Without the illuminating beams of their flashlights guiding the way, only dim patches of light illuminate the corridor. Every few yards, faint slits of moonlight sift in from the bordering rooms along the back of the structure.

"We should go downstairs. I highly doubt the others will be up here, considering our luck with stairs on this shitty island," Helen whispers.

"Good point." He nods, shifting his eyes from one edge of the small corridor to the other. "Just gotta find some stairs first."

Helen sidesteps a small heap of fragmented stones and dust. The air is stale, and the hum of the rain has grown louder. Under any other circumstance, it would be relaxing.

They pass a handful of doors, each opening into what appear to be small boarding rooms or offices, and then they reach another wide-open space. They keep moving.

The further they walk the more the air thickens with moisture. A subtle stink reaches her nose. She flares her nostrils and coughs into her sleeve.

"Do you not smell that?" Helen asks.

"Smell what?"

"Obviously not," she whispers, rolling her eyes.

"Haven't been able to smell well since middle school. Bad

allergies and all. Doctors called it hyposmia or something."
Grady twists around and grins at Helen. "It's just fancy for I
can't smell shit."

"Well, right now you might be fortunate because this
doesn't smell much better." She tries to grin through her
scowl.

Then her eyes open in fright. The smell. She swallows
hard, wondering how she could so quickly forget that rancid
odor in the dark, that violent stink when the creature breathed
in her face. She plants her feet and reaches for Grady. Her
hand grabs at his arm and squeezes. He stops and eyes her
but doesn't utter a word as he sees the terror in her bright
green eyes, dulled under the low light. Grady grits his teeth
and cautiously turns his face back down the hall, staring into
the long-abandoned area with its failing wallpaper and crumbling beams.

A tiny crack jumps through the dark up ahead. A tingling
current spikes up Grady's spine, causing the hair on his neck
to stand on end. He freezes. Helen's grasp tightens, and she
tugs at his arm. He doesn't move.

Another crack breaks over the rain. Helen's eyes dart to
the open doorway leading into a room at their right only feet
away. The noise comes again, like something cracking under a
heavy weight, and a low grumble rolls into the hall. Helen
stumbles back, pulling Grady with her.

A cloud of hot, wet breath hits Helen's nostrils with the
scent of death and rot. She winces and opens her eyes to a
tormented face coming around the doorframe. It lumbers into
the hallway, lacking haste as its nostrils snarl and its deep
brown eyes pierce into her soul. Its chest bulges above a hard
stomach and thick, steroidal thighs under sickly gray skin. It

stands at least a foot, maybe more, above Helen and Grady, like something out of a comic book, minus the playful and comical fantasy of its two-dimensional brethren.

Helen shrinks back, lowering her head into her neck, struck with the queer feeling that it looks human.

She tugs at Grady again, trying to pull him back, wanting to leave but unwilling to move on her own. He staggers back an inch but stops, entranced by the creature's piercing eyes, those black slits against a dark brown. It roars, the force of a tiger on the prowl in its cry.

That does it. Grady snaps from his trance and takes off down the hall with Helen on his heels.

"Go, go, go, go!" he yells.

Helen feels a rush of air sweep across her back as her feet hit the floor, one after the other in quick succession. With stealth no longer in the game plan, Helen flips on her beam and flees down the corridor. Doors flash by. The floor seems to reach up for her, tripping her, but she manages to keep her balance. Another roar screams past her and the horrible odor overtakes her. For every step she takes, another pounds the floor behind her, reaching out for her, seeking her throat, her blood, her life.

Ahead, the staircase comes into view. Helen pushes forward.

Grady skids to a halt a foot before the stairs and his eyes shoot back to Helen, worried. It takes her only a second to see the problem. They're gone. Except for the planks rising to the next floor, the stairs are gone. Where they used to be, a handful of wooden shards jut from the metal railing, the rest likely piled in a heap beyond the black abyss. Lacking the luxury of time, Helen reaches for the rails.

"Up. We have to go up!" she yells back. "Come on!"

She pulls at the metal, and crawls onto the first intact riser before turning to give Grady a hand. His fingers brush against hers as the creature's bulbous hand snaps forward, wrapping its palm around Grady's waist, lacing his stomach in dingy gray claws.

"Grady!" Helen yells, but it's too late.

Its grip tightens, as if in reflex to Helen's voice. Its claws disappear in a gush of scarlet and Helen's face goes pale. She reaches out with a trembling hand, eyes locked on Grady's scared blue ones. Her attention is wrenched away when Grady's head jerks back. Helen's mouth drops open as the creature digs its teeth into Grady's skull and clenches its fist, spilling more blood from Grady's stomach.

"No!" Helen screams, the word trailing on for seconds.

In reply, every muscle in its arms contracts and heaves, pulling Grady away. He screams for a second, but the noise quickly turns into a gurgled moan as his eyes roll back in their sockets, the pain too much.

"No!" Helen cries again as Grady's arm is wrenched from her grasp. She falls to her ass. The stairs shimmy under the impact and groan in protest. Her hands go flat against the riser, eyes wide with new terror.

A new sound escapes Grady's open mouth. It comes out like a scratchy breath. It's indecipherable, but Helen understands the cry. A dying man's last call for help. Shaking, Helen slides her butt to the next riser, hating herself for leaving Grady but needing to put distance between her and that thing.

Its arms flex again, but this time Grady's body offers little resistance. Helen watches in horror as Grady's shirt tears and its claws sink into his skin. She shrieks, watching the skin stretch. Pulled past its limit, his flesh ruptures along a jagged line, revealing a grotesque mix of yellow, gray and red. She scoots back, throwing her face to the side as her stomach churns when something long and glistening drops from Grady's side and bobs against his leg. Helen's whole body quakes, bile rising in her throat. She stands, throwing her face over the edge of the railing and vomits into the black hole beneath her.

The stairs begin to shake as she wretches. She jerks back, trying to steady them, but it's no use. The plank she's standing on gives way and her body drops. Her stomach rises in her throat and weightlessness takes over for a brief second. She throws out her arms aimlessly, begging for something solid. Before the dark can ingest her, her arms hook another riser. It sags dangerously under the abrupt impact, but she curls her arms around the board and refuses to let go.

Engulfed in a thick veil of blackness, Helen heaves her chest atop the board. The spongy plank feels like a spring under her elbows, but the rabid howl and the tearing of skin from bone behind her, drives her upward. She throws her leg onto the board, gritting her teeth to stave back the panic and adrenaline pumping through her veins. She reaches blindly, swinging her hand in the void, hoping for something, anything, to tow her away from death. Her hand brushes against rough, worn wood, but a series of loud cracks split the darkness.

Before her mind can catch up, the stair falls away from her knees and a sense of weightlessness overtakes her again as her stomach lifts into her chest. She screams, her limbs flailing in the air, begging for purchase but finding only air. A howl of primal rage blends into her own shriek and the sound of wood crashing beneath her. Then, without warning, her calves and knees collide with an unforgiving foundation and the fractured remnants of the stairs. Her body topples, given over to the laws of gravity. A screech bursts from deep within her as the she crumples to the floor, wood and metal crashing down on her.

"*Ugh!*"

Helen tries to move, but sharp pangs of electricity seize her leg. She freezes, mouth wide, tiny pained breaths spurting between her gaping lips. Helen clenches her fists and seals her eyes. Debris falls off her back, clanking to the floor. She lifts her head and peers into the dark space above, her body quivering. A frenzied wail chases her down the broken staircase.

Move, Helen!

30: Cooper Bay

The air is thick and moist as I plunge forward, pushing Ava to move faster, but my own heart outpaces my feet. It thuds against its mortal cage in anticipation of the beast's clawed hands.

Behind us, the stairs crack. An ensemble of creaks, moans and groans join in as the wooden planks fail under the creature's careless gait.

Ava's pace slows, and she steals a look back.

"Don't slow down!" I shout.

Unfortunately, I don't need to look back. Its cat-like eyes are branded into my mind, its thick frame outlined in bulging muscles, its threatening claws curving from each fingertip. It gives me the slightest pleasure, amidst the fear pumping through my veins, to imagine it falling through the weakened planks and smacking against an unwelcoming concrete floor. But any glee I feel is quickly extinguished by an irate, almost jungle cat-like roar.

It didn't fall through the stairs.

Dammit.

My beam flashes past Gabe's threadbare stump propped along the wall. I dart my eyes away and swallow back the disgust between breaths. It's not hot in this subterranean corridor, it may even be cool because of the rain, but sweat drips down my forehead. I keep my eyes up and my flashlight beam focused down the center of the hall.

"Maybe we can make it up the opposite end," Luca yells between heaving breaths. "There must be more stairs."

No one answers. I keep my mouth shut and focus on expelling the air from my lungs and dragging in new gulps. I'm already winded, but I know I can do this. I shouldn't be out of breath already, so I spur myself into a breathing cadence. At first I can't concentrate, not with the sound of that thing bearing down on me. It can't be more than twenty yards back now. I blow out one hard breath and then set my lungs into a rhythm.

Over three strides I draw in a single ample breath and then let it out over the next three, and repeat. I angle my chest into my sprint and tap Ava's back, urging her to quicken her pace. The creature is gaining on us. Its roars grow louder between each thunderous footstep.

"Go right!" Nick yells to Luca, flinging his arm out and pointing toward a fork in the hall ahead.

My eyes twitch from left to right, wondering where each goes. Does one lead back upstairs? Is it the right or left hall? Maybe one leads outside, a straight shot into the rain and back into the woods. I envision bursting through doors, and the four of us making a run through the forest and then sprinting for the dock. A second later I lean to the side, less than a stride behind Ava and take the right fork.

"Go back! Go back!" Luca is screaming. His beam blares in my face, and I squint against the glare. I throw up my hands and almost lose my flashlight. When I open my eyes again, he's less than a foot away and his shoulder comes within an inch of clipping me as he barrels by. "There's another one!"

Ava twists gracefully on her toes, like a ballerina, and faces me before taking off. She's confused, and so am I. *Another? What the hell?*

In answer, a distinct roar bellows from the darkness and the rain-drenched form of the other beast materializes from the shadows. My entire body tenses, but I'm quick on my feet this time. I sweep around and race after the others.

There are two of them. There are fucking two of them!

I bear to the right, bolting down the fork we'd thought better than to take earlier, and lean into the stale air. The hall is filled with a mix of grumbling roars and high-pitched howls. They echo off the walls, drowning the sound of our feet pounding against the floor. I scrunch my nose as the smell of death rushes my nostrils. It grows heavier with each step.

What the hell?

Encased in the bounce of my light, Nick diverts to the right edge of the hall and I barely have time to notice Luca drop to the floor. I leap, the tip of my shoes grazing his back. My shoes smack the concrete and my legs wobble under the pressure. I lock my legs and skid to a stop. As quick as I can manage, I swivel around and bring my light about.

It bathes Luca in bright yellow, his body sprawled over the concrete. I dart my eyes past him. The hulking forms of our trackers are yards out. My legs, arms, every muscle in my body constricts at the sight of their ravenous eyes.

They're coming for us.

Nick barrels by, screaming something I don't register, but it's enough. I wrench my eyes away and bound forward. My arms reach for Luca. The pounding of the creatures' feet and the horrendous noises bursting from their maws are like magnets, drawing my attention. I try to focus on Luca, but my eyes dash between the director and the beasts. They're closing in, no more than ten yards now. Luca struggles to his feet and gives us a nod. He must have slipped on something, but I don't really give a fuck right now. Without second-guessing his state of being, I turn and run.

One of the creatures roars. The sound is deafening at this range. I throw my hands up to my ears and wince. That smell, an acrid mixture of rotting flesh, festering wounds and dank, mildew-infested wood is almost palpable now. My eyes shoot wide and I can only imagine how pale my face is as two words punch through my mind's walls of self-preservation.

Slaughterhouse. Oh fuck! No, Cooper, calm it down.

We keep running. The howls and snarls are coming more frequently now, and I swear I can feel their hot breath billow over my back. I dare a quick glance back, but all I make out is the glare of Luca's beam set against a black canvas.

"In here!" Ava yells back.

I snap my attention forward and find a lone door at the end of hall. Another room, but no outlet. It's a dead end. A dead fucking end. With only one option left, I lean forward and will my legs to pump harder. In four long strides I slide to a halt a few feet inside the room. Nick skids to a stop a second later, and I immediately check for Ava. She's to my left, eyes locked on the bumbling white beam from Luca's flashlight.

"Come on, Luca!" Nick screams.

"Quicker, Luca, run!" I join in.

He's hurt. His legs buckle slightly with each step, but he's moving.

We need to shut the door!

My eyes finally adjust to the glaring beam and find the two massive silhouettes hanging behind Luca. He's only a few yards from the door.

"Come on!" Nick casts his voice down the hall, his fingers clinging to the doorframe, probably thinking about dashing down the hall and helping his friend.

I stand on the opposite edge with my hand wrapped around the edge of the door, ready to slam it shut the moment Luca clears the threshold. My heart is racing. I turn back to Ava.

"Get back!" I tell her, needing her to be okay. The deeper she moves into the room, the safer I feel.

I don't know if she moves because in the same moment an ear-splitting scream bursts from Luca's lungs. I jerk around as his chin smacks the concrete at my feet. I look up and all the color in my face flees at the sight of the creature's face hanging feet from my nose. I retreat a step, but quickly jump back to grab the door. Nick is pulling at Luca's arms, but he isn't moving. My mouth droops when my eyes find the set of scythe-like claws dug in between Luca's shoulder blades.

"Help!" Luca shrieks, trying to angle his head up despite the weight of the beast on his back. "Help me!"

A rabid howl escapes the creature's maw. Its breath is rancid, a deeper reflection of the slaughterhouse smell. The same smell that clung to Brooklyn's body and what was left of the man upstairs.

"Luca!" Nick screams, his voice tainted.

I reach down, forsaking the wooden door, and wrap my hands under Luca's armpit, putting fear in the back seat. I hoist him back but instead of pulling him farther into the room, I find my body jerked forward. A clawed hand swipes out at me, but it comes up an inch short, pawing at the air. Time slows as the dingy gray claws pass my nose. I swear they're each at least half a foot long, covered in a tawny glaze like unwashed teeth. I reel back, but I keep my grip on Luca.

He mumbles something, but I can't make out the words, as another set of claws pierce his lower back. The hooks under his shoulder suddenly rip out, cleaving chunks of meaty flesh. Blood drips from the tattered bits onto Luca's shirt. Then the onslaught begins. Ignoring Nick and me, the beasts begin to stab their talons into Luca's body, again and again.

"Pull him in!" Ava screams, her voice like a screeching siren.

I plant my feet against the doorframe and lean back, towing back with every ounce of strength I can muster. He's screaming, begging us to save him, to free him. I don't know what to do, so I slide to my ass and fix my feet against the doorframe and tug. My calves burn and my arms ache under the tension.

The creature roars again, but I barely hear it as meat and blood fly without direction, coating the room. A splatter of thick crimson paints my chest, neck and stains my left cheek. I want to throw my hands to my face, to wipe frantically at the thick mess on my skin, but I don't let go.

In the background something scrapes against the ground, a dull grind under the sound of the ravenous growls, labored breaths, screaming, the ripping and twisting of skin and my own heartbeat. I look back, expecting to see another beast hovering behind Ava. Instead, I find her flashlight focused on a lone bookcase that reaches to the ceiling and spans at least six feet. Looking back to Luca, I grip him tighter and then glance at the bookcase quickly. It's moving.

What the hell?

"It's a doorway!" Ava yells. There's a tinge of hopefulness

in her voice.

"What?" Nick calls back, only now turning to see.

"A doorway!" she shouts again as the bookcase grinds to a halt, revealing a solid metal door.

It looks like a bank vault. Ava's light reflects off its surface and bounces over the nearby wall. She steps toward the door as I tighten my grip on Luca and pull harder.

A broken groan from Luca pulls my attention back to the chaos reigning at our doorstep. He crooks his neck upward with his last bit of strength, trying to find Nick. But his eyes go hollow, as if his soul had decided it had enough. His body goes limp and his face drops like a leaden ball, slamming against the concrete with an unceremonious crack. Without thinking twice, I let go of Luca's flaccid body and skid back on my butt. My hands are shaking, and I swallow absently.

"Come on! Let's go!" Ava yells at us.

I turn, eyes wide, trying to process what just happened, that a man just died in my arms. My friend, however recent it might have been. A person. I see everything playing out before me, but I don't really see it. A haze of something heavy and daunting hangs over my mind. I swallow back the bile building at the base of my throat.

"Come on!" Ava yells again.

I blink and snap my head around to find her. Gruff growls and voracious howls barrage my senses, but like everything else it just bounces off the haze. I feel numb. Ava is waving for us to come, standing by the now open vault. Her mouth is moving. I can hear her, but her words are muted and distant.

"Cooper!" she yells again, snapping me back to reality.

"I'm coming," I mumble and get to my feet. I make it to

the door and signal her to go ahead. As she starts through the doorway, I turn to look for Nick. He's still pulling at Luca. Does he even realize Luca's dead?

Completely ignoring my brother, the beasts are still tearing at Luca's corpse. I find it odd that they don't seem the least bit interested in Nick. Then I catch a tear streaming down his cheek. I grimace, horrified to step toward the creatures, but I jump forward anyway and grip Nick's shoulder.

"We have to go, Nick." I try to sound understanding, considerate, but it comes out abrupt and hurried. I dodge a clawed hand but refuse to lose my grip. "Come on, man. He's gone."

At first, I think he's going to say something, try to explain why he must stay, but he doesn't. He falls back to his butt and drops Luca's arm. I cringe when it smacks against the concrete and his body is dragged into the hallway. Nick's eyes are distant as he watches Luca's body shredded and torn. Finally, he rises to his feet. I pull back, not wanting to stand this close to the two beasts and the dead. Before he can take a step, I see a beefy clawed hand arch through the air at Nick. I pull him forward and shove him toward the vault door. He topples forward, catching himself as I stumble after him.

Every muscle in my body tightens as the first claw finds my skin and breaks the surface under my shoulder. Before my brain has time to process the pain, two more claws slice into my flesh. I jerk forward as they burrow through my skin, carving three distinct canyons down my back. My mouth springs wide, but noise refuses to break the invisible barrier between my teeth. I'm about to crumple to the ground when Nick yanks me up. I wince, a thick moan finally exiting my lips, as he pulls me forward.

Ava's next to me, her eyes imploring, analyzing me. She cranes her neck to inspect my back as Nick pulls me past the vault-like door. A pained expression crosses her lips and her eyes flinch away, finding me again as we run.

"You're going to be fine," she tells me, lacing her fingers between mine.

Despite the pain, a thread of joy needles its way between the electricity spiking through the nerves in my back.

She came back for me. She left the safety of whatever lies behind the vault door to be sure I was okay. She came back.

"Let's move!" I hear Ava yell at point blank range as my eyes finally registered where we are. It's a totally different world.

31: Cooper Bay

I lose my footing on the polished white floor, but my hand catches the wall. The ravenous growls and sickening rip of claws through Luca's body disappear as the door grinds shut. The hard clank of successive metal locks clap into the thick wall and then disappear into total silence.

We stop. Nick first, then me, followed by Ava when I give her hand a tug. I turn, my eyes exploring the new landscape. Everything about the place is the antithesis of the hospital and this whole damn island. The walls and ceiling match the pure white under our feet, with the addition of a subtle granular texture and lack of polish. Light glows over the corridor from two sets of never-ending recessed fluorescent bulbs at the edges of the ceiling. A two-foot brushed metallic panel lines the length of the hall on both sides at waist level. It's all so sanitary.

I squint, letting my eyes grow accustomed to the light. As everything comes into focus, my eyes find the door that now separates us from those creatures. It looks much the same on this end, silvery metallic with an air of indestructibility, like a bank vault.

"Thank God," I mutter between breaths. The sight of the bulky door, sealed shut and solid, injects a sensation of ease into my mind. I smile and swing my gaze between Nick and

Ava. I'm sure my eyes say it all.

Nick grunts, his hands propped on his bent knees, trying to get his breath back.

A laugh escapes my lips. I don't know why I'm laughing, but I can't seem to help it. Maybe it's Nick looking like he just ran a marathon, which he basically did, or the sudden shift in scenery, or that we just escaped death. I don't know. But I'm laughing. Nick grins and slaps me on the forearm.

I glance at Ava. The edges of her mouth rise and her brilliant blues shimmer under the light. I'm about to speak when the adrenaline high wears off and the agony in my back begins to build. I grit my teeth and force a smile. A sob pulls my attention away. I turn to a tear riding down the slope of Nick's cheek. He's staring at the floor, all signs of the excitement behind his former smile gone. He steps back and plants his butt against the wall. His hands begin to tremble as he drops his face toward the floor. His knees shudder and then go limp. He slips down the wall, burying his face in the palms of his hands. I kneel beside him.

"Nick," I start, but struggle to find the right words and the air to push through from my lungs. I've never been the type that knows what to say when things are tough, and it feels awful to be so useless when Nick's hurting. I look to Ava, hoping she's a better person than me. She steps around Nick and puts a hand on my shoulder, as if to say *I've got this*. She rests her other hand on Nick's arm. She doesn't say anything. Maybe that's all right. I feel like I need to say something though.

"Man, you did everything you could. It's… uh…"

I want to tell him it's all going to be okay, but I can't do it. It's a lie, it's a *motherfucking* lie, and I know it. There is nothing *okay* about what happened to Luca or the others. None of it's okay. Not Brooklyn, Gabe, Luca or Riley. They came here to act and to film, to have a good time and entertain, not to have their bodies torn apart like paper dolls. The sight of Brook's dismembered corpse and Gabe's leg flash through my head, tainting the clean white of this pristine hallway. In my mind, a slow falling waterfall of blood overlays the bleached walls.

Fucking dead.

"Luca..." The name croaks through Nick's vocal chords, and his body shakes. "Why?"

"You did all you could," I say again, unable to find anything else to comfort my brother with. I close my eyes, barely holding back my own tears.

A minute passes and Nick's tears wane. He lifts his head. The skin under his eyes is stained a wet purplish-black and the whites of his eyes are streaked with veiny red lines. It hurts to see him like this. I hate that I don't know how to help. He's always there for me, but I can't even think of a damned word to say when he needs it.

Nick nods at me and his mouth trades its downward slant for a flat line. I give him a sad grin and exhale a hard breath. Suddenly the lightning shooting through my back erupts, and my body goes erect, a hard scowl embedded over my face, my mind temporarily forgetting about Nick. I arch my back to alleviate the fire burning under my skin, but the flames keep licking at my muscles. I twist, trying to see the scratches, but I can't turn far enough, limited both by nature's built-in safety to keep me from breaking my neck and the sensation of the meat in my open wound tearing.

"How bad is it?" I ask Ava, letting my head bound back. Streaks of lightning shoot up and down my back. I want to scream, but I hold back and grind a gravelly groan through my clenched teeth.

"It's..." Ava shimmies over and peers around me. She scowls, her eyes uneasy. "It's not good."

It definitely doesn't feel good.

"You've got three...uh...three cuts. They're not too deep, but they're not exactly shallow either." I can feel the pain in her words, as if it hurts her, too.

I imagine how I must look, the back of my shirt shredded, probably coated in blood. The three gashes running down my back like it was trying to mark me. I'm glad I can't see.

"Where are we?" Nick asks, the quiver in his voice only a faint shadow now as he huddles over me.

I shift my feet, scanning the hall, and face away from the vault door. The hall ends abruptly at an intersection that continues in more white and brushed metal. Corridors shoot off in both directions. The walls are uninterrupted by doors or windows. I have to remind myself that we're underground, but that only prompts an overwhelming sense of claustrophobia. I take a deep breath and release it, trying to move past the panic.

"I don't know, but it sure as hell looks better than out there."

"Definitely," Ava agrees, her eyes taking in the hallway too.

"And I doubt those things are going to be getting through *that* door any time soon," I add, struggling to ignore the pain in my back.

"So what do we do now?" Ava asks. Her eyes are on me.

The realization that she's looking to me for an answer comes down hard on my shoulders. She's a strong girl, I know it. Underneath her gentle curves and stunning eyes is a bold and self-reliant mind. She's the type of girl that takes her life by the horns and constructs her own path, and probably bulldozes anything in her way. I saw it from the moment we met in the dark lot by the bay when she sauntered confidently out of the taxi. I saw it in the confidence behind her eyes and the way she commanded attention on every take, not with her words or her body, but her persona. But now she's looking to me. It's both invigorating and terrifying.

"I uh..." the words stutter between the throbs moving down my back and the overwhelming sense of responsibility. "Let's follow the hall, maybe we can find a way out."

I hate how scared and befuddled I sound as I try to be who she's needs. I think Nick senses it. He speaks up.

"Right, and then stick to the coastline until we find the dock."

I nod and look back to Ava. She bites her lip nervously and bobs her head, then takes my hand. I feel a burst of strength race up my palm, past the aching and into my heart.

A *pat, pat, pat* draws my attention back to the hall. I lean forward and step in front of Ava, putting myself between her and whoever, or whatever, is coming our way. Nick hears it too. He stands up and plants his feet next to me.

Footsteps.

Without thinking, I take a step back. My ass bumps against Ava. She braces her free hand on my shoulder, barely missing the marks along my back. I still cringe as the pressure under her thumb moves the skin and muscle and a new pulse travels up my spine.

The footsteps draw closer. My frame stiffens, and I tighten my grasp on Ava's hand. My heart clamors against my ribs and shoots the blood up my back. I grit my teeth, waiting for the steps to break the corner. They're slow and deliberate. I curl my lips, begging it to just be over, for them to show themselves.

What feels like minutes later, a man steps past the intersection and rounds the bend, his pace even and purposeful. My chest relaxes. A stark white, knee-length smock hangs loose over his gray button-up and black sweater combination. An orange and black striped tie is knotted under his collar and disappears beneath the sweater's V-neck

Smile lines form as the man's mouth splits into a warm grin, revealing two rows of bright white teeth. His green eyes are small behind brown thick-rimmed spectacles, further complementing his brown hair laced with silver except where it fully overtakes the patches above his ears.

"Hello, I'm Dr. Markus Fischer," he announces, still five yards down the hall, all smiles. He's foreign, there's no doubt about that. His syllables are stressed, and "doctor" comes out more like "toctor", but I can't place it.

He continues toward us, a calm confidence in his aged face. His gait is steady. I'd peg him at about fifty. He finally stops three feet ahead. When he speaks again, the way his "w" comes out as a hard "v" declares his not-so-distant German ancestry.

"Welcome to Riverside," the doctor says. His voice is upbeat. "Follow me."

With a curt nod, he turns and walks back down the hall without another word. I squint, confused, excited and little angry all the same time. I take a step forward but stop. I crane my neck around to find Nick and Ava and give them a questioning glance.

"Wait. Stop." Nick says what I'm thinking. He jogs forward three steps and comes to a halt only a few feet behind the doctor.

The man turns. It bothers me that he's still smiling, that he seems so calm and in control. He's everything that I'm not. His deep green eyes stare at Nick, unblinking, expectant almost.

"Who are you?" Nick asks.

"Dr. Markus Fischer." His left brow rises, wrinkling his forehead. His expression changes to subtle concern and his eyes widen as if a thought hits him. "Is your hearing damaged?"

"Uh... No..." Nick stutters, his eyes flickering between the walls and Dr. Fischer with a note of indignation. "What's going on? Where are we?"

"Ah. Good." Satisfied, the doctor turns and starts down the hall again. "Follow."

I exchange a curious glance with Ava, hiding the agony in my back, and then take off after the doctor. *Doctor of what?* I stop by Nick and tap him on the shoulder. He eyes me, a haze of confusion and irritation clouding his dark brown eyes. I shrug. Reluctantly, he lowers his head in surrender before taking off after the doctor. I understand how he feels.

Who is this guy? Where the hell are we?

I mean, I know what Dr. Fischer called it, *Riverside*, but *what* is this place?

A tingle in my fingers eclipses the pang under my shoulders for a moment as Ava's soft fingers interlace with mine. She pulls me closer, wrapping her arm under mine, and she gives me a fearful, needy grin. In her eyes I see something that scares me. I'm not sure what it is, but it upends the little confidence I have left, and that isn't much. I cloak the dread in my chest with a subtle grin and continue forward.

"What's going on up there?" Nick asks again. The doctor doesn't answer, and Nick's voice drops an octave but rises in volume. "Dr. Fischer! We've been through hell out there. What's going on here?"

He stops abruptly and he places his hands in his pockets. For some reason, I look down. I can see my reflection in the solid surface, but I don't recognize the person I see. He's dirty, his clothes are torn and filthy. A look of scorn reaches from the surface and taunts me, and the eyes are all wrong. They're the same as Nick's, but there is no vibrancy left in them. Instead, they're dull, dead.

When the doctor doesn't turn, Nick speaks again.

"Please!" Then something seems to click in Nick's mind. He pulls his foot back and tilts his head, keeping his eyes on the doctor. "You've been down here the entire time, haven't you? Did you know we were up there? Did —"

I look at Nick, surprise blossoming across my face. But it makes sense.

How dense am I? Of course he was.

I bore my eyes into the back of the doctor's head.

A sigh escapes Dr. Fischer and he about-faces, a sympathetic scowl propped precariously over his bored features. His eyes find Nick and then move to me, and then Ava, before finding Nick again.

"Yes." The word drops from the doctor's tongue without emotion. Just a statement of fact — no less, no more. He sighs again. "If you'll just follow me, I *will* explain."

"No, the time to explain is right *fucking* now!" Nick jumps a step closer. "Our friends are dying out —"

"Actually, they're *dead*, not *dying*," Dr. Fischer puts up a singular bony finger, enunciating each word carefully. His eyes are calm, but there's something calculating behind them. "There's a difference. Ah, no, I about forgot. I'm sorry, all but one, that is."

My back stiffens and my brain moves at hyperspeed.

What the fucking hell?

I take a step forward too. I don't know why, but I do. Nick's eyes glow as his feet take flight. He leaps forward, his hands reaching for the man's throat.

A glint of black catches my eye at Dr. Fischer's side right before a single thunderous boom explodes in my ears. A yellow flash bursts from the end of a compact barrel, and my hands instinctively cover my ears. I don't hear Nick scream or witness his body tumbling to the floor. All I hear is the acute ringing in my ears. I close my eyes, shutting out the room. My eyes flicker open and shut again, the noise replaying in my head over and over again.

Through squinted eyes, I find Nick on the floor and I forget about the noise. There's blood, but I can't tell from where. It smears the pure white floor in expanding red under Nick's hip as he writhes on the tile. I drop to a knee and lay a careful hand on his shoulder, my mouth gaping. His face is skewed with pain, his eyes squeezed shut.

"Nick!" I scream, but I can't hear the word exiting my lips. Finally, the ringing dissipates, and noise fills the space. A screech from Ava, which comforts me only in knowing that she's still behind me. The clanking of heavy boots sounds around the corner. The doctor is saying something, but I ignore him, instead focusing on Nick. He twists around and plops onto his ass. There's a hole in the fabric of his right shorts leg, bordered in crimson that spreads over his lower thigh. He cups a hand over the wound. The blood is a dark red, almost black against his hand, as it flows between each finger and drips to the floor.

"What the fuck?" I jump to my feet and face the doctor. I don't know what I'm doing, and in the moment, I frankly don't give a flying fuck. Anger floods my veins and clouds my mind. Something else, something deeper, takes over and I stomp forward. "Who do you —?"

"I wouldn't do that!" The doctor raises the pistol level with my nose and refuses to budge. The barrel hangs inches from my face.

I freeze and pull my shoulders back. I stare down the brushed aluminum barrel, forcing my eyes past it to find the doctor. My legs quiver, and unconsciously I hold my breath. My thoughts speed by like the cars at a NASCAR race.

What the hell? He shot Nick, he shot my brother. He's going to shoot me. He's going to kill Ava. What the fuck is going on? What the fuck? I'm going to die here. Where the hell is here? What is this place? What the hell?

As my mind flies, two tan and brown clad soldiers jog around the corner and spot us. They skid to a stop and assume a defensive position, legs spread, each with an arm tucked under their shoulders, fingers wrapped around the stock of M4 carbines, the other cradling the hand guard. They're both men; the one on the left is as black as night while his partner barely holds a light tan and has glasses propped on his nose. *U.S. ARMY* is stamped on the soldiers' left breasts. I find myself creeping back, eyes focused on the soldiers instead of their guns. My eyes come back solidly to the pistol in the doctor's hand, aimed at my temple.

"Freeze!" the black soldier yells. His voice is deep and commanding.

"It's okay, it's okay." Dr. Fischer takes his left hand from the pistol and waves at them. They visibly relax but keep their weapons aimed. The doctor wraps his hand back around the pistol and purses his lips.

"You all could really learn a little patience," Dr. Fischer says. Malice drips from his voice. He works his shoulders in small circles and cracks his neck. The pistol wavers an inch before coming back to a rest, still inches from my nose. His tone evaporates into irritation. "That's the problem with your damned generation. You're so impatient, with all your iPhones and iPads, your Facebook and Twitter, and your one-day deliveries. If you don't get what you want immediately you think you're deprived. So damned impatient."

I can't help but tilt my head at his words.

Really? He shot my brother and is holding me at gunpoint and all this old fuck can think is that we're impatient? Fuck you, old man!

"Now get up, Nick!"

My eyes spring open.

He knows my brother's name?

The eyebrow over Dr. Fischer's left eye rises knowingly.

"Go ahead, help him." Dr. Fischer nods at me, taking a step back. "He is your brother, isn't he? So help him. We'll get him fixed up in a moment. Now, *follow me*."

I step back without turning and find Ava crouched over Nick, her hands coated in a thin layer of red. She's cupping Nick's hands, trying to help stem the blood flow. I finally take my eyes from the doctor and bend down to help them. If I move him, though, he won't be able to hold the wound, and I don't know how far away we are from wherever this mad man is taking us. My eyes dart back and forth in thought and I settle on the first thing that comes to mind.

I grit my teeth and pull my shirt over my head. I cringe and my body quivers as the fabric and dried blood separate, pulling at the scratches on my back. I exhale in minimal relief as I bring my hands back down, my torn and bloodied shirt in hand, and get down on my knees. I twist my shirt into a thick cotton rope.

"I'm going to put this around your leg, Nick," I warn him in case it hurts. It does. He groans when I cinch the shirt tight around his calf an inch above the bullet hole. I hold back the urge to yell at the doctor, while I pull tighter at the makeshift bandage and tie it off. Satisfied, I give Nick a hopeful smile and pull his arm over my shoulder and help him to his feet.

Feeling naked, I nod at Ava. She steps around and hooks his other arm over her shoulder. I retrain my eyes on Dr. Fischer and the end of the pistol. He tilts his head in an appreciative gesture and waves at us with the gun.

I start forward. Nick leans his weight on me each time his right foot touches the ground. I stare at the doctor as we pass by, lips sneering and eyes hard. He looks annoyed as we go by and then disappears behind us. A rush of horror sweeps over me. I'm terrified, not for myself, but for Nick and Ava. I can't fathom my brother like the others, his body torn and limp, eyes lifeless. He's my big brother. Yeah, we fought when we were kids, but I love him. I flinch away the thought. And Ava... I look at her, blinking away the frown on my face and smiling sadly to reassure her. The terror in my gut transforms into something heavier. It should have been so obvious to me before, but it hits me like a linebacker.

I love her too. I love *her.*

"Take a right," the doctor demands.

The soldiers move to the edges of the hall and let us pass between raised rifles. We take a right at the fork and keep going. For minutes, the stomp of boots against the floor and Nick's labored breaths between groans are the only noises. I think we're going down. It's barely noticeable, but there's a subtle slope in the floor. A series of plain doors line the walls. Escape scenarios begin running through my mind, but they all end badly. I don't know where we are. I don't know how to get out. I don't even know where any of the doors lead, and I'm certain that a door like the one that saved us from hell to dump us into something only slightly less hellish has some damned good locking mechanism, so going back doesn't seem like a viable option. Even if we got away for a moment, the island is a nightmare. *Death.* That's the word that keeps flashing across my mind. *Death.*

"Here, go inside," the doctor barks.

I don't nod or respond, I just walk. At the door, we help Nick through. Before I have time to take in the space, the doctor speaks.

"Meet Dr. Nathan Price."

The heat of my blood skyrockets. I don't even see the man. Instead, my eyes lock on the stacks of monitors on the far wall. On each screen a video relays another scene from the island. The old church. The empty forest. The nurses' dormitory and buildings I don't remember. The hospital. The entire fucking island.

32: Helen Harrison

The corridor is draped in shades of gray. The shuffling of Helen's feet on the dirty floor sounds like a bag of dead weight scraping across rocks. She tries to step lighter, even though she needs to get as far away as fast as possible, and the thick veil of black before her eyes only serves to slow her down further.

She holds back a curse when her toe cracks against something solid. She stops long enough for the pang to dissipate and moves on. Her fingers explore the wall to her right. It's coarse and uneven beneath her fingertips, rutted out, warped and chapped with age and neglect. Helen's lips tremble as her eyes dart aimlessly in the dark. The musty smell of damp rot permeates her nostrils.

The board beneath her foot creaks and Helen halts. She swallows, fruitlessly closing her eyes, and holds her breath. Silence envelops her body, itching at her skin and causing the hair on her neck to stand up. The chill passes and Helen cranes her head around and peers down the hall. She searches blindly, waiting, watching for signs of movement, hoping that somehow in the emptiness she might catch it before it's too late. She shifts on her feet, bringing on a stabbing pain down her left thigh. Her face tightens into a grimace and she grinds her teeth, denying her lips the scream that begs to spout from her throat. Except for the quiver of her fingers and lips, Helen holds absolutely still, unmoving, for another half minute. When nothing moves, and no creaks bounce through the hall, she decides nothing is following, that nothing resides in the dark just out of sight and out of reach. She lets out the breath she's holding. It stutters between pursed lips and she drags in another.

She turns and continues down the hall.

Where the hell am I?

It's been minutes since Grady's last scream cut out in the middle of a tormented note and the sickening thrashing and growls stopped. The horror of it had been replaced by an eerie silence, an impending doom that the creature could be waiting for her at any turn, at any doorway. Every tiny noise is suspect, every imagined movement in the dark looks like claws or the slit eyes of the monster. The drone of the rain is a high whisper beyond the walls, bringing the crack of thunder at the worst moments.

Three yards ahead, the wall disappears under her fingertips. Helen stops.

Another hall?

She listens. The sound of the storm is louder here. A wry smile lifts her cheeks, and she reaches for the wall again. At first, she catches nothing but air, then her finger finds the corner. She caresses the corner, trying to determine if it's another hall or a doorframe into another room, a dead end, a death trap. Her finger drifts about the edge, rubbing against the peeling wallpaper. Its frayed and curled edges catch her fingers. The texture becomes grainy, and it's cold under her fingertips. Wooden, but there's no raised part to indicate a doorframe. She changes directions, sliding her finger up the wall.

The texture continues as far as she can reach.

It's a hall, Helen, otherwise you would have hit the top of the doorframe. Yeah, it's another hall.

She tries to reassure herself that she's making the right decision. With a huff, she makes the bend and moves forward carefully.

The adrenaline gone, Helen's mind begins to wander. She sees Arianna on her first day in kindergarten, or "big girl school" as her youngest had called it. She's dressed in a pink and black zebra-striped dress, the one where the bottom half spreads out like an upside-down flower. A pink bow barely holds on to her long, thin hair. Helen remembers reaching to fix the bow, but Arianna had stepped back and told her she was a big girl, that she could do it herself.

Then Jaylen's distorted face mars the memory, his mouth wide in a silent scream, an inch of sharp claw jutting from his forehead. Blood dribbles down his face, falling over his eyes as he stares her down. They beg for relief. Helen's face contorts as his mouth moves, forming a silent sentence. *Help me.*

She blinks away the vision and picks up her pace. A scream breaks the silence.

Grady?

Helen jerks to a stop. She throws her body against the wall and peers down the hall.

It can't be. He's... He's... It just can't be. You're hearing things, dammit. Get a fucking hold of yourself, Helen.

She shakes her head vigorously. Swallowing back the foul stench of fear, she breaks away from the wall and finds the wood with her fingers again. Her breath comes in quick gasps. Her heart beats faster. She quickens her pace. She needs the light, she needs to bathe in it, to drive away the darkness.

Suddenly, her foot catches on something thick, and her hurried momentum carries her body forward. She throws out her hands, catching the ground just inches from smacking her face against the surface. Helen crumples against the floor, but she keeps her head up. Her thigh screams, shooting jolts of lightning up her veins.

"Agh!" she yells, but quickly claps a hand over her mouth. *Are you crazy, Helen?*

She waits and listens, clamping her jaw shut to brace against the pain. A full minute passes. All is quiet. Finally, she pushes off the floor. Her entire body aches, tendrils of pain shoot in never-ending currents through every muscle. She grits her teeth and starts down the hall again, reminding herself to take it slow.

Down the hall, a faint glow washes over the floor and wall. She squints, cocking her head like an investigator. It's not much, but it means the outer hall is close. It has to be.

She takes her time shuffling down the corridor. At the end she leans around the corner. The dim light washes over her face, coating her in splotchy yellows. Around the bend is another hall. It's short, and other hallways branch off at the end in both directions about fifteen feet ahead. A door hangs open at the end of the corridor, and Helen can see the outline of an old window behind it with the fuzzy background of falling rain.

Excitement builds in her chest. Helen slinks around the bend and takes off. She lets her hand leave the wall, no longer relying on it for her sense of direction.

Don't get your hopes up, Helen. You know how quickly things can change. Be realistic.

As if the demons cooped away in the old building heard

her thoughts, a low creak crawls across the walls. Helen freezes.

Where did that come from?

She takes a quick survey of the hallway, sweeping her eyes in a full one-eighty. Ahead is the fork. It spreads right and left, surrounding the door at the end of the hall. Behind her the hall fades into nothing where the light can't reach, like the world simply ends beyond its black shadows. The walls are peeling and two-toned, but the colors appear in grayscale under the filtered light. The segment of wall to her right, set after another open doorway, is shifted half a foot into the hallway. The entire wall leans in dangerously. Helen ignores it, choosing not to dwell on the building's incongruities and how quickly it can come tumbling down.

She fixes her eyes down the hall toward the door with the window behind it. She squints, determined the creak originated from one of the halls ahead of her. She exhales and begins to debate the merits of continuing forward.

It's just the building. It's just the old wood because it's not used to weight. But damn, what if it isn't? What if it's that monster? I should go back. No. It's too dark. That's where the monster is, that's where Grady... Where he... Where he died. No, I have to go forward. It's just the shitty old building. It's okay. Keep moving, Helen.

Helen takes the next step and crosses into the fork. She peers past the door but doesn't push it open farther. The rain is pouring outside but the storm is calmer now. Through the half-open door, the room looks empty. Helen considers going inside, but a chill at the back of her neck won't let her.

Instead, she swivels her head between the two halls like a little kid crossing the road for the first time. She bites her lip and goes with her gut. She starts off down the left corridor.

It's exactly like the others—damp, smelling of mold and sodden clothes. A thick layer of dirt and dust covers the floor. She accelerates into a jog to match the pulse shooting up her temple. Her leg throbs, striking a nerve with each stride. She slows her gait.

What's the plan, Helen? Leave the... Where the hell am I anyway? Never mind. Leave the building or stay? If you leave, you're going to have to make a run for the beach and then find the dock. What if one of those things is out there, or it follows you outside? Can you get away again with a hurt leg? But, if you stay you're stuck in here with *it, and it's like a damned maze in here. But, you can hide. You can wait for daybreak. Yeah. If you wait for the sun to come up, then you can see it coming when you go outside. You can be more careful. That's the plan, Helen. Hide until daybreak,* then *get off this fucking island.*

She passes a door on her right, then left. Empty. Behind the next door her eye catches a flash of red, or maybe it was orange. She stops and peers around the corner. It's dark inside, an interior room, but the light from the other side of the hall sheds a small glow into the space. Helen lowers her brow and her eyes scan over the floor in awed curiosity. It's not just one thing. The floor is littered in books, piles of them from wall to wall like a roiling rainbow-colored sea. She steps in and crouches over the pile.

Helen reaches down and brushes a hand over the edge of a stiff hardback. It strikes her as both beautiful and sad. Books of all sizes and colors, khaki, ochre, and russet among others, some with black bindings and others a single color. Fading foil inlays announce the titles on most.

She chooses the book closest to her and picks it up, checking the spine for the title. *Death Be Not Proud* is stamped down the edge just above *John Gunther.*

Never heard of it.

Helen opens the hardback and flips through the thick, water-spotted pages before gingerly placing it back on the pile. She reaches for another. The smell of old books mixed with the stink of mildew and a helping of dust wafts past her nose. She coughs, forgetting about her problems for a brief moment while she relishes in the nostalgic fragrance. Helen picks up another hardback, its scarlet cover warped by years of water damage. She checks the title, swiping the dust away with her palm. *One Flew Over the Cuckoo's Nest* by Ken Kesey. She grins, remembering the classic story from her college days.

Appropriate. She thinks, considering the island's use. It might not be a psych hospital like in Kesey's story, but the quarantine and drug rehabilitation centers of the early and mid-1900s couldn't have been a cakewalk.

Crack!

She swings her head around. Her green eyes lock on the open doorway. Whatever it is, it's close, maybe a few yards down the hall. She fixes her feet in place and holds her breath. A low creak crescendos over the wood. It's closer this time. A moment later, another *crack* follows. Helen shifts, nudging the pile of books. One of them swims down the edge of the pile and emits an almost imperceptible thud when it taps the floor, but it's like thunder in Helen's ears. She grips the book still in her hands tighter and clenches her teeth, unaware of the pain building in her jaw and how her body shivers.

She wants to close her eyes when a familiar growl seeps through the door, but she doesn't blink, she can't. She wants to move, to cower in the corner behind the door, to become lost in the mountain of ancient books. But she doesn't move, afraid she might slip on one instead or that her shoe might scrape against the rough floor and emit a siren's call to the approaching demon.

The heavy thud of bare feet joins the swelling growl. It grates against her ears and causes her chest to tighten. She wants to run, to pounce from her crouch and sprint past the door. But a deep, paralytic dread freezes her in place. Unable to hold her breath any longer, Helen releases the air in her lungs in one long, slow puff, trying to lessen the hiss between her lips. She drags in another breath, and almost chokes on the smell. Her mind is thrown back to the office space upstairs where she smelled the same rancid scent, her body pressed against a rotting cubicle wall and Grady in the dark. Her body quivers. She fights back the nausea as the smell looms around the corner and poisons every molecule. The footsteps are so close.

A dark shape interrupts the light flooding the book-filled space until its shadow drapes Helen in one massive blanket of gray. It's tall, the sleek top of its round head looming an inch below the doorframe. The light seems to bend around it, casting its sinuous form in a mix of grays. Its muscles ripple and move as it stomps forward, filling Helen's eyes with horror. She swallows, crouched only a yard from the threshold, only feet from death. A scream builds in her throat, but she restrains it. Droplets form at the edges of her eyes and she struggles to hold her breath. The pressure rises in her chest.

Its head scans the hall lazily and its eyes sweep over the doorway. Helen fights the urge to drop to the ground when its bloodied claws sway past the door. Her eyes cling to the talons, enthralled by their sharp tips and the fresh carmine splotching them. But somehow it doesn't see her.

It moves its lumbering head and massive arms past the door and aims back down the hall, its silhouette disappearing around the corner. Helen stays put, her lips pressed firmly together. Pressure blooms in her head, a combination of pain and the air held hostage in her lungs. The edge of her vision begins to fade, and she finally opens her lips, letting the air whoosh from her lungs in one long exhale. She slumps and inhales rapidly but quietly.

Listening to the creature move down the hall, Helen lets her muscles relax. She almost forgets the book clamped in her hands and it teeters in her grasp. She stifles a yelp as it slips from her grasp and over her other hand. She throws her palm down, desperate to prevent it from announcing her hiding place. An inch from the floor, she clamps her fingers around the binding and locks her body into a statue, terrified to move an inch. She closes her eyes and takes a deep breath.

Calm down, Helen. Calm down.

She waits another minute, crouched over the discarded books. Her lungs contract and release slower, the sweat no longer courses down her cheek and the beat of her heart ceases to feel like a freight train smacking against her chest. She puts the book down, careful not to disturb the pile, and stands up. She starts toward the door.

The anxiety behind her ribs grows again as Helen closes in on the door. She balls her hands into tight fists and releases them, flexing her fingers, and then does it again, over and over as she walks forward.

It's gone. You can make it. Go, just go.

She fights the urge to pump all her strength into her legs, rationalizing the chances of success versus the possibility the creature might not actually be gone. But the omnipresent throb in her thigh wedges its way into the equation. A sprint was never an option in the first place.

Helen claims another inch. Her face and arms are shivering, and her lips form a frightened oval as she approaches the door. She stops when the tip of her nose breaks the invisible plane. She closes her eyes and swallows back the angst lumped in her throat, taking long, slow breaths of the musty air and the lingering scent of mortality. She unclenches her fist and lets her eyelids slide open after a long moment, and without giving herself time to think better of it, she bends around the doorframe. Helen grasps the decaying wooden frame for both physical and mental support and peers around the immediate space beyond the door. It's empty.

She swings her head around and glances behind her. The hall is empty, save the occasional pile of scattered debris and the residual odor left by the beast's feculent breath and death-coated claws.

Just go!

She puffs out a quick breath and takes the right branch, away from the creature. Slivers of light glide over her reedy form as she passes door after door. She quickens her pace and the corridor grows brighter with each step. She ignores the throb pulsing up her thigh and presses on.

Crack!

A thin piece of rotten doorframe breaks beneath her foot. An icy chill scales her leg and bites at the root of her brain. Her eyes barely have time to snap shut before a vicious roar engulfs the hallway. Helen stops for the shortest of seconds, taking only enough time to steal a quick glance toward the sound of rumbling footsteps. The blush in her cheeks evaporates as the beast materializes from the shadows. It clambers forward, thick arms swaying, legs pumping, its eyes frenzied.

"*Fuck!*"

Helen screams and takes off. Her leg cries in protest, nearly bringing her to her knees, but the adrenaline kicks in just in time to keep her from crashing to the floor. It lessens the pain and gives her the strength to move. Doors streak by. Her vision tunnels her focus down the center of the hall toward the light.

Run, Helen! Run!

The creature's heavy feet smack against the floor, vibrating it like thunder beneath her. Its roar echoes off every wall and corner, past every doorway.

The end of the hall is close now, only another ten feet at most. Helen leans forward, grunting past the agony, and pushes on. It's gaining on her. Her mind recounts fleeing from the same beast up the stairs, the sound of Grady's screams and the sudden void when the wails had stopped.

No. No! That's not going to be you! Move, dammit!

Finding an extra burst of energy, Helen forces her legs to run quicker. She breaks past the end of the hall and spills into the veranda where she had entered the building only an hour ago. Then, she was begging for cover to escape this damned creature, and now she wants out, but not yet. She knows if she makes a run for it now, the creature will simply follow, so she shoots across the open space, swooping around an obstacle she doesn't have time to identify. Dull light bathes her skin as she passes through the space.

A gigantic roar stops her in her tracks. Her eyes bulge, fear painting her face, as another beast lumbers into the veranda from the other corridor, its feet cracking the floor. She locks her legs, the soles of her shoes skidding on tiny bits of broken concrete and thick dust. She stares into the beast's silvery blue slit eyes, but she's unable to stop her forward momentum like a conveyor belt into Hell's stomach. The world slows as the creature's thick arm rises, its clawed hands spread wide. Helen's heart sinks deeper into her chest with each pump. It rears back and then swings forward.

Helen is about to close her eyes, to submerge herself in the emptiness behind her eyelids before welcoming the void of the hereafter, when her feet finally catch. Her eyes widen, and a tiny spark lights beneath her bones. The thick, sharp tips of five sharp claws fill her vision only feet from her face. She ducks, and without thinking, twists on the balls of her feet as the talons swoop inches above her head. She plants her heels on the floor and bolts in the opposite direction, back into the veranda. In the split second before her feet move, her eyes inventory the space. The scattered debris, a cart or hamper — she can't tell and doesn't care—a set of open double doors leading into a large open space shadowed in even more darkness, another hallway drenched in heavy shadows and empty walls.

On adrenaline-induced autopilot, her brain chooses the hall. She darts forward.

The beasts scream behind her as they clash into each other. Wind tickles her neck as another hand swipes at her but misses. She gasps but keeps moving. It doesn't take long for the creatures to regain their pursuit, but their collision gives her a head start. She leans into the hall, hastening her step, laboring to ignore the spasms shooting up her leg with every step.

Crazed cackles murder the airwaves about her ears as they close in on her. She tries to ignore it, instead focusing on the quick rhythm of her own breath and the beat of her heart. A car length away, the hall angles off to the right and a door sits to the left. Her mind races.

Keep going or hide...

Without time to weigh the pros and cons, Helen banks left and dives into the room. Her thigh falters under the new pressure as she leans on her hip to make the sudden turn. Her leg goes numb and Helen pitches to the right. The cold floor comes up to meet her and the rough concrete scrapes against her leg just before her head hits the floor. A sudden, abbreviated scream jumps from her mouth. Before her body can come to a full stop, she shoves her hands against the surface. Her palms scrape the floor, determined to find purchase. Finally, her slide comes to an end and Helen opens her mouth, willing her head to stop spinning.

A wild howl rocks the room and overrides the pain long enough for Helen to jump to her feet. She wobbles drunkenly, her head light and dizzy. She throws her hands out to balance herself and shakes her head to clear the fuzz from her eyes, but pain floods her head. Helen groans, blinking in a useless effort to wash away the ache. In her peripheral vision , she catches the sight of blood. It laces below her knee in tiny vein-like rivulets. Her eyes sweep the room in panic as the thud of sturdy legs pounding closer fills the room.

The first revelation that enters Helen's mind is the lack of an exit unless she decides to go back into the hallway. Directly ahead the wall is bare, covered partially in heavy, dust-covered tiles, the rest showing a bare, unfinished wall. Her head snaps to the left. There's a set of glass doors covering a recessed closet, but the glass is nothing but shards. Another empty closet sits in the adjacent wall. A set of odd black metallic contraptions hangs from the ceiling, one stocked with the remnants of an ancient light fixture. Another gravelly howl panics Helen further. She twists and turns, searching for a way out, unwilling to chance fleeing into the hall again. Her eyes stop in the corner next to the entrance. What little color that's left in her face drains.

Gabe?

She stumbles backward and flattens her back against the wall. A tremor quakes through her body as she lets out a shrill scream. He's dead. His body is torn, shredded. Blood trickles from the stump where his left leg used to be and the bottom half of his body clings to his torso by only a few strands of sickly, bloody muscle. His entire chest is carved open, his ribs jutting out like ghastly fingers reaching for relief.

Helen slides against the wall. She doesn't bother holding back when her body convulses. She bends over and wretches, spilling the contents of her stomach across the floor.

Her eyes snap to the open doorway just before its wooden frame shatters and the two monsters invade the space.

It's over.

Their lips snarl over gaping jaws as their eyes beg for flesh, her flesh. One of them emits a high-pitched roar, and Helen flinches away, cowering in the corner. She waits, knowing what's about to come, waiting for them to pounce, waiting for their weight to hit her, waiting to feel her flesh ripped from her body, for the claws to slice through her skin and curl between her organs. She waits. But nothing happens.

Helen squints, confused by the sudden quiet. The roars no longer come, and only the heavy breaths of the creatures fill the space. For a long moment, she continues to cower, frozen in the corner, still unable to unclench her frozen bones or open her eyes the rest of the way. The seconds move on and life still pumps through her veins. Confused, Helen forces herself to look.

Shaking, she carefully angles her head and torso around. They're just standing there. Their cat-like eyes are still. They're filled with a ravaging intensity, a burning desire to feed, but somehow, in that moment, they're frozen in place. She stands erect, ignoring the flagrant reek of their breath against her nostrils, and faces them, her heart beating against her ribs.

Why?

She wants to run, to swoop around them and make a break for it, but there is no room to get by. Their large bodies standing side by side block any route out of the confined space, and any attempt to slide beneath their claws would surely end with them embedded in her skin.

It's over. Just do it!

"Go ahead! Kill me! Fucking do it!" she yells.

33: Cooper Bay

It's so much worse than I thought. The black and white monitors on the wall say more than Dr. Fischer could ever utter.
My knees buckle, making my legs nearly crumple beneath the
weight of it all: the searing pain in my back, the weight of
Nick propped on my shoulder, the fear of dying here, of them
hurting Nick or Ava. It all washes over me as the feeds blare
one pointed thought through my mind.

They watched it all. They fucking watched it all!

Nick grunts as his bad leg hits the ground. I pull my eyes
away from the camera and giving him an apologetic nod before looking to Ava. The shine in her blue eyes is gone, replaced by a dejected melancholy.

The doctor's mouth is moving but my mind hasn't caught
up yet. The two Army guards have taken up positions behind
us on either side of the door, their rifles held stiffly against
their chests, no longer recognizing us as an immediate threat.
Sitting in a simple metal swivel chair with a thick fabric seat is
another doctor — at least the long white smock trailing over his
plump shoulders and belly matches Dr. Fischer's. An abrupt
snapping breaks into my thoughts.

"Are you listening to me?" It's Dr. Fischer. His left eyebrow is arched in disapproval. "You do know it's rude to ignore people when they talk to you, right?"

I don't answer. *How the hell can you lecture me on etiquette?* The other man rises from his chair. His face is round and fleshy. Wavy brown hair covers his head, leading to thick, coarse sideburns and a beard that overtakes his cheeks, chin and upper lip, highlighting a set of gray eyes. The smock rolls over his stomach like grass atop a hill.

"This is my associate, Dr. Nathan Price." Dr. Fischer dips his head toward the man.

"It's good to finally meet you." Dr. Price actually grins while he extends his hand.

My brow rises. *What the hell?*

I don't move. I refuse to play this sick game. He holds his hand out for another second before swallowing and shifting his gaze to the floor. He lets the arm fall to his side and brings his eyes back up. I thought guilt would be behind those dull gray orbs, but instead they're clouded with embarrassment. My blood boils.

You watch my friends fucking die out there, you sit back with your fucking military guard in your safe fucking lab and watch us get picked off one by one, and you think I'm going to shake your fucking hand?

In that moment, a black hate rushes my veins, coating my pounding heart like hot oil. I hate him more than I abhor Dr. Fischer, more than the man who shot my brother and still expects us to follow like dogs. This man, Dr. Nathan Price, is a coward. I can see it in his eyes. He's a stupid fucking coward hiding behind a title and a steel door.

He coughs before opening his mouth again. "Ah. Yes."

Dr. Price turns and faces the monitors, his eyes searching the grayscale screens. Dr. Fischer rolls his eyes and shifts on his feet. The room fills with silence under the muffled hum of the ventilation system.

"So you've been watching us this entire time?" I'm surprised to hear the words pour out of my own mouth. Each syllable spits a dose of venom, shock and distress.

"Yes." The word seems to fall involuntarily from Dr. Price's lips and he goes silent again, as if one word was enough to atone for all we've been through.

"My friend here is a man of few words," Dr. Fischer explains, his voice thick with apology.

I don't know how to process it all, everything that's happened and this man, how he talks to us, one minute consoling, the other ready to put a bullet through my head, the next apologizing for an awkward co-worker.

"But yes, we have been watching you, Cooper. And your brother, Nick, Ava and the others."

The way our names glide from his tongue causes my stomach to drop. I suddenly don't know if I really want to know more. I just want to leave, to be done with this place. I want to put it all behind me like it never happened, but I know that's the scared part of me talking, the part that wants what it can never have. But what part of me isn't scared? My arms, legs, hell, my whole body is shivering and my heart pounds against my ribs like I'm running at full sprint. I can feel fear building in my chest like a locomotive drawing closer and closer, like the blood in my veins has broken free and is flooding over my organs, filling every crevice of my body. It all weighs me down. The pressure in my chest threatens to burst at any moment.

"But why?" Ava speaks up. Her voice is quiet, saying what I can't seem to get out anymore as my fists clench up tight.

"Well," Dr. Fischer clears his throat, "first, you *weren't* expected. It's not like we planned all of this, if that consoles you any."

He waves a hand in the air and continues. "You trespassed in a restricted zone. You're not even supposed to be here, really. But you are, so you can thank yourselves for all of this. You see, this isn't just some avian reserve, a place for some stupid bird that doesn't even grace our shores anymore to take refuge. It's *much* more."

My eyes are glued to the doctor. I've almost forgotten about Nick's weight on my shoulder as he goes on, shifting the blame for every atrocity we've faced to us. My mind cannot fathom how, but he does it anyway.

Dr. Fischer shifts to his left and puts a hand on the back of Dr. Price's chair. He huffs dramatically.

"You don't know how hard it's been to keep people off the island since the herons stopped coming. Everyone clambering on about why the island's still closed, going on about silly conspiracies and stories. Most of it's crap, but you know how that goes now, I guess. We even tried importing the damned birds, but they won't stay anymore. They don't appreciate the company, it seems."

His voice trails off, the look in his eyes is almost nostalgic. The lab, everything around me, starts to wobble. I blink, pushing back the anxiety building in my chest and behind my eyes.

This is really happening.

"That's neither here nor there though. You want to know *why*, right?" The doctor stops, eyeing Ava, head tilted expectantly.

She doesn't answer, and I find myself wanting to go to her, to stand between them, but I can't move with Nick over my shoulder, and I'm not sure I could even if I didn't have to hold him up. Instead, I maneuver my hand up a few inches on Nick's back and grip Ava's arm. After a moment of silence, Dr. Fischer starts up again.

"Well, this laboratory is a facility of the Defense Advanced Research Projects Agency. DARPA. You've probably heard of it; the agency isn't exactly a secret. We're the agency tasked with the development of cutting-edge technologies and research for military applications. This is a…lesser-known wing of the agency."

There is pride in the doctor's voice, his chin held high as he explains. I know what DARPA is, and for us, it can't mean anything good. Suddenly the realization that we're never leaving this place hits me. I fight it, pushing against a fate my mind isn't ready for, but I can't help how it seeps in despite my best efforts.

"You see we—" He's cut off by Dr. Price's hand patting against his coat aimlessly, his eyes still on the screens.

"Markus!" he finally says. "You might want to see this."

"What is it, Nathan?" Dr. Fischer is clearly aggravated by the interruption, but he looks down at the corpulent doctor anyway. "I'm trying to explain…"

His voice trails off as his eyes land on one of the monitors. I squint and try to find what he's looking at. My eyes pass over a set of empty woods. The storm has slowed, and the rain is almost gone. Then I spot a vague building overshadowed in vines, the interior hallway of another, and then another. It all starts to look the same, and then Dr. Fischer speaks up.

"Ah. Perfect timing." He looks back and gives us a half grin. "How about I just show you what we're doing here?"

I frown, confused. *What?*

"The third screen from the left, top row." Dr. Fischer nods toward the wall of monitors. "It's your friend Helen, right?"

My eyes shoot to the monitor. I find her just as she disappears from the feed and comes into view on the next. She's running, her arms swinging in the dark. My heart sinks when one of the thick-legged, clawed beasts enters the frame. I swallow back a taste of dread and retrain my vision on Helen, letting my eyes chart her course forward. If I've got the monitors right, she's about to enter the veranda at the center of the hospital. My eyes sharpen. There's another one waiting for her around the corner. I take an unconscious step forward, warranting a sideways glance from Dr. Fischer, but his frown quickly morphs into a satisfied grin.

Unable to do anything, I watch in horror.

Dr. Fischer loses interest in me and looks back at the screens. I catch a glint in his eyes as he rubs his palms together in excitement. My lips tighten and my brow furrows.

Helen runs into the veranda and comes to a sudden halt. It's obvious she sees the other creature. She skids to a stop, barely out of its reach. I want to scream for her to move, but it's useless, she can't hear me over the airwaves. For a second, I wonder if she's overhead, maybe standing directly above me in the hospital. I shake away the useless thought as she darts backward and takes another hallway, now with two of them on her tail. She barrels forward. I tighten my grip on Ava's arm unconsciously. She flexes, probably in pain, and I loosen my fingers but keep my eyes on the screen. I can see something in Helen's gait that isn't right, like she's hurt. She's near the end of the hall now, and suddenly she breaks off to the left. I want to scream, to tell her to go right as I check the other screens. A right would have taken her back around and given her a chance to get out, but taking a left corners her.

In the room she falters and tumbles to the floor.

Get up, Helen! Get up!

It doesn't take her long to jump to her feet. Immediately she snaps her head back and forth, searching the empty space. But it's not empty. I notice a huddled mass in the corner next to the door. I squint, seeing the creatures racing down the hall on the adjacent monitor, and then I realize what it is. My mouth drops open, and a tear escapes my eye.

Gabe.

I can't make out much detail, but his body is strewn against the wall. The job those *things* did on him is obvious, and now they're both attempting to burst through the door at the same time. Chips of wood fly across the screen.

In front of the monitors, Dr. Fischer raises his hand under his chin and presses his thumb against his wrist, as if to take his own pulse. Then he speaks.

"Stop."

Inside I scream for Helen to run, to do something, but instead she presses her back into the corner, her arms curled against her chest. Then I notice something odd. The creatures aren't moving. They're standing still, looming maybe four feet from Helen. Their bodies are tensed, palms reaching for her, claws extended, but frozen in place. I watch as their hands fall to their sides, and one of them twitches its head spasmodically. Helen steps away from the wall and throws her arms up. She's screaming, but I can't tell what she's saying.

What the hell?

I pull my eyes from the screen and find Dr. Fischer. He's staring back at us, a sheen of excitement in his eyes. The look sends a wave of fear through my body. I want to reach out and save Helen, to pull her away from the creatures, but I take an unconscious step backward without taking my eyes off Dr. Fischer. I'm horrified. Whatever is happening here is beyond simple military tech.

Dr. Fischer lowers his wrist and grins. The guards don't move. I want to scream at them to go help Helen, to do their job as American soldiers, but it suddenly hits me that we're the enemy here. One line crossed, one *no trespassing* warning ignored, and here we are on the other side of the battlefield.

"Intrigued?" Dr. Fischer asks.

"Let her go," Ava demands.

"No questions?" His face falls in disappointment. "Only demands. Next you'll be demanding I let *you* go."

"Please. Let her go," I try.

"Are you dense, boy?" Dr. Fischer jumps at me, eyes glaring angrily. His abrupt change in demeanor is disturbing. I recoil another step, brushing the ragged edges of my torn back against the cold metallic surface of a rifle muzzle. Instinctively, I jump forward again before settling down, and I lose my grip on Nick. He wails as his bad leg hits the ground and his wound is aggravated. I regain my footing and get my arm situated again under Nick's shoulder.

"She's standing right in front of Bellator and Miles. Do you really think if we let her go that she's just going to go back home and never speak of this again? That she'll just leave you all here to rot? Unfortunately for you, *I'm* not that dense."

I swallow, glancing at Nick and Ava, not even registering the two names the doctor spit out. Nick is standing straighter, carefully placing his weight on his injured leg and offloading the rest on my shoulder. His eyes are still moist. I can read his thoughts without trying as he looks at me. *I'm sorry.*

Ava's face is drawn tight, her lips sealed. Beyond the fear I can't read her, and I hate it. Out of the corner of my eye, Dr. Fischer raises his wrist to his mouth again.

"Kill her." The words are quick and forthright, emotionless.

My mouth falls open and my eyes dart to the screen as the creatures pounce. I want to turn away, to cover my eyes, but I don't. Instead, I step forward, throwing my free hand forward as I witness the first claw disappearing into Helen's stomach in pixelated grayscale. Then the other one makes its move. It jumps on Helen, wide arms wrapping around her shoulders, its maw coming down hard on her cheek. It takes less than a second for Helen to drop to the floor under its immense weight. Even in the low-resolution feed I can see the skin being peeled from her chest in ribbons. Thick chunks of muscle and fat trail after the white layers and smack to the floor. Gray droplets splatter the exposed concrete floor. Her body writhes and jerks, as the beasts rip and pull at her head and waist.

A wave of nausea sweeps over my stomach as her body stretches and twists unnaturally. They pull at her frame without mercy, like two tigers fighting over a deer. Then, as if the bone and meat under her skin is nothing more than butter, her body rips apart across the stomach in a haphazard line of tattered skin, sinew and guts. A long, gelatinous mass flops uselessly to the floor from her lower half. I swing my head away and wretch, unable to hold it back. When I look again, the mass is still hanging between her separated body, but her face is still.

I pull my eyes from the screen and hold back another

heave. I stare at the cold white floor, thankful there's no audio. When I straighten back up I keep my eyes away from the wall of surveillance feeds and fix my gaze on Dr. Fischer. He's watching me, a sly grin across his face. I refuse to look away even though I want to.

"So that's a good little sampling of what we're doing here," Dr. Fischer's voice is steady, unaffected by the coldness of his own words. "Though it may be hard for you to see right now, we're in the business of saving American lives."

34: Cooper Bay

"We've been here since the forties in some capacity or another," Dr. Fischer explains.

Nick is lying on a thinly cushioned examination bed with both doctors leaning over his leg. Dr. Price balances a set of tiny plier-like scissors and a curved needle in his pudgy hands. He plunges the needle into Nick's thigh, piercing the bloated edges of Nick's bullet wound. He threads another stitch through the skin while Dr. Fischer holds Nick's leg in place and prepares the next suture.

One of the guards stands behind me, while the other is positioned a few feet beyond Dr. Fischer, at the ready. Five minutes ago they ushered us away from the surveillance room, after taking our cell phones, and guided us another five yards down the stark hallway to this room. It's some type of medical or surgical chamber. Glass shelves are filled with dozens upon dozens of marked translucent bottles above waist-high counter space, and mobile medical equipment crowds the head of the singular patient bed. Ava is sitting in the room's only chair. I guess stool would be more accurate, it's nothing more than a metal seat atop a cylindrical support rod and wheels.

She hasn't let go of my hand since we deposited Nick on the bed. Some support I am though. My face is still pale and my stomach's weak. I can't get the image of Helen's skin stretching and tearing like thick, hot mozzarella out of my mind. It sends my stomach into knots every time.

"The island was more or less a natural outgrowth of the Riverside Hospital in its last days, around the end of World War II. The research was elementary compared to the leaps we've made in recent years, but it laid much of the groundwork. They were looking for quick solutions to use against the Nazis." Dr. Fischer looks at us, still holding down Nick's leg like it's an ordinary task. His nostrils flare. "But that was long before my time. I'm told that research boomed when the island became a youth rehabilitation center in the fifties. The constant influx of the East Coast's unwanted and troubled kids finding their way to the island apparently served the lab's purpose well."

"Markus," Dr. Price interrupts, nodding toward the tray of threads.

"I'm sorry, Nathan," the doctor apologizes and hands his colleague another black thread. I watch Dr. Price thread the needle through Nick's skin, and then loop it, pulling the open wound closed. The stitches pull unnaturally at his skin, like tiny black trenches along a landscape of dirt, but they do the job. Dr. Price dabs a clean white gauze against the web of threads, and Nick's blood blooms through the dressing.

"Where was I?" Dr. Fischer asks, biting his lip and looking at the floor. "Ah, yes. The point is that the lab has been here for years, conducting research on possible biological weapons in a controlled environment where people don't ask questions because there *are* no people to ask questions." He smiles a little too happily for my taste. I want to rush him, fists swinging, and knock the grin from his lips. I want to see the blood trickle down his nose. But no, instead, I feel like I'm going to vomit again.

"When the rehab center closed on the surface in the seventies, DARPA wasn't finished with Riverside. It took some pushing, from what I'm told, but eventually they were able to have the island cordoned off as an avian reserve without it being connected to DARPA. Naturally it took on the namesake of the hospital that sat above it during the time. It wasn't until the late eighties, though, that the lab officially encompassed the surface as a testing ground. The agency wanted to be sure the island was empty and overgrown to provide some natural cover. But it didn't take the researchers back then long to realize the island could bring in its own research subjects."

The words send a pang of regret and agony down my spine. He's talking about us. About Brooklyn, Gabe, Luca and Helen.

Wait. What about the others?

My mind shoots back to the video screens as Helen sprinted to her death. Where are Grady and Jaylen? And what about Riley? We still don't have a clue where he is. Did one of those things take him, too?

"All fixed," Dr. Price announces. He steps back and puts a hand behind Nick to help him sit up. I grimace as Nick swings his leg over the bed and carefully puts his weight back on his feet as he slides off. He grunts, gritting his teeth and squinting, but he doesn't complain. Dr. Price leaves the bedside and holds out my bloodied shirt. "Here's your shirt back."

I take it, letting the fabric droop over my hand. It looks like a tie-dye that someone decided to only use shades of red on. I gulp back the urge to vomit again and toss the shirt to the ground as Nick comes up on my left.

"Your choice." Dr. Price shrugs.

I grit my teeth and let my eyes tell Dr. Price how much I hate him. He flinches away, turning and busying himself with discarding the leftover supplies from Nick's stitches. To the right, Dr. Fischer picks up a white plastic package and scans a barcode on the computer next to him. I furrow my brow when he tears open the package, pulls out a thick syringe and starts walking toward us.

"I don't suspect that we'll really need these, but just in case, I'm going to inject each of you with an RFID tracking chip." He lifts the syringe and places his thumb on the plunger, eyeing Nick. "Your wrist."

Nick doesn't refuse. He puts out his arm, wrist facing the ceiling, and lets Dr. Fischer shove the thick needle into his skin. I clench my hands, gripping Ava's hand a little tighter.

"Very good," Dr. Fischer says. "See, that's not so bad, is it?"

Before he can finish the question, Dr. Price hands him a second syringe. I know it's coming, so I hold my hand out and let him plunge the needle into my wrist, watching my flesh glide up over the metal tubing as the tiny cylinder inside slips beneath my skin. I flex my fingers, my eyes glued to the tiny hump under my wrist. It doesn't hurt. I can barely tell it's there.

Dr. Fischer turns and deposits the last of the syringes in a metal trash can. I look to Ava, surprised that the doctor had already chipped her, too, but the tiny red entry dot at the base of her wrist confirms it.

"All right, it's time to give you a close-up look at our little experiments," he says and turns to face us again.

I cringe at his words, and instinctively I steal a glance at

Ava and then look back at the doctors. A close-up? I don't want to be anywhere near those beasts. My instinct is to step back, but I hold my ground and find Nick's eyes. He grimaces but nods.

"This way." Dr. Fischer leaves the bedside and walks into the hallway before taking a right. With the guards behind us, Ava follows after me. The doctor's voice trails over his shoulder. "Did you know that there were nearly twelve hundred patients in quarantine just above our heads at Riverside at the peak of the typhoid outbreak? And the infamous Mary 'Typhoid' Mallon herself was among them."

No one answers him, not even Ava. Had one of us known Dr. Fischer's factoid about the surface just hours ago, Ava probably would have been fascinated, but now it appears to mean nothing to her.

Instead, we follow in silence, our shoes tapping against the gleaming floor. We pass a set of closed double doors, their bright gray surface breaking the hall's monotony. Twenty yards down, Dr. Fischer opens a door off to the left and steps back into the hall. He waves toward the opening, his palm up, like a rich host trying to appear modest as he ushers us into his mansion.

I refuse to meet the doctor's eyes as I follow Nick inside.

It's a small, unlit space. There's just enough room for the three of us and Dr. Fischer. Dr. Price stands in the open doorway and crooks his neck from side to side to get a look around us while the guards take up positions on either edge of the doorframe. Dr. Fischer runs his hand over a smooth panel along the wall and the darkness flees, lighting part of the room in a dim golden glow. My brow lowers as I take in my surroundings.

Less than two feet in front of me, the gentle reflection of the overhead lighting betrays the slab of glass dividing the space. The cold white tiles of the lab, shadowed in gray, end at the glass, and the wet, grassy overgrowth of the forest takes over. The sudden patches of moss green and deep browns is jarring at first, and I have trouble believing my eyes. I search for the forest canopy and the stars, but it only takes me a few seconds to realize I won't find them. Rather than stars, a thick layer of vines race along a stony ceiling. We're still underground. It's a cave. My mind wonders where the end might spill out. Could we get out this way?

"I know you've already met our pets, but I want to give you a closer look." Dr. Fischer raises his wrist inches from his mouth again and speaks. "Come back to base."

As the words roll easily off his tongue, my gaze jerks from the cave and lands on the doctor. *What? No.*

"It's okay," he says, and raps his knuckles against the glass, creating two low thuds. "The glass is thick. They can't get through, I promise."

"I don't want to be here." Ava's words are little more than a whisper, and I hear even less as she pulls me closer, her arm nudging against my bare side. I can feel her trembling, but I don't know what to do, so I squeeze her hand.

A minute passes and the room remains empty. I glance between Nick and Ava. Nick stands on his own despite the pain I know he must be biting back. His eyes are set forward, staring through the glass where the subterranean cavity twists out of view. A clicking noise draws my attention, and I fasten my gaze on the spot where it came from. I wait. I force my lungs to expand, pulling in a quick drag of oxygen, and then constrict, purging it from my body. I can feel the steady thump of my heart and the rhythmic surge of my pulse in my temple as I unconsciously clench my teeth.

The clicks turn into low thuds. The thuds grow and become more defined, building into heavy crashes against the earth. The low growl that haunts my thoughts emanates from the tunnel, and I have to remind myself there is a wall between us to keep from stepping back. I tighten my grip on Ava's hand as the first one comes into view.

I'm struck by how adept its movements are, how it maneuvers with purpose, and despite its rigid muscle-bound appearance, it displays a cunning dexterity. But that's where my appreciation ends. It's unnatural, something more fitting of a Tolkien novel than reality, with its thick and dirty brown skin stretching firmly over every bulging inch. I catch its eyes just as the second one comes into view. I'm surprised by the color behind its black vertical slits. Instead of the dull gray or bloodshot crimson I fully expected, a deep gold bursts from between its lids.

Almost human.

But then its claws click together, and I'm reminded of its savagery, of how it ripped and tore and gouged. Even now they're coated in a film of crimson. The blood of my friends. I swallow as they stomp closer, tilting their unnaturally large and boxy heads as they approach, as if to examine us.

"They're human." Dr. Fischer breaks the silence and continues without allowing reply. "At least they were. The one on the left is Bellator, and the one to the right is Miles. Those aren't their human names, of course. I believe Miles was a guy named Omar Laity. I don't remember Bellator's, he's been with us for over a year now. He's simply Bellator now. Miles only arrived here, what? Three weeks ago?"

He turns and finds Dr. Price, but my eyes never leave the beasts...the humans, on the other side of the glass.

"Just under. Nineteen days as of tonight, actually," Dr. Price agrees.

"Yes, that's right." Dr. Fischer turns back to the glass wall and admires his work, sighing with a confident satisfaction. "He and another were snooping around the island much like you were, and he became part of our work. See, we're looking for ways to produce the most efficient and ruthless killer. And as you can see, we've made significant progress. They are ruthless, and they are compliant."

The doctor raises his hand again. "Sit."

My eyes widen as the towering beasts calmly lower themselves to the ground and sit. In a way it comes off naturally, like they simply made the decision, but Dr. Fischer's irritating accent doesn't allow me to forget that it was by his command. They look about the small cave aimlessly, and for a second, I pity them. Humans, their humanity sucked out of them and replaced by...what?

"You see, we've managed to tap into the cerebrum and hijack the electrical currents that control thought and action. That's how I'm able to simply *tell* them what to do and they listen, sort of like a Jedi mind trick. Of course, it's all much more technical than that, but it would take some time to explain. Simply put, it's a key step in the project, one we only recently accomplished."

"Can they see us?" Ava speaks up, her voice quiet.

"No. The divide is a two-way acrylic mirror. All they see is themselves." Dr. Fischer nods. "Otherwise they'd be all over the glass just at the sight of us. It's a byproduct of the chemical exposure we put them through. Miles doesn't exhibit as much senseless aggression as his predecessor, but it is there."

"What did you do to them? If they're human, how did they get like this?" I ask, my voice cracking.

"Genetic and chemical alterations." Dr. Price pokes his head around the corner. Dr. Fischer purses his lips and lets the man continue. "We wanted to see not only how absolutely compliant we could make them, but how strong. In the most recent subject we managed to splice the genetic material..."

"Yes, yes," Dr. Fischer waves his hand, hushing Dr. Price. "The point is that we're close. Very close."

"But you said..." I search for the name that Dr. Fischer mentioned just moments ago. Once I find it, the name comes off my tongue in a stutter. "Mi...Miles only arrived three weeks ago. How is such a transformation even possible in that time frame?"

"Let's just say it's painful," Dr. Fischer says plainly, though the German accent puts a harder edge to his words. "We are trying to work that out though. A weapon like this is no good in stealth situations or where blending in is of the utmost importance. We're very close though."

With that, Dr. Fischer turns and starts to leave, but I've already opened my mouth.

"You told them to kill us, didn't you?"

He stops, his head dropping a fraction of an inch, and then rising to look at the ceiling as he exhales a deep breath. He turns and meets my stare, his eyes lacking any real conviction or emotion. Not even the tiniest ounce of sorrow.

"Yes."

35: Cooper Bay

"Well, not all of you." Dr. Fischer corrects himself and shakes his head dismissively. "You see, the Proeliatorum are not simple automatons, they're... Sorry, how rude of me. Proeliatorum is plural for Proeliatoris, or Homo Sapien Proeliatoris. It's what we call our creation. A new step in human evolution designed specifically for warfare."

"How the hell is that evolution?" I surprise myself as the words shoot out. "*You* created them."

I catch a sly grin spread on Dr. Fischer's face as he turns and walks into the hall. The soldiers and Dr. Price follow behind as Ava and Nick exit the room with one last glance through the glass.

"What else is war but survival of the fittest? It's one of the most basic acts of survival, one group fighting back the other for its own hegemony and right to go on. *How* we advance is not the prerequisite to evolution. No, it's the undeniable fact *of* advancement that defines the evolutionary process. Who is to say that every evolutionary change, small or great, especially in this day, is always natural? I mean, what *is* natural, how do you define it?" Dr. Fischer twists his head about and gives me an inquisitive look but keeps walking down the hall. I don't answer, holding my lips together sternly. But that doesn't dissuade him.

"What is the difference between the peppered moth's evolution in response to its environment and us mutating human hosts into something greater for our survival? The principle is the same—survival. How the change happens makes it no less evolutionary."

I keep my mouth shut, not wanting to hear more from this madman and unsure why I even bothered asking. I look away when he glances back again. I don't want to hear his rationalizations or the glee in his voice as he explains why he's building creatures that tear people into pieces.

We walk another ten feet before the doctor stops and turns to face us. He looks past me.

"Please escort Nick and Ava to the holding cell." His words are curt, and before I can question why my name wasn't mentioned, he turns and starts off again. "You're with us, Cooper. We need to stitch up that back."

I turn, searching for Ava and Nick.

"No, I'm staying with Cooper," Ava nearly yells, sprinting forward. She doesn't get far. The black guard snaps forward and wraps a hand around her upper arm. She jerks against the man's grip, but it does no good.

Nick starts to move, but I can see the hesitation in his eyes as he thinks twice about it. He looks at me, not knowing what to do or say. I think that scares me more than realizing I'm about to be escorted off alone with this crazed scientist, but I give them both a reassuring nod and let Dr. Fischer lead me away. I peek back a few steps down the hall and meet Ava's scared blue eyes. I try to give her a grin, but I can't do it.

Less than a minute later, I'm lying face down on the same bed where Dr. Price stitched up Nick's bullet wound, a heart monitor attached to my finger. The plastic cushion is cold against my bare chest, and every movement feels like I'm peeling my skin from a rubber mat.

"I'm sorry about not attending to you earlier, Cooper, really. I got ahead of myself. I wanted you to see the Proeliatorum. Fortunately, your cuts aren't that deep." Dr. Fischer's words are genuine in their own fucked up way.

In my peripheral vision I can see Dr. Fischer eyeing my back with a scowl and Dr. Price setting up a small tray. "We need to get you patched up before an infection sets in though."

"Why thanks!" I blurt sarcastically, hot anger lacing my voice. I thought I couldn't feel more scared than I did in the hospital, or when the man giving me his sad song of apology shot my brother, or when Ava looked at me with horror and fear clouding her eyes, but I was wrong. So hellishly wrong. Lying here on this bed, alone, in the hands of these vile men, prompts a new level of fear to pump through my veins. It takes everything in me not to jump off the bed and make a run for it, or maybe it's the opposite. Maybe my reality is that the thick fear suffocating my lungs and clamping its cold hands around my heart has tainted any hope that running can be an option.

No, Coop, calm down. You're still alive. Nick is still alive. Ava is still alive. They're helping you now, fixing your back. Yes, they might be mad, but they're helping you right now. You'll be with Ava and Nick in no time.

"Calm down, Cooper, your heart rate is climbing, and I've not even introduced the anesthetic." It's Dr. Price. I hear the *beep* pulsing rapidly in time with my heartbeat from the stack of monitoring devices somewhere behind me. I'd forgotten the heart rate monitor attached to my finger. I take a deep breath and attempt to slow my breathing. The beeps slow a little. "That's better. Now, you might feel a slight sting —"

"Agh!" I grunt as the needle prods one of the peeled back layers of skin. Electricity shoots up my spine.

"And again."

I clench my fists and grind my teeth as the needle pricks my tender flesh again and a dose of anesthetic liquid gushes under my skin. The *beep* quickens again, but the medicine kicks in quickly.

"All right, Cooper, I'm going to begin stitching you up now," Dr. Price says. "This might take a bit. The lacerations are rather long."

"Look at how clean the cuts are though." Dr. Fischer's voice is academic. A dull, tickling sensation flutters in my lower back, and I roll my eyes at the doctor. "I doubt we'll get these types of results in future subjects. Nothing this massive at least."

Dr. Price coughs and goes back to work.

I try to ignore them. I feel the stitches tug at my back, but I ignore them, too.

"What are you going to do with us?" I ask bluntly, holding back the shiver that tries to escape through my voice.

"I haven't fully decided yet." The candor in Dr. Fischer's words is effortless. I can imagine his calm demeanor as he watches Dr. Price do his work. "But whatever it is it'll be useful, it'll serve a purpose, just know that."

A tear escapes my eye as I think what those words could mean, of the unimaginable terrors we've already gone through, of how *useful* they were. My body quivers.

"Please don't hurt Nick and Ava. Please!" A tear seeps from the corner of my eye and gravity pulls it down my cheek.

"Hold still unless you want these stitches botched really good," Dr. Price barks.

I ignore him, not caring about my back when all I can think of are the bodies of my brother and the woman I love lying in pieces in that cage.

"Please! I beg you. Do whatever you want with me, but let them go, please!"

"No. You're damn well insane if you still think I can just let them prance out the door and back into their little boats." Dr. Fischer's words are cold and numb. "I'm not going to hurt them. *I'm* not going to do anything to them."

36: Cooper Bay

My back aches, but the most violent of the pain is gone. I don't bother to ask how many stitches it took, and I don't really care. Neither of the doctors said much after I broke down. Although they did give me a plain clean t-shirt so I wouldn't have to walk around half naked. Of course, it's white, too, like every other damn thing in this laboratory.

Now I find myself being prodded down the hall by the tanned soldier, a rifle trained squarely between my shoulder blades. I glance back, giving the guard a stern glare that I'm sure he's laughing at inside. *Castillo* is stamped across the right breast of his fatigues. The doctors left me in his "care" to attend to "other matters", whatever the hell that means. I want to say something, to appeal to his patriotism or humanity, anything to get him to see what's going on here. Inside I already know it's pointless, but I have to try.

"Castillo," I start and immediately hit a blank.

"What do you want?" he barks without a hint of the accent I expect. Instead, I realize he must be a Brooklyn native as the sentence came out more like *Whaddya waant?*

"You've got to let us go. This isn't right." I try to appeal to the soldier. "Yes, we shouldn't have come to the island, that's clear, but how could we have known? We're American citizens, we have rights. This isn't even close to how it's supposed to be."

"Oh, so I'm just supposed to disobey my direct orders to protect this lab because you have rights," Castillo mocks me and then prods my back with the rifle.

My right leg buckles and I stumble from the pain as the barrel nicks my stitches and shifts the cuts underneath them. I throw a hand out and catch the wall, managing to keep myself upright as a yelp shoots from my lips. My mouth hangs open, air stuttering out in pained gasps. I want to lash out, but I know it'd be the wrong choice. Instead, I start off again, regulating my breaths and collecting my thoughts.

"I get you don't like being stuck down here. That makes two of us." I can hear the irritation in his voice, but it doesn't sound like I'm winning him over. "But don't be thinking that you can make me go all righteous. Sure, I hate this assignment, it sucks, but it's my job. So shut the fuck up and walk."

"Come on, man, you —" I clench my jaw shut as his gun pokes my back again.

"I said shut the *fuck* up!" Castillo's voice reverberates off the hallway walls.

It's not worth it. With my body shaking from the pain, I exhale my pent-up breath and continue down the corridor.

How the hell are you getting out of this? In a body bag, that's fucking how. No, Cooper, calm it down. You'll figure something out. Nick will think of something.

"Stop," Castillo orders.

I still my feet in front of one of the many plain gray doors lining the hallway. They all look the same, not even a nameplate to distinguish them, but this one does have a control panel. The soldier motions for me to back away from the door. I purse my lips angrily and step back. Putting his body between me and the panel, he types in a code and the door unlocks with a gentle thud before Castillo opens it.

"In you go."

I'm about to give Castillo an angry glare when I hear my name yelled from inside the room.

"Cooper!" Ava jumps up from her place on the floor by Nick and races forward, but Castillo puts a hand in front of her. She stops, eyeing the soldier like I was going to, and waits for me to enter.

As I cross the threshold, she rushes forward and almost knocks me over. A grin spreads across my face. If I didn't know any better, I'd think she had known me for years and hadn't seen me in months. I squeeze her, letting my eyes find Nick. He steps over and pats me on the shoulder.

"Are you okay?" he asks, peering into my eyes like he's looking for a lie.

"I'm all right. They just stitched me up. I feel better, actually," I tell him. It's only half a lie. I do feel better, but I'm definitely not all right. I'm anything but all right, and I think they both know that. I think we all feel the same.

As the door is pulled shut without another word from Castillo, my eyes go wide, and I suddenly forget about the pain in my back and even the anger that's built up in my chest. Standing in the corner is Riley. He eyes me cautiously, alive and in one piece.

"Riley?" I say, but it comes out like a question. "I thought you were..."

"I know, dead." The words come out flat. It's only then that I see the tears running down his cheeks. I scrunch my brow and release my arms from Ava's back, but I keep a firm grasp on her hand. A row of stitches starts at his temple and climbs over his left eye. Below a bad batch of bruises on his left leg is an even longer row of sutures. I think I know what caused that, but at the same time it seems mild compared to what I've witnessed on this island. I pull my eyes back up to face him.

"What's wrong?" I ask.

"We told him, Coop." Nick squeezes my shoulder and gives me a grave look. "We told him about the others, Brooklyn..."

His voice trails off and I immediately understand. It's not my best memory, but the noises in the woods the first night out here when I stumbled upon Riley and Brooklyn's not-so-quiet lovemaking comes to mind. I push back the thought and lower my head.

"I'm sorry, Riley," I say weakly. I want to tell him I know how much she meant to him, but I don't.

"Can you tell Coop what you told us?" Nick steps around me and takes a seat on the floor next to Riley. His words are careful and sad. I can't tell whether it's Nick's grief showing through or if he's treading carefully.

"Uh...yeah," Riley starts, his voice shaking as he drops his butt to the floor and props his arms on his bent knees.

I crouch down to be eye level with him.

"I just remember running in the woods, for the scene, you remember that, Cooper, right? We were running towards you."

"Yeah, I remember." I nod. Shame tugs at my mind.

I should have done something. But what?

"You just disappeared," I say and try to hide the guilt in my chest.

"I guess so. I was running, and I heard a noise, but before

I had time to stop and look, something hit me hard, and I blacked out. Then I woke up here. I mean, not here, but in the lab. I woke up on a hospital bed. Nick told me you already met the doctors."

I dip my chin slowly, trying to push back the wave of hate that starts to overtake me at their mention.

"They were hovering over me. I think the one's German or something, Fischer I think it was." Riley pauses, trying to remember something. "I can't remember the other's name, they haven't come back much."

"Price. Nathan, I think," Ava speaks up. She's leaning in the corner of the small room by my side, a balled up fist set over her mouth and her eyes studying the floor.

I nod, trying to make eye contact with her, but her scared eyes don't move. Mine shift from her to the floor, and I make myself look back to Riley.

"Yeah, that's him. Price." Riley nods vigorously. It feels too pushed, too emphasized, but I know how he's feeling.

No, you don't, Cooper. You don't have a clue what he's feeling. You still have Nick. You still have Ava. He's lost so much more and even worse, he had it all dumped on him at once. What a brain fuck that has to be.

The thought of losing Ava hits me like a rock. I start to stumble back, but I catch myself. I have to stop and control my breathing. My chest is suddenly heavy and my legs are leaden.

She's still here, Coop. Don't think about it.

And Nick. I clench my fists and fight back the wave of emotions. I have to look away as a tear threatens to breach the corner of my eye.

Stop it, Coop. Stop!

"Well, they were there when I woke up," Riley starts up again. He uses the hem of his dirty sleeve to dry his cheek, not worrying about the strands of long hair hanging in his eyes. "They said they stitched me up. Said I'd hit my head pretty hard and I had some good cuts on my legs. They claimed they didn't know how I got the cuts, and I believed them. They said something about how I must have hit my head on a tree or rock or something. I know better now."

I shift on my feet and tilt my head inquisitively. *I know better now. What?*

"You didn't know what was going on out there this whole time? They didn't tell you?" I ask.

"No. They just said they'd found me and stitched me up," he says before his voice grows gruffer, tinted with anger. "They didn't tell me a damn thing. I even asked where you all were, but they acted like they didn't know who I was talking about. I even thought maybe I was imagining things or that I'd knocked some memories around or something. But I knew something was off when they threw me in here. I mean, it's a damned prison cell, basically." He pauses a second, then looks around the room, stopping on each of us for a moment. "You three are the first people I've seen in hours. I've been sitting here completely clueless. I couldn't make sense of why they locked me up after helping me. I mean, it didn't make any sense."

"No, I bet it didn't." I stand but keep my eyes on Riley. I nod at the stitches along his leg. "They know damn well where those cuts came from and how you got that concussion. Their Proelia-somethings. Those beasts. Whatever the hell they are."

"Yeah, that's what Nick was saying." Riley looks down at

his leg and runs a finger lightly over his black stitches. "I haven't seen one yet, but apparently it saw me." He pauses, a worried grin overtaking his lips. I see him swallow hard before he speaks up again as new tears accumulate in the corners of his eyes. "But why didn't it kill me? Why did it let me live, but...but not Brooklyn?"

He wipes his arm over his face and sniffles. His lips tremble, and before anyone can say anything he turns his face to the floor again.

"Why?"

"Did they ask you any questions when you woke up?" I ask, hoping I don't sound too insensitive.

"Just w-what my n-name was," he stutters between sobs. "Nothing else. I've already told you, they stitched me up and threw me in here. That's it. That's all I fucking know."

I shift against the wall and pull my eyes away from Riley. I don't want to push him any more, he's been through enough.

"I'm sorry, man, I thought..." I stop, hanging my head. "I don't know what I was hoping for. Never mind."

Ava's hand wraps around mine again, sending a flurry of warmth up my arm. I look up and meet her crystal blues. Even with the glint of excitement replaced by a dulling shadow, they're beautiful. I let my mouth sag open, releasing a stuttered breath. I'm so scared and angry, and she knows it. For a second, I feel weak for letting her see, but I push against my need to be strong for her. I'm human, too. It's okay. She doesn't need me to put on a false facade of bravado when inside I'm shaking. She needs to know that I understand, she doesn't need me to be fake, to be something I'm not, something I've never been.

"Are you okay?" she asks me, her eyes peering past mine, into me. My first instinct is to say *Yes, I'm good*, but I decide to tell the truth.

"No," I tell her and exhale a long, deep breath, then draw in another. "No. I'm not, but that's okay. Because there's nothing okay about what's going on here. None of this should have happened. None..."

She puts a finger over my lips to stop me. I lower my brow, confused at first, then it hits me as a sad smile pulls at her pale lips.

"You're mostly right. There's nothing okay about what's happening, but if we hadn't come, I might have never met you, Cooper. And even if that means dying here, somehow... I'm not sure how I can feel like this right now, but even if it comes to that, I'm all right with it, because I met you. I love you, Cooper."

Before I have time to utter a word, the heat radiating through my body mellows into something more pleasant, a calm yet excited spring of joy in the midst of Hell's deepest flames. I smile back at her and let my own admission slip through my lips.

"I love you too."

37: Cooper Bay

It's been at least an hour or two, maybe three, since the door to our tiny white prison last opened. I've never been any good at telling time, and without my phone I don't have a clue. Either way, it's well after midnight...I think.

None of us can sleep though. Everything that's happened sits too heavily on our minds. At times it feels like some fat dude is doing a balancing act on my shoulders, like all his weight is about to crush me.

I'm done with bottling it up. We all are. We even have a plan now; well, we think so.

It's Nick's idea. I think it might work, but I'm worried it won't end like we hope. Basically, the next time they come to fetch us or bring us food, or whatever they plan to do, if it's only one of the doctors, and we know he has the gun, we're going to ambush him and make a run for it. It's not much, but what else do we have? In the end, one way or another, we'll wait until we're with just one doctor and try to wrestle the gun away.

We're going to fucking die down here.

I shake the doubt from my mind and exhale.

"You okay?" Ava asks, brushing her fingers under my chin.

I nod without grinning and she lets it go.

"Luca loved concerts. He loved meeting the band members." Nick's voice trails off under the dim overhead lighting as he thinks back on his friend. We've spent the last hour talking about our pasts, of each other, family, anything to brighten our spirits even a little.

"The last concert we went to was uh… Actually," a quiet, spasmodic laugh jumps from his throat as Nick holds back tears, "it was all three of us. Luca, Grady and me. We went to a concert in Richmond at the Canal Club. Two of my favorites were playing that night, Bad Omens and Imminence. I'd been waiting for Imminence to come to the States for at least a year. But that's not the point. The point is that we went, and I remember getting to meet Noah and Nicholas from Omens and Eddie from Imminence. They're great guys, and let me tell you, Luca was so excited. He was like a damned little fangirl."

I let myself grin and chuckle a little at the image that pops in my head of the short, nearly forty-year-old director jumping up and down, about to meet some dudes. From the looks on Riley's and Ava's faces I imagine they're having a similar visual.

Nick looks to the ground and curls his lips in, trying not to cry, then looks back up with a forced smile. He changes the subject. "Hey, Coop, do you remember back when I was like twenty and we went to the science museum down in Raleigh? I think you were fourteen or something."

I roll my eyes and bob my head. I know exactly where he's going with this memory and I can already feel my cheeks begin to blush. "Yeah, I do."

He laughs, looking down at the floor again, but this time it's amused contemplation on his face. Ava snuggles up closer, her warmth radiating through my side. Nick looks up again, talking more to Riley and Ava than me. I know the story already. He grins.

"We were at the museum, in the aquatic animals section. I think we were standing under the skeleton of a blue whale or something huge, and I'm walking up behind Coop when he starts reading an animal's name off one of the tanks. Oh my God," Nick leans back, a burst of quiet chuckles escaping him, "Coop looks back at Mom and me in all seriousness and says, 'Ah look, sea enemas.'"

A massive grin pushes its way across my face, equal parts amusement and embarrassment. I remember it like it was a week ago, not six years ago. I wait for him to go on as laughs erupt from Ava and Riley. Ava eyes me and slaps playfully at my chest.

"I was in tears. It's a sea anemone, of course, not a damned enema, that'd suck! And while Coop's standing there all confused, I'm crying I'm laughing so hard, and Mom's literally on the ground, clutching her stomach because she's lost it in the middle of the museum. Literally on the floor. My, did we get some looks."

"Wow, Cooper," Riley punches me lightly on the shoulder. "Hope you don't plan on shoving one of those up your…"

I raise my left brow, giving Riley a stern but joking look. He grins and stops. I focus my eyes back on Nick, ready to give it right back.

"Wasn't it you," I start, letting my hands float in the air, with my pointer finger dancing around as if I'm trying to find an answer, "that had to ask Mom and Dad why that building was called a topless bar? I think Mom said you were confused because you said it *did* have a top."

Laughs ring out in the small room again. They're more

subdued than with Nick's story, but they're laughs all the same. I grin at Nick and he bobs his head with a wry smile.

"Yeah, that was me. But in my defense, I was like eight or something, and I hadn't exactly been to one."

"I think that's fair," Ava pipes up. She pats my leg. "But at fourteen I think you should have known the difference between an anemone and an enema."

"Yeah, yeah." I shake my head.

The laughter dies down and the space fills with a lonely silence again. I know it's silly, but in this room, between these four walls, sitting here between happiness and fear, love and loss, watching my friends' and brother's faces sag numbly, not sure how to feel, the silence is heavy. It hangs over me, coiling between my fingers and wrapping its way around my neck like the vines choking at the hospital. For a moment I wish it would cinch the noose tight and seal the deal, but I take back the thought as quickly as I let it slip.

"Do you remember our last beach trip, Nick?" I ask without looking up.

"Yeah, to Myrtle, right?"

"Yeah, to Myrtle. Two years back," I agree. An image of the beach forms in my mind. It's not the most beautiful beach, and it's definitely no Gulf Coast, but we always enjoyed it anyway. A gentle smile breaks the flat line of my lips before I start again, my words slow and thoughtful. "I can see it in my head. The beach. The sand wasn't scorching hot like usual that day. I think it was mid-September maybe."

Nick grunts in agreement over in his corner. I don't look up, but I imagine he's thinking about the same day through a different set of eyes.

"I was sitting on the beach with a book. What was I reading?" I think back, but despite all the other details I can't remember the title. "That's not important. I was reading, though, and Mom was sprawled out on her beach chair, glasses on, sunbathing like usual. I remember lowering my book for a moment to look at the ocean. The sun was high in the sky, but it still reflected off the water enough that I had to shield my eyes. You, Kaylie and Dad were out in the water, jumping in the waves or something. I never really liked the water on the East Coast, but you three seemed not to care how murky it was. I remember the cool breeze. It was one of those perfect moments."

I exhale, reliving it, sure I'll never experience another one like it again. Actually I'm not sure I'll experience many more moments at all as I raise my head and look around the room.

"I met Brook a little under a year ago." I'm surprised to hear Riley speak up. Other than the occasional nod and laugh, he hasn't spoken more than a few words in the past hour as we fill the time with memories. "It was through Luca, actually. He told me he knew this cute chick that did some work for him sometimes. He thought I might like to meet her."

Riley huffs. I can see in his eyes that he's thinking back. He grins, not looking at anything in particular in the tiny room.

"So yeah, he set us up. We went to a movie. It was a disaster. Two different families brought their babies in and they screamed the entire time. I was so angry because I wanted to try to enjoy my date with this new girl, but it's sort of hard with that going on. But she didn't seem fazed by it." He lifts his head and looks at Nick and then Ava and me.

"We went out to some half-decent burger joint down on West 46th Street, not too far from Times Square. It was one of those organic, eco-friendly places. She was all into that natural lifestyle stuff, as long as it didn't involve giving up any of her makeup and such." Riley grunts more than laughs. I see a spark of happiness behind his sad eyes. "Burgers and pop. Heck of a first date, right?"

I laugh gently with the others and nod agreeably. I can't say I see anything wrong with it. It sounds nice to me. I find myself wondering if Ava is a burger joint type of girl or more of a fine dining lady. I give her a warm smile, and she returns the gesture before leaning her head in the crook of my neck.

"It was great though. I mean, except for the screaming kids. I could have dragged them all out the door, kicking and screaming, if I thought I could've gotten away with it, but still... It was..."

His words trail off into sobs, his body quaking under the sadness. Nick puts a hand on his back and Ava leaves my shoulder to put an arm around his shoulders. I watch as she tries to comfort him. I've only known her for a few days, but I know if I were to lose her, I'd be no different than Riley. I clamp my eyes shut and breathe slowly.

For a long time, no one talks. Riley's tears lessen, and his sobs come to an end on the outside. I can only imagine the current that wails inside him though. Ava scoots back over and leans her body against me again, placing her head on my shoulder and wrapping her hand around mine.

We sit quietly in the shadows, each an island of thought, waiting for what might come next. I'm about to ask Nick how his leg is holding up when Ava's head squirms on my shoulder. She clears her throat under a quiet cough.

"This year's been tough for me." I can hear the quiver in her voice. She clutches my hand and draws in a breath, then lets it out. "I bottle up a lot. Internalize, you know? To appear strong, but all this... I..."

I put my other hand over the top of her smooth hand. She's shaking. I want to be here for her, but she pulls her head from my shoulder and refuses to look at me. I hold tight to her hand and try to meet her eyes. She keeps her brilliant blues aimed at the floor. The shadow of a tear drops from her cheek.

"Just this week I tried to kill myself. Seems silly now, I could have just waited..." Her voice breaks and she pulls her hands away and balls them into fists. I want to reach out and wrap her hands in my fingers again, but I don't. I don't know what to say to that, how to respond. She turns her left hand palm up and runs the middle finger of her other hand across an imaginary line along her wrist, tilting her head back and forth as she watches her finger move. "I put a steak knife right here. I was...I was about to do it when my phone rang. It was Luca."

She looks up, her eyes lost in the shadowed wall behind Nick. My heart suddenly aches, replacing the faint warmth that moments ago occupied the same space. I want to hold her, to tell her it's okay, but I also want to step back and ask why, to question who she is. The thought sends a pang shooting through my heart and I chide myself for even thinking like that. I shift my butt along the floor until I find her eyes again. They're sad, terrified, drowning in an abyss of something painful and deep. She looks away and wipes the tears from her eyes.

"My mom died when I was seven," she starts again over a sniffle, regaining a small portion of her composure. The dull overhead light casts a shadow over her face when she shifts and then goes away when she settles back down. "My dad raised me on his own while he took care of his business. We were never close to my mother's side of the family. They didn't approve of their daughter working for some country boy without a college education, from what I'm told. And my dad's family lives down in Tennessee, so we never saw them much. It was just the two of us, mostly. He put me through college, encouraged me to pursue acting, scared off would-be boyfriends." She laughs at the memory, her eyes flicking to meet mine for a split second before shooting off to a spot high on the wall and speaking again. "He didn't just hand me everything, but he did what he could."

I lean forward, waiting for her to say more.

"He died two months ago of a heart attack."

My heart breaks for her. I reach out and take her hands, refusing to let her go. She looks at me, lips trembling, a river of tears trailing down her cheeks, and I can feel the tears falling down my own cheeks now. The closest people to me that I've ever lost were my grandparents on my mom's side, and that was so long ago. I was still a kid. I know I can't fully understand her pain, but I know it hurts.

"I didn't know what else to do. He was all I had. I don't have any other close family, and I drove away all my friends who tried to help. I just felt numb." She looks up and meets my eyes. "Then I found you."

"I'm so sorry, Ava," I pull her into a hug, wrapping my arms around her, determined never to let her go again. "I'm so sorry."

I let her sob on my shoulder. The weight of her pain in tangible tear as I feel her tears soak through my shirt. I hate myself for being so blind, for not seeing it earlier. But how could I have seen it? How could I have known?

You couldn't have known, Cooper. And that's all right, because all that matters now is that you hold her.

"I almost did it, Cooper, I almost—" she cries, but I interrupt her, unwilling to allow her to continue berating herself.

"But you didn't. That's behind you," I tell her, mustering every bit of conviction I can find inside my burning chest. I wrap my arm around her shoulder and let our foreheads touch. Her adorable nose is less than an inch from mine as I look at her eyelids, waiting for her to look at me again. When she does I smile and stare into her crystal blues in the dark. Her tears catch the slightest glint of light and sparkle even through her grief. All at once I'm filled with the weight of her pain and the joy of everything about her. I lean in and kiss her softly, lingering long enough to taste the hint of strawberry on her lips.

"I'm here now, and *I* need you. *I* need you."

38: Cooper Bay

I wake to Nick tugging at my shoulder.

"Cooper," he calls through my half-comatose state. I blink and yawn before my eyes find confirmation that this hasn't all been one horrid nightmare. Dr. Fischer stands in the open doorway with Castillo staring over his shoulder. His eyes sweep over me then make their rounds to the others.

"Up," the doctor commands, but the only harshness about the word is his German accent. A slender grin is set above his thick chin. "Come on now, we have things to accomplish."

Ava groans on the floor next to me, still not realizing we have company. I give her shoulder a gentle jolt and her eyes flutter open. I give her my best weak grin and then jerk my eyes toward the doctor. She gets the message and slides to her butt. I get to my feet and help Ava do the same.

"What *things*?" My voice croaks from the lack of sleep. The combination of cold hard tile as a bed, mad DARPA doctors and what today might hold didn't serve well for sleep. Plus, all I could think about once we did finally try to get some sleep was how much I wanted and needed to protect the girl wrapped in my arms.

Nick looks at me questioningly. I can only assume he thinks I should keep my mouth shut, but I'm past that now. I want answers.

"You'll see." Dr. Fischer steps aside so I can see the end of Castillo's rifle, and I raise an eyebrow at Nick. "Remember, patience."

I want to lash out at the doctor, to scream out the hypocrisy of a man like him lecturing me on virtue when he stood behind a screen in his underground laboratory and ordered my friends' executions. I want to curse him, to tell him to go fuck himself, but I listen to the silent words hanging from the tip of Castillo's barrel and choose to hold my tongue instead.

Pursing my lips and taking a step forward, I let him know I'm ready, but the expression on my face tells him I'm not happy about it. Dr. Fischer's smile widens, a knowing gleam in his eyes. He knows he has my attention and compliance, and it burns me in the depths of my heart.

"Come on, let's go." Dr. Fischer waves and immediately walks out of the room and starts down the hall.

Castillo remains stationed at the door, eyeing us, waiting for us to move. Riley goes first, his head angled low, never looking into the soldier's eyes as he passes. Nick urges me forward with a nod of his head. I take Ava's hand and move past the guard. She follows, the warmth of her hand diffusing a bit of the tension in my chest. Nick takes up the rear.

A few steps down the hall, I look back, squinting at how bright white everything is. My eyes adjust quickly, but it still feels unnatural. Castillo falls in line behind my brother, the thud of his standard issue Army boots clunking against the floor. I turn back around and leer past Riley to see the doctor. All I get is the back of his head, a full head of salt-and-pepper hair, the thick black ends of spectacles, and the high collar of a medical smock.

I wait for him to start talking, certain he's about to proclaim how amazing and useful his little project is, but he doesn't speak. We walk in silence for about two minutes before he leads us on a detour down another hall. I'd say it's one we haven't been down yet, but at this point I'm not sure where I am. Less than ten steps into the new branch, Dr. Fischer leans into a set of double doors and disappears around the corner. Through the swinging doors is a generous space with two sleek gray rectangular tables with simple metal chairs arranged four to a side.

"Take a seat," Dr. Fischer says, holding his hand out toward the four chairs on this side of the nearest table.

It still strikes me as odd how his orders lack any of the traditional qualities of someone commanding obedience. Instead, they sound more like requests, coming off kind and even thoughtful at times.

As we take our seats, the doctor walks around the table and faces us. He looks at each one of us in turn, his eyes calculating but bright with a morbid happiness I have no desire to understand. I wish he'd stop smiling or that I could have the pleasure of wiping it off his face permanently. His shoulders rise and lower as he sighs and bobs his head.

"All right, then," he starts, the grin never leaving his chiseled face. "You want to know why you're still here, as opposed to being in our morgue in pieces, right?"

I don't know what to say. The contrast between the actual words streaming from his mouth and the calm normality of his tone leaves me baffled. I look to Nick. He's faring no better, his nose crinkled and lips parted in disbelief.

"Do you not?" he asks. A look of amused confusion slips across his grin for a moment.

"Ye—" Nick starts.

"Of course, you do," Dr. Fischer interrupts him. "You'd have to be imbeciles not to wonder, right? You don't have to answer that. The hick is already dead, and I think the rest of you are at least marginally in—"

"That hick was my friend, you fucking cunt!" Nick screams and jumps to his feet. His chair scuttles back and a screech bounces off the solid white walls. I jerk from the sudden outburst.

Sit down, Nick!

I clench my jaw and dart my eyes between Nick and Dr. Fischer. The rage in my brother's eyes matches his voice as his fists pound the table. A click draws my attention back to the doctor and I find the pistol drawn again, but this time Nick stares down the barrel. I inch forward in my seat and tighten my grip on Ava's hand. I lift my other hand and place my palm on Nick's arm, begging him to stop.

"Sit back down." The doctor enunciates each word slowly, his eyes narrow and beaming, but the grin is still there. "The first thing you all need to know is that I don't *need* all of you. So if I were you, Nick, I'd sit the fuck down."

Nick gulps and reaches for his chair. His hand swats behind him aimlessly until he glances back long enough to find his seat and then brings his eyes back to Dr. Fischer. He retrieves the chair and takes his seat at the table again. I eye him, begging him to calm down. He shuts his eyes, processing the loss of another close friend.

The doctor sighs before his smile returns.

What the fuck is wrong with this guy?

The door swings open and Dr. Price scurries in.

"I take it that I missed something…" His words trail off, his brow rising as he finds Dr. Fischer aiming the pistol.

"Indeed, you did. Our guest here took offense to my candor, it seems. We were just getting down to business though," he tells his counterpart without taking his eyes off us.

"What *did* I miss?"

"Nothing, really." He waves the pistol in front of me and passes the hollow end by Ava and Riley before coming back around. I tense, gritting my teeth and restraining my arms at my sides.

Dr. Price nods and takes a seat across the table near Dr. Fischer like this is all common practice. I glance at each in turn.

"Nathan, can you get them something to eat and some water?" Dr. Fischer asks. Once Dr. Price starts off to the silver fridge in the corner, Dr. Fischer continues. "So, now that we skipped to the end, let's move back a few steps. The first point I wanted to make is that your misfortune here is not all for nothing. It's *not* meaningless. I understand that you might not be able to see it, but your unexpected visit to the island has filled a need. Even your friends' deaths serve a purpose."

I can't believe what I'm hearing. It shouldn't surprise me, but I still can't wrap my brain around the mental fucking it takes to say the things coming out of Dr. Fischer's mouth. How could someone believe this shit? I would think that someone intelligent enough to work in a DARPA facility would possess the same ability to empathize and to see the morbidity of his actions.

"As I told you yesterday, we're doing research here for military warfare applications. We're finding new ways to protect American troops, to provide them with an edge on the battlefield and maybe even keep them out of the battlefield altogether." Dr. Fischer pauses, lowering the pistol to his side.

"Any sacrifice you make here is to protect American lives. It's truly that simple."

"What? You've got to be shitting me!" Ava's hand tightens around mine as the words jump from her lips. "What about *our* lives? We're Americans too."

Dr. Price jumps at her words, almost spilling one of the waters, before depositing the clear plastic cups in front of us.

"Yes." Dr. Fischer doesn't lose a beat. "But you made the mistake of trespassing on the clearly restricted grounds of this *reserve*. It's cliché, but this is a top-secret facility and the rules are a little bit different here. The moment you stepped foot on the island, it became our job to protect its secrets. We could have called the authorities and had you removed, but we were ready for the first testing phase of our eighth generation Proeliatorum. We've been at this for a number of years, and if you haven't noticed, people don't frequent the island often."

He bends forward, planting his palms on the table. The metal frame of the gun smacks against the solid surface under his hand, and my eyes snap to it. I tear my eyes back up to the doctor, but my mind stays on the gun. It's so close, maybe two feet across the table, and Dr. Fischer's grasp on it is weak. It's under his hand, but it could easily be taken. I shift my butt in my chair, wondering if this might be our moment.

Dr. Price walks around the edge of the table and puts down two more cups of water. He leaves again and quickly comes back with a bowl of cereal for each of us. Reese's, I think.

The gravity of Dr. Fischer's words pulls me back in. They could have kicked us off the island when we arrived, but they didn't because it served *their* purpose.

"We *were* using the city's homeless population, but that

required abduction. The agency was never overly happy with that, plus it took more resources, but research isn't always clean. They prefer we take the opportunity to exploit the rules on the island where possible. Hence where you come into the picture." Dr. Fischer lifts his hands from the table, extending his pointer fingers and waving to encompass all of us. No one says a word. I glance to Nick and find his eyes fidgeting up and down, too, from Dr. Fischer to the gun. "I think you all have a general idea what we're doing here now. Riley, I'm assuming your friends filled you in on the rest. Sorry for keeping you in the dark, but we weren't ready yet."

I flinch when the pistol scrapes across the table. Dr. Fischer slides the weapon along as he takes a step to my left, eyeing me, then Ava. His eyes shift to Riley before he turns and walks back in the other direction, continuing to drag the gun over the table. The noise grates my ears, but that's the least of my concerns.

"Our Proeliatorum are the next soldiers. Initially we thought cybernetic enhancements were going to be the next step, our upper hand to give our soldiers increased strength, dexterity and mobility. Just think if they could trek the mountains or the desert without tiring, or implants in the mind that could exponentially increase the soldier's reaction time and mental processes. But other labs are working on that. We thought a different approach was needed."

Dr. Fischer grins.

I don't want to know. I just want to get out of this place. My eyes twitch toward the gun again. It's still sitting under his open palm. I lean forward and have to calm my breathing. It's so close.

"We were brought to Riverside to explore the possibility

of genetic mutations and enhancements to create the perfect the soldier. One with the reflexes of an animal, an increased ability to process information, and split-second decision-making with the best positive outcome. But most importantly, we wanted a totally compliant soldier." He shifts his feet, looking up to Dr. Price and then back to us. His haughty air only grows with my obvious distaste.

"As you've seen, we've accomplished most of our goals. Of course, our research, once perfected, would only be used in select groups, like special task forces. My personal suggestion has been to use enemy combatants as the Proeliatorum rather than locking them up for an eternity on some offshore hellhole. Why not put them to use for us?" Dr. Fischer's eyes gleam with excitement. "Wouldn't that be the ultimate punishment for their crimes? To fight *for* the very ones they were fighting *against*?"

I let my gaze drop, mulling over the implications of their research and the slopes they're not just slipping down, but falling at full speed. He's talking about taking prisoners of war, terrorists, enemy combatants, whatever you want to call them, and taking away their humanity without trial, without consideration for human will or dignity. I know they're the enemy, but right now, from where I sit, I feel like he's looking at me as the enemy.

He is.

"You can't do that. The government will never go for that. People will—" I start, unsure where the sudden burst of courage is coming from.

"Oh, just shut up," Dr. Fischer interrupts. He leans his back in the corner of the stark white room. Dr. Price smiles and shakes his head like he was expecting the outburst. His brow rises expectantly.

"Yes, the human rights groups will march. The constitution thumpers will jump all over it. So? It's time we make some changes, and once they realize how many American lives it takes off the front lines, the mothers, the fathers, the wives and husbands of our servicemen will be clambering to keep them."

I lean back against the cool solid back of my chair. He's mad. He's *fucking* insane.

"But then again, we're a long way from that day. There's no need to rush — that only causes backlash and would prove you right. No. Just like this lab, the American people don't have to know. Like I said, the Defense Department will keep it small at first, just small special forces type groups for quick, targeted actions." He glances to Dr. Price and then back at us. "Hell, they've already drafted up a possible timeline for implementation. I don't know the specifics, I'm not a military man, I'm a scientist. The point is that by the time the media ever has the chance to break the news of these new super soldiers, the people will applaud them and beg for them. There will always be resistance, but that won't stop progress."

"You're one sick fuck." I snap my attention to Ava and let a small grin of approval paint my lips. Dr. Fischer raises his hands to correct her, but she keeps talking. "You really think yo — "

Beside me, Nick lurches forward and grabs for the pistol. My head snaps to the right as his fingers grab the barrel, his other hand simultaneously swatting Dr. Fischer's unprepared hand away from the weapon. Nick reels back, but not before the doctor grapples for the weapon, the balance of power. It's stuck between the doctor's and my brother's hands. I dart my eyes between them and the gun. Suddenly I'm not ready for this. After all our planning, now that the moment is here, I freeze.

"Let go!" Dr. Fischer screams, grasping the grip. "You don't know what you're doing!"

We know exactly what we're doing.

The thought jolts me back into the game. I lurch forward, clamping my fist into a tight ball. I swing with every ounce of hate in me. My knuckles connect with Dr. Fischer's chin and his face snaps back. Spit and blood spurt across the table and the doctor stumbles back, both arms flailing in the air to guard his face from another impact. I shoot my attention back to the table as Nick hoists the pistol and solidifies his grip. He rises to his feet and aims the weapon.

"What do you think you're doing?!" Dr. Fischer bellows.

I step back and put a hand on Ava's shoulder, urging her to get up. She understands and leaves her chair. Riley follows along as I step between Ava and the doctors. Dr. Fischer raises a finger to his chin and lip, touching the bleeding skin. He stretches his jaw with an angered grunt.

"What does it look like!" Nick yells. His eyes are outlined in dark circles, but there's an intensity in them I've never witnessed before. I glance between him and the doctor. "We're leaving, and you're going to help us. How do we get out of here? Start talking!"

I raise my brow at Nick, excitement and anxiety sparking through my veins at the sudden shift of power, then I fix my gaze on the doctor. His eyes lack that annoying self-sufficiency they had beamed so confidently since we walked through the vault door, and his chin shakes. He swallows and licks the blood from his lip.

"You're going nowhere," he says slowly, the rage in his voice building with each word. "You have no idea what you're doing. The moment you walk through those doors and the guards realize you're escaping, they'll cut you down without blinking. And even if you managed to evade them, you can't open the exit doors without a key card."

The doctor raises the ID badge hanging from his pants and wiggles it triumphantly for us to see.

That could be a problem...

"Give it to Cooper," Nick barks. My eyes snap toward Nick, and he nods for me to go along. I nod half-heartedly and extend my hand toward Dr. Fischer. "Now!"

"I'm not giving you anything," Dr. Fischer responds in defiance.

Nick straightens his arm and lifts the pistol an inch higher, holding the barrel level with the doctor's nose. I can see the gun wavering in Nick's nervous hands. He knows how to handle a gun, we were raised around them, taught how to use them and to respect them, but holding one on another human being is something altogether different.

"I don't want to hurt you," Nick tries again. "Give Cooper the key card and tell us how to get out of here."

"I think I can get us out," Ava speaks up. "I think I remember the way."

I keep my eye on Dr. Fischer while my arm remains outstretched, fingers splayed open awaiting the key card.

"I'm not giving you shit." Dr. Fischer curls his lips. "Price!"

My eyes dart to the other doctor as a flash of yellow accompanies into an earsplitting boom. I jerk my hand back and stumble against Ava in surprise. The bullet ricochets off the wall before Dr. Price pulls the trigger again. I flinch as another boom fills the space. Next to me, Nick gasps.

No!

I twist to the right and find Nick stumbling back as his finger curls around the trigger. A burst of yellow explodes from the barrel, but Nick loses his footing and falls to the floor, the bullet flying high. The pistol smacks against the white tile, but he manages to raise it again as I drop to my knees beside him.

"Nick!" I scream, dropping to the floor next to him. He turns to face me, his motions overemphasized and dazed. I find the bullet hole in his upper chest. It's a small fray of singed cloth and blackness beyond. Blood begins to soak his shirt. "No, Nick! No! You're going to be okay!"

I don't know why the words come out, but I say them anyway. Footsteps clamber around me as Ava drops to my side. It doesn't even register that the gunshots have stopped or that the doctors are simply standing behind us, watching.

Ava puts a hand on Nick's shoulder and gives me a determined look. I don't know what to do, but I press my hand against his chest, covering the wound. He grunts as the thick blood pushes between my fingers and over my palm. My mind is a flurry of emotions. Love. Hate. Horror. Fear. Hope, irrational hope.

"Stop!" Dr. Price yells over my thoughts. "It doesn't have to be this way."

I swing around and glare at him. I can see how shaken he is, his eyes wide and buggy. His pistol is held awkwardly in front of him in unsteady hands. Dr. Fischer raises a brow at his counterpart and then finds me looking.

"He's going to die, Cooper." Dr. Fischer juts out his chin again and plants his fist on the table. "You can't win. This only ends one way for you, and that's giving up."

He means dead. The words blare in my head. *Dead. Dead. Dead.*

I pull my eyes away from the doctors and back to Nick, trying to forget Dr. Fischer's words as they play between my fears.

He's going to die, Cooper.

"Come on, Nick!" I refuse to look down at the wound again, instead keeping my eyes locked with his. They're scared, weak. He swallows hard. I'm shaking, wishing that somehow this is all a terrible nightmare or some vivid simulation as my brain tries to cope. "We can get you fixed up. Remember, they fixed your leg."

An look of amusement breaks past the fear in his eyes, and a little part of my brother shines through again. I begin to cry, hot tears streaming down my face.

"I...I don't think...they're going to help me this time," he stutters.

"Nathan, give me the gun," Dr. Fischer commands impatiently.

"You can't go, Nick." My voice is a whisper, but the words are quick. "I don't know what to do. We need you."

Nick reaches out with his left hand and cups the back of my head, pulling me closer. My chin rests on his shoulder and I feel his irregular breaths hot against my ear.

"You have to run..." he whispers. Then I feel something cold and solid press against my right hand. It only takes me a second to realize what it is as my fingers wrap around the warm grip. "Get...out of here."

As the last word exits his lip, Nick's body slumps against the floor and emptiness invades his eyes. My vision blurs as tears fill my eyes. I lean over his body and place a palm on his cheek, waiting, hoping for him to say something, but he only stares past me, through me. I bite my lip as Ava begins to cry, and she places a hand on my back.

A voice shouts something behind me, but it's all a haze as the air stutters between my lips. My eyes bounce between Nick's lifeless eyes, hoping that I'm dreaming, determined that this can't be real.

Come on, Nick. Come back.

Ava squeezes my arm gingerly and I pull my eyes away to find her. Somehow the sadness in her eyes is comforting.

"Turn around!" Dr. Fischer screams.

I close my eyes and pull my hand back from Nick's empty face, clenching my fist and letting my breath out in a staccato choppiness.

"Now!"

My whole body quakes as a dark sensation, a black concoction of hate and pain and loss swells in my chest. I let it boil in a place deep beneath my heart that I've never felt before. It's overwhelming.

I spin around. The world moves in slow motion. I straighten my arm, grasping the pistol with both hands and aiming the iron sights as Dr. Fischer comes into view. He's reaching for the gun in Dr. Price's hands. I turn until the iron sights settles on Dr. Price's chest; only then do I see the horrified expression in his eyes as he realizes what's about to happen. I pull the trigger.

The pistol recoils, sending a jolt through my arms and a flash from the barrel as the slide snaps back and then falls forward again. The bullet punches into Dr. Price's chest and knocks him into the countertop. Metal clangs and falls from the counter as he flings his hands to stop himself. I pull the trigger again, bracing for the recoil as Dr. Price's body absorbs the impact of the second round.

Dr. Fischer jumps back, a deep confusion clouding his eyes. He watches as Dr. Price slumps from the counter. The doctor's back scrapes against the shelves and falls limply to the floor, a swath of blood streaking the cabinets.

"What have you done!" Dr. Fischer yells, wheeling around to face me, his eyes both scared and enraged.

I swing the pistol toward him and begin to pull back on the trigger, but I stop, fighting against the adrenaline pumping through my veins. I grit my teeth as the reality of what I just did sets in. I remind myself that I'm justified while I fight back the tears and the tremors building in my chest. The gun still shakes in my hands, but I hold it true and ignore the doctor's question.

"Give us the key." I don't scream, but I still put force behind my words. He doesn't seem to react at first. He stands there, glaring at me as if trying to decide whether he can survive a bullet or not. My patience gone, I scream at him. "Now!"

He flinches and his hand hurries to his side and unsnaps the badge from its belt loop. He huffs, "You're not going to make it off this island."

"We might not, but we're damn well going to try," I tell him. "And we're going to tell everyone about this place." I take a step forward. "Toss it to Ava."

He begins to toss the badge, but stops in mid-swing, a haunting smile growing over his face. He laughs at me. It strikes me as odd, even as scared as I am, and I'm horrified that a man in his place could laugh down the barrel of a pistol.

I keep my aim nonetheless.

"No," he rebels with a huff of indignation. "You'll have to…"

I angle the pistol down and finish his sentence with a squeeze of the trigger. He drops to the ground, hands clutching his calf, and the badge tumbles from his grasp, landing under the table. "No problem. Ava, can you get that badge? Be careful."

"Got it," she says as she drops to her hands and knees and crawls under the table.

My mind racing, I step back and take one last look at Nick. My stomach tightens, and tears threaten to obstruct my vision. I open my mouth and let out a terrified breath to hold back the tears before looking back at Dr. Fischer and letting the rage build again.

"I'll get the other gun." Riley runs around the table, but he's careful to keep his distance from Dr. Fischer. He pauses in front of Dr. Price's corpse and takes a deep breath before leaning down and grabbing the pistol.

"We have to go before the guards get here, Cooper." Riley aims the gun at Dr. Fischer and comes back around the table as Ava gets back to her feet, key card in hand. "They had to hear all that."

I nod, my body quaking. I tighten my grasp on the pistol and raise it, letting my shaky hand bring its cold metal frame in line with Dr. Fischer's head.

You deserve to die.

I curl my finger around the trigger and begin to pull.

Why? Why Nick? Why not me?

"Cooper." A gentle hand wraps around my wrist. I gasp, but I don't let my eyes waver. The man deserves to die. Ava speaks softly. "Cooper, let's go."

You deserve to die, but a bullet's too quick for you.

She tugs at my arm as I let my finger fall from the trigger and purge the air from my lungs in one long breath. I lower the gun. A hopeful smile finds its way across Dr. Fischer's face and I almost raise the pistol again.

"Come on, Cooper, we don't have much time." Riley's voice is urgent but shadowed by a subtle understanding.

I turn to look at Nick one more time. He's lying on the floor, his messy mop of hair dirty and splayed on the ground. His body is still, floating in a growing pool of blood against a pure white backdrop. I skip over the hole in his chest and find my brother's eyes. They've lost their depth, buried under something not quite human, something distant and unknown.

"Cooper, we have to go." Ava tugs at my arm again.

"Okay."

39: Cooper Bay

I feel like I'm moving on autopilot. My feet are keeping pace with Ava. The white tiles slip by underneath me like a conveyor belt. My eyes are locked forward, staring past her and Riley, but I can't focus on anything but my thoughts.

How can Nick be gone? Dead.

The word grinds though my brain like a foreign object inserted into the gears of a clock. My throat and heart feel like its hands, stopping, jerking, desperately wanting to be free of the burden buried down deep, but unable to shake it.

"Cooper." Ava pulls at my hand.

I glance down, my eyes blinking, and find her fingers laced between mine. I don't remember taking her hand. I raise my eyes and meet her worried expression. She's glancing between me and the path ahead, trying to be eyes for both of us.

"We have to speed up, they're coming."

That's when I finally hear the footsteps charging behind us.

The soldiers!

A surge of understanding rushes up my spine and I quicken my pace.

"Stop!" one of the soldiers bellows down the hallway. Judging from the accent, I think it's Castillo.

"Come on, guys!" Riley yells back.

Suddenly, the veil clouding my thoughts falls and I realize that if I don't get my head back in the moment, it won't just be me who pays for it.

Ava.

As the sounds of boots and orders being shouted from behind reaches my ears, I draw in a deep breath and bury the dead feeling in my heart, pocketing it away. In its place I fill my chest with how it felt to tell Ava I loved her last night and the pit that burrowed in my chest at the thought of losing her, too. I close my eyes, fighting to focus on her. When I open them again, I glance back at the soldiers and swing the pistol around. I pull the trigger without waiting for a proper aim and let the bullet fly. It cracks against the wall a few feet ahead of Castillo. He jerks to a stop and props his rifle against his shoulder.

"Oh shit!" I mutter. I turn and urge Ava to move faster.

I jerk forward as a piece of lead scrapes the wall to my right. Sparks fly. I flinch away, almost knocking Ava off her feet, but we keep running.

How many rounds do I have left?

My mind suddenly needs to know, my eyes jumping between the walls and the turn coming up ahead, trying to make a mental inventory.

Somewhere between three and five…I think.

Riley makes the bend first. He stops and leans his shoulder against the wall, waving us by as he takes aim. I rush forward. A bullet ricochets off the floor and lodges in the wall ahead of me. Its brass case is distinctly visible in the smooth white walls. I burst by Riley, and he takes his shot, then a second. I hear one of the soldiers grunt, but I don't look back.

"Come on, Riley!" I yell, slowing long enough to glance

back. He's already abandoned his post and his feet are pounding against the floor.

Ava's a few paces ahead now, her lean calves pumping with each step. I focus on her, hoping she knows how to get us out of this white hell.

I can't lose her. I can't bear to lose anything else.

A round of semi-auto fire bellows over the sound of my breathing and footsteps announcing the soldiers' turn into the corridor. I think Riley's shooting back, but I can't tell the shots apart. Then, over it all, a bloodcurdling roar washes the hall, coating every inch of my body in a palpable fear. I fight the urge to freeze as my limbs tighten, threatening to lock up at the thought of the beasts. What did Dr. Fischer call them?

Proeliatoris.

Ava jerks her head around and catches me in her sight. Her eyes are filled with a deep fear that makes them glassy, but instead of causing my heart to swoon, it drops. Before I have a chance to look back, Riley screams.

"Run!"

I know better, but I swing my head around anyway. It makes no sense, but despite the roar and the way the hair on the back of my neck stands up, I have to see, to know what's behind me. The first thing my eyes catch is the vicious open maw in mid-growl. Then blood bursts from one soldier's chest as four sharp claws bury themselves deep into the man's side. The creature lifts him from the ground. As the soldier's body seizes, his finger clenches the trigger of his M4 rifle. Bright flashes burst from the barrel as bullets fly. I duck as lead ricochets against the ceiling, floor and walls.

"Go, Ava! Run!" I scream.

For a brief second, the knowledge that Nick died by the

bullet rather than the ravaging claws of the Proeliatoris sends an uncomfortable calm through my body. My feet strike the tile without slowing, but I realize that if I do die tonight, today, whenever the hell it is, I want it to be by the bullet. I glance at the pistol in my hand, but I'm quick to look away. The *clack, clack, clack* of the firestorm ends abruptly, culminating in a pained scream for its grand finale. I keep running but glimpse back. Riley's catching up. His face is a warm red. He waves me on, but I peer past him. Castillo is sliding on his back, using an elbow to drag himself across the slick white tile, a messy crimson glaze left in his wake. Beyond him, the other soldier lies in a heap of his own organs under the unbreathing body of one of the Proeliatorum.

My eyes widen in surprise.

They killed one! They actually killed it!

A wave of screamed curses and obscenities pull my attention back to Castillo. He's not going to make it. I check my twelve o'clock to be sure I don't miss a turn or lose Ava, then turn my head back around. I grimace as the creature scrabbles atop the soldier, its spike-like fingers tearing into his skin like knives slipping through cake. An anguished scream assaults my ears as blood splashes the walls each time the creature stabs and pulls at the man's flesh.

"Cooper!" Riley snatches my attention and nods forward. I turn to find a wall but no Ava. Where is she? Which way did she go? I'm about to panic when Riley yells again, "Left!"

I lean into the turn and let my weight pull me through. Around the corner I find her again. She's making good time. A spark of hope pours through my body when I catch the vault door at the end of the hall. Ava reaches it first and wastes no time swiping the key card. I clench my teeth, fully expecting it to be deactivated.

I should have killed him.

A green slit along the card scanner blinks to life and a series of staccato *clanks* sound around the edge of the door. A flood of relief drenches my mind.

It worked.

"Come on!" Ava turns and waves.

I barrel forward. The screech of steel against concrete pierces my ears. There are only a few more yards of hall left before it spills into the hospital basement. I throw my arm forward, signaling Ava to go ahead.

"Go on! We'll catch up!" I scream. I don't want her to linger. I don't want her waiting any longer than she has to or being any closer than necessary to this place.

Before she turns, an all too familiar howl fills the air. My body seems to grow heavier under the bellow. I yell again for Ava to go. She steps over the threshold into the black abyss beyond the vault door, but instead of running she takes up a centurion-like position behind the door.

By the look on her face, I know the creature has made the turn even before the pounding of its feet offends my ears. I push myself to move faster. In seconds I bolt past the threshold, welcoming the shadows and the musty air. I take Ava's hand and start off again, but she doesn't move. Her dead weight yanks me back. I peer at her, confused.

"Wait," she exhales over quick breaths. "Maybe we can shut it in."

I start to protest. My primary thought is getting as far away from this place as possible, but finally it hits me. She's right. I take up a spot next to Ava and search the hall. Riley's racing up the corridor with that thing on his heels. I snag the key from her hand, unwilling to let her take the risk. She eyes me.

"I can't lose you," I tell her.

She doesn't stop me.

I step back across the threshold, tightening my grip on the card. Riley's maybe ten yards down the hall. My heart pounds and sweat beads on my forehead as I take another leaden step and plant my feet by the locking mechanism. I can see the beast bearing down on Riley, gaining inch by inch. I stare it down as Riley rushes down the hall. A cold intensity radiates behind the silver-blue of its cat-like eyes, but somehow, I can see the human behind them now. I shake my head, tossing the thought away. Its thick calves contract and stretch, its brawny chest flexes, and its claws clink with each swing of its arms.

"Shut it! Now!" Ava barks.

I raise the key card to the lock but stop long enough to scream to Riley, "Hurry!"

I swipe the card, generating a double beep from the panel and a screech from the vault door as it scrapes against the concrete. Never letting my eyes leave the giant beast on Riley's heels, I slide back and slip over the thick metal threshold into the hospital. I drop the card and wrap my fists into tight, nervous balls. The air in my lungs is tight against my chest and the blood in my veins moves with an urgency I've never felt. It's taking an eternity for the door close.

Three feet... Two feet...

Come on, Riley!

I can feel the quake under me with every pounding step of the creature's feet. The door slides closer and the dark begins to overtake the glow on our side of the door. I take a step forward. There's nothing I can do. Once the door shuts, I won't be able to open it again.

What if he doesn't make it? What... You just run. Take Ava and run.

A pang of shame runs through my chest, but I know if it comes to it, that's what I'll do. Bellator, Miles, whatever the fuck Dr. Fischer called it, snarls at us as Riley twists his body and slides through the heavy vault door, falling and skidding on his butt across the rough concrete of the hospital floor.

The door inches closer, but it's too slow. I beg it to speed up as the creature's form swiftly overtakes the space between us. Using the tiny sliver of white light jutting between the slimming separation, I step back and help Riley to his feet. Upright again, he turns to face the door, watching the light fade away, needing to know it holds. Only four more inches until it closes. Three...

The sound of the vault door closing sends a shot of relief rushing through me. A colossal crack breaks my temporary comfort, and my eyes widen in shock as the wall encompassing the vault door shudders. I imagine a series of spiderweb fractures cracking the concrete at the around the doorframe, but I can't see it in the dark.

"It's not going to hold..." Riley's voice trails off as he steps back. He pulls me back. "We need to go. Like now!"

I step back as another boom sends a tremor down the wall and into the floor.

I spin on the balls of my feet and aim for the open door leading into the hospital's subterranean hallway, taking off feet behind Ava and Riley. We rush through the doorway and spill into the unlit corridor.

Blackness engulfs us, and I find myself wishing I had a flashlight. I can't see a thing.

40: Cooper Bay

"Cooper," Ava's voice cuts through the darkness over her racing breaths.

She should still be in front of me, but I reach out to be sure. At first my hand finds nothing but air. Then my fingers touch something soft.

"Ava? Is that you?" I ask, my legs pumping.

"Yeah." She reaches back and takes my hand.

Without a flashlight to guide us we're running blind, engulfed by an opaque darkness. I keep my hand holding the pistol stuck out ahead of me with the hope it'll be enough to stop me from slamming into a wall. I can't remember if there were any turns when we came down originally.

Please just be straight.

I put off the thought and call out to Riley. "Riley? You up there?"

"Yeah, I'm here," he answers, panting.

A hard-hitting boom quakes the floor under my feet. I steal a glance back to find a sliver of light piercing the hallway yards behind me. Another crack shakes the floor and echoes through the tight space. The sliver grows.

Oh fuck! It's not going to hold long.

"Let's get the hell out of here!" I scream, not waiting for a reply before injecting a new burst of energy into my legs. I take up a position next to Ava and urge her to move quicker.

A howl slices through the darkness between the massive blows against the steel door. It cracks one last time and I hear the thud of the creature's feet crossing into the hospital.

We have to get out of here!

"Gotta move faster, gotta move!" I yell ahead.

"I know!" Riley screams back.

Ahead, a new sliver of light materializes. In seconds, the pale brown of the wooden stair planks come into focus. A grain of hope falls on top of the tension swelling in my chest. We mount them, climbing up each stair without thinking twice about the age and weakness of the boards, ignoring how each plank creaks and bows under the sudden pressure.

Over the last stair, a misting of morning sunlight seeps into the expansive open space. My foot leaves the last step a second after Ava and we sprint after Riley. We weave between wooden planks and rotten chairs, rushing through the auditorium-like room before entering the veranda. Warm yellow rays sift through the broken windowpanes and past the overgrowth, which covers them like green spiderwebs.

"Come on!" Riley dodges the overturned clothes hamper and jumps over a stack of fractured wood.

Following close behind Ava, I let go of her hand so she can focus on running. I refuse to look back when the crack of wooden planks pierces the air, and claws clamor against something solid. It's gaining on us.

Riley rushes through the glass front doors, pushing the double doors out of his way. In a full sprint, I brace myself before my shoulder pounds against the door as it swings back. Glass shatters and digs into my shoulder, eliciting a sharp scream deep from within my lungs. The door swings out and its hinges, weakened by years of neglect, break. It topples from its posts and careens down the stairs, glass cracking and clinking against broken concrete. I constrict my fists and grind my teeth to stave off the pain and keep my legs moving. Ava bursts through after me, and we make for the forest.

"I think we're going to make it!" Ava yells at me, trying to stay beside me as we break the tree line and head into a light fog. I squint. The warm haze isn't bad, but it's enough to muddle my vision.

I try to grin, but I can't. Instead, I focus my thoughts on her. I think about seeing Ava for the first time under the streetlights when she stepped out of the taxi and the excitement that surged through my lungs and chest. I remember how my heart reached out to her when her eyes filled with tears as she talked about losing her father. I relive the feeling of her skin under my bare body and the passion we shared, the taste of her lips.

There's no giving up, Cooper.

"Of course, we—" I try, but before I can finish the sentence a crescendo of breaking glass and wood explodes somewhere behind us. I know what it is. The beast is out. "— are. Dammit! Can't we get just one break?"

Its roar permeates the forest, sending the birds above us scattering in panic. I glance back, but I can't see it through the thick grouping of trees between us. I turn forward again and put an extra burst of energy into my legs and catch up with Ava again.

It takes no time for the creature's heavy steps to invade the forest in muted thuds, each one reaching out like claws for my neck. I dodge a low branch. The wind whistles through the spindly trees, leaves and undergrowth, and washes over me, cooling my sweat-soaked skin. Ava sidesteps a tree. I try to follow, but I don't react quickly enough, so I take the opposite side.

As we run I realize I've lost the sound of the creature's footsteps. I let my pace slow and turn my head from side to side, listening for its harsh footfalls, its ragged breaths and that horrendous roar. In its place I find the ruffle of leaves as another bird takes off from a branch overhead, the stamping of my own feet on damp dirt and the faint chaos of the city across the river, but not the Proeliatoris.

"Ava, Riley..." I call between breaths. "I think it stopped."

When they turn, I come to a halt. Riley skids to a stop a few yards ahead and stares back. Ava stops, too, and looks at me questioningly. I peer up into the trees as if they're going to speak to me and tell me where it is. I listen. Still nothing.

"Are you sure?" Ava whispers.

"I can't hear it," I tell her. A dark sensation seeps into my stomach and I swallow back the sudden need to dart forward. It doesn't make any sense. It's nearly silent, but I feel like we're being watched. I wave Ava forward. "Let's keep moving. Are we going the right way?"

I start toward Riley before she can respond.

"I think so," she says, but there is a subtle doubt in her silky voice. "But I don't have a major frame of reference here. I mean, it's just forest."

I bob my head; I can't blame her. "Yeah, not exactly the city."

We stay on our path, making our way through trees on a long untraveled trail. It's warm and humid, and the sweat on my brow only makes me feel worse. The smell of bark and dirt sift into my nostrils under the faint wetness of the mist. But it's eerily quiet. I wish I could see past the fog, but it only grows thicker. I quicken my pace to come up by Ava and take her hand. She eyes me, her blue eyes wondering but beautiful. "This doesn't feel right. Why would it just stop?" I look around but find little more than trees and fog. "It doesn't make sense."

Before she can answer, Riley speaks up a few feet ahead. "Maybe it gave up."

If only it were that easy, but it can't be, it just doesn't *feel* right. After all we've been through on this damn island, I can't accept that answer. I squeeze Ava's hand, the scared boy inside me wanting to spill out.

"I don't think so," Ava whispers, biting her lips nervously. "That's too easy."

"Why can't it be easy?" Riley comes back, his tone rising. I crinkle my brow. "Why not? Don't we deserve a *fucking* break?"

"Yeah, we deserve a break, but do you—" My words are sliced short by a guttural scream to my right. It booms in my ear a second before the hulking mass of my worst nightmare materializes behind the fog, its claws reaching out as its body flies through the air.

Before I have time to react, its claws wrap around Ava's ankle and its feet pound against the forest floor. The ground quakes beneath me as Ava's hand is wrenched from my grasp. I stumble forward, reaching for her.

"Ava!" I scream, and without thinking, against every reasonable thought and fear, I bound after her. Blood pumps through my veins, and the current pulsing through my nerves overloads my brain. The sound of Ava's screech cleaves my heart in two, and the sight of her terrified eyes reaching for me causes my stomach to sink to depths unknown.

Kill it, Coop.

I stop and swing the pistol to eye level and take aim, but it's moving too erratically. I'm afraid I'll hit Ava.

"Dammit!" Without giving myself time to think it over, I charge forward. Ava's arms are flailing, trying to grab onto anything that will release her from the powerful grip on her leg. I don't know what I plan to do, but I rush forward, closing the gap anyway.

With only a few feet between the beast and me, I raise my weapon at near point-blank range, but before I can pull the trigger its free hand swings through the air and swats at me like an overgrown fly. I gasp as the hard claws and leathery skin pound against my chest and shoulder, and a flurry of misery breaks through my muscles. My body spins away in a swinging arch. Wind rushes over my back, curling under my side before my time in the air comes to a sudden biting stop against a thin but sturdy tree trunk. I fall helplessly to an un-forgiving forest floor. A groan tries to escape my air-deprived lungs, but the pain squelches it, my face flattened against the wet soil. Every inch of my torso screams, but with Ava's cries for help filling my head, I inhale, ignoring the flaring pain in my chest, and push off the dirt.

I stow the pistol under the band in my shorts and start af-ter the beast again. Before I take two steps, Riley blurs past me. I stumble back, not expecting him to sprint by, and strug-gling with the pain overwhelming my body. I start off again, pumping my legs, willing myself to ignore the discomfort and burning in every inch of me. Riley is easily ten yards ahead, and the creature, dragging my Ava through the woods, is at least another five yards out.

I weave between a set of bushes and have to make a last-second adjustment to miss a branch I didn't see coming a moment before. Shifting to the right, I avoid another branch, then a fallen trunk. Ava's desperate screams fill the forest and drive me forward. I'm running as fast as I can, but I can't match its stride. Nonetheless, I keep my eyes up, locked on Ava, darting in and out of the trees and thickets. Her body bounces and shudders against the ground. My blood boils and my lips curl as I push my legs to move quicker.

Between us, Riley begins to close the gap, his body shooting through the tiny rays of sunlight pricking through the forest canopy and dispelling the mist in his wake. My eyes widen when his feet leave the ground and he tackles the beast. He wraps his arm around its thick neck and tugs and yanks. Despite my shock at seeing it slow and its grip on Ava loosen, I keep running. She slides from its hand, flopping to the ground like a rag doll. I close the gap and drop to my knees feet from her side, skidding on my bare knees through the dirt, leaves and twigs.

"Ava!" I yell and scoop her into my arms. Before I can get out another word or make sure she's okay, the creature bathes the moist air with a high-pitched yelp, followed immediately by a harsh crash.

Ava's eyes flutter, and her voice escapes her lips in a harsh moan. I smile down at her. "I've got you."

Riley!

My eyes jerk up. I find Riley and the Proeliatoris on the ground, his arms still locked around its neck. I let Ava lean back on the ground, giving her a reassuring grin, and get to my feet.

This is bad. This is so bad!

I start forward, unsure what I can do, but I move anyway. Ahead, the creature shakes Riley's grip, and he tumbles off, his back landing firmly on a rotting trunk. Its bark caves on impact, and he falls through to a bed of decomposed wood and insects. I lean forward and start to run, but within seconds Riley is back on his feet, bobbing like a boxer. He sprints forward, faster than I've ever seen anyone move in all my years in track.

What the hell?

He drops to his butt only feet from the beast, his legs fully extended, sliding across dirt and compost. I stop in my tracks as the creature's thick legs are hammered out from under its own body. A mini thunderclap booms through the forest as its weighty form smacks against the ground. Before it has time to react, Riley is back on his feet and clambering over its muscular back. He reaches around the creature's face, wrapping his hand under its chin and grasping the back of its head with his other hand. Then he reels his hands in opposite directions.

I stumble back as a stomach-wrenching crack pierces the fog and the beast's body goes limp. Riley tumbles off its back and onto the ground, and as if it was normal, he jumps to his feet. His chest is rising and falling in quick succession, and one thin line of red trails his arm. But otherwise, he's unscathed.

What the fuck?

"Riley?" I step back again, eyeing him.

How the hell did he do that?

He steps around the beast's lifeless carcass and approaches me. I can see the adrenaline running through him in his steel-blue eyes.

"It's dead." His words are curt and quick. He stops a few feet away and lowers his head, wiping a shaky hand through his dirtied blond hair. "What the *hell* just happened, man?"

"Huh?" I don't understand, my eyes searching his dazed face. "What do you mean? You killed it. You fucking killed it with your bare hands."

"But I..." His mouth shuts before finishing the sentence.

I step forward and put a hand on his shoulder. I don't understand what just happened, but all that matters right now is that we're all alive and that thing is dead.

"Don't worry about it. It's dead." The realization blossoms in my mind. With the creature dead, we only have to get to the boats and contact the authorities once we hit the mainland. Hope tingles down my arms. We're going to make it. We're really going to make it.

I swing around and find Ava standing uneasily on her feet, leaning against a nearby tree. I smile at her, the joy radiating off me. "We're going to make it, Ava!"

She grins back, though her face is laced with pain. I rush to her side and place my palm on her cheek, taking care not to cause her any more agony. Peering into her eyes, I find that well of strength and happiness shining again; I remember seeing that when we first met. I lean in and bow my head closer, letting our foreheads touch. I lay my palm on her dirty cheek. They're still beautiful beyond the grit and scratches. I caress her skin, sliding my hand down to her neck.

"Are you okay?" I ask. "You took one hell of a ride there."

"I'll be okay. I'm just a little sore and beat up." Ava diverts her eyes for a moment and chews cutely on her lips. I lift my head and examine her. A handful of crisscrossing scratches interrupt the pale tint of her arms and legs, and I feel a welt is rising at the back of her head, but otherwise she looks okay. Who am I kidding? She could be caked in mud and I'd still think she was gorgeous. A silent giggle rises in my throat.

We did it.

"Are you sure?" I shift forward, still worried about her.

"I promise, Coop, I'm okay." She grins and as if to reassure me, she lifts herself on the tips of her toes and kisses me. "I love you, Coop."

Elated, I couldn't wipe the grin from my filthy face if I tried. I want to rush back into another kiss, but first I let her know I feel the same. "I love you too, Ava."

A pang of shame and guilt washes over me as I consider how Riley must feel right now. Here I am with Ava, enjoying the fact that she's still here, loving the taste of her lips and the simple way she looks at me, while Brooklyn lies discarded somewhere on the island. My mind says I should pull away, but I don't want to. I can't.

Then, all at once, with the adrenaline diluted and my brain no longer running for its life, an image of Nick's scared eyes begging for one more breath jumps into my mind. My shoulders slump and a lump builds in my throat as my hands slide from Ava's neck and dangle limply at my side. I lower my eyes when the tears begin to seep from the corners of my eyes and the memory of my brother's last moments plays through my head. It's like a movie in vivid detail. I see the sanitary white tile floor, the walls, the lower quarter of a silver metal chair reflecting the room's florescent lighting a few feet away. In my arms, lying on the ground is Nick, the singular bullet hole seeping crimson rivulets. I can even hear him telling me to go, to get away from this place.

"Cooper?" Ava steps forward as I turn away.

I stumble, then regain my footing, but the weight of Nick's loss brings me to my knees. He was always there for me. He was *the* big brother, the one person in my family I felt most comfortable talking to, even if he wasn't always around or we didn't always see eye to eye. I love him in that way only brothers can. The lump in my throat releases in uncontrolled sobs, the loss setting in after the shock. I fall onto my side, into the dirt, and roll among the insects and soil. My body quakes and I can't imagine ever feeling okay again.

"Nick..." I finally manage to push his name through my lips.

A finger gently swipes the tears and the dirt from my face and then strokes my hair. I open my eyes and find Ava kneeling beside me, blurry through my teary eyes. She's frowning, her lip quivering.

"I'm so sorry, Cooper." She hooks a hand under my arm and pulls me to my knees. I squeeze my eyes closed and wipe the still flowing tears away before meeting her eyes again. Ava leans in and wraps her arms around my neck, planting her cheek against mine. "I'm so sorry. We've all lost someone, but Nick. Your... I'm sorry."

All I can do is nod to let her know I understand, but it does little to assuage the pain in my chest or to remove the images in my mind. I can't sit here in my pity forever, though, so I force a cough and blink my eyes as I push back the tears and try to gain control of myself. I release a pent-up breath and find her again.

"We need to go," I tell her, forcing my words to come out smooth and confident.

She nods, but the look in her eyes tells me she's worried about me. I get back to my feet and help her do the same. I find Riley standing between two trees, his eyes aimed at the ground. He swipes at his cheek when he realizes we're looking. I dart my eyes away and then back at him, the same shame that had invaded my mind earlier returning.

"Uh…" I struggle to find the simplest words. "You ready, Riley?"

"Yeah." The word slips quietly through the woods, his head lowered again.

"So which way?" I turn to Ava, hoping that she'll know where to go. To me everything looks the same in every direction. Trees. Bushes. Vines. Dirt. So many trees.

She eyes me for a moment with a sad grin painted on her lips before answering.

"I…" She holds the single word out for a few seconds, her head twisting and turning. I catch her eyes twitch in apparent pain as she turns her body. She extends her hand, pointing in front of her and then to the left, trying to get her bearings.

My eyes narrow, afraid that after all of this, we might now be lost on this damn island. It can't be that bad, though, it's small, and we should be able to find our way to the shore eventually. I'm about to resign to wandering aimlessly when Ava speaks up.

"This way." Ava plants her feet in the dirt and waves her hand. Some of the confidence seeps back into her voice.

I force a half-grin and start after her. When I reach her, she takes my hand and weaves her fingers between mine. I give it a squeeze and push my shoulder against her in a gentle gesture. Little does she know that I think I need her more right now than she'll ever need me. I swallow back a gulp of sadness and shame and keep my feet moving.

I look back to make sure Riley is following even though I

can hear his feet plodding along behind us. He's there, his face downcast. I lower my eyes for a moment and then meet his when he looks up, giving him a gentle smile. He bobs his head forward with a sad, tight-lipped smile.

The mist is lighter now. It disperses in twirling billows as I plow through the thinning condensation. The sun splits through the treetops with more warmth and force now, and the wind wisps under my neck in delicate wafts. I inhale a deep breath of humid air, but my heart still sags over the edge of a cliff, unable to take my mind off my loss. I hold back the fountain of tears, but my eyes still drip at the edges like an old leaky faucet.

"Riley?" I squint when the name slips from Ava's lips.

I turn to find Riley's hand grasping Ava's shoulder. She half turns to see him. His eyes are blank; there's no sign of the torment that plagued them just minutes ago.

"Riley…" she says again, and she lets go of my hand to turn around. Riley's hand falls back to his side, and I turn as well, waiting for him to say something.

"You okay, man?" I ask. "All of this sucks, it's *okay* not to be okay."

He steps forward, his hand reaching for Ava's shoulder again. It finds purchase and then begins to slide closer to her neck. A confused expression overtakes Ava's face, and she looks to me with a question in her eyes.

"Riley?" I move half a step closer to the boy. Something doesn't feel right. He doesn't answer, and there is an eerie lack of emotion in his blank face. It's like he isn't there. "Riley are you —"

My chest explodes in a deep eruption of agony as I'm thrown from my feet. I fly through the air, and my eyes catch

Riley tightening his grip around Ava's neck and wrenching her from the soil she stands on. My back hits the unwavering trunk of a strong tree, and it feels like I've landed atop a pit of the most venomous jellyfish as thousands of agonizing tendrils shoot up my spine. I drop to the forest floor in a heap, my eyes snapping shut.

As I gasp for breath, a shrill scream rips through the air. *Ava*. I remember how Riley had only minutes ago snapped the neck of the Proeliatoris and my heart plummets as my eyes fly open.

"Get up!" Riley's voice barks, but there's something distant about his tone.

I lift my head, fighting back the ravaging pain at the base of my neck, and meet his stare. His eyes are cold. It's him, but it's not at the same time.

"I said get up." His voice rises, but he doesn't move.

I let out a painful breath, sending the dirt and leaves by my mouth away in a haze. I inhale a new breath and mentally brace myself for the pain I'm about to cause my own body before pressing a hand on the wet soil and pushing off the ground. Either I'm doing okay or shock is keeping it from hurting as bad as I think it should. Huffing, my hand finds purchase along the bark of a tree and I pull myself up. A lightning bolt of pain races up my thigh and back, threatening to bring me back to the ground, but I tighten my grip on the tree and let my weight fall against its bark instead.

A grunt escapes my firmly clamped lips and I look up again to find Ava. Her hands are clasped over the backs of Riley's hands, her fingers trying to break between his palm and her neck. Her eyes reach out to me, begging me to do something, and a tiny shriek jumps from her throat when Riley's fingers contract for a split second, a threat aimed at me.

I bury the pain gushing through my body and get shakily to my feet. I moan and grit my teeth but meet Riley's stoic gaze.

"What the hell is going on, Riley?" I question through clenched jaws.

"Riley?" he asks, emotionless laughter bursting from his mouth. "No, my dear Cooper. This is Dr. Fischer."

41: Cooper Bay

I stumble against the tree as my legs threaten to go numb. I can feel the color flee my face, and I swallow back a gulp of fear and realization.

How? It can't be. It's not possible.

I jerk my eyes to Ava. I can see the same wheels turning in her eyes, the same confusion and fear. I consider making a run at him. No. That would be suicide and it would practically give him the order to kill Ava. I can't do that. Even if I do die, I can't have that on my conscience for even a moment.

The gun!

I let my hand fall to my side, trying not to look obvious. My fingers touch the waist of my shorts and my stomach sinks. It's not there. Nausea threatens to push bile up my throat.

What? Where the hell is it?

I yank my eyes back up and lock my gaze on Riley, suddenly understanding. I must have lost it when he threw me against the tree. I may be eight feet from him. The gun couldn't have gone far, but I keep my eyes forward, not wanting him to know my thoughts.

"Well, don't you want to know what's happening?" Riley's mouth moves. It's his voice, but the words are not his. I cringe at the phenomenon. Somewhere behind those eyes,

Riley is stuck in the passenger seat while the doctor, the man I should have killed in the lab, holds the reins.

I puff my cheeks angrily, trying to release my pent-up rage, and push my weight off the tree. I lower my eyes, looking for the gun as I shake my head, trying to look angry. It isn't hard. Finding nothing, I center my eyes on Riley again, and give Ava a worried grin.

"I'll take that as a yes." Riley's voice is tinged by the doctor's maddened joy. It sends a chill through my spine. "You see, Riley is our latest model. When you kids wandered on the island it was a perfect opportunity to try our new formula, so we captured Riley. It only took a few hours to complete the procedure, plenty of time before you arrived at the hospital. The changes take time to manifest though. We're fortunate you didn't escape any earlier than you did. Had you, the mental link wouldn't have been ready yet and it would have been harder to get our property back."

Property?

My body recoils at his words, him speaking of Riley like a plaything with no regard for the person beneath the skin. I shoot my eyes away in anger, an excuse to search for the gun again. This time I find it. Its barrel is tucked under a growing bundle of fallen twigs literally right next to my foot.

"Of course, this wasn't how we planned it, and my friend, Nathan, will never get to see this moment of achievement because of you ungrateful punks. But nonetheless, the moment is here." With every sentence, his words continue to confuse my sense of reality. How he can think like this is beyond anything my mind can understand, and the fact that the words are coming from Riley combine into one exquisite mindfuck. "I can deal with the cards I've been dealt. How about you?"

I'm about to answer just before I make the decision to end this. Instead of giving him the joy of seeing me trip over my own words and revel in the way he's tearing at my heart, I let my legs fold beneath me and I drop to the ground. I scoop the pistol into my hand and lock my eyes on Riley again. In one smooth motion, aided only by the adrenaline coursing through my veins, I throw my arm up and align the iron sights with Riley's body.

No. It's Riley.

"Stop right there, Cooper!" Riley spouts, his head twitching. "You don't want to do that."

I stop short of pulling the trigger. I can't do it. The thing my mind had planned hits me like a speeding freight train. It's still Riley standing in front of me, not the doctor. If I take the shot, I'm killing Riley, not the true beast.

I can't do it. It's not the doctor.

Riley's not in control. He's just as much a prisoner, more so even than we are.

"Put the gun down. You can't hope to win this." The doctor's words continue to demean me. He flinches Riley's wrists, causing Ava's head to twist an inch to the left. I gasp and my gun hand sags. "Before you can pull the trigger, she'll be dead. Oh yes, and Riley, too. Don't forget about that. You'll be killing your friend."

"Do it, Coop." Ava dares to defy Fischer while in the reaper's grasp. Riley's hand squeezes tighter around her neck, eliciting a pained shriek. I narrow my eyes and jerk forward a step.

"Ah, ah!" Riley chides me. "Stay right there, Cooper. And you might want to tell your little bitch to shut up."

I want to pull the trigger, but I don't. I should feel powerful and in control with the gun in my hands, but instead I feel weak, scared, conflicted. His words repeat in my head, spurring my hate as they play again and again.

What the hell do I do?

My hands tighten around the pistol and I have to remind myself to loosen my finger on the trigger. Scenarios play out in my mind in hyperspeed. My aim is decent, but it's far from perfect even at short distances, and perfect is what I need. If I take the shot and hit Riley, this whole nightmare will be over. But then again, my aim might be off, and the bullet could glance off his skull or uselessly hit his cheek. Then he'd surely kill Ava. Even worse, what if my bullet, meant for Riley, for Fischer, hit Ava instead? I couldn't live with myself. But I can't lower the gun.

You're not just going to give up, Coop. You have to get her off this fucking island.

As a busy highway of questions and schemes crash through my mind, a singular question breaks through it all. My mouth opens, bypassing the fear and anxiety rocking my body.

"Why did you let him kill the...your Proeliatoris?" I ask, my voice shaking as I bring the pistol level with Riley's head again, refusing to give in.

"Ah, I see you've adopted our naming. Very nice." Riley's mouth moves with. Fischer's words. "You really should put down the gun though." He waits, angling Riley's head. When I don't respond, he huffs and continues. "It was no longer needed. It was an outdated model, a failed iteration of the experiment leading up to the true Proeliatoris, my pride and joy. Riley."

It all makes sense, but that doesn't block the disgust and

hate rolling through my veins.

"That was his first test, and I must say it was a smashing success. The strength and agility he displayed, the increase in mental acuity, all within an unassuming, fully human form. With your help we have realized our project's goals, Cooper. For that I must thank you."

He pauses, eyeing me through Riley's numb blue eyes. "You should have killed me when you had the chance, you know. You were so close. So very close. But you didn't, and here we are. I have your girl and your friend. Your brother's dead. All your friends. Drop the damn gun and let me bring you and Ava back to the lab. At least you'll have more time together that way."

My lips purse as the anger and hatred builds to even greater heights in the depths of my heart. I force myself to breath, letting the fear and newfound adrenaline pump through my veins. For a second, his offer tantalizes me. The guarantee of another hour, another day with her. I shake my head and wipe away the stupid thought. It would just end in death. It might be delayed, but it would still lead to certain death. I raise the gun and retrain my eye down the iron sights as my hands steady.

"I said put down the gun!" Riley's mouth opens wide, his words spewing his frustration. His hand slides up Ava's neck and grasps her chin, fingers spread wide like some long-legged spider. He threatens to wrench his hand to the side, his empty eyes glaring.

"No!" I yell before I have time to think. "Don't hurt her!"

"Then put down the gun," he growls. I refuse to give in even though my heart says to listen, if only to see her another minute, to hold her against my chest and feel her warmth, to look into her eyes.

But I can't. I can't put it down.

Ava's crystal blues plead with me. They melt my heart, uncomfortably blending my affection and need for her with the raging hate for the man behind Riley's unwilling eyes.

Do it. The words never leave her mouth, but her naked lips form them.

I swallow back the fear and doubt overriding my body and switch my gaze to Riley. I look into his eyes, trying to find him.

I'm sorry, Riley.

I release the breath I've been holding and let the sights settle on Riley's nose. I pull the trigger.

The sound of the wind whistling through the trees, the scattered birds squawking in the treetops and the muted tones of the city are erased by the rocking blast of the firing pin as it ignites the bullet. A flash bursts from the end of the barrel and my ears ring with the percussion of the round exiting the muzzle.

I want desperately to close my eyes, but I also want to see this—I need to see it. I keep my gaze steady, frightened of what I might see when the gun, tilted up from the recoil, lowers. My heart is in my throat as everything plays out in slow motion.

My mouth drops open, and I suck in a deep gulp of the moist air as my eyes find Ava past the barrel. I let the air pour from my lungs in elated stutters. An excited grin spreads across my face, replacing the fear with a joy I've never felt. Still held in Riley's arms, Ava is shaking but alive. A small hole dots Riley's head above his right eye. Before I can move my arms and legs, his head lolls back and his body falls like a heavy sack to the ground.

I gulp, the realization of what I just did sinking in. A flurry of emotion floods my soul, overwhelming the simple joy I felt moments before. Excitement, guilt, joy and discomforting panic. My arms and hands are shaking. Hell, my whole body is shaking. I still have the gun aimed, like he might somehow rise back to his feet, a creature from some Stephen King or George A. Romero story.

Ava lets out a pent-up breath, her whole body shaking like mine, and sprints toward me. I let the pistol fall from my grip. It smacks the forest floor with a dull thud.

"Cooper!" She throws her body against me, enveloping me in her arms. Nestling her face in my neck, she sobs. The pain in my back and legs begins to come back as the adrenaline wears off, but the warmth and closeness of her body soothes me and gives me the strength to stay on my feet. Still, I grunt as my thigh shoots an especially painful tendril of electricity up my side. "Are you okay, Coop?"

"I'm good, what about you?" I lean back and cup her face in both hands, looking her over, horrified that my eyes might have tricked me. "I didn't..."

"No, I'm fine, Cooper. Really." She grins wide and pulls my hands away from her face, then leans forward and plants her lips firmly against mine. I breathe her in, ignoring the way her body shakes under me, and I cherish the taste of her lips.

I don't know how long we stand like that, lips locked, arms wrapped tightly around each other, enjoying the peace of winning our lives back and melting into each other. Eventually, Ava leans her head back and looks me in the eyes. That bright glow fills her beautiful eyes again.

She whispers, "We did it, Coop. We're getting off this island."

42: Cooper Bay

My hand tingles in Ava's gentle grip. A stir of tranquility floods my body, and the balmy morning sunlight warms my skin as I walk between the pinprick-like rays shooting past the leaves high above us. Even in full daylight, the light struggles to break through the green canopy.

I smile at Ava and lean my shoulder into her, but inside, my heart is in the midst of a civil war. The excitement in my chest from her nearness and knowing that we're getting off this godforsaken island wars with the hanging despair and loss that looms over my heart like a balloon about to burst. I feel like it might seize up at any moment inside my chest and drop me to my knees from the sheer weight of the struggle, but I keep a grin on for Ava.

Does she feel the same?

I look forward, diverting my eyes to the ground.

She does. I know she does.

"It's going to be okay." The words glide from her up-turned face. "It's not all right, but we're going to be okay."

I bob my head and mimic her grin. Nick would be happy for me, this is what he'd want. He had helped talk me through my break up months ago, kept me going through those hard times. I can see him walking the beach in the memory I'd brought up in our cell. The smile on his face, the warm air whipping through his messy hair—that's how I need to remember him.

I bite my lower lip, holding back the urge to cry. Instead, I let out a gentle laugh and look at Ava.

"Yeah, we're going to be okay," I tell her, and let go of her hand to wrap my arm about her shoulders. I stop and hug her, taking in a deep breath, our foreheads touching, my eyes locked with hers.

"Do you hear that?" Her eyes light up.

I angle my head, squinting as if it might help improve my hearing, and listen. My brow rises in excitement. Somewhere up ahead, I hear the gentle lapping of the river against the shoreline.

"Yeah, I do." I almost yell the words, excitement taking over my body again. "It's the shore. We're close."

"Come on!" Ava darts forward and my arm falls from her shoulder. I smile and bolt after her.

It only takes a few strides to catch up. We weave through the woods. The sound of the water rises, and the dense patchwork of trees begins to open before us. I can see the city now. Its towering metal high-rises and century-old brick-faced buildings paint the base of a blue sky like a "welcome home" sign.

I want to sprint forward, but the pain is already getting to my legs, and I know Ava can't feel much better. I settle for a quick jog. I let out a sigh as my feet hit the rocky shore and the river expands beyond the tree line. The sun sparkles off the water and a cool mist plays on my skin. I search for the dock but find a set of water worn dikes dotting the shore instead. The water sloshes around them gently and laps at the rock-covered coast.

"So which way now?" I ask Ava. "You're the walking map, remember?"

She grins and shakes her head but eyes the coastline anyway. She casts her gaze over the river to the city and then looks up and down along the coast. "This way."

She points to the left, south I think, and starts off. I join her. The small pebbles and larger rocks crackle and slide under my shoes.

Before we make it another ten yards, my eyes catch a dot out on the water. I turn to check it out. A boat. I squint to make out more detail as it turns in our direction, but one thing is certain. It's mostly orange; its brightly painted sides shout the color across the water.

"Hey, Ava." I stop. "You see that boat? It's headed our way."

"I see it." Her voice is breathy with excitement.

She waves her hands in the air and starts jumping, trying to make sure they see us. I'm certain they already do, but I join her and wave my arms anyway.

"Over here!" Ava screams.

"I think they see us," I comment, trying not to sound sarcastic.

With the boat drawing closer I can finally make out more detail. Its shell looks more like a raft, painted in bright orange, and a small control room housing sets in the middle. A man sits at the front ledge behind something small and long that I can't quite make out yet. It makes a slight turn before angling back again, and I catch three precious words. *U.S. COAST GUARD*.

"Ava, it's the Coast Guard!" I shout.

"Definitely better than rowing across the river," she says

and lets her arms fall back to her waist.

I lead her closer to the water to await our lift when I remember we're not even supposed to be here. I inhale a breath of humid river air and come to a halt at the river's edge as the bow of the boat makes land and the machine gun attached to the front comes into view.

I hold back the urge to run to the boat and jump in just to get my feet off the island. But it doesn't stop my mind from imagining how great it'll feel to leave this place.

The soldier sitting behind the machine gun rises to his feet. He's dressed in a dark blue uniform. The bright red floatation vest strapped over his shoulder hangs inches over a black utility belt and the pistol holstered at his side. A matching blue helmet covers his head. Behind him, another soldier exits the control house and the two jump over the edge of the orange shell, their shoes smacking loudly against the rocks.

"What are you two doing here?" I can't see the man's eyes past the dark black sunglasses, but his dark features and thick arms complement the gruff tone in his voice. "You're trespassing. This island is an avian reserve. It's off limits."

At first, I don't know what to say. *Thank you* comes to mind, but it seems out of place. Running and slinging my arms around the man seems unwise, but it still feels like an option. Instead, I stand among the rocks, my face holding a dumb smile for a moment before I finally speak. The other guardsman keeps his feet in sync with the bigger man. He's thin but radiates an air of strength and confidence behind cool eyes and tanned skin.

"Uh..." I stutter, both excited and somehow nervous. "I know, we shouldn't have come, but...our friends...my brother... They killed them. There's a lab under the hospital."

As the words gush out I realize how crazy I sound, but I can't stop myself. It all wants to rush out at once. An amused grin surfaces on the black soldier's face and his shoulders bounce as he chuckles, looking to his partner, who joins in.

"A lab," he laughs, "under the hospital, you say? Well I definitely have to report this."

I know he's mocking me, but just maybe someone will listen eventually. I look at Ava hopefully. She's lost most of the glow she had moments ago, washed away by the reality of how these soldiers must see us.

He reaches for the walkie-talkie attached to his uniform at his shoulder and reports in. My mind glazes over the formal radio talk until he starts to tell them what's going on. "I've got two kids out on the shore of North Brother. Trespassers. Advise."

"You have to check," I say. "There's a door in the basement of the hospital that leads into the lab. He's still down there. Dr. Fischer, he's the only one left."

He waves dismissively at me. A surge of contempt ripples over me, but I force myself to understand, to put myself in his shoes. I'd do the same thing.

"You have to—" I start, but he cuts me off.

"What are your names?" he asks.

"I'm Cooper Bay," I tell him, then point to Ava. "And this is Ava Thompson."

Ava nods at the soldier but doesn't speak.

"Names are Cooper Bay and Ava Thompson," he reports in the walkie-talkie.

He eyes us for a long moment, undoubtedly listening to someone giving him orders on how to handle the two loons on the beach. He shifts his feet on the rocks and nods, before looking at the other soldier.

"You heard the man," he says.

Before I speak another word, my eyes expand in shock. In one fluid motion both men swipe their pistols from their holsters and point them directly at us. I want to scream at them, to reason with them, but all I manage before the first trigger is pulled and a *bang* fills the air is to snap my neck around to find Ava.

She never has the chance to look my way. Panic and confusion mar her face as a red mist is dispatched from the back of her skull. My mouth drops like lead as her body falls backward and lands unceremoniously on the rocks. Every muscle in my body tenses, my whole world taken away from me when we should be going home, when we should finally be safe. I swing around to face the soldiers.

A burst of yellow flashes from the other soldier's gun and my vision goes black.

ABOUT THE AUTHOR

Jordon Greene is the Amazon Bestselling Horror Author of *To Watch You Bleed*. He is a full stack web developer for the nation's largest privately owned shoe retail company and a graduate of UNC Charlotte. Jordon spends his time building web applications, attempting to sing along with his favorite bands, and reading when his not writing. He lives in Concord, NC just close enough and just far enough away from Charlotte.

Visit Jordon Online
www.JordonGreene.com

If you enjoyed this story,
please consider reviewing it online at retailers like Amazon
and recommending it to friends and family.

CPSIA information can be obtained
at www.ICGtesting.com
Printed in the USA
BVHW030217090119
537407BV00001B/7/P